# THE SPOILS OF VICTORY

## Book 1 in the Prisoners of War Series

## Daniel J. Markowitz

Flint Hills Publishing

Cover design by Amy Albright

Author photograph by Dave Leiker

Flint Hills Publishing
Topeka, Kansas
Tucson, Arizona
www.flinthillspublishing.com

Printed in the U.S.A.

Paperback Book ISBN: 978-1-966323-20-4
Hardcover Book ISBN: 978-1-966323-21-1
Electronic Book ISBN: 978-1-966323-22-8

Library of Congress Control Number 9781966323235

For my grandchildren

Christopher, Alexander, Graham, Dominic, and Delilah

# CONTENTS

# PART

I

# Chapter 1
# AWAKE

He was floating in an amorphous cocoon. Incorporeal and timeless, his only connections to whatever lay beyond were incongruent memories as jagged as lightning bolts...sweaty soldiers double-timing in rigid lines...a boy and girl skipping along a still blue lake surrounded by trees ablaze in autumnal reds and oranges...charcoal shadows lurking behind a mound of rubble...other children processing around a candle-lit church...inhaling pungent incense as a priest in rich vestments placed a figurine in a manger...human remnants lying contorted on blood-drenched sands...adoring crowds welcoming their leader with stiff arms and raucous cheers...giant red flags with black swastikas flying off thick staffs to envelop him. On and on they came.

Too dry and disjointed to arouse real emotion, these shards of some other existence played to a mad cacophony emanating from divergent sources—choirs, engines, birds, bombs, jackboots, bodies (as bullets tore into them with wet, squishy splats). Underlying it all rang a sonorous ding-dong-ding-dong, as if he were a fly inside a giant, slow-tolling bell.

Now and again, he sought to will himself to greater clarity, to escape his prison or at least quell the dissonance, but unseen chains held him fast.

Until something changed. Different sounds seeped in—utterances from someone outside himself. English! These anomalous words formed a lifeline tossed in his direction. As he reached for them, the dissonance faded. With Herculean effort, Rolf Mueller opened his eyes. More words became louder and clearer, and tangible objects came into view. His mind began to process the information that his senses were again gathering.

"Hello. Can you hear me?" The voice was now less tinny.

His gaze found a man in spectacles and a khaki uniform. The young, tall stranger looked up from a clipboard, and their eyes met.

"There you are. I can speak German if you prefer. Would you like that?"

It took time to muster an indignant response. "Of course I prefer

German." He thought, *How do I even know English? I'm German, aren't I?* His voice was raspish, his tongue thick. It was incredibly difficult to speak. He knew what he wanted to say, but words hid, then wouldn't align with the thoughts that inspired them. And when they finally came out, it was like he was listening to someone else. "Where am I?"

"In a German field hospital in Bizerte. In Tunisia." The man's accent was odd.

"You're German?"

"No, I'm American. You're our prisoner."

Rolf stared past the man at new scraps of memories, grim desert scenes. Wait! Americans were the enemy!

"Would you like some water?"

"Yes." Rolf eyed his helper warily.

The man held a paper straw to his mouth. A short sip of cool water was enough to soothe his parched, viscous throat.

"Where is my company?" he demanded.

"The entire Afrika Korps surrendered, so your unit is being held somewhere, but I don't know where. It doesn't matter anyway. The war is over for you now. North Africa is liberated."

He rolled his head on the pillow in disbelief. "Liberated? What do you mean, the war is over? I'm a prisoner? This can't be. Where are my men?" he asked again. Getting only a shrug from the American, he saw a nurse next to a nearby bed and called to her. After several tries and much throat-clearing, he made himself heard. "Fraulein, where am I?"

She turned. "You're in our field hospital."

"How can I be a prisoner then, if I'm in a German hospital?"

"The hospital was captured too. We're all prisoners now, even me."

The American said, "Now do you believe me?" but got no answer. "Soldier, what's your name, rank, and military number? I'm taking a census of everyone in this hospital. I can't find your *wehrpass* or your *soldbuch*. Do you remember who you are?"

The nurse interjected, "His documents were not with him when he was brought in, and he was unconscious, but his identification tags are around his neck."

The American moved in to check them, but the fear in Rolf's eyes stopped him. Or was it anger? Or malice? He glanced back down at his clipboard impatiently.

The young German was silent a few moments longer, then mostly to himself, he said, "Yes," and more words rolled out. "I am Rolf Mueller, *gefreiter*, 334th unit, second battalion, first infantry regiment, 21st Panzer Division, Afrika Korps, serial number 6204-7533-16."

"*Gefreiter*, a lance corporal, yes? You're an enlisted man?"

"That's right, I think."

"Corporal Mueller, what is your date and place of birth?"

"I was born 8 July 1920 in Olpe, Germany. What day is it?"

"It's Friday, 14 May 1943. You were wounded just before Bizerte fell. German doctors treated you, and American doctors are here now too." He held up the glass and straw again.

"Bizerte fell," he repeated as his face hardened. "Where are my men? I must know."

The nurse spoke quietly. When the American nodded his approval, she turned to Rolf. "You were brought in alone. We don't know about the rest of your unit. I'm sorry." He frowned. "Bullets and shrapnel were removed from your legs. They are bandaged up. You also had a concussion and head wounds that required another surgery. Then the doctors put a drain in to reduce swelling in your brain. You've had morphine, which is partly why you've been asleep and are confused. Have you any pain now?"

He hadn't thought about how he felt physically. At the question he tried to sit up but immediately collapsed back onto the mattress. His head exploded into bursts of pain; excruciating jolts wracked his entire body. "*Gott in Himmel*!" he panted.

The American spoke again, "You probably shouldn't try to move around yet. but I'm not a medic. I'm just here for information. Looks like you're a lucky guy. I'm glad you made it."

Lucky? Why would an enemy be glad that he was alive? He glanced around again to see if he could recognize anyone without moving. Flat on his back, it was impossible to tell. He saw human shapes, but no one recognizable. "I must know about my men."

Without responding, the American continued, "One last thing—do you remember your mailing address in Germany so the Red Cross can notify your family of your status?"

"Yes." He recited it by rote, which brought to mind his parents, Anton and Klara, and his older brother and younger sister. How they would worry when they heard that the Afrika Korps was no more. The throbbing worsened. He touched the bandages, moaned, and closed his eyes.

"That's all I need for now," said the American as he moved away.

The pain was beyond anything he'd ever experienced. The nurse stepped back into his line of sight with a morphine syrette. In one fluid motion, she opened the tube with a needle and drained its contents into him. In seconds, he was floating again. The last thing he heard was the nurse saying, in a sing-songy voice that slowed and deepened with each word, "This will help, now...get...some...sleep."

In the days that followed, he hung between pain and morphine. The first time he woke after the interview, he wasn't sure it had happened. He couldn't tell awake from asleep. He heard people talking over him, changing bandages, knew he was in a hospital. He felt himself being bathed and rolled on his side, but then there were familiar battle noises and sounds from home. Everything—and nothing—was real. Being here and there was worse than being completely out. And now his muddled recollections churned intense, unwanted emotions. He saw himself shooting at people, mostly other soldiers, but once he shot a child in the face, and the obliterated face turned into Maria's, his little sister. Then he was spraying a dozen well-dressed women, old men, and children, with machine gun fire as they pleaded in French with him and with God. He watched them fall limply to the ground, just as he did when he was shot. He remembered that now. Over and over, he saw people blown up. How grotesque that a man could be speaking while his intestines were lying outside his body. He retched at the sweet, acrid stench of burning flesh, shuddered at anguished howls, Some came from a battlefield, some from across the room. At times he woke himself with his own cries or hysterical laughing. Once he was high above the desert strapped into a *Luftwaffe* plane with no propellers and no one else on board. All he could do was wait for it to crash and destroy him, but it never did.

Gradually, nights lifted away from days like cream rises from milk, and life regained a more recognizable rhythm. The dreams and hallucinations continued, but he could stay awake longer. Memories came more naturally when summoned. He still stumbled over thoughts and words, but less frequently. He began to grill doctors and nurses about his condition.

Two weeks after being wounded, Rolf demanded to stand. Two orderlies, one German and the other American, came to help. They were joking with each other when they approached his bed, which irritated him. As they swung his legs over the side of the bed. he nearly fainted but then gritted his teeth and pressed on. He was going to get back on his feet. Arms around their shoulders, he slowly rose, staggered for a moment, and shuffled a few steps. He couldn't go far that first day, but it was enough.

While still standing, he surveyed the room. It was in an old, European-style building with high ceilings and cracked pastel stucco walls. Uniformed men and women nonchalantly chatted and reviewed papers near a door to a hallway. Shades were pulled down to keep the morning sun at bay, but the room was still bright enough. Considering how crowded it was, with at least four dozen beds squeezed in, Rolf was surprised that the odors of human waste and suffering weren't overpowering.

All the beds were occupied by patients with casts and all manner of bandages, dressings, and slings. Limbs were frozen at odd angles. A few men were playing cards. Others were prostrate and silent. A few heads were completely enshrouded in gauze, except for black holes for eyes, noses, and mouths. He recognized one man's moaning from the nights.

Back in bed, though gaunt and exhausted, he'd confirmed that he would recover. As his head was propped up, Rolf said quietly, "I'm too young to die. And I will find my men."

Before the orderlies left, he pointedly thanked just the German, then addressed the American in the condescending tone of an officer addressing a subordinate, "There was another American here asking for my family's address in Germany. Do you know who he is?"

"No, but I think I know where to find him."

# Chapter 2
# FRIEND OR FOE?

It was several days before the first American returned. "Looks like you're feeling better," he said as Rolf finished a set of push-ups.

"I am. And tired of laying around." He rose stiffly from the floor and toweled sweat off his face and arms.

"Is there much pain still?"

"No." A quickly-concealed grimace betrayed the lie.

"I'm John Schmidt, PFC, with the MPEG unit assigned here." He held out his hand.

"I'm Gefreiter Rolf Mueller, 21st Panzer Division." He pretended to not notice the American's outstretched hand.

"I heard you wanted to see me again. And, please, call me John."

"Thank you, Private Schmidt, but I prefer that we follow military protocol."

"As you wish, Corporal Mueller," the American complied with an almost imperceptible roll of his eyes. "What can I do for you?"

"My memory is still a little cloudy, but I think when you were here last you asked for my address in Germany?"

"Yes, and I gave it to the Red Cross so your family would be notified."

"Do you know if that was done?"

"No, but you can write home yourself if you'd like. That would be better anyway since you probably want to update them on your condition. Plus, the Red Cross is so busy now with a couple hundred thousand prisoners that their notices may be slow in getting out."

Rolf's eyebrows raised. "A couple hundred thousand?"

"Yes, all the Axis troops that were captured are still here in North Africa. Only a few got out before the surrender. Rommel was back in Germany, but Von Arnim and most of the other senior officers were captured too."

The magnitude of such a loss was incomprehensible, especially following the death or capture of the tens of thousands of other Germans at Stalingrad earlier that year. "What are you going to do with all of us?"

"I'm not sure. Plans are being made, but it will take time to get it all sorted out."

"How do I go about sending a letter to my parents?"

"Well, first you write one." The American smiled to lighten the mood. "I have everything you need," he said, handing Rolf a pen, paper, and envelope."

"Will we be kept here?"

"I doubt it. There's no infrastructure in place for so many POWs. It would be a logistical nightmare."

"All right, I will write this afternoon."

"Then I'll try to come back tomorrow sometime." With a wry smile, Schmidt snapped to attention and saluted his superior officer. Rolf blushed, then saluted back.

Since he was drafted in 1939, he'd written home regularly from camps in Germany and from the fronts. He'd also been home on leave several times, most recently the previous December. He cringed wondering when he'd see his parents again. And this letter would be a hard one to write. He wanted to ease their minds, but things were in such flux that he wasn't sure how. His parents were worriers, especially his mother. Having both sons, Rolf and his older brother, Kurt, in the *Wehrmacht* for so long had been a great strain on them.

He fretted most of the afternoon, afraid that he'd saturate the pages with too much information about all he'd gone through and too much speculation about what Germany's recent losses might mean. Finally, he forced himself to begin, determined to keep his message on point. He'd been wounded but was better. There was no need to mention the continuing pain, the cane, or the scars. Hopefully that would all be temporary anyway. He told them the Allies were treating him well so far and that he loved and missed them. That's what they needed. He would comfort them, even if writing worsened his homesickness.

It was warm and stuffy the next afternoon when Schmidt woke Rolf from a nap. Putting the letter in his satchel, he said, "Do you want to go back to sleep, or are you up for a walk?"

Rolf tensed up. "What? Where?"

"Do you want to go outside for some fresh air?"

"I suppose, if it's permitted. I've not been outside in weeks. I didn't know I could."

"This building belonged to the French government before it was turned into a hospital. There are some gardens, and one is for POWs. I can show you, if you'd like."

"All right." He was on his feet so quickly that it made him wobbly.

"Okay?"

"Yes, I just need to remember to go slow."

A dozen paces past the entrance to the ward, down a hall and to the right, were oversized front doors. They slowly made their way in that direction. After passing through the high, graceful stone archway onto a broad front porch, Rolf stopped and looked up into the clear, blue afternoon sky. He closed his eyes and inhaled deeply, momentarily oblivious to everything except the warm sunshine and the clean air that wafted over him on a gentle sea breeze.

Buoyed by the freshness, Rolf hobbled down the stairs, and they turned into a walled courtyard. Overgrown bushes covered with waxy green foliage and sweetly-scented pink blossoms shaded the wide stone pathways. In the back wall was a gaping hole left by a bomb or artillery shell. The debris had been removed, and the breach was filled with barbed wire. Through it they could look down into Bizerte. The hospital stood slightly above the city center.

Every structure in sight was damaged. Dusty stone heaps rose everywhere. Few of the remaining buildings still had windows or shutters. Jagged pipes and splintered wooden beams stuck out of the mounds; walls were stained black with soot. Here and there lay tree trunks stripped bare and metal vehicle chassis and rotting animal carcasses. It was hard to tell where streets were supposed to be.

The men sat on a stone bench and looked out through the gap. Quietly, Rolf said, "I was out there somewhere." Then he added pensively, "It must have been a beautiful city at one time."

"How much do you remember about getting wounded?"

Lost for a moment, he finally said. "I was alone and exhausted. I was in a second-floor window of some building. I don't recall how I got separated from my men. It was an apartment because I was in a bedroom. I stood up to shoot at..." He cast a sideways glance. "I stood up to shoot at some Americans across the street. I got off some rounds. As I did, I was hit in both legs. What got me came from another direction, from up the street where I couldn't see anyone. I fell, then there was an incredible explosion and a loud ringing and everything went black. After that, the next time I was awake was when you spoke to me. I have no idea how I got to the hospital." He stood up. "Let's talk about something else."

"Sure," said the American. "That first day, you spoke in English, and you seemed to understand it well. Where did you learn?"

Rolf stretched and sat back down. "I studied it for many years, first in gymnasium and then at the University of Berlin. I haven't had much opportunity to practice."

"We can speak it now if you'd like."

Rolf hesitated, then replied in English, "I guess there's no harm in that."

"What were you studying in college?"

"Medicine. Before the war, I was going to be a doctor. I only got through one year and part of another before I went into the *Wehrmacht*."

"Maybe one day you'll go back to school and become a doctor."

Rolf smiled. "Maybe, but that dream was a lifetime ago. What should I dream for now? Survival?" He looked edgy. "What about you? How did you learn German?"

"My family came from Germany, as you can probably tell from my last name." Rolf nodded. "My grandparents emigrated from near Hamburg in the 1880s. They settled in Nebraska. I was raised on a farm near Columbus, a small town. You know where Nebraska is?"

"In the middle of the country, isn't it? I also loved geography and looking at maps. Why did your grandparents leave Germany?"

"One reason, my grandfather told me, was religion. Our family is Catholic, and Opa said Bismarck hated Catholics. Then, when his older brother inherited the farm, he was left out. He wanted his own land, and there was plenty of it, good and cheap, in Nebraska. Nebraska also had a lot of Germans by then, so they got their own farm and could still be around their people."

"I'm Catholic, too, and was raised on a farm as well. My hometown, Olpe, is in Westphalen, about sixty kilometers east of Köln." Rolf smiled. "It's not so far from Hamburg. I have cousins named Schmidt, though it's a very common name in Germany."

"Maybe we're cousins." The American grinned.

Rolf wasn't sure what to make of that. "Your family still speaks German?"

"Yes, at home, but not at school or church anymore. Opa's gone, but Oma is still alive and that's about all she speaks," John said. "When the war started, Uncle Sam assigned me to the MPEG because my German might come in handy. I guess it does."

"What is MPEG?"

"It stands for Military Police Escort Guard."

"I see. And what will you do when the war is over?"

"I'll go home and farm with my father and brothers. There's enough land for all of us." Now it was John's turn to pause. "I miss Nebraska. I get homesick sometimes."

"I understand."

After a few more minutes, Schmidt said he had to go. They walked back in, and the American promised to post the letter. "Thank you for getting me outdoors," Rolf said, but his tone had changed. His expression was now vaguely, but unmistakably, hostile.

"You're welcome. Is something wrong? Did you want to stay out longer?"

"Can I ask you a question?"

"Sure."

"Why are you being so nice?"

"Why not? You seem like a good guy. Aren't you?"

The response irked him. "A month ago we were trying to kill each other. Someone almost got the job done on me. So why treat me so well now?" Rolf sounded accusatorial.

Schmidt shrugged his shoulders. "Well, first of all, not all Americans want to treat POWs nice. Some of us think we're coddling you. Do you know the word 'coddling?'"

"I'm not sure."

"'Coddling' means to be too easy on someone who's done wrong, to not punish them when they deserve it."

"But you don't feel that way?"

The American looked directly at him. "I think we should treat POWs fair and square because it's the right thing to do." Rolf cringed and shook his head. "You disagree?" Rolf didn't reply but turned away and stared down at the floor. Schmidt noticed his left leg was twitching. "Look, we're all stuck in this damn war, aren't we? Why bring it in here if we don't have to? We have a lot in common. We should be glad to be alive. There's no reason to hate each other."

"Perhaps you're right," Rolf mumbled through gritted teeth.

"I want to look back on all this knowing that I did the best I could to make it through without sacrificing my beliefs, including being kind to strangers, even enemies and prisoners."

Rolf listened, then smiled cynically. "Wouldn't that just be wonderful." Now he turned back to glare at the American. "May I ask one more question?" then proceeded without waiting for a reply. "Have you and the others in your MPEG unit ever been to the front?" Louder, faster, and with growing disdain, he continued, "Have you ever even been shot at? Have you watched friends die from enemy bullets or bombs? Do you think you would be so kind to people if they'd just tried to kill you? Are you telling me that's what I should do?"

"That's more than one question," Schmidt chose his words carefully. This was not his first time talking to a German POW in distress. "No, I've not served on the front lines, that's not where I was sent. How would I feel about it if I was the one you were aiming at that day when you got shot?" He paused. "I don't know, but I hope to God that once the shooting stopped, I'd treat you as a human being, even if you had tried to kill me. And no, I'm not telling you how you should feel."

Rolf looked out the window, his foot tapping an angry cadence against the metal railing at the foot of the bed. Without looking back, he snarled, "Please leave me alone, Private Schmidt." He'd reverted to German, which made his words sound even more insincere.

"I hope you keep getting stronger. You can go out in the courtyard any time you like." Schmidt tried to defuse the tension in a measured, friendly tone, but didn't offer to shake hands, nor did he salute.

Rolf was left to flounder in a black sea of anger and resentment. Flashes from countless battles seared him, and there were other flashes, too, from all the times during and before the war when Germany's leaders pronounced that all their many enemies deserved only the severest punishment, never mercy. And he had agreed. Suddenly, he was gasping for air.

The American had to be wrong. Schmidt's love-thy-enemy bullshit and friendliness was absurdly naive. That was it! Schmidt had the luxury of self-righteousness because he'd never been shot at or had to follow the kinds of orders Rolf had been given. He was probably in the MPEG because he was weak, unfit for real military duty, less than a real man. Rolf was suddenly more ferociously angered by this one American's sanctimony and condescension than by the enmity of all those who'd tried to kill him at every turn since this damn war began. What an arrogant, judgmental bastard!

Especially-terrible nightmares tore through his sleep that night. The dead were taunting him again. Several times, he woke up startled. The last time, the fear was so palpable that he was crying, which shamed him deeply. What if his fellow soldiers heard him? Instead of trying to go back to sleep, he turned to distracting himself with happier memories. Nothing worked until, at last, he thought of a favorite lullaby his mother sang when he was young. He quietly whispered the words to himself and was, for a moment, a child in her arms. God damn it! How humiliating that a decorated soldier of the Third Reich would have to sing children's songs to calm himself. But that's where he was.

## Chapter 3
# ETERNAL TRUTH

Feeling more aggrieved by John Schmidt than he should have and frustrated that he didn't understand why, Rolf gave up trying to figure it out and escaped by focusing on a more tangible goal—physical recovery. He began pushing himself to the edge of his endurance. Always proud of his lanky, athletic physique and superior strength, he would will himself back into fighting shape, injuries be damned. He sweated through intense daily calisthenics sessions and made himself walk farther and faster until he was jogging around the crowded little garden. He ignored the chronic pain, eschewed painkillers, and refused to use the cane unless he had no choice. The doctors and nurses advised him to slow down or risk re-injuring himself. He ignored them. If he couldn't sort his feelings out, at least he'd get his body back to normal. More than anything, that's what he wanted—a return to normal, to be back with the 334th fighting for the Fatherland, or at least fighting for himself and his comrades. Even with the dangers and deprivations, soldiering in the *Werhmacht* was all he'd known for the past four years, nearly his entire adult life. And he was good at what he did. He'd received commendations for bravery, was admired by his fellow soldiers. *If I'm still alive*, he thought, *I must have done something right. I did what I was supposed to do. I did what I was told to do. I did what I had to do. I knew who I was then.*

One afternoon, he came in to find two GIs rifling through his footlocker. They weren't guards. One had already pocketed Rolf's wallet. The other was examining his watch, which he took too. "What the hell are you doing?" he demanded in English. "Put that back!"

One of them, a crude dullard with bad teeth, drawled, "What's it look like?"

"Like you're stealing!" Rolf moved closer to the Americans, who reeked of alcohol.

"We're looking for contraband, asshole. Wanna try to stop us?" asked the other man. Slowly and deliberately, he put a cocky hand on his holster. "You gonna hit me with your cane?"

"I wouldn't need a cane." He pressed in further. Instantly, his training came back as he assessed which one he should strike first, and how.

The Americans moved ominously toward him, too, clearly spoiling for a fight. But just before the confrontation turned physical, a German orderly—the one who'd helped Rolf earlier—hurried up and said, in German, "Gefreiter Mueller, you don't want to fight these two."

"They're stealing from me!"

"Let it go," said the orderly. "It's not worth getting into a fight. You won't win, even if you beat the shit out of them both. Remember your place." He put a reassuring hand on Rolf's shoulder and spoke to the thieves. "The guards are on their way." The Americans pocketed a couple more items and casually walked away.

"Why are you such a coward?" Rolf asked the orderly, still agitated.

"What choice do we have? Those bastards have guns. I've seen them pistol whip others."

"But I could have taken them. Even now, I'm stronger than they are."

"Maybe so, but then you'd get written up and confined to your bed. And they'd come back with their friends and beat you senseless. Look around, we don't hold any cards here."

Rolf did just that, began to pay closer attention. He soon saw how right the orderly was. Utilizing his good English, he could hear how crude and demeaning some Americans were, and now he began to listen. Guards were impatient or insulting to prisoners and even the German doctors and nurses. Sometimes they intentionally roughed up patients. Demeaning their captives was a new sport. Reveling in their authority, some Americans acted with impunity, and the few officers who visited the ward were either complicit or didn't care.

Not long after he was robbed, three American enlisted men strode up to a prisoner near his bed. With no explanation, they forced the man, whose arms were in casts, into a wheelchair. The German asked repeatedly where they were taking him, to no avail. The Americans pushed him out of the ward and into another room at the far end of the entry hall. A short while later they returned. The German was dripping blood from his face; his eyes and lips were badly swollen, and a tooth had been knocked out. He was barely conscious. One of the attackers nonchalantly said to a shocked German nurse, "We needed to talk to heinie here. He got all excited and came at us, but the stupid son-of-a-bitch lost his balance and fell." The Americans all laughed uproariously. Rolf seethed, but not one of the Germans said a word.

In a strange way, this vulgar, brutal behavior was comforting because it was familiar. Hadn't this been the way of the world and warfare since the dawn of history? Hadn't this been ingrained in him since he was a boy? Might makes right. Power is the only absolute. After dominance is established on the battlefield, intimidation is a valid tool for maintaining authority. Victory carries with it no mandate for leniency.

The *Fuehrer*, who'd been in power since Rolf was twelve, espoused these principles clearly, but he wasn't the first. As every German knew all too well, the same reasoning guided the victors after World War I, when the United States, Britain, and especially France, demanded Germany's subjugation. Then in 1940, it was Germany's turn to humiliate France, and now it was the United States' turn in North Africa. If the American guards treated their captives harshly, who could complain? Hadn't he himself acted similarly? He may never have been so crass as to steal just for the sake of stealing, but he'd done much worse without giving it a second thought. Victory had been as intoxicating to Rolf then as it was to his keepers now. Every time he thought of the naive American, Schmidt, and his self-righteous sermonizing about how enemies must become friends, Rolf grew angry. Once he said aloud without realizing it, "Fuck you, Schwuchtel! You know nothing about victory or honor or war."

One evening, he recalled a conversation he'd had with his brother the previous December. Kurt Mueller was three years older. He had no interest in university but stayed on the farm until he enlisted in the *Wehrmacht* in 1937. Kurt was happy as a soldier and good at it. He was in the vanguard of the armies that marched into Austria, Poland, and Russia. He'd been awarded numerous combat medals, commendations, and citations, many more than Rolf had, and had never been seriously injured. Rolf was proud of his brother, one of the toughest characters he knew. He epitomized what an Aryan soldier ought to be.

By coincidence, the brothers earned overlapping three-day passes home to Olpe in early December 1942. It was a great occasion for the family, the first time in four years that Anton and Klara had all three of their children home at the same time. They hosted a big celebration in spite of rationing and the other inconveniences of war.

One cold wintry night during their break, after too much schnapps and with their parents and sister in bed, Rolf and his brother were alone at the kitchen table. Kurt, very drunk, started talking about the German juggernaut in the East. "Little brother, you can't imagine how invincible we are. I know you've seen battles, but Russia—it's incredible! We've gone so far, nothing will stop us from conquering the Soviet Union all the way to the Pacific. It's only a matter of time." He called Stalingrad a temporary setback and wanted to be back at the front in time for the capture of Leningrad or Moscow.

"Do you really think Russia's that close to collapse?" Rolf was still hopeful about the war's outcome, but he knew how formidable Russia was because of its sheer size, natural resources, and population.

"Fuck the Russians!" Kurt's words were slurred and passionate. "They're running out of troops. We kill them as fast as they mobilize. Some have switched to our side, and we've captured so many that they won't be able to field full armies before long."

"Really?"

"Yes, really. I know what I'm talking about. I myself have seen thousands of Russian prisoners. What a pathetic lot. Many of them didn't have decent gear to begin with, not even uniforms or boots. After they're disarmed, we get them away from the front and neutralize them. Stalin will soon run out of his rag-tag communist cannon fodder!"

"Doesn't it take a lot of time and resources for the *Wehrmacht* to accommodate so many prisoners?"

"Accommodate?" Kurt laughed. "First of all, it's not our problem; the SS takes care of POWs. And it's not a problem for the SS, either. They come in behind us and handle the 'problem,' you know what I mean?" Recalling the SS's work in France, Rolf nodded as his brother went on, "I don't see us feeding them or building them cozy *dachas*." Kurt smirked. "The SS shoots stragglers and troublemakers, I've seen that myself. And the wounded, well they aren't any use to us, are they? As for the rest, if we get a little work out of them, fine, but if they die, there are plenty more where they came from." The bottle almost slipped from Kurt's hands as he held it upside down to drain out the last drops of schnapps, then he staggered up the stairs to bed.

Then and now, Rolf understood. Casualties are an inevitable result of war. People die on and off battlefields. Some would say casualties are the goal of war. The Russians should have expected such treatment when they lost. Why, now that the shoe was on the other foot, should he want the Americans to behave differently? Even the thieves and bullies were only exercising their prerogatives. The world was black and white, clearly delineated into the victors and the vanquished, as it had always been. John Schmidt was just too naive to see that.

Or maybe he wasn't naive at all. Maybe he was only pretending to be kind to gain Rolf's confidence so later he might lure him into speaking out against Germany for propaganda purposes. Or maybe he thought Rolf would inadvertently spill valuable information that would help the Allies in the war effort.

Whatever the American had been up to, Rolf's emotional reaction to Schmidt's nonsense was justifiable. He must have mainly been feeling guilty for having almost been taken in by all the talk of mutual respect and friendship and the war being over. But he hadn't fallen for it. He would have to be very careful now—among so many enemies—not to do or say anything that could cause anyone to question his loyalty. The eternal rules still applied.

When Rolf was a child, his family was in a feud with their closest neighbor, Frau Schneider, whose cow trampled much of the Mueller garden. Frau Schneider refused to acknowledge the damage or her wrongdoing for not minding her cow. Animosity was high for weeks, until Rolf's mother said it was time to move on. So, she spoke to the neighbor and forgave her with no apology or acknowledgement of guilt. His mother said it was time to forgive and forget.

*No!* thought Rolf. *I am a warrior for the Reich. I am not my mother arguing with a cranky neighbor, and this is not the time for women's sentimentality. And this is not some minor spat, it's all-out war. I don't have to get along with the Americans. We are not friends, we are enemies, and I will not be taken in by such talk. I want to see America and all its John Schmidts soundly defeated.*

The words of the oath he took when all this started were as unequivocal and meaningful in 1943 as they were on that frigid day in 1939 when he raised his arm and proudly proclaimed them for the first time:

I swear by God this sacred oath that to the Leader of the German empire and people, Adolf Hitler, supreme commander of the armed forces, I shall render unconditional obedience and that as a brave soldier I shall at all times be prepared to give my life for this oath.

*At all times.* It was not his place to question how the war was being conducted or to choose to be friendly with the enemy. His faith was in the *Fuehrer* and the Reich. He would not be taken in by disingenuous offers of friendship or succumb to defeatism. He would not curry American favor. He'd fought bravely, he did what he had to do, he did things he never wanted to do for the *Fuehrer*; now he must accept his new circumstances with the same courage, remain loyal to the Fatherland, and serve his *Fuehrer*. That was what was true and good and normal. His war was not over; the battlefield had merely changed. Fuck John Schmidt!

# Chapter 4
# TRUE BELIEVERS

With his body mending and his emotions momentarily quieted, Rolf learned of the next step in his prisoner's journey. He would soon be transferred to a small camp at the edge of Bizerte, then to the larger facility at Mateur, farther to the southwest. He wasn't sure what to expect. The first camp was said to hold thousands of Germans, but only a few had tents. And Mateur was worse. The orderly told him that the tens of thousands of men there all spent twenty-four hours a day out in the open. Americans called it "The Cage." Water was in short supply, and the camp latrines were open cesspools. Cholera, dysentery, and malaria were rampant.

Whatever he encountered, Rolf would not complain. He would be glad to be outdoors. Early summer on the Tunisian coast was generally nice. Days were warm, not hot, and nights were cool. There wasn't much rain, and the Mediterranean breezes were quite pleasant.

He was tired of the hospital. Being surrounded by seriously-wounded men was depressing. Patients were still slow-dying, and their final hours were often messy, gut-wrenching affairs. He was ready to put some distance between himself and death's grim reach.

And there was the boredom. By the middle of June, he'd read every German publication he could find, plus the few English materials left by Americans or the Red Cross. He played Euchre with other patients a few times, but quickly tired of that. There was no one from his unit in the hospital, and he'd still not found out about any of them. He didn't enjoy talking with the others, who were fixated on speculating about what would happen next to them. At best, it was undignified, so he kept to himself. He wrote more letters to his family, not knowing whether they were received, but it felt good to write as long as he kept it light. A Red Cross representative started weekly inspections and delivered and collected mail, so it was no longer necessary to use an American as an intermediary.

Early in June, Schmidt stopped by. When Rolf saw him at the door, he closed his eyes and pretended to be asleep. A few days later, the American caught him in the courtyard, where he could not be avoided.

"How are you doing, my friend? You look great!"

"I'm good." he bristled at being called an American's friend, especially in front of others.

"Glad to hear it. I'm not surprised. You seem very determined to recover."

"I am."

"Are you getting outside much?"

"Every day." He hoped his curt responses would get his point across.

Schmidt carried on cheerfully. "That's good. I guess it won't be long before you're discharged from here. Is there anything I can do for you? Do you have any letters to send?"

"No."

"Well, all right then. I'll look for you here or at the camp outside of town. If you need something, let them know and they'll get word to me. Even if you just want to talk."

"I'm sure I won't."

"Okay." Any disappointment Schmidt felt stayed hidden. "Oh, I have something for you." He handed him a copy of *Auf den Marmorklippen.* "Do you know this author?"

"Ernst Junger, yes, I read his earlier work, *In Stahlgewittern,* about World War I."

"I came across this and thought you might find it interesting. It was written in 1939. It's not related to medicine, but it's something to help pass the time, right?"

"I suppose." It was cloying that Schmidt remembered that he'd studied medicine. Was he this damned familiar with all the Germans?

He decided to throw the book away, but by the time he got to his bed, he'd changed his mind. Having anything new to read would be good, and Junger's books were uncensored in Germany. His first one made him famous. He was pro-German, so how bad could it be to read his new one? If Rolf remembered correctly, Junger was serving with the *Wehrmacht* in France. He was not a Nazi but was definitely a loyal German. Just like Rolf.

On a sunny Wednesday, June the twenty-eighth, he was loaded into a truck and taken to the small camp just outside of Bizerte. Because his uniform had been ruined, he was issued a new set of clothes: A long-sleeved blue work shirt and a pair of blue cotton trousers with a thick white "P" stenciled on one leg and a "W" on the other. He also received a German cap and jacket, both used. The jacket had faded blood stains on the back and one sleeve but was otherwise in good condition. No bullet holes, at least. He wondered what happened to its previous owner. It wasn't the first time he'd used clothing from someone who'd been injured or died. In the early days of the blitzkrieg through Belgium, he lost his cap and took a replacement from the head of a fallen comrade.

The camp was not as crowded as Rolf had heard. Only a thousand POWs or so were there, and everyone had a cot in a tent. He learned from another POW that several thousand had already been taken away.

"Where'd they go?" he asked.

"Some to Mateur, some to America," another man told him.

"They're taking us to America?"

"Yes, I heard another group will depart soon."

He was initially surprised they'd be being taken across the Atlantic, but it made sense. American troops were undoubtedly now streaming east across the ocean—he was sure the Allies would eventually try to invade Europe—and POWs could be ferried back to the U.S. aboard those empty ships. That didn't explain what would happen once they got there. He wondered if the Americans had their own SS. Maybe they'd be forced to do hard labor on a starvation diet. From thousands of miles away, who would know what abuses they suffered? He twitched involuntarily but refused to allow himself to worry over something he couldn't control.

A day after arriving at the camp, Rolf had a greater surprise. Wilhelm Stultzman, his best friend from his company in the 21st Panzer Division, was there too. He'd often thought about Willy and feared he'd been killed. Coming in and out of a latrine, they nearly ran into each other. "Willy! My God! It's so good to see you! How are you?" The men hugged.

Beaming, Willy said, "I'm good, and so glad to see you! I figured you were dead."

"Close to it," Rolf said, pointing down and up. "I got shot in the legs and hit in the head, knocked out cold for a week. How about you?"

"I only got a twisted ankle and some fractured ribs. I was lucky to make it through those final days. Even luckier to make it through surrendering. Giving up was more dangerous than fighting."

"What do you mean?"

"Just that. After you and I got separated, everything went to hell. Several of us were assigned as snipers to slow down the Americans. You were put on sniper duty, too, remember?"

"Yes."

"Anyway, four of us, Dietz, Hillermann, Shultz, and I, got pinned down near the harbor. After being trapped for hours, we had to surrender. Hillermann was bleeding badly. We couldn't stop it and were out of ammunition, so we shouted in German that we wanted to come out. Someone answered in English, then switched to broken German and told us to put down our weapons and put our hands up. We did as we were told, except Dietz shouted over that Hillermann couldn't walk, so he and Shultz were going to help him. I wish you'd been there because none of us speaks English like you."

"Why would that have mattered?"

"Because I'm not sure if the Americans didn't understand or didn't care, but when we came out, they shot the others. All three of them died right there. I was a short distance away with my hands up. I have no idea why they didn't shoot me, too, but they didn't."

"My God!" Rolf patted his friend on the shoulder and inhaled slowly. "I'm so sorry. I've been trying to find out about you guys since I woke up. You're the first one I've seen since then. I'm the only one here that I know of. This fucking war."

Willy sighed. "Tell me about you, what happened to you, where you've been."

As they walked, Rolf shared his story. He glossed over his injuries, but Willy could see his limp. Rolf described the hospital, but didn't mention Schmidt. In his tent, they took seats on Rolf's cot some distance from a few others, who were writing, reading, dozing, or staring blankly off into space.

"How are the guards here?"

"There are a few bastards who love being in charge. The ones who were forced into guard duty after being on the front lines are the worst.

They'd rather shoot us than guard us. A few guys have had their things stolen," he said. "Overall, though, I have to say most of the Americans I've met are decent enough."

"Really?" Rolf said in a frosty tone. "Even the ones who shot our friends as they were surrendering?"

"Of course, not them. That was unforgivable, but that's what war is, one unforgivable act after another, linked together like a never-ending chain. My God, how I'm sick of this war, and Hitler, and Nazis!"

"Willy!" Rolf quickly grew upset.

His friend spoke more quietly but went on. "I mean it. I blame our goddamn *Fuehrer* for getting us into this mess. I hate him! What in the hell were we doing in North Africa anyway? The Italians screwed up, couldn't defeat the British, then we had to come to their rescue, and then the Americans showed up and kicked our asses."

"Stop it! I don't want to hear such talk." One of Rolf's legs began to shake nervously.

"I'm sorry, but that's how I feel."

"You weren't saying that two years ago. Back then, you said you believed in our cause."

"Maybe I did. Maybe I was just stupid. What have the last two years achieved? Nothing, except death and destruction. Dead Germans, dead Englishmen, dead Italians, dead Americans! Bombed cities, even in Germany. Have you seen Bizerte?"

"I nearly died there."

"So much destruction, and for what? After two years of fighting in this godforsaken desert, what do we have to show for it? Sun-baked leather for skin? Broken bones and scars? Friends gone forever? Glory for the Fatherland?"

"No more of this talk! I'm still a German soldier, Willy, I stand by our oath. And you must too." Rolf was very animated. He and Willy had always been candid with each other, more so than with anyone else. They hadn't always agreed, but this was going too far.

Willy looked at him with tired, sad, knowing eyes. "I'm sorry." Then he changed the subject. "Let's not argue, my friend. I'm so glad to see you again. Knowing you're alive makes it so much better for me." He lowered his voice even more and added, "And you're right, you have to be very careful in here about what you say. It's not just Americans we have to worry about."

"What do you mean?"

"Our officers still think they're in charge. They think we should be carrying on the war in here and taking orders from them. They don't want to hear any criticism of Germany or the *Fuehrer*. I've heard stories of prisoners being beaten for speaking out—by other prisoners. I should be more careful. You're right. There are still some true believers in here." They looked around to see if anyone in the tent was eavesdropping. None appeared to be.

"Maybe I'm still a true believer. Maybe I also think we should do what we can to promote the Reich, even now."

"That's your prerogative." Willy looked at his watch. "Are you up for a walk around the camp to get some exercise and fresh air before dinner?"

"Yes, I'd like that. I'm trying to get back in shape." Relaxing, he winked, "And it looks like you could use a little more exercise yourself."

Willy hit his stomach with a thwack, and the friends laughed as they stepped out. A gentle breeze filled the camp with sweetness from white and pink blossoms in nearby gardens. On the north side, just inside the perimeter, the ground rose slightly. Standing there, Willy and Rolf admired gnarled olive trees and ancient fig orchards. Beyond lay the ruins of Bizerte, and on the far horizon, a thin blue sliver of the Mediterranean was visible.

"It seems so peaceful now." Willy sighed, lost in thought.

# Chapter 5
# GOODBYE, AFRICA

Some POWs were put to work clearing clogged roadways, but Rolf and Willy didn't get assigned to crews, so they spent their days exercising, eating, and discussing everything, except the war and politics. Uneasy around supercilious guards, zealous Nazis, and gossip mongers, they mostly kept to themselves. What a relief it was to have a friend to pass the time with.

Willy was from München, two years younger than Rolf. He was drafted in 1940, right out of school. North Africa was his first campaign. The two met when Rolf returned from France and was reassigned to what became the 21$^{st}$ Panzer Division. They hit it off at once, enjoyed the things that appeal to men their age—women, sports, drinking—but they shared deeper interests as well, in literature, history, music, art, philosophy. The others in their squad didn't, so the two quickly gravitated to one another and formed a deep bond. Because he'd already experienced combat, Rolf took it upon himself to look out for Willy like a big brother when they deployed. He was strong and athletic, smart, and a good soldier, but Rolf worried about him on and off the field, fearing his outspokenness could get him into trouble.

Side by side, they spilled blood across the continent. More than once, one saved the other's life. They hardly ever talked about what they'd lived through, but each took comfort in knowing the other had been there and understood.

For his part, Willy was a constant source of encouragement. No matter how bad things got, he found a way to be upbeat. Rolf marveled at that. Since his own first **battles in France, he'd been prone to periods of unrelenting darkness and anger when** it felt like evil was leeching right out of his soul into the world. Willy would see his friend withdrawing and try to help him back to the light. His zany, frequently-sarcastic humor could always make Rolf laugh.

They never found out what happened to their comrades. They heard that a few had spent time in their camp before being sent elsewhere, but they never saw them. They did learn that casualties in their unit were extraordinarily high.

July 8th was Rolf's 23rd birthday. He was glum at the thought of a birthday in captivity, and the unusually cool and overcast weather added to the drear.

"Happy Birthday!" Will said when they met for breakfast. "You probably thought I wouldn't remember, but your birthday is the same as my father's, so it was easy." Rolf's face brightened. "I have an idea, let's ask the guards for passes to the beach. We'll say you're a VIP, a Very Important Prisoner, and would like a swim. We'll promise to be back by dinner. And maybe the Yanks will give us the keys to a jeep so we don't have to walk. And cake! What do you say?"

Rolf smirked. "Being a VIP might get me shot. And I'd prefer strudel."

Willy took a package from behind his back. It was wrapped in crumpled newsprint and string tied into a sad little bow. "In the meantime, here you are." Inside was a hand-carved wooden pig figurine, about four inches long and two inches high. It was a three-dimensional puzzle made up of fifteen odd-shaped and various-sized pieces that had to be put together in the right sequence in order to assemble the animal. Seeing Rolf's pleasure, he added, "For luck and to help you with the boredom. If you take it apart, it will be a challenge getting it back together, even for a genius like you."

"Thank you so much!" Rolf would have been glad to have anything to open, but a pig—a German good luck talisman—was especially nice. "Did you carve this yourself?"

"No, Papa did. He gave it to me when I was a boy. I've had it with me since I left home."

"Then you shouldn't give it away."

"I want you to have it. Maybe it will keep you from getting blown up again."

"Maybe." Rolf danced the little pig around the table and patted his friend on the back.

As they were finishing their meal that evening, Willy stood up on his chair, to Rolf's great embarrassment, and proclaimed *"Herzlichen*

*Glückwunsch zum Geburtstag*, **Rolf!" As the men sang**, one of the guards slipped out and returned with a small bottle of vodka. "It's okay to bend the rules a little for a birthday," he said, taking a swig. Then he passed the bottle to Rolf, who initially refused, but finally drank and gave it to Willy to shouts of "*prost*!" and "*zum wohle!*" Everyone was cheered by this small, kind gesture.

As they were leaving, Rolf approached the American, but wasn't sure what to say, so he just stood there. The guard, an older, heavy-set man with a thick Southern accent, laughed, "You looked at first like you thought I might be gonna poison ya." Before Rolf could respond, the man continued. "But don't worry, son, I'd never waste good liquor. Happy birthday."

A day or so later, a load of art supplies and other materials arrived, courtesy of the IRC. Willy was excited because he loved to draw and was thinking of becoming an architect. That same day, he began sketching scenes of Tunisia beyond the camp. In spite of all the havoc they'd wreaked, there was still beauty to behold for those who looked. Willy wanted to capture some of it. He used his imagination to supplement what his eyes saw to try to convey what a building or a scene might have looked like before the war. For an amateur, his paintings were quite good.

Rolf selected a writing tablet and pencils and started a journal. He wasn't sure why but felt the need to record his thoughts. Maybe he'd want to remember these extraordinary times someday. Or maybe it was just to relieve the boredom.

In the beginning, he wrote protectively, would not spell out anything that he wouldn't want someone else to see in a place that offered no privacy. Or perhaps he didn't yet want to share his truest thoughts with himself, so his entries from Tunisia were stiff and shallow, mainly remarks about the weather or meals or his health. Little did he know that this would be the start of a journaling habit that he'd come to cherish. And along the way, his writing blossomed from superficial sprigs into deeply personal, sometimes elegant blooms of self-revelation. Gradually, he'd commit it all, his joys and sorrows, successes and failures, to paper. But it was never his intention to let anyone else read his journals. When asked why he wrote if not to share his reflections with others, he'd glibly say that keeping a journal was just a hobby, nothing more.

One afternoon Rolf was reading *Auf den Marmorklippen* when Willy stopped by his tent. "So, you like Junger?" he said.

"A little. I finished this a few weeks ago, but it was confusing, so I'm trying again."

"I've read it, too, and also found it hard because of all the metaphors. I think Junger's hiding a very negative message about Nazism in there."

"I'm not sure about that, but I am a little surprised he could get away with some of this."

Willy snickered, "It's too intellectual for the Nazis to comprehend."

"Maybe, but it can be taken different ways. Junger is so clever. It might actually be an indictment of communism, not National Socialism. That must be how he got it printed."

"Where did you get it?" Willy asked.

"From an American at the hospital. I don't know where he got it."

"Why did he give it to you? Was he a friend?"

"He's a guard, not a friend." The exasperation in Rolf's voice surprised Willy. "We spoke a few times, that's all. I'm not sure why he gave me the book. Maybe he agreed with you, thought it was anti-Nazi and that it would encourage me to be disloyal to Germany."

"So, he had you pegged as a seditionist, a collaborator with the Americans? You?"

"I didn't say that, and it sounds silly when you do. But you never know."

"Whatever the reason was, when you're finished, I'd like to read it again."

As they spoke, another POW came in and said a notice was posted outside the mess tent about 500 prisoners departing for America the next day. Rolf and Willy hurried over and pressed into the gathering crowd. They were happy to see both their names on the list and relieved to be going to America instead of Mateur. The notice did not say where they would be taken once they got to the U.S., only that they were leaving the following morning.

"Before the war, I wanted to visit America one day, but this is not how I envisioned it."

Willy was more animated. "Look at it this way, at least we don't have to buy a ticket, and it will be a helluva lot easier to pack than when we shipped out to North Africa two years ago."

Rolf added, "Yes, I just hope we don't end up paying some other way once we get there."

Willy grinned. "I'm glad we'll be together so you can translate if I get into trouble."

"And how much trouble are you planning on getting into?"

Willy just flashed a grin.

With the rising sun came orders instructing those listed for transport to dress, go to the mess tent, and be lined up in thirty minutes. Rolf and Willy met in the mess, where they were handed a day's supply of C-ration kits. Heading for the gate, Rolf saw John Schmidt standing with some other guards. He looked away, but Schmidt saw him and walked over.

"Good morning. It looks like you'll be seeing America before I do. Good luck to you."

"Thanks."

"If you make it to Nebraska, please be sure to tell my family hi."

Rolf was flustered. "I doubt I'll be seeing your farm. Goodbye."

Schmidt smiled, then turned to rejoin the other Americans.

"Who's that?" asked Willy.

"The guard who gave me Junger's book."

"He seems like a nice enough fellow."

Rolf smiled. "I suppose. But I was always told it's the nice ones you have to watch out for. And he is still an American, and I am still a German."

"You've such a pessimist. There are still good people in the world, even Americans."

"We're about to learn more about that, aren't we?"

The drive to the port in open Army troop transports was slow due to their winding route around still-blocked roadways. Rolf hoped to glimpse the neighborhood where he was shot, maybe recognize a building, but nothing looked familiar, in part because Bizerte's survivors were already renewing the landscape, restoring the city to itself. The place had a noisy air of defiant resurgence. Merchants hawking their wares in re-opened bazaars could be heard even over the vehicles' engines and the crackle of tires over rock-strewn streets.

In one destroyed building where only the stone walls remained and everything else had crumbled into itself, an old couple had cleared away enough rubble just inside the front archway to create space for a little cafe. At each of the six tiny tables, grey-bearded men in tired kaftans and well-worn babouches gathered for kabobs sizzling on a small grill and mint tea served from a lone tea pot sitting beside a dented old samovar. Rolf and Willy both commented on how ironically normal the restaurant looked in the middle of such devastation.

The old men in the cafe barely noticed the Allied military trucks passing by, but as they made their way toward the harbor, a few younger Tunisians began shouting when they saw the Germans, then a fast-growing crowd began to pace the slow-moving trucks. Men and women surged in, spewing vulgar epithets in Arabic and French and gesturing their deep antipathy. They spat and threw bricks and stones and babouches, whatever they could find, at the captives. American guards couldn't quell the commotion. Neither Rolf nor Willy was hit, but others were. A man near them was struck above the eye and bled profusely. Several Germans tried to shield him from further injury until they reached the docks. They tried to wipe his face, but instead smeared blood all over the man and themselves.

Willy looked, as if to say, *What should we expect after what we did to their country?*

Rolf glared at him. "So much for the Americans protecting defenseless prisoners, eh? Can you imagine how they're going to love us in America?"

The harbor was alive with soldiers, sailors, merchant and civilian crews, stevedores, and locals moving in every direction. The Germans were handed off to a new group of guards, lined up, and walked to a wharf where a mismatched flotilla of self-propelled barges, whale boats, and other small craft waited. The guards cleared a path through the throngs with shouts and whistles so the POWs could pass.

At the wharf, they came alongside an odd group of fifty or sixty American soldiers. They wore war-soiled uniforms, but weren't moving, in marked contrast to everyone else. Some were sullen and downcast. Most avoided eye contact. Others were nervous and flinched at the constant loud noises. Some were muttering. One particularly wretched looking young man was cursing loudly in between outbursts of gibberish, all the while spraying those near him with his spittle. These men were all unarmed and being guarded by other Americans. Rolf and Willy were trying to make sense of it when one of the guards detailed to the Germans shouted to one guarding the Americans.

"Hey Jonesy, what you got there?"

"Crazies. Supposedly they cracked up. Couldn't take the heat so now they get to go home to mommy. The bastards! I think it's a bunch of shit. They're faking it. Shell-shocked, my ass!"

"I sure as hell hope they ain't on my ship! It's bad enough I gotta cross the pond with a load of sauerkrauts. Sure don't need any crazy Americans too."

"It might be fun. Put 'em together and see what happens. Maybe they'd toss each other overboard. You could take bets on who'd sink and who'd swim!"

Neither the American detainees nor most of the Germans seemed to understand what was being said, but Rolf heard it all. He pitied those who were the butts of the others' cruelty and wondered aloud whether those callous, arrogant guards had ever been in a real battle.

At the end of the wharf, Rolf and Willy were pointed onto a barge. As soon as it filled, its civilian crew pulled off, and they headed out over glassy-smooth water toward a large gray ship anchored among too many others to count. Vessels were crammed into the harbor and stretched out across the water as far as the eye could see. Scuttled ships littered the beaches, along with burned-out plane fuselages and all other manner of war's waste and detritus.

"Look at all that," Rolf said with a sweeping gesture. "I guessed it. The Allies are gathering here and getting ready to head north. And we're going to miss the party."

"You're not sorry about that, are you? You've been to enough parties already."

"I'm a soldier, Willy. I'm well enough to fight again, to do my duty. I wish I could help stop what's coming." He thought of his parents and sister doing their chores on the farm near Olpe that morning, unaware of what was coming. A chill ran down his spine.

Willy took off his backpack and dug around in it until he found a pencil and a small tablet of paper. Immediately, he began sketching something in broad strokes.

Rolf was puzzled. "Are you drawing the American armada or the sad remains of our *Kreigsmarine*?"

"Neither," said Willy without looking at him. He pointed to a spot out in the distance between the large foreign vessels, where a fleet of local fishing boats had gathered. Willy surmised that one of the boats had come upon a school of sardines or anchovies or Atlantic bonito and their full nets and excitement had summoned the other boats to partake. "Some Tunisians are going to eat well tonight," he said with a smile. "I'm glad."

"Me too."

By the time the barge had turned and Willy lost sight of the fisherman, he had enough of a sketch done that he could complete it later. Turning, Bizerte came into view one last time. "Goodbye, Africa. I wonder when I'll see you again. Maybe someday I'll come without a gun in my hand, see the pyramids, ride a camel." Eyes glazing over, he added under his breath, "I'm sorry for my part in all this."

"What day is this? Willy asked.

"Thursday, 15 July 1943. A good day for sailing, I hope."

# Chapter 6
# LIBERTY

When the barge was beside its assigned ship, the two were lashed together and the men climbed up the Jacob's ladder hung over the larger vessel's side as oblivious seagulls screeched and swooped and scoured the water. The air was heavy with salt, seaweed, and acrid exhaust. On deck, POWs were counted into groups of twenty and sent down into the ship's five holds.

When it was their turn, Rolf and Willy were handed more C-ration kits and descended a steep, narrow stairway into the cavernous hold #4, second from the stern of the ship. It was at least two stories high. Built to transport war materiel, the ship had been retrofitted with scaffold-like metal flooring that divided each hold into more levels to carry as much human cargo as could be crammed in. Dozens of sets of bunks were jammed onto each of the floors, separated by aisles barely wide enough to allow a man to pass. Each level was less than six feet from floor to ceiling. The entire hold smelled of pesticides, cigarettes, and lingering human odors that liberal quantities of bleach had failed to erase. They took upper bunks next to each other, made up their beds, and settled in to wait the several hours it would take before all the passengers were aboard. Until then, they weren't allowed on deck.

Windowless, the hold's few naked bulbs cast a surreal, dim light. Rolf's bunk was close enough to a bulb that he could read and write, though barely. Hunched over to keep from hitting his head on the ceiling, he recorded the date and wrote a few lines, but the warm, damp darkness soon made him and everyone else drowsy.

Mid-afternoon, the ship rattled to life. Turbines opened and a windlass creaked slowly and rhythmically as it cranked the anchor up from the seabed. The propeller created a different humming pulse and horn blasts sounded departure. The entire ship groaned and swayed, more and more noticeably as forward movement began. Rolf and Willy both opened their eyes.

"Do you know the name of this ship?" Willy asked.

"No, it wasn't painted on the sides."

"Why not?"

"Probably to keep our side from knowing where it's headed and what's aboard."

"I was wondering about that. Let's hope our side doesn't decide to sink us. That would be a shitty way to go, torpedoed by ourselves."

"I know." Rolf sat up slightly. "I think this is called a liberty ship, which the Americans are building quickly and in great numbers. Our leaders say they may not be seaworthy."

"Thanks for that!" Willy said sarcastically. "So, we're going to prison aboard a ship called 'liberty?' Wonderful!"

Toward evening, a dower American guard came down with a translator. While they were at sea, he said, they would be eating only C-rations. Each kit consisted of a meat can with beans, potato hash or vegetable stew, a bread-and-dessert can with an instant beverage, and an accessory can containing sugar, gum, cigarettes, matches, a can opener, and toilet paper. Kits would be handed out three times a day on deck, weather permitting, and meals could be eaten there or taken below. When a few prisoners grumbled, the guard scowled. "You're getting fed for sitting on your asses. These rations are the same that our men get in the field. If it's good enough for them, it's sure as hell good enough for the likes of you." The translator paused until the guard ordered him to translate exactly what he'd said. After he did, a few Germans scowled back.

Toilets were in the midship house in the center of the ship, below the bridge. There were no showers but wash basins would be set up daily on deck. Seasickness pills were available, and there was a small medical staff on board for emergencies. Drinking water would be kept in coolers on deck. The following morning, the guard said, POWs would be shown the lifeboats and given instructions on how to use them.

Normally, prisoners could come and go between the deck and their holds during the day. They were admonished not to speak to the crew, which included civilians and the merchant seamen responsible for the ship's defenses. They were banned from any hold, except their own, and emphatically warned that anyone found near the guns or any military equipment would be shot on sight. Other, less serious misbehavior would be punished with confinement in the brig.

Shortly after sunset, the POWs were all allowed up to the deck. It was soon crowded, but the cool evening air was a huge relief. Already, the hold was stifling and hazy with cigarette smoke. In the dusky light and with a full moon rising behind the ship, Rolf could see the shadows of other ships in formation with theirs. Standing portside and facing what he thought should be south, he tried to see the African coastline, but they were already too far out into the Mediterranean. Looking back, he saw the cannon and anti-aircraft guns at the stern. He had no doubt everyone on board would know it if those guns started shooting and noted with irony that his life might now depend on those American guns protecting him from his own country.

After just fifteen minutes, the prisoners were ordered below. Reluctantly heading down the stairs, Rolf's legs buckled without warning. He almost fell as he was overcome by waves of vertigo and nausea that grew more debilitating by the minute. It surprised him how quickly and unexpectedly the seasickness hit, and in calm seas. His entire world was spinning. He stumbled to his bunk and barely managed to get his outer shirt, trousers, and shoes off and lay down. He was afraid he'd vomit and was panting for air as a dull pressure inside his head transformed into an exquisitely bad headache. It was like every nerve in his brain was firing at the same time, and everything, even the air, was pushing down on them.

"Are you okay?" Willy asked when he saw his ashen friend sweating profusely. "Want me to get the seasickness medicine for you?"

"Yes," was all he could muster. Eyes closed and curled into a ball, he thought that if the *Luftwaffe* or *Kriegsmarine* was going to attack, it should be right now. He wouldn't care, as long as it put an end to this misery.

# Chapter 7
# SITTING DUCKS

The seasickness was slow to abate. For days, Rolf laid on his bunk, tried to sleep, and drank as much water as possible, but he couldn't eat and didn't even try to read or write until after he'd finally dragged himself up onto the deck. The ship's rocking motions were less debilitating up there, and the fresh air breathed life into him. When he forced himself back onto a daily exercise schedule, his recovery accelerated. Good weather and calm seas also helped.

Even so, moving too quickly would cause dizziness, and there was periodic nausea throughout the entire voyage. But at least the hold wasn't spinning round and round, and the sea's swelling and sighing no longer made him feel like he was going to fall down or throw up.

As they steamed west by southwest, Rolf saw thin dark strips on the far horizon a few times, the African coastline. Near Algiers and Oran, more Allied ships joined their convoy—more personnel transports, destroyers, and cruisers. British corvettes and armed trawlers took up defensive positions on the perimeters. One evening, they counted sixty-two ships. Rolf wondered how many more were out there beyond his vision.

After Oran, the ships bunched closer together as they started their passage through the Strait of Gibraltar. At its narrowest between Spain and Morocco, the Strait is just nine miles wide, a bottleneck that made it a favorite spot for German and Italian attacks. For years, they'd hit Allied ships there utilizing bombs, torpedoes, mines, even frogmen.

"What do you think?" asked Willy. "Are we heading into danger?"

"We're sitting ducks," Rolf recalled news accounts at home early in the war. "All these ships so close to each other will have to slow down, and that will make us attractive targets."

That same evening as they finished eating, loudspeakers blared, ordering prisoners and guards below deck at once. "Already? Damn!" Rolf said. Willy watched in amazement as every American on board spring into action. Men ran toward weaponry while others rushed crates to predetermined locations and broke out equipment and ammunition. Watchmen scanned the clear evening skies and others raced to the bridge while horns and loudspeakers blared from nearby vessels. Coded messages flashed urgently between ships in the fleet.

Standing in line to go down, Willy asked a guard, "What's going on?" The guard, an older man in a too-tight uniform, was named Pat O'Leary. Willy and he had gotten acquainted while Rolf was incapacitated. O'Leary was almost fatherly to Willy and spoke a little German.

O'Leary frowned. "A transmission was intercepted. Germans are supposed to attack us by 2200 hours." He gestured with his hands and arms to supplement his rough German.

"Tonight?"

"Yes."

"Is there a way to let them know this ship is carrying Germans?" Willy asked hopefully.

O'Leary smiled at Willy's naiveté and shook his head. "Sorry, kid, your air force and navy don't seem to care. You and I are on the same side tonight."

"Oh." Willy looked forlorn. "By the way, what's the name of our ship?"

"It's the Daniel G. Bitler, AK-126. Now get down there, son."

To Rolf, Willy said, "If we're going to die on it, we should know its name."

"It would be more useful if you remember how to use the lifeboats," Rolf said. "I was sick when they gave instructions. And let's hope our countrymen aren't good shots tonight."

Willy laughed nervously. "I never thought I'd hear you say that."

The POWs made their way down to their bunks, followed by O'Leary and another guard, who took seats near the stairs. Everyone was fidgety, but the hold was eerily quiet as they strained to hear anything that might clue them in to what was going on up above.

The wait wasn't long. Moments after the hatch was secured, the ship's anti-aircraft guns opened up with quick, loud rat-a-tat-tats. Its cannons' thunderous ka-booms were less frequent and deeper, but each one of their concussive blasts reverberated through every sliver of the ship.

Then came the German attack—bombs whistling in, planes buzzing down, dull kerplunks in the sea. Bombs that missed?

The clamor faded into a pregnant silence that was followed by another round of the same booming, zinging, and buzzing, only louder, closer, and more threatening this time. To this frenetic second movement something new was added, something familiar to Rolf and Willy—staccatoed machine gun bullets chewing up the deck on top of them. The lights flickered, momentarily throwing the hold into complete darkness. When they came back on, Rolf saw Willy's boyish face, wide-eyed and drained of color. He tried to calm him with a reassuring smile, but didn't speak so he could stay focused on what was going on.

It was more frustrating to Rolf than frightening. In the *Wehrmacht*, he'd been cool even in the worst fights. But here, not only was he being fired upon by his own side, but he was unarmed and had no control over anything, which left him feeling exposed. On solid ground, he could shoot whoever was shooting at him, and he was an excellent marksman. And there was always a foxhole to dive into, a tree to hide behind, a building to hunker down in. Here, the whole damn ship could be blown to smithereens with one bomb, or one torpedo, and he had no way to respond, or even to know until it was too late. He hated being the sitting duck he'd just joked about.

Waves of attack continued for an hour. Sometimes explosions were close enough to rock the boat, but Rolf was about ready to think they might make it through when there came a high-pitched whistling. It sped in louder and louder until there was an enormous crash. The ship lurched sideways violently, then bounced up and down like a rubber duck in a bathtub. Gasps and curses in the hold were followed by crunching sounds on deck. The ship's guns went silent, and the hold went black and stayed that way. They held their collective breath. One man prayed earnestly and annoyingly loudly. Rolf wondered if they'd burn to death in a fireball or drown when water rushed in. He cursed both options.

After waiting for what felt like forever, it became apparent that whatever had happened, it wasn't going to kill them, at least not yet. It grew quiet above. A few men lit matches. Cigarette ends glowed bright, then dim, as smokers inhaled and exhaled.

The lights finally sputtered back on after several tries. Shouts came from people moving around above them. The men in #4 didn't move, as if any movement might cause the ship to tilt and sink. Just before Rolf couldn't stand it any longer, a young American guard opened the hatch and practically jumped down the stairs. "It's over!" he reported excitedly. "The krauts threw everything but the kitchen sink at us! A couple other ships were hit and sunk, but we're okay!"

O'Leary interrupted him, "So what was that big blast toward the end?"

The first guard caught his breath. "A direct hit! A German bomb hit the deck right above #2 and went straight down. Made a helluva hole, but it didn't explode! It's still there. You can see it from the deck. Some debris got us from a *Luftwaffe* plane that our guys shot down. It exploded midair and mostly ended up in the water, but some landed on deck." Rolf translated the gist of what he was saying to Willy.

"Casualties?"

"Yes, some in #2. Medics are getting ready to transfer the wounded to a destroyer with a bigger infirmary. Most were Germans, but I think a guard got it, too, I don't know who for sure. You're supposed to stay put down here for the night. They're trying to disarm the bomb now. I'll let you know as soon as we know more."

As soon as the younger man left, O'Leary told the POWs to try to get some sleep. When he finished talking and sat down, he began to shake, from exhilaration maybe, or perhaps the realization at how close he'd come to dying. O'Leary had never seen combat. Most of the battle-hardened Germans were more impassive, but for them all, relief mixed with what-ifs and thank-Gods and why-nots. Rolf pulled out his journal and started to write:

This evening, aboard an American ship, the Daniel E. Bitler, I, a *gefreiter* in the *Wehrmacht*, and 499 other loyal Germans were attacked by the *Luftwaffe* and *Kreigsmarine*. Apparently, the German High Command doesn't care about sacrificing us as long as American ships are destroyed. I am alive thanks to the American crew. If Reichsmarschall Goering were here, I might be tempted to say, 'I have been loyal to the *Fuehrer* all my life and served the Reich honorably. Now I must ask, is the Reich loyal to me?' What the hell?

As soon as he finished the entry, he read it, ripped it out of the journal, and tore it into tiny pieces, which he soaked in water. He wondered, *Am I destroying it because it's traitorous? Or because someone might use it against me?*

Drills, saws, and winches made noise all through the night. Smaller boats came and went. Finally, the Daniel G. Bitler's engines grew louder, and it picked up speed. Rolf was glad they weren't going to linger in the Strait and give his comrades another chance to kill them all.

# Chapter 8
# STORM CLOUDS

It was foggy when the POWs in hold #4 were allowed to climb through the hatch. They had thirty minutes to use the latrines, wash off, and collect their day's C-rations. As each man stepped out, he was handed a small towel.

The damaged portions of the ship seemed especially eerie in the fog. Zigzaggedy bullet trails had transformed the deck and other topside structures into giant connect-the-dot puzzles. Rolf and Willy stepped carefully over and around debris; a few pieces still smoldered. No plane parts were recognizable, nor did they see any human remains.

"I hope we're not going to need the lifeboats." Willy said, pointing to several that had been shredded in the attack. "Those wouldn't hold us for long."

Rolf smiled. "No, but a hearty ocean swim might get you in shape."

Willy snapped him with his towel. "What do I need to be in shape for, so all the girls on board will admire my bulging muscles?"

Restricted to the back of the ship, they caught only glimpses of the damage inflicted from the midship house to the bow. At least half the deck up there was cordoned off. After washing up, they leaned against the starboard railing to eat and make the most of their limited time outside. Due to the damage, only small groups of POWs could be allowed on deck at a time. Before he opened his can of breakfast, Rolf stretched and hurried through his morning exercises.

"Do you think we'll be attacked again?" asked Willy.

"Maybe, but I think we're past Gibraltar and in the Atlantic now. It's hard to tell, but I think we've spread out and are moving in a more westerly direction now, maybe northwesterly. I can't see any coastline."

"What difference does that make? Don't we rule the Atlantic?"

"Yes, but the U-boats usually hunt closer to the coasts. The farther out in the sea we are, the less likely they'll find us. It would be like searching for a needle in a haystack. We should be safer until we approach the American mainland."

"That's fine with me," Willy smiled. "I don't want to go through another night like that."

"Me, neither."

"Were you scared?"

"Of course, but it does no good to panic, does it?"

Before they'd finished eating, it was time to head back down, where they helped squeeze more men in. The unexploded bomb had been deactivated and the gaping hole it left was covered with huge canvas tarps, but #2 was now uninhabitable, so dozens more POWs were reassigned to the other holds. Some would have to sleep head-to-toe in pairs in single bunks. Rolf and Willy still had their own bunks, but they were butted up against one another.

Life on the ship was even more monotonous than in the hospital or camp, and tedium wasn't the only problem. Having so recently been exposed to relentless, traumatizing injury, death, fear, fatigue, and deprivation in the field, many POWs were still easily agitated. Some bore deep emotional scars. Many were demoralized at having fought so hard, only to lose. Others grieved the loss of friends or ached with homesickness and worry about loved ones. All their raw emotions and pent-up frustrations were amplified in the tomblike hold. Sleep was hard to come by. Fist-fights sometimes broke out over a card game, or the war, or nothing.

Willy and Rolf kept to themselves. They each finished Junger's book a second time, then read and discussed the others they'd gotten in Tunisia. Rolf especially liked *Great Expectations*. He also wrote letters to his family which he hoped to post in America, and he wrote in his journal every day, more cautiously so he wouldn't have to tear out any more pages. Writing was becoming cathartic for him; he saw how it was helping to organize his thinking. He was thankful the seasickness had passed enough for him to read and write.

The best part of each day was their time on deck, where they were unshackled from the hold's claustrophobic grip for a few minutes. And something else happened up there. While Rolf contemplated the vastness of the sea and sky, tiny seeds of confusion planted deep inside him since his capture began to sprout into uncertainties about life that he could not yet express, not in conversation with his best friend nor even to himself in a journal entry.

In the Third Reich, doubt was *verboten*. Hitler gave the German people intoxicating purpose and unassailable certainty, about Germany's invincibility and especially about the righteousness of their cause. When the war began, Rolf knew without having to be told that he was going to be part of a historic mission to make his country safe and strong for centuries. He was going to help Germany avenge past wrongs and command the respect it deserved from the rest of the world. For decades, Germany had been on the receiving end of some very bad deals, and now Hitler promised them only good deals.

But now, looking out over the waves and absorbing new truths—about what defeat felt like, about the war's now uncertain trajectory, and about enemies who were not all cruel or vengeful—his youthful certitude began to slip away. Never before had he had to navigate through such ambiguity. The ship's crew may have known where they were headed, but Rolf was starting to drift.

Mid-voyage, the convoy was struck by a powerful storm. For two days and nights, the sea raged beneath ferocious winds. The skies thundered ceaselessly, and torrents of rain pelted the ships as they slogged on. The Daniel G. Bitler listed dizzyingly every time it climbed or descended a mountainous wave. There were moments when the entire structure sounded like it was coming apart at the rivets.

All but essential crew members were confined to quarters. Food was stockpiled below, but no one could eat. Seasickness reclaimed Rolf and everyone else. They retched constantly. Towels, sheets, blankets, even clothing had to be used to sop up the most awful messes. Unable to reach the toilets in the midship house, they made do with buckets for latrines whose fetid contents slopped onto floors every time the ship tilted. The stench was terrible and made sick men sicker.

When the tempest finally drifted off, Rolf was among the first to stumble up the stairs as soon as it was allowed. Blinded by dazzling sunshine, he stripped off his clothing on the way to a wash basin, where he doused himself with cold water. He soaked his clothes, too, hoping to rid them of the foulness that permeated everything in the hold. As he waited for his shirt and pants to dry, he took long drinks of fresh water and ate his first C-rations in days.

Revived, he took it upon himself to organize a cleaning crew. With approval from the Americans, he and others went down with disinfectant, soap, mops, and buckets. They scrubbed floors, walls, and bunk frames. They removed the slop buckets, aired out mattresses, and did their best to freshen up the place. As they were finishing up, O'Leary stopped Rolf. "Thanks for organizing the clean-up," he said.

"You're welcome."

"What a mess! You boys got it looking and smelling a lot better."

"Thanks."

"You're a friend of Willy Stultzman's, aren't you?" O'Leary's unusual accent made his English hard to understand. It was unlike anything Rolf had heard.

"That's right. We were in the same unit in Africa."

"I'm Pat O'Leary. Private O'Leary." Instinctively, he put his hand out instead of saluting.

"I'm Corporal Mueller." Rolf looked at him nervously, hesitated, then tentatively put his hand out too. As they shook, he relaxed and went a step farther, "My first name is Rolf."

"Nice to meet you," said O'Leary. "Willy and I met while you were still sick."

"I see."

"He told me you're a good guy and looked after him."

"We looked after each other."

"Willy's a good kid. Very positive, smart. Hell, all you Germans seem nice so far. I got a son not much younger than you. I was drafted last year even though I'm 42 goddamn years old. Too old for a fighting unit, so they put me in the MPEG."

"You weren't in the army before the war?"

"Hell no! Do I look military?" O'Leary laughed. "I drove a bakery truck in Boston. I'm a Southie! That's where my family lives. This is the last place I ever expected to find myself."

"Me too," said Rolf, and they both grinned.

"I bet that's right. Here you are, in the middle of the Atlantic riding out storms on a ship, cleaning up puke and shit, talking to an American with a funny accent, and getting shot at by your own people." Rolf smiled. O'Leary seemed genuinely friendly and non-threatening. "You know where Boston is?"

"Yes, sir."

"Good for you! It's a great city. Lots of Germans there, but more Irishmen like me."

"Are we headed there now?"

"No, I think we'll make port in Virginia. Probably Norfolk. After that, I don't know where they're taking you. Someplace away from the coast. I won't be going with you after we land. I'm stuck with these transports for the time being."

"I see."

"Well, I gotta get back to my rounds. It's good to meet you, Rolf. I'm glad you're looking out for Willy. He seems kinda innocent, a babe in the woods. This war's a helluva thing, ain't it?"

It took Rolf a moment to follow, then he said, "Yes, sir. Good to meet you too."

"Thanks again for cleaning things up." O'Leary started to walk away but turned back. "One more thing. We're not supposed to be fraternizing with you guys, but if there's anything you need, let me know and I'll see what I can do."

Rolf put both hands on the railing, squatted, stretched, and let the brine-infused air flow deep into his lungs. When he opened his eyes, a perfect rainbow graced the eastern sky. The water surface was calm, except for the ship's wake that churned out diagonally and dolphins splashing as they arched gracefully in and out of the water. They seemed to be racing the ship. Rolf was savoring it all, amazed at how the sea could rage so furiously one minute and be so tranquil the next, when he heard footsteps approaching from behind. Thinking it would be Willy, he said without looking, "So, Stultzman, are you ready for some push-ups?"

An unfamiliar voice replied curtly, "Is that how you address an officer?"

Rolf turned to find a *Wehrmacht* major in an immaculate uniform staring at him coldly. He was squinting in the bright sunlight, which made his eyes look especially dark and beady.

"No, sir! I'm sorry, sir. *Heil!*" Rolf brought himself to attention and raised his right arm to the superior officer in a stiff Nazi salute.

"*Heil* Hitler." The major saluted back as he continued to stare in the icy, authoritarian manner that was so familiar to Rolf. "What is your name, your rank, and your unit?"

"I am *Gefreiter* Rolf Mueller, sir, 334th unit, second battalion, first infantry regiment, 21st Panzer Division, Afrika Korps, sir."

"Do you not wish to wear your uniform any longer, *Gefreiter* Mueller? Are you ashamed to be in the *Wehrmacht* now?" His voice was a mix of condescension and sarcasm.

"It was destroyed when I was wounded, sir."

"Are others from your unit aboard this ship?"

"Only one that I'm aware of, sir, Private First Class Wilhelm Stultzman, sir."

"So, you've not been under the command of an officer from your regiment in some time?"

"That's correct, sir." The familiarity of formal, deeply ingrained habits of conduct had once been reassuring, but it seemed strange to Rolf that he and this officer should now be maintaining strict military decorum in such a one-on-one encounter, especially in the present circumstances. Still, he continued at attention since the major had not given him permission to stand down.

"I am Major Eduard Streicher, also from the 21st." No hand was offered for shaking this time. "I am the highest-ranking officer aboard ship. As such, it is my duty to assume temporary command of all *Wehrmacht* personnel on board until further orders are received."

And further orders would be delivered out here how, by gulls or dolphins? Rolf smiled inwardly but maintained his stolid composure.

Major Streicher continued, "I am organizing our men into provisional companies. There are some thirty officers on the ship. We are housed in hold #1. What hold are you in, *gefreiter*?"

"Hold #4, sir."

"One of my subordinates may be in touch with you. I expect you and the rest of the enlisted men in your hold to comply fully with all orders given by myself or any other German officer as if we were your old battalion and regimental superiors. Is that understood?"

"Yes, sir." But it wasn't clear at all; in fact, it seemed ludicrous. How could a German officer, himself a POW, expect other prisoners to follow *Wehrmacht* orders when they were all under American control?

"Lastly, *gefreiter*, some advice: We are still at war, in case you haven't noticed. The Americans are our enemies. Each of us owes our *Fuehrer* and the Fatherland a duty to prosecute this war to the best of his abilities, even now. Contact with Americans is forbidden unless it is necessary, for meals or medical treatment. Socialization with guards is a punishable offense. If you do have communications with the enemy, I expect you to immediately report any useful information you learn to me or one of my officers. Do I make myself clear?"

"Yes, sir." He wondered if the major was an ego-maniac or crazy or just excessively military. It didn't matter; he was a threat, and Rolf hoped he was being appropriately deferential.

"Do not let me see you fraternizing with the enemy again, or you will be punished."

"Yes, sir."

Major Streicher saluted again and barked "*Heil* Hitler!" then turned crisply and strode off.

Rolf returned the salute and waited for the major's clip-clopping boots to carry him away while he grew angrier by the minute. This arrogant man's plans to organize the POWs into fighting units was a pointless parody, a mockery of the *Wehrmacht,* and his threat to punish a loyal soldier for being polite to an American was offensive. Not only that, but he'd ruined the few perfectly good moments Rolf had for enjoying the sun and the view.

It took until the next day for Willy to be well enough to come back up on deck. That evening, Rolf asked him, "Do you know a Major Streicher?"

"Yes, he commanded the second infantry regiment. I know of him from some men in units under him. He's a real son-of-a-bitch."

"Why? What do you mean?"

"Some men I met in Bizerte told me how reckless he was. After El Alamein was lost and we began the retreat to Tunisia, Streicher repeatedly put his troops in harm's way when it could have been avoided. His regiment had even more casualties than ours. His men hate him."

"Hate?"

"Yes, the story is several units were completely wiped out at Medenine due to Streicher's refusal to see what was happening, or maybe he didn't give a damn. He never tried to save them, even when there was no point in fighting on. Their deaths were avoidable and unnecessary, yet he remained indifferent. He has no honor. I heard he was reprimanded by General von Arnim." Rolf snickered. "That's funny?" asked Willy.

"No, of course not, but do you believe that any of our officers were worried about 'avoidable and unnecessary' casualties? Remember how many men we lost on the race to Tobruk, then on the way back to Tunisia when we were covering the retreat? There's a reason we haven't seen anyone else from our unit since we were captured. They're probably all dead. And none of our officers gave a *scheiße* if any of us lived or died, as long as they stayed in Hitler's good graces."

Willy looked at his friend. "Now you're starting to sound like me."

Rolf smiled, then a blank expression crept over his face and his glassy eyes stared out to the ocean's horizon without looking or seeing. Willy had seen this expression before.

"Are you okay?"

Rolf was back in Libya, stepping inside a large Bedouin tent with bright-colored rugs with beautiful designs. A group of women and children huddled together at one end of the tent, crying and praying and clutching prayer beads. None of them would look at Rolf except for a boy of eight or nine years, who stared at him defiantly. Now he was sweating, and one foot was tapping the deck.

"Hey, what's going on?"

To no one, Rolf said, "I was only doing what I had to do. What you made me do. I did things I never wanted to do." Then, hearing Willy call his name again, he slowly came back.

Willy waited quietly with a hand on Rolf's shoulder.

"I'm sorry, I was just thinking again." His pulse was slowing back to normal.

"I know. I understand, and I'm here. We're here. We're not back there."

Rolf remained quiet for a bit longer, then returned to the subject of Streicher, "Anyway, he's on this ship. I met him yesterday afternoon."

"Shit! Someone told me he was in camp, but I never saw him and thought he must have gotten sent out earlier."

"He's the senior German officer on this ship."

"And he thinks that's somehow important?"

"Yes, he clearly does."

"He's a Nazi, one of those true believers I was talking about, and maybe crazy too. I'll bet he thinks he's still in charge of all of us."

"He does. Yesterday he saw me talking to O'Leary and reprimanded me. He all but called me a traitor for being friendly with an American and threatened me if I did it again."

"Good God! O'Leary's a good man. He does his job, but isn't an ass about it. It's ridiculous if we're not supposed to be polite in return."

"You may be right, but we have to be careful in front of our officers."

"Does he want us to try to sabotage the ship? Sink it and kill ourselves in the process? Should we try to escape?" Willy's words were laced with contempt.

"It seems ridiculous, I know, and it's insulting. I've been a soldier for the Reich for four goddamn years, with the scars to prove it. I fought harder than that fancy-pants bastard ever did. I am a loyal German, but present realities must be taken into account. Things change." Rolf was surprised by the clarity of thought underlying the words he spoke, but then he stepped it back. "But what am I changing into?" He paused and shook his head.

Willy nodded. "I understand."

"Sometimes I feel like I'm a man without a country. Who can we trust?"

"You can always trust me, Rolf."

Rolf smiled, "I know. Just as long as you don't get us into any fights like that night somewhere in Libya I think, when you were mouthing off to those Italian guys."

Willy grinned, then laughed. "I was a little drunk. It was our first day off in months, and I didn't know those guys would take it personally when I started making fun of Mussolini."

"You called him *Er Puzzone*, which I believe means The Stinker, and you said if Hitler thought *Er Puzzone* was such a genius, why were we getting the shit kicked out of us." Rolf rolled his eyes and laughed.

"I was drunk, but I knew you weren't and you could take 'em. And you did!"

"Yes, but this is exactly what I've been warning you about. You really must be careful now, maybe even more than before."

"I understand, Rolf, and I am grateful for how you look out for me. So now, what do we do to satisfy a Streicher? Pick a fight with the guards? Taunt them? What good would that do?"

"I'm not sure. I didn't trust the Americans at all at first. The only one I really talked to in Bizerte was John Schmidt, and he pissed me off. But now I don't know. What if Schmidt was just trying to be friendly and that's why he gave me the book? What's wrong with that?"

Willy nodded. "Nothing. That's what I've been saying."

"Some Americans are asses, but the few I've actually spoken to so far aren't bad people. Men like O'Leary and Schmidt and the guy who shared his vodka with us? I think we need to get along with them. That's not being disloyal."

"What do you think we should say to Streicher? Or O'Leary?"

"Nothing. I think we should stay away from the officers and watch what we say and not be overly friendly with the guards. It may be as dangerous to speak out now as it was at home. I'm getting damn tired of being intimidated by men like Streicher."

"The world is upside down," Willy said sardonically, "like when we were attacked at Gibraltar by Germans and it was the Americans who were protecting us."

"No, we're protecting ourselves now."

After several more days came the announcement that the ship would dock in Norfolk during the night. The POWs prepared for lights out as usual, but stayed dressed, ready to disembark when the order came. Rolf was too curious about what lay ahead to sleep, and he also worried about another U-boat attack. More than anything, he looked forward to standing on solid ground. He may have grown to tolerate the ship's constant rocking, but he'd not miss life at sea.

# Chapter 9
# 'BOARD!

Shortly after midnight on Tuesday, August 3, 1943, the Daniel G. Bitler steamed up the Chesapeake to the mouth of the Elizabeth River, found its berth, and eased to a stop. Minutes later, Rolf and Willy were on deck waiting their turn to cross a gangplank when a familiar voice called out, "Good luck to you guys. I hope you enjoy your stay in the U.S. of A."

Rolf looked around to see who might be listening like a deer sensing a predator nearby, but Willy stepped out of line and went up to O'Leary. "Thank you for all your courtesy," he said.

"I wish I could stay, but it's back across the pond for me. Otherwise, I'd take you boys up to Boston to see the Red Sox!" O'Leary winked.

"What is a red sox?"

"Only the best damn team in America! Don't let anyone tell you it's the Yankees. You gotta learn to play baseball while you're here. It's the best game in the world!"

"I hope they let us do that. And I hope you remain safe."

"Thank you. I'll do my best. You too." O'Leary moved back toward the hatch as the Germans headed for American soil.

In spite of the hour, the Norfolk port was incredibly busy. Blinding-bright searchlights crisscrossed the sky in broad sweeps. Ships slowly moved in and out of berths up and down the river and trucks and all other manner of vehicle sped through the dockyards loaded with cargo and personnel. People on foot seemed to be everywhere, too, and everyone was in a hurry. Despite all the moving parts, the entire scene felt much more organized than madcap Bizerte.

As soon as they stepped off, the POWs were lined up and sent to a large warehouse several hundred yards east of the ship for delousing. Each POW took a turn seated on a stool. Using a cylindrical hand pump, an American liberally doused each one with DDT at the front and back of the neck, around the waistband, and up each sleeve. After his turn, eyes burning, Rolf moved as close to the warehouse doors as possible to escape the cloud of noxious fumes.

As the sun rose, the enlisted POWs were lined up again, this time to march several miles to Norfolk's railroad station. Officers got to ride. Rolf thought he saw Streicher from a distance.

"Are you ready for a march?" asked Willy.

"Can't wait! Finally, some real exercise on solid ground!"

"Your legs won't bother you?"

"They're stiff, but I'll be fine. It's you I'm worried about," Rolf said, smiling. He should have been tired, but adrenalin kept him going. He couldn't help it; this all felt more like the start of some strange, surreal adventure than incarceration.

At the gate, IDs were checked under a cloudless sky, then the men were organized into units of fifty POWs and four guards. Rolf was glad to be on the outside of his line, the better for viewing the city on their route on side streets that avoided Norfolk's main thoroughfares. A few people, mostly uniformed, came in and out of buildings, but no one paid the Germans any attention. As they marched along, he saw American houses and buildings for the first time and marveled at all the wood in most of the structures, which made them look flimsy compared to the stone and brick construction that was the norm in Europe.

Most of them were panting when they reached the railway station, but not Rolf. They wouldn't get the chance for strenuous exercise once they boarded a train, so he wanted to make the most of it, especially on such a pleasant morning. He was sorry when they turned a corner and there was the depot, but his disappointment immediately gave way to surprise.

"Where are the troop cars?" he asked as they came to a stop. Ahead was a covered boarding area and next to it a single train with more than a dozen passenger coaches.

"I don't know. Perhaps on the other side of that one?" Willy was just as confused. "Or maybe we have to wait here until it comes."

"Hold on, some of the men from our ship are already getting on this train. Look, up there." A couple cars behind the engine, German officers were entering the first passenger car, and enlisted men were moving into the second one.

"Excuse me," said a German who spoke fluent English to an American guard near them, "are we going to prison on this train?"

Amused, the guard replied, "Yes, of course. How'd you think we were gonna get you to Kansas, in freight cars?"

"Why, yes," said the German sheepishly, "That's exactly what we thought."

Loud chatter rose as the news spread. In his four years in the *Wehrmacht*, Rolf had never traveled in anything other than overcrowded box cars, notoriously cold in winter, stiflingly hot in summer. Sometimes there were rough benches for seats; often there was only straw on the floor. The only time he'd been in a train car built to carry people since the war started was when he went home on furlough. "Amazing!" he said. "And to Kansas. That's even more remarkable."

"Why?" asked Willy.

"Because Kansas is a very long way from where we are."

"O'Leary said we'd be going into the interior of the country."

"Yes, but Kansas is near the very middle of the continent. We have a long trip ahead."

"At least we'll be traveling in style. Nothing but the best for us!" Willy pursed his lips and pretended to squint through a monocle and hold a cup to his lips, pinky finger out, while he blew on imaginary tea. "I do hope they've not forgotten my luggage, or there will be hell to pay! And where is my manservant!" Rolf laughed. So only his friend could hear, Willy added, "Oh Streicher, please, do fetch my things!" Rolf cast a wary glance, then couldn't help himself and laughed even louder.

When they were beside the next car to be filled, a guard told them to step aboard and take the first available seats. The interior was divided into sixteen sections, eight on either side of a narrow aisle. Each section, two upholstered benches facing each other, was designed to hold four people. A section in the front and one at the rear were reserved for guards; this car would carry fifty-six prisoners and four guards.

Rolf and Willy stepped up and in, turned into a tight hallway that led past a small lavatory, and entered the main part of the car. They took seats facing each other by a window about halfway down the aisle. Large windows lined both sides of the car, but all the shades were pulled completely down. As the men stowed their gear and took their seats in the muted light, a guard at the back of the car said in broken German that the shades must remain drawn until the train left Norfolk.

Reveling in the car's luxury, Willy heard a door slide open behind them, looked up, and was stupefied. "Look!" An elderly black porter in a crisp white railway uniform was carrying a tray and slowly making his way down the car. He politely gestured for the men to take sandwiches wrapped in wax paper and coffee in paper cups. When his tray was empty, the porter went back for more until everyone, prisoners and guards alike, had been offered refreshments. Rolf and Willy smiled shyly and nodded to thank him as they took theirs. Few of the Germans had ever seen a Black person, except for French and Commonwealth troops from Africa, certainly never in a situation like this. Rolf had encountered a few Black musicians at cabarets and jazz clubs in Berlin, but still he stared at the porter and shook his head in disbelief.

"Am I dreaming?" Willy said quietly. "What is going on?"

"I'm not sure, but if you're going to talk instead of eat, then maybe you won't mind if I have yours?" Rolf grabbed at Willy's sandwich, but Willy pulled it back.

"No, I'm not sure what it is, but I don't care. I'm eating it!"

Rolf took a tentative bite. "It's ham with maybe some sort of mustard. The bread is different, but it's good." He gobbled up the last crumbs and leaned back against the starched white-cloth-covered headrest. He wished his parents could see him now. *Just this morning*, he thought, *I've seen houses made of sticks and a Black man and boarded an American passenger train and tasted American food.* He dozed off thinking of all that he'd have to write about.

A shrill whistle sounded, and the train convulsed from one end to the other. Couplers rattled in a chain reaction from front to rear. With guttural chug-chug-chugs, sooty black belches from the engine's smokestack, and more screechy blasts, the linked procession slowly pulled out. A man outside, hidden from view by the shades, shouted, "Board!" Rolf, still watch-less, opened his eyes and wished he knew the exact time his long journey to Kansas was beginning.

In a few minutes, as the train picked up speed and swayed gently, an officious, pear-shaped American with dark sweat rings under each arm entered with a short, nervous German. "Attention, men, attention. I am Corporal Louis Carson." His high-pitched voice was more comical than authoritative. "I'm in charge of this car's guard detail. The other guards are Privates Barnhart, Glaser, and Thomas." The corporal pointed to the other three. The unnamed German lieutenant at his side translated and fidgeted; it was soon clear that his language skills weren't good. Rolf wondered if he was a Streicher lackey.

"We are on our way to Kansas," Carson continued. "It will take several days. Exactly how long is unknown because this train does not have high priority and will stop to allow more important transports to pass. It is critical that the shades not be raised unless a guard gives you the okay to do so." Rolf wondered how anything the isolated POWs might see could possibly make any difference to anyone.

Carson explained that the seats converted to upper and lower sleeping berths and directed the porter to demonstrate. Then he asked for volunteers to work in the kitchen car and continued with more rules. Smoking was permitted during the day, but never in the berths at night. POWs could move about in the coach but must not leave the seating area unless instructed to do so by a guard. And when a prisoner wanted to use the washroom, he must raise his hand and ask first.

The Germans had listened respectfully until the corporal told them about needing permission to use the bathroom, but then several groaned, and a few laughed out loud. Willy looked around and said, "He's kidding, right? Are we in kindergarten again?"

Without thinking, Rolf raised his hand. When the nervous corporal called on him, he pretended not to speak English, but addressed the translator awkwardly and earnestly. "What if more than one of us raises our hands at once? Who decides who gets to go first? Does the guard flip a coin? How will he know who has to pee the worst?"

The Germans laughed, but not Carson. As he was about to respond, another POW interrupted him without first raising his hand, "What if we go to the toilet without first getting permission? Will you shoot us?" That led to more snickers.

A third POW chimed in, "In that case, what would the notice of death say, that I was shot for using the bathroom? Would I have been 'killed in action,' or would that only occur if I died while actually peeing?"

Another one stood up. "Should we raise two hands if we need to shit?" Now the car erupted with derisive laughter and cat-calls. Even the translator had to smile. The other guards didn't understand all that was being said, but they got the gist. A couple of them laughed, too, but not Carson. He raised his hands to demand silence, but his growing indignation and inability to maintain control only made the Germans laugh harder.

Red-faced, he finally shouted, "Silence! These are the rules, and I expect them to be obeyed!" He sounded like a petulant child and looked like he was about to stomp his feet.

At this, the Germans laughed even harder, then a few gave the corporal the Nazi salute with shouts of "*Heil*!" A couple more cried out, "Me! Me! I have to go right now!"

Seething, Carson stared out in frozen silence until the ruckus died down, when he spat out through gritted teeth, "Insubordination will not be tolerated. You are prisoners and will do as you are told. Violators will be punished. And you are never to give your filthy Nazi salute to an American. Never! Do I make myself clear?" The POWs wondered if they'd pushed the corporal too far. No one was willing to keep taunting him and find out.

Back in control, the American asked if there were any serious questions. A prisoner asked for the correct time. The translator responded that it was noon on Tuesday, August 3rd. As Carson turned to leave, he singled Rolf out for a parting glare. Rolf blushed and looked down.

Willy said, "That guy makes me miss O'Leary already."

"Maybe I shouldn't have been so rude. I don't know what came over me."

"He deserved it."

"You're right. There are decent people everywhere, and there are self-important asses everywhere too."

Willy feigned surprise. "Except in Germany, right? Surely you don't mean there are any pompous asses in Germany, do you? Especially not any Bohemian corporals!" He put two fingers above his upper lip and looked fiercely at Rolf in a crude imitation of Hitler.

"Knock it off!" Rolf was not laughing now. "For Christ's sake, that's exactly the kind of crap I've been saying you need to stop, especially in front of others." Willy nodded an apology.

# Chapter 10

# JOURNEY OF A THOUSAND QUESTIONS

Since he was a boy, Rolf loved to travel. Learning about other people, seeing new places, discovering different customs—it all fascinated him. Now, sinking into the car's gentle rhythm after a long, harried day, he quietly reflected about his other trips—a few with his family, several to and from university in Berlin, and the many military expeditions he'd been part of. How dissimilar this one was, even beyond the most obvious difference—that he was now a captive being transported somewhere without his consent. His past journeys had all been grounded in certainty. Almost always, he'd traveled a known route with clear starting and ending points and an expected duration. His just-completed transatlantic voyage was more ambiguous in that its length and the port of arrival were unknown at the outset, but even then there was a tangible goal—dry land. Now, nothing could be predicted. Where exactly were they going? He could find Kansas on a map, but it was a land of uncertain proportion on an unfamiliar continent of unfathomable scope. There was no mention of the city or town or place where they were being taken, and as for duration, who knew? Since he awoke in Bizerte, uncertainty had been the new norm, and he'd had to accept that. But now, life's capriciousness was deepening with every passing mile.

While thinking such thoughts, Rolf dozed off. He fell quickly into deep sleep, but only for a few minutes before he suddenly awoke with a loud snort, eyes wide and confused. His body jerked.

Willy jumped. "Jesus! You scared me. Bad dream?"

Rolf rubbed his eyes, stretched, and smiled. "No, well maybe. I don't know." He pressed his chin down to his chest and pushed his arms back to stretch his tight shoulder and neck muscles. "I guess, well, I guess I'm trying to comprehend all that's happening."

Willy nodded. "I think I'm a little numbed by it all."

"Who am I?" He looked over to Willy as if he could answer, but his friend could only shrug. "Am I the kid in school in Olpe? The student in Berlin? The soldier in France and Africa? The unconscious POW in a hospital in Bizerte? A few days ago, I was lost at sea. And now I'm lost on a train going to who-knows-where. Everything feels completely out of control."

Willy smiled, "But we didn't have any control when we were in the 334th."

"Yes, but at least we knew who was in charge and what the objectives were. There was some certainty. Now there is no certainty about what the next five minutes will bring, let alone the next five years."

Willy thought for a moment. "Would you rather trade this for where we were a few months ago, getting pushed out of North Africa?"

"Of course not." The question irritated Rolf. Suddenly his thoughts flashed back to that Bedouin tent. His jaw tightened as he shut his eyes and folded his arms.

An hour or so after leaving Norfolk, Carson returned and announced that the shades could be raised, to everyone's relief. As the windows were opened, the car's already-thick cloud of smoke began to dissipate. Several men politely raised their hands and were waived to the toilet.

Rolf opened his eyes, revived by the fresh air, and took in the Virginia countryside. It seemed familiar, yet different. There were forests, but the types of some trees were unfamiliar. There were large and small fields with crops, but he couldn't tell what they were growing. And the size of the herds and flocks spread out on the rolling hills they were passing was surprising. Here and there were small cities and even smaller hamlets, many no more than a few structures clustered along a main road. And everywhere on the roads were automobiles and trucks, many more than in Germany.

People completed the tableaux. Women in polka-dotted bonnets and men in overalls bent over fields and gardens. Mothers pushed baby buggies into stores while grocers in white aprons arranged merchandise out front. Old men in Panama hats grinned and gesticulated on sidewalks. Elders fanned themselves in lawn chairs under ancient, moss-dripping shade trees. Children rode bikes and played in the dirt. Now and then, a barefoot boy tried to pace the moving train, waving frantically for acknowledgement, but mostly these pass-through people were ambivalent.

Rolf wondered if they would be so indifferent if they knew it was loaded with enemy soldiers.

Most of the young Germans were quickly bored by the scenery, but not Rolf and not Willy. The first time the train came to a squeaky stop in the middle of nowhere to let another train pass, Willy pulled out his pencil and sketch pad and began the outline of what he was seeing out the window. Which reminded Rolf to take out his journal and begin writing:

Date: 3 August 1943, Location: Somewhere in America. This is the first entry that I'm writing in the United States. It will not be possible to mention everything that's happened since I wrote a day ago on the ship. Was it just a day ago?

Now we're on a train. Willy and I are sitting across from each other looking at the countryside. He's capturing what he's seeing in a drawing that may become a painting. I'm trying to do the same, but with words. But I don't have enough words to describe what I'm seeing. All I have are questions, and there's no one here to ask.

I'm going to start writing down all my questions. Then I'll try to find answers and write those down too. I'll probably have at least a thousand questions written down by the time I get to Kansas, that's where we are heading. I'll have to write smaller or I'll run out of paper.

The questions came quickly: What was sold in this store? What kind of church was that? When did they hold services? Why was that man walking so fast toward the village? Did he always walk that way? Were there snakes in that field? Fish in that stream? Do Americans eat such fish? Was that forest native or planted? Was this Black woman related to the porter? Was she a descendant of slaves? Did that old couple in that car have a son in the American army? Had he fought in North Africa? Who lived in the manor house? Were they rich? How did they make their money? Had they been slave owners?

Around six o'clock, he raised his hand to use the toilet. Carson happened to be the first guard to notice and nodded his permission. Without thinking, Rolf thanked him in English.

The American grinned, "Ah, so you do speak English? What's your name?"

"Mueller, sir, Lance Corporal Rolf Mueller. I apologize for showing disrespect earlier."

"It's all right. I'm sorry we got off to a rocky start. I apologize too. I'm new at this, and I think that showed. I'm not really the asshole I made myself out to be."

Rolf smiled. "And I'm not usually such a smartass. It's been a long day."

Carson was waiting when he passed by on his way back to his seat. "Mueller, you guys were right. It's stupid to make you raise your hands just to use the head. Please tell the others they don't have to from now on."

"Thank you, sir. I'll tell them."

"But be sure to let them know they are not to go past the lavatory. The outside doors are locked, but if they try, I'd still have to shoot them."

"And are you a good shot?"

"Good enough. Say, your English seems pretty good, is that right?"

"I understand most of what's being said."

"Would you mind translating for me? I don't think that other guy was any good."

"All right."

"Thanks. You can start by telling your men that dinner will be here soon."

When Rolf got back, Willy said, "So, you have a new best friend?"

"Ha! No, but maybe Carson's not as bad as we thought. He says we don't have to raise our hands to piss any more. Pass that along and tell the others that we'll have food soon."

The meal was a most welcome change from C-rations. They had pork, potatoes, green beans, and bread. The coffee was real, not chicory, good and strong, better than any Rolf had had in years. As the mess kits were collected, he looked back out the window. The terrain was hillier now, and in the fading daylight, the roads and fields were quieter. People must be home now and settling in for the evening. Would they be reading? Listening to the radio?

At around eight, they made up their berth for the night. Rolf was so deliriously exhausted that he didn't care how claustrophobically low and tight it was. He was out as soon as he laid down. There were interruptions all night—train whistles and rumbles, light flooding into the compartment as they passed through towns and cities, stops that brought the swaying to a halt—but none of it kept him awake for long.

"Wake up, Mueller." Rolf opened his eyes to Carson's words in the dimness. "Tell the others it's time to turn the berths back into seats and let them know that breakfast will be here in thirty minutes." Rolf stretched, yawned, rubbed his face, and jabbed Willy, who was still sound asleep. Shortly after the beds were stowed, the porter came through with coffee.

"I thought I dreamt being served by a porter, but he's back." Willy smiled.

"How'd you sleep?"

"Like a rock, except for your snoring and yelling."

"And you're a bed hog."

After the breakfast trays were removed, Rolf self-consciously stepped into the aisle for some push-ups and sit-ups. Not a full workout, but enough to accelerate his heart rate before a long day of sitting. His legs were healed, but still grew stiff and ached, especially around the scars. Daily stretching helped. He still had headaches from his injuries, but exercise seemed to lessen that pain too.

Exercising had been important to him for years as a way to exert at least a little control over his life. Early in the war, working out kept him strong physically and gave him mental stamina. Even when he was glad to be a soldier, army life was often bureaucratic and stifling. So much of what they were ordered to do was unnecessary, redundant, or even counter-productive. A good work-out usually restored his equilibrium. By the time he was on his way to Kansas, he was addicted to exercising, so down he went, even in the aisle of the crowded car.

"Such a fine soldier, one of the Third Reich's best," chided another POW from across the aisle as Rolf began his second set. "Are you working for a commendation or just showing off?"

Willy looked over and said, "Shut up, asshole."

Otto Hecht glared. "Oh, I didn't realize you two were girlfriends. Such a cute couple."

"Jealous? Too ugly to find someone yourself?" Hecht might have punched Willy, but couldn't get to him over Rolf, who ignored them both. After several fast-paced sets, he toweled off and walked to the bathroom. As he passed by, Carson nodded.

Back in his seat, Rolf settled in for a look at the changing scenery, which prompted more questions for his journal. The second day on the train was much like the first. Rolf wrote and Willy drew, including a couple sketches of the inside of their train car. They chatted a bit, read some, and napped frequently.

Travel fatigue crept in with the start of their third day on the train. They'd come to that in-between place in a long journey where the excitement of heading somewhere has faded, but the promised arrival is not yet within reach. He still scanned the sights and formulated questions, but his queries grew more repetitive and less effective at carrying him off into sometimes whimsical speculations about what he was seeing. And without those distractions, he fell prey to other thoughts and haunting memories that were difficult to suppress—recollections about doing what he had to do, and what he never wanted to do.

When the train entered Louisville, Kentucky that morning, a shift-change was underway at the sprawling factories lining the tracks. Women and men were entering and leaving mammoth buildings pulsing with industry. At one large complex, dozens of new army jeeps were lined up in neat rows. Close to the city's center, the train crept into a large rail yard crowded with freight cars and switch engines. To one side was an imposing stone depot with towers pointing skyward at each corner. Stylish passengers flitted from platforms and trains like bees at a hive.

The car was warm even before the train stopped in a cluster of glistening metal carriages, and it quickly grew worse. Fine coal soot wafted in from a dozen nearby engines to mix with perspiration and coat the men with a grimy black paste. Trying not to think of how miserable he was, Rolf asked, "When we were going past those factories, did you see any signs of damage?"

"No, why?"

"I was just thinking about the reports we used to get about how the *Luftwaffe* and our saboteurs were inflicting heavy damage here in America. Remember?"

"Maybe we've not struck this far into the United States yet?"

"Or maybe we haven't attacked America at all yet. Did you see any damage in Norfolk?"

"No."

"Me, neither, and it's right on the coast."

As soon as they were rolling again, the men tried to wipe Louisville's gritty patina from their seats and clothing and bodies. Some played cards, most slouched with blank stares or dozed. Conversations were subdued, and the rumor-mongering and speculating about what was waiting for them in Kansas grew even more tiresome. Rolf ignored everything his countrymen had to say about what was going to happen, since none of them could possibly know.

After lunch, Corporal Carson approached. "I need you to make an announcement. Tell your men that we have a little surprise ahead."

"Is it a good one or a bad one?" Rolf couldn't tell by the corporal's expression or tone.

"What, don't you trust me?" Carson smiled. "Relax, it's a good one. We're going to be pulling over on a siding in a few minutes. They're going to let us all get out while we wait for the line to clear. And the best part is there's a water tower, so they're going to let you get hosed off."

"Really?" Rolf was surprised at what sounded like a very kind gesture by the Americans.

"The men will have to stay away from the other cars so we don't lose track of anyone. Do you understand?"

"Yes, sir."

"There's a field where we'll wait. When it's our turn, you'll strip down to your skivvies and get wet. The Army has used this siding for some of our own troops."

"I'm sorry, I don't know the word 'skivvies.'"

"Underwear."

When the train stopped, the Germans were escorted to a grassy area. When some men a few cars ahead began to line up for calisthenics, Rolf looked at Carson. "May we?" The corporal nodded, and Rolf took charge, crisply ordering the group into lines. A few grumbled, including Hecht, but they complied. Rolf stood at the front of the formation and led the group in rigorous stretches, jumping jacks, push-ups, and knee bends. The Germans were soon shouting out *eins-zwei-drei-viers*. Perspiration and lethargy poured out in equal measure. When they finished, he shouted, "Company, halt."

The men responded in unison, "*Seig heil*!" A couple of them clapped.

As they broke ranks, Carson instructed Rolf to tell them to leave their pants, shirts, and shoes and follow him in formation about a hundred yards down the tracks. There they waited until their turn came, then they stood in a tight group under a large cylindrical wooden tank on stilts while a railway worker turned a crank to open a large tap and poured water down on them for a minute or so. For men who'd not showered or bathed in weeks, the water was cold and wonderful! There was no soap, but just getting drenched by clean water felt incredibly good. They shouted and laughed, jumped, and waved their arms like children in a rain shower. Rolf could have stood under that spigot all afternoon. It reminded him of the times when Kurt and he splashed each other with buckets of cold well water on hot summer days.

Rejuvenated, someone started *Deutschland Uber Alles*, and soon those from other cars joined in, but as they started the third verse, a guard ran up to Carson, who came over to Rolf.

"Tell them to stop. Now!" he said tensely. The men did as they were told, but some were resentful. They drip-dried, dressed, and waited until word came that it was time to re-board.

Moving into the car, Hecht said, "We should have kept singing. Who are the Americans to tell us we can't sing our own national anthem?"

Rolf scoffed. "They're our captors, and we shouldn't forget that."

"And you shouldn't forget that you're a German. When I see you talking to that American, I wonder whose side you're on. And watching you commanding us today, even though you have no authority to do so, it seems you've forgotten your place."

Rolf calmly replied. "I know who I am and whose side I'm on. And what my place is. I don't owe you or anyone else an explanation. I, for one, was glad to have the chance for some outdoor exercise, and I'm grateful for the shower." Others nodded their agreement.

Back in their seats, Willy leaned in. "You show such restraint. I just want to punch him."

"Hitting him wouldn't do us any good, and it might make things worse."

"You think he's dangerous? Even in here?"

"Especially in here. We're wild animals in a very small cage."

"You really don't trust anyone, do you?"

"I trust you," Rolf smiled. "Beyond that, probably not."

The porter made the rounds with tea after they were moving again, and high clouds and a steady breeze kept them cooler across southern Indiana and into Illinois. Rolf was mesmerized watching the clouds precipitate in the distance. Undulating purple sheets of raindrops formed opaque curtains through which sunlight still passed. The shower moved languidly across the countryside away from the train.

# Chapter 11
# SPOILS OF VICTORY

Sometime during the third night, Rolf woke when he felt the train make a wide turn onto a long bridge. In the morning, Carson told him they had crossed the Mississippi River and were now in Missouri. By the time they'd trudged the breadth of Missouri to reach Kansas City around one the next afternoon, the car was torrid and the men were miserable. For two hours, they suffered until, mercifully, the train began to slide west on shimmering rails. Carson, who looked like he'd been dunked in a river, mopped his brow as he announced that they would arrive at their destination, Camp Concordia, sometime that evening. He barely got a reaction.

Rolf's first glimpse of Kansas, though he didn't know it, came when the train crossed an invisible line between Kansas and Missouri and turned to run parallel to a slow-moving, muddy river. Along its banks, trees were already shedding leaves. Unlike the Sahara, there was ample vegetation here, it was just toasted brown and crackling dry.

When the train rumbled into a sizable town nestled between the river and a prominent bluff, Rolf saw a sign—Lawrence, Kansas. He tried to call to mind all he knew about the state. He recalled that the central states were sparsely populated and primarily agricultural, and the climate was said to be harsh. He didn't know about winter but could now attest to the brutality of its summers. This day was hotter than anything he'd ever experienced in Germany. It was worse even than the Sahara because this humidity-laden air clung to humans and inanimate objects—everything— like a thick, hot, wet blanket.

He knew that Germans had immigrated to Kansas, including Westphalen cousins of his, and his parents received letters from them. Now, he'd traveled much more circuitously to arrive at the same place. He wondered if those relatives still lived there and what they'd think about having a *Wehrmacht* cousin in the neighborhood.

As the breeze revived them, talk resumed around the car about what lay ahead. In spite of decent treatment to date, whispers about torture and forced labor and summary executions began making the rounds again. Some adamantly claimed that the Americans' niceness was only meant to placate them until they came to some secret place where Allied justice would be meted out. Drawn in, Willy turned to Rolf. "What are you thinking about?"

"About how tired I am of riding in this train," he replied dismissively.

"C'mon, Rolf, what do you think is going to happen to us now?"

Sensing his friend's angst, he said, "Look, we're going to a prison camp, not a spa, deep in enemy territory. But they've treated us pretty well so far, haven't they? You shouldn't worry."

"Can you tell where we are?"

"Somewhere in Kansas, but I don't know where exactly."

"Then it shouldn't be long?"

"Kansas is big. I don't know where this camp is. We may still have hours to go." He went back to looking out the window. The fields here were the largest he'd seen. Golden wheat stubble covered large swaths of land. How could farmers plant, cultivate, and harvest such huge tracts, even with large, sophisticated machinery? Each of the several fields on his family's farm could be tilled and harvested by his father, his brother, and himself using a single horse and small implements, as generations of Muellers had done before them. He grew pensive. "The thing that gets me most is just how big this country is," he said with a gesture to the window. "We've been on this train for three days and we're maybe only halfway across it!"

"It's incredible."

"If we had sufficient *lebensraum* like this, we'd never have had to pursue expansion. The *Fuehrer* was right, we need more space."

"Do you still believe that?"

"Yes, of course, because it's true. The last war left us trapped between vengeful powers in the west, especially France, and communists in the east. Our resources were stolen, huge chunks of our territory were lopped off, along with millions of our folk. What were we supposed to do, sit idly by and wait until they dismembered the entire country? We had to act or be destroyed. At a minimum, restoration of our lost territories was critical to our survival."

For twenty years, variants of these arguments had fueled German antipathy toward their neighbors and then served as justification for the rise of Nazism. Rolf and Willy were both weaned on them, so Willy wasn't surprised to hear them expressed again, but for the first time he detected ambivalence in Rolf's tone. "You neglect to mention that German aggression helped start the last war. Didn't we deserve some of the blame for what happened when we lost? Some measure of punishment?"

"There was no need for the entire nation to be humiliated, starved, and cut into pieces. Both of our families barely survived after Versailles."

"There were no winners the last time around, and I doubt there will be any after this one."

As the last rays of sunlight dimmed, the POW train coasted to a stop at a tidy depot in Concordia, Kansas. It was Friday, 6 August 1943. Tired as they were of being cooped up for days, the Germans still hesitated as they stepped out into a foreboding holding pen. It was brightly lit and surrounded by a high fence topped with barbed wire. And just beyond the fence, some fifty yards away, a crowd of animated civilians clapped as they de-trained. Mothers and fathers knelt to point out prisoners for their children. There were jeers and taunts. An old man shouted, "So you're Rommel's super-soldiers—you don't look so super now!" A circus had come to town, and the Germans were the main attraction. Someone launched a rotten cabbage in their direction, and a man yelled, "Make some sauerkraut out of that, you sons-a-bitches." It was unnerving, even for arrogant men like Hecht.

Since their capture, the Germans' contact with Americans had mainly been with military personnel. They'd seen a few civilians in Norfolk and from the train, but those people hadn't seen them or paid much attention. Now the POWs were on display for America's citizenry as the human spoils of war. To what end? Thoughts of ancient Rome came to mind, when captive soldiers were sold into slavery, forced to fight as gladiators, or fed to wild animals for the rabble's amusement. Rolf shuddered to think the gossip-mongers might be right, but then he breathed deeply, stretched, and forced himself to focus on the moment—the immediate pleasures of standing on solid ground again and breathing cooler, fresher air. As they were herded toward the gates, where Army transports awaited, the gawking and taunting grew more intimidating. Rolf avoided eye contact with everyone, except other POWs, and tried not to seem nervous or haughty. Willy followed his lead.

The convoy left the depot and turned onto Highway 81 for the short drive out of town to a large installation surrounded by high fences and guard towers. Because of the lateness of the hour, the newly-arrived prisoners were assigned to temporary quarters for the night. As identification papers and delousing tags were checked, guards counted off groups of fifty and sent them off to the barracks. Rolf noticed how clean and new everything was. There were even wooden sidewalks. If this was all a hoax, it was very elaborate and very convincing. And these guards looked nothing like the SS, and they treated the prisoners without roughness or rancor. The entire scene was orderly and efficient, very business-like. His group was sent into a long, narrow building in an area marked EM Compound 3. On each bunk was fresh, neatly-folded bedding, and at the foot of each was a small footlocker. Rolf would have liked a shower, but an American announced lights-out in fifteen minutes and pointed in the direction of the latrine building. Fifteen minutes gave them just enough time to use the toilets and return to their bunks.

The minute the lights were off and the Germans were alone, they began to talk excitedly. Some crept to the windows to see what they could see. A few laughed nervously. Several said what Rolf was thinking—these accommodations were better than any they'd had in years. But even saying that might be deemed traitorous. Rolf and Willy both stayed quiet.

The chatter initially muffled rumbling from outside that rapidly grew more insistent and was soon accompanied by broad flashes of light. Rolf was disoriented until he realized this was not the noise of battle, but the prelude to a storm. In minutes, the entire camp was engulfed in it. Blinding shafts of light split the darkness. Brash thunder sounded like madmen were beating on dozens of giant drums. Gale-force winds wooshed in to challenge the camp's very right to exist. Rain drops splatted one by one on the ground and rooftops, then came faster and faster until the sprinkle became a deluge. As they fumbled with shutting the windows, hail began thudding on the tar paper roof, the building rattled and creaked, and the storm-symphony became even more intense. Rolf wondered whether this wooden structure would hold up against the straight winds or if a tornado would descend from the clouds and suck them all up into the heavens.

Then the tempest passed, and the camp was silent, except for a few final grumbles tossed over the storm's shoulder as it moved east and slowing trickles from rooftops. The Germans inhaled the storm-sweetened air and settled into the darkness.

Exhaustion-induced sleep came easily after their rousing welcome, but somewhere in the night, Rolf admitted that he was more awake than asleep and had been for a while. Maybe for minutes, maybe for hours. He turned on one side, then the other, fluffed his pillow, rolled onto his back with his arms at his sides, palms open, fingers at ease. He straightened his sheets, laid as still as he could so as not to disturb the others. He shut his eyes, told himself he was relaxed. He slowed his breathing and sank into each inhale and each exhale. He tuned into the yelping cries of a pack of animals beyond the fence. He conjured up pleasant memories. But nothing could override a long, slow loop that was playing over and over inside his head. He wasn't agitated or afraid, just stuck in an annoyingly insistent stream of thoughts that seemed to rise and fall in time with the cadence of the tapping of his foot against the footboard.

*I'm twenty-three years old*, it began. *Five years ago, who would have thought that I'd be on my back in a prison so far from home, or that my journey to get here would have been so—so what? Dangerous? Exciting? Painful? I'm twenty-three. Look at where I've been and what I've done so far. I dedicated myself to my home and my country. I tried to advance our interests. I swore an oath. I should be proud of that. I am proud of that. I bled for my country, almost died for it. I've slept in too many different places to count, on three continents. I did things I never wanted to do. I did what I had to do. I'm twenty-three. I was supposed to be starting my career as a physician about now. I was supposed to be with a pretty girl, maybe already married, maybe already a father. I was supposed to be going to dances and movies and reading good books and hiking in the mountains and drinking beer and managing my life and visiting my parents on Sundays. But instead, I'm twenty-three and I'm in a place that I've never even seen in the daylight. I haven't done any of the things I planned to do by this time. I did things I never wanted to do. I did what I had to do. I'm twenty-three. I've never even been with a girl, not really, not for long anyway. And whatever I have done, I did because I was told to, not because I wanted to. I'm twenty three. I should be a full-fledged adult by now, but I'm not. How could I be? I've been treated like a child my entire life. First it was my parents, then the Reich and the Wehrmacht controlling my every thought and action. And now it's the Americans who brought me here and are telling me what to do. I've done so much and accomplished so little.I did things I never wanted to do. I did what I had to do. I'm so old. I'm so young. I'm twenty-three and I'm a prisoner. But I'm not imprisoned for what I did, only because of who I am. Nobody asked me how many people I killed. I'm only in prison because I was on the losing side and got caught. Every other soldier on the other side did the same, but they aren't in jail, only the losers who got caught. How did I get here? I'm only twenty-three.*

# Chapter 12
# HONORABLE MEN

It was a blessed relief when a guard finally stepped into the barracks at 7 a.m. and shouted instructions for the Germans to be dressed and be ready for breakfast in fifteen minutes. Freed from the tyranny of his thoughts and confinement to his bunk, Rolf was the first up and dressed.

"How'd you sleep?" Willy asked, still groggy and moving slowly.

"Good," Rolf lied, lest his friend think he'd been worrying all night. "You?"

"Great! It's so quiet here. Once the storm passed, it was almost too quiet for a city boy like me. No trams or sirens or horns or taverns. I did hear something howling out there, though."

"Those were the wolves they're going to feed us to after they fatten us up."

"Ha ha. Are you ready for today?" Willy asked hesitantly.

"Do I have a choice?"

The men looked around curiously as they were shown to the compound's mess hall. The walk wasn't long enough to see much, but Rolf sensed undeniable calm and normalcy about the place. Their first breakfast in Concordia included ample portions of eggs, bacon, fried potatoes, toast with jam, and coffee, all prepared and served by POWs.

As they stood in line, Willy exclaimed, "My God! Is this how much we're going to be fed every day? There's twice as much food here as I've ever seen in the *Wehrmacht*."

Rolf smiled. "I told you, they're going to fatten you up."

"Welcome," said one of the Germans tending to the food line, a man their age with a crooked smile, as Rolf and Willy got their trays. "How was the trip?"

"Long and hot," Rolf replied.

"Kansas is definitely hot."

"Where are you from?"

"Dortmund. I was captured in North Africa. You?"

"Tunisia. How is it here?" Rolf looked around to see if anyone cared that they were talking without permission. Not only was no one paying any attention, but he then realized that there were no Americans in sight. He had nothing to compare it to—he'd never been in a real prison before—but thought it strange that this one had so few guards.

"Not bad. I got here a couple weeks ago. We were the first ones in Concordia."

"And you're still alive," Rolf said, smiling at Willy. "Where are all the guards?"

"We don't see them much, mainly first thing in the morning, then at night, and at roll-call. They don't come into the compounds very often." He saw Rolf's surprise and added, "They treat us all right. You'll see." The server picked up an empty food pan and headed for the kitchen.

Willy smiled. "That doesn't sound too bad."

"No, and the food looks decent, and the coffee smells strong."

Over the PA system, someone instructed the men to return to their barracks when they were finished eating and to be ready to go to the front of the camp for processing at 9 a.m. The way was clearly marked. Until then, they were free to move around their compound, but nowhere else. The off-limits areas were clearly marked. They were also told to stay away from the camp perimeter. The guards in the towers had orders to shoot any prisoner who approached the fence.

There was time after breakfast to exercise and shower, then Rolf and Willy headed to the designated processing area, a large field. At the far end was a small platform with chairs and a podium with a microphone and speakers. Another microphone stood off to the side. German officers were already seated in front, conversing quietly. As the enlisted men from the train arrived, they stood behind the officers.

Promptly at nine, the Camp Concordia commander, Colonel Phillip C. Jones, crossed the field from the direction of the administration buildings with a small entourage. The German officers stood and saluted. The colonel returned their salute and briskly strode up the steps with the other Americans in tow. He looked around, smiled, tapped on the microphone, cleared his throat, and began. A translator at the other mic efficiently converted everything the colonel said into German.

Colonel Jones, a confident, amiable-looking man in his sixties, first welcomed the newly-arrived POWs in terrible German, then returned to English with a laugh and a promise to never do that again.

Authorized in December 1942, construction on Camp Concordia only began in February, just six months earlier. It was turned over to the Army in May. As if he were showing honored guests around his home, Colonel Jones described the sprawling facilities in detail, its administrative buildings, hospital, workshops, fire station, mess halls, warehouses, garrison, officer quarters, the internee barracks contained in several compounds, and the recreation fields. He gestured to different buildings as he spoke.

After pausing for effect at the end of his verbal camp tour, the colonel said, "For you and the thousands more who will be interned here in the coming months, the war is over. You will be incarcerated until the end of hostilities in accordance with the terms of the Geneva Convention of 1929 concerning the treatment of prisoners, to which both the United States and Germany are signatories." Colonel Jones said the full document would be posted in German, but he would outline the most important provisions for them now. For starters, POWs would be housed in facilities of the same quality as provided for American military personnel of equal rank. They would receive the same rations, and they would receive the same pay that Americans of the same rank received when the Geneva Convention was signed. For enlisted men, the pay would be twenty-one dollars per month, while for officers it would be up to forty dollars per month.

Willy was baffled. "Did he say the Americans are going to give us our military pay?"

Rolf, who understood the colonel's English well enough to follow him as well as the translator, shared his surprise. "That's exactly what he said."

"Paid to be a prisoner? By the Americans? This is unbelievable!"

Colonel Jones went on. A portion of each man's monthly pay would be available in camp scrip and could be used to purchase items in the canteen. The balance would be held until the end of the war, then paid to them upon repatriation. Some looked skeptical, but others cheered and clapped until their officers turned around and scowled. The enlisted men quickly quieted down.

The colonel and the translator went through more provisions, slowly so the men could follow. POWs would be allowed regular exercise; they were entitled to safe and sanitary conditions; they could not be interrogated for information about the *Wehrmacht*; they could send two letters home per week, plus one telegram per year; they could receive packages from their families. All mail would be censored. The camp would be regularly inspected by the International Red Cross and representatives of the Swiss Government, who would share their findings with the German government.

Next, Colonel Jones introduced Lieutenant Colonel Walter Lutzke from the 15th Panzer Division, North Afrika Korps. He was the senior German officer in camp and, as such, the POWs' designated senior spokesman. "All officers, German and American, are to be saluted and afforded the respect due their rank. Either the American or the German form of salute is acceptable. However," Colonel Jones paused again for emphasis, "make no mistake, the Americans are fully responsible for the operation of the camp and treatment of all internees. Our orders must always be given priority."

POWs would be given clothing and shoes but could wear their uniforms if they preferred. Military insignia could be displayed, but Nazi symbols, including swastikas, were forbidden. Their private property would be respected. German doctors and chaplains were classified as exempted persons. German doctors would work in the camp hospital, and German chaplains would be allowed to conduct religious services for POWs.

Colonel Jones said any POW who attempted to escape could not be punished, except to be placed under closer guard. No prisoner could be tortured for any reason, but fighting among POWs was a punishable offense. All serious offenses would be handled pursuant to American military rules through courts-martial. Food and water could not be used as punishment, except that prisoners who refused to perform assigned duties could be restricted to a diet of bread and water for up to fourteen days at a time.

He went on, "All able-bodied enlisted men will be expected to work as jobs are available. Officers are exempted from work but may volunteer to do so. Non-commissioned officers may be required to work in supervisory roles only."

Willy nudged Rolf, "He doesn't have to worry about our officers volunteering. They're much too important for menial labor. They might get their hands dirty."

"Most of the work here, in the kitchens, laundry, and latrines, plus landscaping, maintenance, and mechanical work, will be done by POWs. Those assigned to perform these duties will be paid at the rate of eighty cents per day in addition to their military pay." The men were still digesting this when Jones added, slowly and deliberately, "There are more of you than there will be jobs in camp. Since labor is in such short supply due to the war, German enlisted men may also be assigned to work outside the camp on farms or in businesses, as long as the work is suitable and not war-related, unhealthy, or dangerous. Many farmers have already requested workers to help bring in their harvest. Wage for these workers will be set by the Army and employers. The Army will retain a portion to cover expenses. All men who work outside the camp will be paid at least eighty cents per day. And all wages earned, whether inside or outside the camp, will be paid partly in camp scrip and partly held for each worker until repatriation."

Willy was dumbfounded. "You mean we might get to work outside camp, and we'll get paid more, on top of our military pay? Good Lord!" Rolf shook his head in disbelief.

Colonel Jones ended by saying, "Gentlemen, as I said, the war is over for you. You fought for your country, but now your part in the fight is over. We remain enemies until peace comes again, but that should not preclude us from treating one another civilly. We assume you are honorable men. You will be treated as such unless and until proven otherwise." The enlisted Germans applauded enthusiastically; even their officers' displeasure couldn't curtail it.

Queues formed at tables set up on the field, and Americans and translators soon motioned the first men in line to come forward. As each German's name was checked off a list, he was given an internment number, a barracks assignment, and fingerprinted. Rolf's number was 6GT-5607. Once again, he and Willy were assigned to the same barracks, which they took as a sign of their continuing good fortune. They would be in Barracks #3, EM Compound 2.

Behind the registration tables were tables piled high with toiletries, clothing (three sets per man), and shoes. Starter bags of toiletries and personal items were free, but henceforth, such could be purchased in the canteen with camp scrip.

On their way to their new quarters, Willy was effusive. "This clothing is all new, and the shoes are sized to fit! I've never had so many new clothes in my life!" He could barely contain his excitement, but Rolf was slow to respond. He needed to organize his swirling thoughts—there was so much to take in.

In the barracks, they recognized a few men from the ship or the train, including Otto Hecht. They nodded to him, but Hecht ignored them. Willy rolled his eyes.

As soon as they'd chosen their bunks and stowed their gear, Rolf and Willy practically ran to the latrine to shower and shave. They'd both forgotten what it felt like to be truly clean. It didn't matter that the shower water was lukewarm or that the trousers had the now-familiar white "P" and "W" stenciled on each leg; they were clean! Afterwards, it was still too early for lunch, so Rolf asked Willy to go with him to find out where to post letters and to check the duty rosters. Near the barracks' only exit, however, a group was talking loudly and blocking the aisle. Pushing through didn't look feasible, so they stopped.

"This is better than anything I could have hoped for," one young soldier said. "Thank God we were captured!"

Another man bristled. "Glad you were captured, are you? What a coward!"

"It's too good to be true," another one interjected. "There's no way the Americans will feed us and pay us and all that other shit. It's not even logical. This has to be a set-up."

"A set-up for what, exactly?" someone scoffed. "Is this camp a mirage? Are these new clothes just my imagination? Isn't your belly still full from breakfast?"

Hecht pushed his way into the crowd and held his hands up to demand attention. "You're idiots if you don't see what's happening. They're going to pretend to be nice to get us to think they're our friends, then they'll start grilling us for information. What they want is for us to betray the Fatherland. The Americans are very sly with this crap about the Geneva Convention."

A few nodded in agreement. Rolf thought back to a few short months earlier, when he believed the same things about John Schmidt. How long ago, and how inaccurate, that now seemed, but he listened without betraying an opinion one way or the other.

Someone shot back, "How could anything we say help the Americans? We've been out of the fucking war for months. We don't even know where they're fighting."

Hecht glowered. "The slightest things you do know could be used against Germany. How the *Wehrmacht* is organized, how battles are conducted, how supplies reach front lines, where we are weak at home. Do you have friends still fighting and family at home? Do you want them all to suffer because of your big mouths?"

An especially-agitated young man spoke up, "What about those crews going out? Is that just a way to get rid of us, a few at a time? Once we're out of sight, they could torture us, then execute us. Who'd know?" Pleadingly, he added, "You saw that crowd last night—they hate us! We're just a burden on the Americans. They're not going to feed and house us while the war is going on and give us spending money too! That's absurd! We're thousands of miles away from Europe, a perfect place to bury us and any evidence that we were ever here. I doubt the Red Cross or the Swiss will even find this shithole! Who the hell even heard of Kansas before now?"

"That's bullshit and you know it, Gunter," said another. "They need able-bodied workers as much as we do. They may work us hard, but they also won't kill us."

The talking turned to shouting. Tensions grew, some got into others' faces, there was some shoving. Just when a full-scale brawl was about to break out, a tall, uniformed figure appeared in the doorway.

"Officer in the barracks!" someone shouted, loudly and authoritatively enough to snap the others to attention. "*Sieg heil!*" they said in unison.

The officer returned their salute and stepped in the door. The crowd deferentially stepped back and parted to allow him to enter the room. It was Streicher.

"As you were, men. Tell me, what is this about?" he asked firmly.

It took a few seconds before one of the loudest ones replied, "We were discussing the commandant's speech and our situation here, sir." He averted his eyes.

"That was quite a 'discussion,'" said Streicher calmly. "What is your name, soldier?"

"I am Private Erich Zimmerman, sir."

"And which unit were you with in Africa, Private Zimmerman?"

"The 244th unit, third battalion, second infantry regiment, 15th Panzer Division, sir."

"Do you know who I am?"

"No, sir."

"I am Major Eduard Streicher, 21st Panzer Division. I now report directly to Colonel Lutzke. My responsibilities include command of this barracks." Turning to the rest of the men, he said, "Is that clear?"

"Yes, sir!" came the obligatory response, though a few looked confused.

"I came here to inform you that the POW representative for this barracks is Private Otto Hecht." Streicher pointed to him. "Any grievances or concerns you have, about the Americans or one another, you are to bring them to him, and he will communicate them to me. Is that clear?"

"Yes, sir." This time, their reply was more subdued.

"Now, I overheard some of your comments about the Americans." Condescendingly, he asked, "Would you like to know my thoughts on the subject?" then proceeded without waiting for a response. "They are cunning, which is why they transported us so far into the middle of their country, for whatever they have planned. Your officers are evaluating the situation and will be in touch soon regarding counter-measures. In the meantime, conduct yourselves cautiously. Regardless of what that naive camp commandant said, we retain true authority over all enlisted German soldiers here. First and foremost, you must follow our orders, and you must report all violations of *Wehrmacht* regulations to us. Need I remind you of your oath to our *Fuehrer*? You are still bound by it, to him and to his officers. Do you understand?"

"Yes, sir." Some looked away nervously, others shifted from one foot to the other.

"Finally," Streicher looked from man to man, "on the subject of working outside the camp," he paused, "here is the only opinion that matters: It is traitorous to aid the enemy in any way. Let the Americans starve; no good German would consider helping feed them. Some of you may be forced to work, but that does not mean you should stop trying to advance the interests of the Fatherland. There are ways to pretend to comply with American orders and still not betray your sacred duties, even now. Perhaps by sabotaging a building or ruining a crop or poisoning a well or disabling a vehicle." He paused to emphasize what he would say next. "You are soldiers for the Reich, for the *Fuehrer*, you are trained to inflict the ultimate penalty—death—on those who oppose us. Today we find ourselves among our sworn enemies. For us, the war is most definitely not over. Do you understand?"

Rolf and Willy did not add their yes-sirs to the others'. Willy was visibly agitated, while Rolf's jaw locked and he looked down in anger, muttering under his breath so no one would hear, "Goddammit." Streicher did not notice them, but Hecht did.

"Of course, some of you will disregard what I've said and gaily skip off to work on your American farms or in your American factories with enthusiasm and energy. You may even try to justify your abhorrent behavior but remember this: You do so at your peril. You are endangering the lives of all Germans who long to see the Third Reich prevail. That is all for now." With an icy smile and a final nod to Hecht, the major turned and stepped out.

Willy couldn't contain himself any longer. Streicher was barely out of earshot when he said, "What an arrogant son-of-a-bitch! Did he not hear anything the commandant said? Does he really think he's in charge in here?"

Hearing his friend speak so audaciously snapped Rolf out of his conflicted thoughts. In one motion, he grabbed Willy's elbow and nudged him through the disbanding crowd. "Let's go," he muttered, his face turning crimson.

Willy shook off Rolf's grip. "What the hell? You don't think he was right, do you?"

"What I think is irrelevant! Weren't you listening? Hecht isn't just an ass-kisser, he's a lackey, an informant. Goddamn it, Willy! You've got to be more careful."

"But I'm tired of all the bullshit, the *sieg heils* and the *heil* Hitlers! And pompous, self-important officers. Who's guarding whom here? Who has the guns? The Americans are in charge, and I, for one, am happy about that because they're going to treat us fairly." Rolf glanced around furtively and hoped no one was listening, while Willy raged on. "After listening to Jones, I feel like I'm free for the first time in years. Free from the *Fuehrer* and the Streichers! How's that for irony? It took getting captured and sent to a POW camp in the middle of America for me to feel free."

"Streicher may be an arrogant ass, but he's right about this: We are Germans and they are Americans. I'm sick of hearing about it, too, but we did swear an oath. How are we still obligated to the *Fuehrer* in here? I don't know, but I'm also not sure how in-charge the Americans are. Do you see any guards? No! But the German officers and their henchmen, they're all around us."

"But the Americans run this place, Rolf. They do. We're in their prison! All our officers and their henchmen have is their insane Nazi ideology, oaths, and threats."

"They don't have to be armed to be dangerous to us!" Rolf snapped. "And I don't feel at all free right now; I feel more trapped than ever. You seem to be so damn sure of who's in charge, which is fine, you're entitled. You and I haven't always agreed on everything, and I've never judged you for our differences, but you don't want to be wrong in here. It could cost you."

"How? How could it cost me?" Before Rolf could reply, Willy went on with rising emotion. "I don't give a shit who hears me! Like I told you in Tunisia, I hate Hitler, I hate what he's done to Germany. I hate what we allowed him to do. For years, I helped promote his insanity, and now I regret that every day. I'm done defending Nazis. Now, I'll say what I feel."

"Then you're a fool!"

"Better a fool than to continue to prostitute yourself for a mad man!"

The words cut deep. Rolf's fists tightened. He'd never struck his friend but suddenly felt a terrible urge to do so. His arm was already pulling back when he regained his composure and stopped. Willy realized he'd gone too far and said no more.

They continued a few steps farther, then Rolf stopped and looked away, still bristling, while Willy waited awkwardly. After a few deep breaths, Rolf's jaw relaxed slightly, and they continued on in silence. At the mess hall, Willy saw that he was assigned to kitchen duty beginning that afternoon. He grumbled about not getting assigned to work outside the camp, to which Rolf responded curtly, "Jesus Christ. Be happy you got an assignment. My name's not up there at all. I'll go crazy if I have nothing to do."

"Maybe it's because you were wounded?"

"Who the hell knows. but I'm well enough to work."

Willy tried to placate his friend and make amends. "You're more than well enough. You're in better shape than you were before." Rolf said nothing, so Willy added, "It says that more assignments will be posted tonight, so maybe you'll get something then."

"I'm going to go find the mail drop. You should head back to the barracks since you have to work before long."

"Are you sure?"

"I can find it," he snarled as he walked away. At the mail drop, he posted two letters, then took his time returning to the barracks. He took no pleasure in the gorgeous noontime sky or the sweet fragrances of new-mown grasses and wildflowers that were floating into the camp on a southerly breeze. By the time he got back, Willy was gone.

Rolf skipped lunch and tidied up his space. He started a letter to his parents, but couldn't finish it. He'd been looking forward to telling them about all the colonel said and about the camp, but now all he could think about was the argument. He was angry as his friend's reckless indiscretion, but Willy's personal attack was even worse. *I am a loyal German, goddamn it,* he thought. *And I'm supposed to be! I'm not a prostitute for anyone.* And yet, deep down, Willy's words rang true. Conflicting emotions weighed him down like a millstone hung around his neck. His thoughts were tyrannizing him again. *I did things I never wanted to do. I did what I had to do. I did things to protect you, Willy!*

It was almost ten and lights out, when Willy returned. Rolf was exhausted and still unsettled and angry, but glad to see him in spite of himself. "How was it?" he asked.

Willy looked at him warily. "Not bad. The work isn't hard and I like the other guys in my crew. It felt good to be doing something."

"That's good."

"I didn't see you come in for dinner. Were you there?"

"Yes, I can't believe how much meat they gave us. Everything was good." Then, to ease the lingering tension, he quipped, "Except, I found a fingernail in my soup. Was it yours?"

"Asshole!" Willy replied with a relieved smile. "For your information, I didn't work on the soup. I did lose a fingernail in the potatoes, but that couldn't be the one you found."

"That's good because I know how dirty yours are. I know where they've been."

Willy grinned. "So, what about you? Did you find out anything about work?"

"No. Others got assignments, but not me. I'm not the only one, though."

"I'm sorry about that."

"The commandant said they need manpower. I wish they'd let me provide some of it."

"I'm sure it's just a matter of time. The American Army is probably just as bureaucratic as the *Wehrmacht*. It will take twice as long as it should to finish the paperwork to get everyone assigned to something. Some dim-witted paper-pusher is sitting around with his thumb up his ass, and final assignments must wait until it comes out."

Willy jumped up on Rolf's bunk and sat down. "Listen, I'm sorry about earlier. I've got to learn to keep my big mouth shut, even if I'm right. And I'm really sorry for what I said about you prostituting yourself. I didn't mean it. I apologize. You know I think you're a good man."

Rolf grimaced. "Apology accepted. I'm just worried about you."

"Thanks." Willy smiled. "My mother always said my mouth was going to get me into trouble someday. She's already been right more than once."

"Let's hope she's not right this time. And I'm sorry for lashing out at you. Much of what you say is true. About the *Fuehrer*, about the war, about how the hell we got here. But it's not easy to think about that." Willy nodded. "I'm not saying I agree with everything you said, but at least some of it I do." Rolf looked off and spoke quietly. "I'm starting to feel like everything we've done the last few years was for nothing. That's very hard to admit. And we have to keep that between ourselves, Willy. Understand?"

"I do." In his friend's contorted face was more conflict than Willy had ever seen. "But let's not talk about all that now, okay? Let's just figure out how to make it through our days here, okay?"

"That's all we can do now."

"And I'll start by keeping my mouth shut more."

"It's okay if you want to say what you're thinking to me, but just me, no one else."

"I promise. And if you ever do want to talk about all of this, you know you can with me."

Boredom can be a fearsome enemy. While Willy easily settled into his new routine, Rolf had too much time on his hands. He exercised religiously and played soccer with other enlisted men in the recreation area a few times. He cleaned up around the barracks and helped with the landscaping. He volunteered in the library and read voraciously, but it wasn't enough. In small increments, he tried to sort out his thinking in his journal entries. He also wrote letters home and fretted because he hadn't heard anything from his family since April. But that wasn't enough, either. Had it not been for Willy, who once again was as optimistic and upbeat as ever, he'd have had no one to talk to. They didn't speak about politics or the war or what they'd been through but knowing Willy's views about everything was somehow comforting.

Finally, a month later, on September 9th, a Thursday, a work roster was posted with Rolf's name on it. He couldn't wait to share the news with Willy that evening.

"Good for you!" Willy said with genuine enthusiasm. "On a farm?"

"Yes."

"Excellent! I like the kitchen, but I'd still love to go outside. When do you start?"

"On Saturday."

"That's just two days from now. Are you worried after what Streicher said?"

"You mean do I still want to avoid him and lay low? Yes, of course."

"No, do you think you're obligated to sabotage the farm you're sent to, like he said?"

"No. I've had a helluva lot of time to think. I still don't know exactly how I feel about everything but working on a farm isn't traitorous. That's just bullshit. Any food I help harvest will be feeding us too. It's no different than you cooking here. I'm not going to poison livestock or burn down barns. That's not required of a *Wehrmacht* soldier."

"You know I agree. Are you afraid of going out of the camp?"

"Of course not," Rolf smirked. "All that speculation is bullshit too. The guys already working outside all come back, don't they? Everyone's accounted for, and they're not being abused. They say most American civilians are friendly enough, just like in camp. There's no secret

American agenda here. I don't know exactly what I'll be doing or who I'll be working for, but it will be all right. And anything will be better than sitting around."

The next morning, Rolf noticed something troubling, something he'd missed the previous afternoon: He was being sent to a sub-camp in Peabody, Kansas, a hundred miles south of Concordia. He hadn't considered the possibility that he might be sent to a different place altogether and have to leave his only friend.

Willy smiled at the news, but his disappointment was unmistakable. "How many are going?"

"Around a hundred of us altogether. You'll be happy to hear that Hecht's going too."

"Really? He has his head so far up Streicher's ass that I assumed he'd have gotten himself assigned to be his personal valet or maybe his chauffeur by now."

"I know. But now I'm sure he's looking forward to becoming a saboteur."

"You'll have to keep an eye on him." Hesitantly, he asked, "How long will you be gone?"

"I don't know. It says it's for the harvest, so I'm betting we'll be back by Christmas."

Early on Saturday morning, September 11th, Rolf, Hecht, and fifty-eight other POWs were handed C-rations and canteens and loaded into green Army trucks. The convoy included several more trucks loaded with supplies and gear. They were told the drive to Peabody would take several hours. The day was surprisingly hot and windy.

While Rolf packed that morning, Willy sat nearby. His silence spoke volumes. When the time finally came, he managed a pained smile as they shook hands, then hugged.

"Take care of yourself, Willy." In a near-whisper, he added, "Please be careful. Work hard and keep your head down. Please."

"I will. I've done better these past few weeks, haven't I?"

"Yes. But when I'm gone, trust no one, and don't let the entire world know your feelings about everything. And keep your fingernails out of the potatoes," he added with a smile.

"I will. I'll miss you. Take care of yourself too. Don't get run over by a tractor or gored by a bull. Or pushed down a well by Hecht."

"I'll be fine. I have my birthday pig for luck."

Willy smiled faintly. "Let me know what some real Americans are like."

"Will do. And maybe by Christmas, you'll know how to make a proper *roggenbrot*!" Rolf joined the others walking toward the trucks at the gate. Willy watched him go, then turned the other direction with a sigh and slowly and sadly headed to the mess hall for breakfast.

# PART

## II

# Chapter 13
# PEACE PILGRIMS

"Mama, they're here, Aunt Dora and Uncle Peter and the others." Carol Ann Unruh called toward her parents' bedroom as two black sedans came up the long drive to the grassy area between the large white clapboard house and an even larger barn. The cars rolled to a stop in the shade of a towering elm tree with gnarly ashen limbs that turned skyward like arms raised in supplication.

"Tell them I'll be right out. Where's Loretta?" Clara Unruh poked her head around the bedroom door, still buttoning her dress and smoothing her hair.

"She's outside with Papa. Should I go get her?"

"No, let them finish. Show Aunt Dora and the rest into the front room, then go upstairs and get yourself changed. Have you washed up?"

"Yes, Mama. And I'm already dressed." Carol Ann hurried to the kitchen door as Dora and Peter Jantz, her great-aunt and great-uncle, were helping each other up the porch steps. She held the screen door and welcomed them in, along with their adult children and grandchildren, all from McPherson.

"Hello, dear," Dora said as they hugged, "I'm so sorry for your loss."

"Thank you, Aunt Dora. I'm sorry for you too," Carol Ann said. "Mama is almost dressed, and Papa and Loretta are still doing chores. Mama said to show you to the front room."

"Thank you, child. You remember everyone, don't you?"

"Of course." Carol Ann kissed her great-uncle and smiled at the others. Turning back to Dora, she said, trepidatiously, "You don't mind, do you?" She paused, not sure how to go on.

"Mind what, dear?"

"I mean, um, well—going in there." The teenager nodded toward the front room.

Dora understood. "Of course not, child. That's why we came. Don't be afraid."

Using Carol Ann's arm and her cane for balance, Dora slowly walked through the arched doorway into the large front room and stopped. In spite of the sun blazing in a cloudless sky, the room, located on the protected north side of the house, was dim and not overly warm. Lace curtains at the windows filtered out most of the afternoon sunlight, while two floor lamps brightened their corners, but little else. The only two pictures on the lathe and plaster walls, the Last Supper and a landscape with tall mountains and a river splashing through a forest while deer grazed on the opposite bank, were barely discernible in the shadows. Opposite the kitchen was the front door and a porch. Hardly anyone ever came or went through the front door, but it stayed open all summer to coax in as much fresh air as possible.

The sofa, armchairs, and tables had been moved back to make room for a makeshift bier, a pair of sturdy sawhorses covered with a crisp white sheet. On it rested an open pine coffin cradling a body. A large bouquet of fresh-cut garden flowers—multi-colored zinnias, lavender asters, and spiky blue and white delphiniums—gave off sweet fragrances, and the flame from a thick beeswax candle swayed and flickered gently in the parsimonious breeze. This ordinary room had been transformed into holy space, where this world and the next converged, where death could be greeted and contemplated.

Dora reached into a pocket for her hanky and entered, clutching Carol Ann's hand. Her husband and the rest of the family were close behind, including Clara Unruh, who'd finished dressing and joined the group. They all waited for Dora to react first. At the bier, she said nothing for a moment, just looked down with sad eyes at the dead woman, so tiny and frail. Her white hair was pulled back into the traditional starched white kapp favored by some Mennonite women. Her face was remarkably smooth and soft for one so old. Only her tired hands, folded on her chest over a simple violet dress and gnarled as tree bark, told her age.

Dora stopped breathing, then gave a heave of a sigh and whispered plaintively, "Sister dear, I miss you already." She dabbed wet eyes. "Now you're home with our Lord and all the faithful who've gone ahead. Your long journey is ended." To the others, she said resolutely, "God be praised!" Then she cupped the dead woman's hands in her own and prayed quietly in German. In Elizabeth Unruh's serene face, Dora saw much more than death; she was carried back through decades of companionship and shared experiences with her older sister and oldest friend.

Wiping a last tear winding its way down her cheek, Dora said to Carol Ann, "Your grandma looks like she's sleeping, doesn't she?"

Carol Ann fidgeted. "I suppose."

The screen door squeaked open and thwacked shut behind Harold Unruh and his older daughter, Loretta. Harold quickly came forward to greet his aunt and share her sadness.

"Harold, I'm so sorry for you. Your mother was such a beautiful soul."

"Thank you, Aunt Dora, and thank you for coming. I know how hard this is for you too."

"We were the last ones in our family," Dora said. "Now it's just me."

Loretta stood back a moment, then she came forward to hug her great-aunt. "I'm so sorry," was all she could get out before her tears began.

"There, there, dear. Your grandmother is with Jesus now. She's free." Dora held her tight.

"I know. It's just hard." Loretta continued to cry quietly.

"It is, child. You and your grandmother were very close. She was so proud of you and Carol Ann, all her grandchildren. She wrote so many lovely letters about you all. And you look just like she did at your age. Such beautiful girls."

Loretta managed a weak smile and wiped her face. "Thank you, but I must look a mess right now, and I'm sure I don't smell very good. It's so hot today, and Papa and I just finished the chores. Please excuse me while I go get cleaned up and change."

"Of course. We'll have time to talk later." Dora held Loretta's face with both her hands a moment longer, then gently kissed each cheek.

Harold and Loretta took turns washing off barnyard grime in cool water in the kitchen sink, then went to their rooms to change while Clara and Carol Ann entertained their guests.

"Would anyone like tea or water?" Clara asked as the men removed jackets and they all took seats in the kitchen. Carol Ann was already getting out glasses.

"That would be nice, dear," Peter said. "We ate before we left home, but something to drink would be nice. We stopped in Peabody to get copies of the *Gazette-Herald* for the obituary, but the paper won't be published until tomorrow. Has it been written yet?"

"Yes, Loretta wrote it on Monday, and we took it to the newspaper office this morning. Would you like to read it? Loretta wrote out an extra copy for us."

"Yes, please, that would be nice." Dora accepted two sheets of white stationery with neat, evenly spaced handwriting from Clara and handed them to her husband. "Peter, your eyesight is better than mine, would you please read it aloud?"

The old man took a pair of wireless spectacles out of his vest pocket and began in a voice still thickly accented with German, the language of his childhood:

*Mrs. Elizabeth Unruh, aged 86, died on Monday, August 2, 1943 at the family home on Doyle Creek east of Peabody. Mrs. Unruh was born Elizabeth Siebert on August 27, 1856 in Karlswalde, Russia to Joseph P. and Maria Siebert. She immigrated to Kansas with her family in 1874, married Jacob Unruh in 1880, and they settled in Marion County. The Unruhs farmed here all their married life. They were blessed with four children, three of whom, Harold Unruh, Tobias Unruh, and Mrs. Joseph (Margaret) Koehn, live in the area. Mrs. Unruh was preceded in death by her husband, one daughter, two sisters, and two brothers. She is survived by two sons and one daughter, seventeen grandchildren, four great-grandchildren, and a sister, Mrs. Peter (Dora) Jantz of McPherson. Her funeral was held on Thursday, August 5, 1943 at Catlin Mennonite Church, with burial in the church cemetery. A wake for Mrs. Unruh was held on Wednesday evening at the family home.*

"Very nice," said Dora. "Such good grammar and beautiful penmanship."

"I'll mail you copies from the paper when it's published."

"Thank you, dear. Is the rest of the family able to make it tonight?"

Clara said, "Yes, we're expecting everyone around six, except John and Joseph."

"I'm going to step out for a little fresh air. Clara, would you care to join me?"

"Of course. I'm dressed and everything is ready in here." She helped the old woman up from her chair and escorted her to a porch swing with their glasses of iced tea. They sat next to each other and relaxed, letting the swing sway slightly.

"Ah, that's better."

"Yes, it is. And I was hoping you and I could talk a bit tonight, just the two of us."

Dora smiled and sipped from her glass, "First, please tell me, how are the boys?"

"Oh, you know, we think they're all right, but we don't know for sure. John is still in Bethesda, Maryland. He talks about the long hours at the hospital where he's an orderly."

"And Joseph?"

"We had a letter from him a few days ago, but it was written a month earlier. As usual, he couldn't tell us anything specific, but as of then he was safe and healthy. But that was a long time ago. Today, who knows?"

"That must be so hard for you," Dora looked at her empathetically.

Clara looked down. "This is not the path we intended for him."

"Such terrible times."

"Aunt Dora, can I ask you something?"

"Of course, dear."

"I've been thinking about this more since Mother Unruh died." Clara took a breath. "Should we have stopped Joseph from enlisting in the Army and going to war?"

Dora tucked a few strands of thick white hair back under her kapp. "Could you have?"

Clara sighed. "Probably not, but should have tried harder? He was twenty years old and out of high school when he made the decision." She fought back a tear. "A decision to abandon everything he was taught."

"He didn't make it lightly, Clara. I remember him telling me how much he prayed about it. He wasn't going to war for fame or glory or because he loved violence. He felt God was calling to help stop some of the most evil characters the world has seen. After Pearl Harbor and after the reports of the atrocities in Poland and Russia, he said he was sure that for him, fighting this evil was what God was calling him to do."

"I remember, but still."

"He didn't abandon everything you taught him. In the letters I've had from him, he says he prays all the time and tries to be faithful to what God has called him to do."

Clara was near tears. "But your parents gave up everything in Russia rather than abandon their faith and be forced to go to war. And now, just two generations later, one of your sister's grandsons has taken up arms voluntarily and is committing acts that our church teaches are abominations. How must your sister have felt? Was her family's sacrifice all in vain?"

"Did Elizabeth ever condemn Joseph for his decision?"

"No. She prayed for his safety and asked God to bless him every day, including the day she died. She wrote him letters, spoke of him often, and worried along with the rest of us. There was no shunning by her or anyone else in our church, although that has happened in other communities."

"She placed her trust in the Lord and knew that Joseph was acting in accordance with his conscience, after prayer."

Clara began to cry. "Yes, but to abandon one of the pillars of our faith? To go against Harold's and my beliefs?"

"But isn't he acting in accordance with his beliefs? God gives us free will, and each of us must decide whether to follow Him and, if so, to discern in what way He is calling us."

"Yes, but to be a Mennonite is to forswear all violence as sinful. And a sin is a sin."

"If Joseph earnestly believes that the Lord called him to go to war, he must have concluded that his actions would not be sinful in the eyes of God. Who are we to judge?"

Clara wiped her eyes and looked at Dora. "You're right, of course. I shouldn't judge Joseph. It's just so hard to stand by when one of your children hears the Lord in a different way than you do."

Dora smiled, "That's been the human condition since Adam and Eve."

"Yes, but it's getting harder today. There are so many influences affecting our children that we have no control over. So many new ideas to compete with. Just in our family, Loretta is only home from Bethel because of the war, otherwise, she'd still be in college, something I strongly opposed. And I'm sure Carol Ann is planning on going there too. John is twenty-four now and showed no interest in marrying before he went to Maryland, and he was dating a nice girl from here. It's time he settled down, but I wonder if he ever will, especially now. Who will be left to farm? Will any of them stay true to our beliefs? Nobody listens to me anymore!"

Dora patted Clara on the back and laughed, "Clara, you have four godly children!"

"That's sweet of you to say."

"It's true! You and Harold raised them well. Now they're leaving the nest and you're wondering if they can fly. I felt the same way when mine were starting out. I tried to protect them, but they all made their own mistakes, just like we did. And they've all turned out pretty good. Yours will too. Continue to show your children the path of righteousness, encourage them to listen to the Lord, and all will be well."

"It's hard to know when to demand and when to let go."

"Yes, but if the Lord entrusted these beautiful children to you, He knew you and Harold were up to the task."

Clara smiled now. "Thank you for listening to a mother's worries."

The screen door swung open and Carol Ann stepped out. "Mama, what are you doing out here? Loretta and I are looking for you, it's time to get the food out. Are you planning on sitting out here all night?"

"Don't be disrespectful! I'll be right in." Turning to Dora, she said. "See what I mean?"

"You'll have your hands full with that one in a few years! God bless you all! I'll start saying extra prayers now."

Dozens of mourners soon arrived, including Harold's brother and sister and their families. Exchanging condolences with everyone was initially sad, but the gathering slowly eased into more of a pleasant family reunion than a wake. Catching up with one another was good, regardless of the circumstances.

The house, porches, and yard were soon overflowing with relatives, neighbors, and friends. A few at a time, they cycled into the house to pay their respects to Elizabeth's immediate family, then stepped back out to make room for more. Clara and her daughters and other women relatives were kept busy serving drinks and offering a light supper to everyone. Many had brought food. Over-flowing platters of bread, ham, roast beef, cold chicken, and cheese vied for space on the large kitchen table with pickles, fresh vegetables and salads, and pies and cakes. Anticipating a crowd, thoughtful church friends had even brought over extra plates, glasses, and silverware so there would be enough.

Surveying all the food, Loretta said to her mother, "We're running out of room!"

"It's like the parable of the loaves and the fishes. Jesus blessed a little bread and a few fish, and it turned out to be more than enough to feed a multitude."

Carol Ann added, "It's a good thing, because we Mennonites sure know how to graze our way through grief! Look how much everyone's eating!"

Clara shushed her younger daughter but smiled too.

Elizabeth Unruh's life was long and full, and she enjoyed good health until shortly before her death. There was much to be grateful for and celebrate. People recalled how beautifully she sewed, and shared stories about her, like the time she was chased by a bull in the south pasture and barely made it over the fence in time, losing her kapp and a shoe in the process. Many recounted the quiet acts of generosity for which she was known throughout the community. Loretta loved hearing how much others appreciated her grandmother.

At sunset, the presiding elder from Catlin Mennonite Church stood by the coffin and said a prayer. In Mennonite simplicity, no eulogy was offered, except to acknowledge Elizabeth's unswerving commitment to and faith in the Lord.

It was nearly ten before the last guests were gone, except Dora's and Peter's family, who were all spending the night with the Unruhs. "I hope you don't mind sleeping in Mama's room," Clara said to Dora and Peter as she finished the last of the dishes with her daughters, draped a tea towel over the oven door handle to dry, and sat down at the table. Carol Ann cringed. Earlier, she'd emphatically told her mother, and anyone who'd listen, that she would not want to sleep in the bed where someone had just died.

"Of course we don't," Dora said. "I hope we're not too much of an imposition."

"The boys' room is ready for you," Clara said to Dora's sons and their wives. "There won't be much privacy, but the beds are comfortable. And we've put blankets and pillows out on the sleeping porch for your children.

They'll have the coolest place to sleep tonight."

"We'll be fine," said Dora's eldest son. "Thank you so much."

"It's no imposition," said Harold, with Clara nodding in agreement. "We don't get to see you often enough anymore. Mama's passing reminds us once again how fleeting life is."

"Very true," said Dora, looking into the front room with a sad expression.

Loretta saw the look on her aunt's face. Hoping to cheer her up, she said, "Aunt Dora, would you mind telling us about what it was like when you came from Russia as a girl."

"Didn't your grandmother talk to you about these things? I was only twelve or so, but she was eighteen. I'm sure she remembered much more than I did."

"Grandma didn't talk much about the past, and now I'm sorry I didn't ask her."

"Are you too tired, Aunt Dora?" interjected Clara. "I'm sure it's past your bedtime."

"I don't mind. It's been seventy years since we left Russia, but in my mind I can see our home there more clearly than I can remember what happened yesterday." She smiled.

"If you're sure you're not too tired, it would be good if you could share some of your memories," said Harold.

"I know the name of your village in Russia was Karlswalde, right?" said Loretta.

"That's right, dear, Karlswalde. It was in the Wohlynien area of western Russia. Actually, it was in the Ukraine, which is part of Russia. It had once even been part of Poland."

"But our family wasn't Russian or Ukrainian or Polish, was it?"

"No, we're German. We came to Karlswalde from Prussia, and before that, our ancestors lived in Holland. They may have been in Belgium before that, but we've always been German and spoken German."

"That's a lot of moving," said Carol Ann.

"We had no choice. We're peace pilgrims. Many times since our people came to know the Lord, we've been hated for our commitment to Christ and for our refusal to shed blood and serve in armies. Some were burned alive for their faith. Our folk were constantly searching for a place where we could be left alone and live in peace."

Loretta asked, "What about Karlswalde? What was it like?"

"Cold and primitive. The village was in a deep, dark forest. When my grandparents arrived in the early 1800s, it was no place at all. They had to clear trees and drain swamps just so fields could be opened, and they didn't even own the land. It all belonged to Russian nobles."

"Why did they pick a place like that to live? Were they trying to hide in that forest?"

"They weren't hiding. The Russians invited them to come and promised that they would never have to serve in the Russian army if they did."

"But Russia is a huge country. How did they choose that particular spot?"

"No one knows for sure. Thousands of Mennonites and other Germans were moving to Russia around the same time. Most of them went further south, along the River Volga and around the Black Sea, but our grandparents' party didn't make it that far."

"The hand of God can be seen in all our migrations," said Peter. "Mennonites have always been under God's protection, even in the darkest times."

Loretta asked, "Were all the forests gone by the time you were born?"

"Heavens, no!" Dora laughed. "There were still lots of trees when I was little, but they'd cleared enough land by then so that we could raise cattle and hogs and enough food to feed ourselves and sell the surplus to pay the rent and purchase necessities."

"I can't imagine creating a farm in the middle of a forest," Loretta shook her head.

Dora smiled. "There's an old saying that my parents were fond of: '*Der Erste arbeitet sich tod. Der Zweite leidet Not. Der Dritte erst hat Brot.*' Can you translate that, Loretta?"

"I think so." She paused, then, "'First generation dies working. Second generation suffers severely. Third generation has its daily bread.'"

"Very good! You remember your German well."

"We still speak it here at home sometimes, and at church," said Harold. "We want our children to know the language and keep our traditions."

"That's good." Dora returned to her story, "Well that's the way it was in Karlswalde. By the time your grandmother and I were born, the area was mostly settled, and we had a comfortable home. Half of our building was a barn for our animals, and the other half was our home. We lived in one big room, our parents and all six of us children."

"That doesn't sound comfortable at all." Carol Ann turned up her nose. "Didn't it smell?"

"Maybe," Dora smiled, "but we didn't think so at the time."

Loretta asked, "Why did your parents decide to leave Karlswalde?"

"As I said, when they moved there the Russians promised them exemption from military service. They were also told they could run their own schools and use the German language. But over time, the Russians reneged on all those promises."

"Did the Russians just say okay to everyone going?"

"Definitely not! They made it very difficult."

"How could you afford to just leave and travel so far away?"

"We scraped together as much as we could, but it wasn't enough, then Mennonites and Amish people already here heard of our troubles. They took up collections and sent money to us. Their generosity saved us."

"Were you able to bring anything over with you?"

"Each adult ticket entitled the passenger to bring twenty cubic feet of freight. Our parents, Elizabeth, and one of our brothers had adult tickets, so that meant we could fill four crates. Let's see, we brought some cooking utensils, bedding, clothing, a little farm equipment, garden tools, a few small pieces of furniture, personal items, and several bags of turkey red wheat seed—not a lot. Most of what we had was left behind."

Harold said, "Loretta, you know the gas lamp in our bedroom? And the old quilt that your grandma slept under?"

"And the big kettle we use for making soap?" added Clara.

"Those things all came over from Karlswalde," said Harold. "And the large crate in the barn, it's about eight feet long, where we store the bridles? That's one of the crates they used."

"Really? Grandma never said anything about that."

"She was never one to make a fuss about things."

"So, Aunt Dora, after the decision was made, how long did it take to leave?"

"Even after the Mennonite Board of Guardians paid for our tickets, there were still delays. It took months to get our passports, then we had to travel across Europe to Belgium where we boarded a ship, the S.S.

Vaterland. It carried us all the way to Philadelphia. We arrived there on Christmas Day 1874 and thanked God for being on dry land again after a rough voyage."

Carol Ann said, "You were a world traveler at the age of twelve! And once you got to Philadelphia, you were still a long way from Kansas."

"Yes, it took more than a week before we arrived in Hutchinson, in the middle of the night. It was bitterly cold and we didn't know where to go. We were just dumped off at the depot, hundreds of us. Some kind souls took pity on us and let us into some empty buildings for the night or we'd have frozen to death. After a day or two, the Mennonite Board and Santa Fe Railroad people came and took some of us to Great Bend and the rest to Florence. We were given railroad cars there to live in, several families in each car, and that's where we spent our first winter in America. In Florence, in a boxcar."

"Really? You didn't have houses?"

Dora laughed, "Oh my, no! We were lucky to have any shelter at all. The cars were crowded and smoky and cold, but at least we were off the ground and mostly dry. Still, many of us got sick. It was in Florence that our youngest brother, Andrew, died of pneumonia. He was only eight. Elizabeth and I got it, too, but we recovered. I always thought God had some reason for letting us live through that winter."

When Doris paused to sip her tea, Clara said, "You're a blessing to us. I've heard stories of the Mennonite exodus many times. You're all so inspiring, living testaments to God's love."

Dora smiled sadly, "But now that Elizabeth has gone home, Peter and I are the last *living* testaments." She took her husband's hand and gave it a squeeze.

Loretta said, "I don't know if I would have been strong enough to survive all you went through, Aunt Dora."

"Every generation has its own problems, its own suffering." Recalling her earlier conversation with Clara, Dora went on, "I am grateful that I don't have to face some of the decisions your generation is facing. Whether to serve in the army, whether to go to college, how best to love and serve the Lord when the ground is changing beneath your feet. Times were hard when I was young, but they were simpler too." Looking at Loretta and Carol Ann, she added, "Remember, with so much changing, sometimes it's hard for your parents to keep up. I think I'm glad I'm an old lady from a simpler time."

Carol Ann said, "Maybe you're an old lady, but you've lived an adventurous life, Aunt Dora. Now, please finish your story, how did you all get from Florence to McPherson and Peabody? Why didn't you just stay in Florence?"

"In the spring of 1875, a Mennonite group and the Santa Fe helped those of us in Florence move to McPherson County. Our parents homesteaded on some of the Santa Fe land and built our first house, out of sod. A few years later, your grandparents got married and homesteaded here on Doyle Creek. I stayed with our parents until I married Peter in 1883 and we got a place of our own." As she spoke, Dora seemed to be reliving the events she was describing.

The clock in the kitchen chimed eleven. Clara said, "Thank you so much for sharing all this. One day, Loretta and Carol Ann will pass your stories on to their grandchildren."

Carol Ann was pensive. "We will, I promise. It makes me proud to be part of this family and to know the stories. I hope to be as adventurous as you."

"I'm proud of our family too child. And I'm grateful. God led us to a land of plenty. We are all richly blessed." Dora smiled.

"Amen," said Harold, and the others nodded in agreement.

"And now, look at the time," said Clara. "We have a long day ahead; it's time for bed."

Dora looked off. "If you don't mind, I'll sit with Elizabeth for a bit."

"Of course." Clara and the rest of the group rose from the table. Before taking turns in the outhouse and going to their rooms, Harold led everyone in evening prayer, then Dora walked into the front room and took a seat near the coffin. Holding her Bible, she looked at her sister in the candlelight for a few moments, shut her eyes, and was lost in the remembering.

# Chapter 14
# THINGS ARE DIFFERENT NOW

The undertaker arrived around noon. Prayers were offered as the coffin was closed, then the family formed a procession of vehicles behind the hearse. In times past, they would have followed the coffin on foot, but the church and adjacent cemetery were several miles from Doyle Creek, too long a trek under the torrid August sun for elders like Dora and Peter.

After the service and commendation, male congregants in work clothes filled in the grave while ladies served lunch in the church basement. Then it was time for goodbyes, the moment when Elizabeth's passing would become final. To stave it off a bit longer, Harold and Clara invited the Jantzes to spend another night, but their sons had to get back to work.

"I hope you'll come see us sometime," said Dora as she hugged her nephew. Then she sat back down on a white bench in the shade of the church while the rest of her family used the outhouse and said their goodbyes before driving home. Loretta and Carol Ann sat down on either side of Dora. She smiled and said, "I'll tell you more about our family history if you come see me sometime, and I have some things from Russia to show you."

"I'd like that," answered Loretta. "Maybe we can when we're done with the harvest."

Carol Ann said, "Aunt Dora, now that Grandma's gone, you're the family matriarch."

Dora smiled. "I don't know about that. Sounds like an important position. Does the title come with any pay?" Her grandnieces both laughed.

"Not likely, except maybe an extra slice of pie once in a while." Carol Ann snickered, then she jumped up to chat with a friend of hers who was still at the church.

Loretta looked a bit nervous. "Can I ask you a question?"

"If I'm the matriarch, I suppose I have to let you ask me anything," Dora smiled.

"How do you feel about Joe being in the Army? I don't know if I've ever heard you say."

"That's probably because usually I only offer my opinions on such matters if I'm asked."

"I am asking, and I would like to know."

"In that case, I'll tell you what I said to your mother last night when she asked me something similar."

"She did?" Loretta looked surprised.

"She did, and I told her that Joseph is a fine young man who loves the Lord. He's doing what he believes is the right thing for him and that God is leading him. It was not my decision to make, and I will not judge him for it."

"You told Mama that?" and Dora nodded. Loretta thought for a moment. "Can a person still be saved if he does things that are contrary to church teaching?"

"God alone knows what's in a person's heart, child. And God alone judges. The church guides and instructs, but each of us has to find our path to salvation. And thank God, our God is also kind and loving and forgiving." She saw puzzlement in Loretta's eyes. "Do you agree?"

"Yes, I do, but sometimes it's hard to reconcile our actions with church teachings."

Dora squeezed Loretta's hand. "Over the years, I've tried to do what's right, what God wants *me* to do. And along the way, I've learned that it's best if I let others figure out what's right for them." Then she laughed. "It's hard enough just keeping track of me."

"Thank you, Aunt Dora. You really are wonderful and wise."

Dora rolled her eyes. "Now let's not get carried away."

Loretta laughed, "I'm not getting carried away. I just appreciate your wisdom."

Dora smiled. "Thank you for saying that. And I want to say that I think you've grown into a wonderful woman. And although you didn't ask me, may I offer one more opinion?"

"Of course."

"I think you'd make a fine teacher."

Loretta was almost startled with her comment. "You really think so?"

"I do. You're so bright and you have such a sweet disposition and so much compassion. And there are many ways to serve the Lord."

Loretta blushed. "Mama doesn't think so, as you probably already know. And I don't know if I'm strong enough to challenge her if the war ends and I am able to return to college"

Dora laughed, "Of course you are! Trust in the Lord, my dear, and you'll have the strength to do whatever God calls you to do." Loretta smiled. "And now, may your sweet grandmother rest in peace." Dora wiped a last tear from her eye, then was helped up and walked over to her son's car. Before they pulled away, Dora held Clara's hand through the car window for a long moment before releasing her with a promise to pray for John and Joseph every day.

It was after five when the Unruhs pulled into their driveway. They planned to change quickly and start choring, but a group of neighbors was there doing everything that had to be done before sundown. In the garden, two women were filling five-gallon buckets with produce. They waved when they saw Clara and the girls coming toward them. Harold headed to the milk barn, where Cletus Slaymaker was minding the Unruhs' fifteen Holsteins while others inside were milking them. Cletus, middle-aged and stout, pulled a crumpled blue handkerchief from his grey and white-striped overalls and lifted up his sweat-stained straw hat to wipe his shiny bald head. He acknowledged Harold with, "It surely is a hot one again."

"That it is," Harold replied. "Thank you. I don't quite know what to say."

Cletus smiled. "We knew you could use a hand. We're about done with the milking. We got the rest of the animals fed and watered too." Nodding toward the big barn, he added, "A couple of the boys is back there finishing up now, and we'll get the chickens in for you. We made ourselves at home and found everything pretty easy. I hope that's all right."

Harold was humbled by their kindness. "We're much obliged."

"Don't mention it. Last year, when I fell out of the loft, you came over to my place for a week until I could move again. Now you go on up to the house and change. You've had a long day. We'll finish up and see ourselves off. And I'm sure sorry about your mother. She was a fine lady.

I woulda gone to the funeral but figured being here was a better use of my time."

"Please tell everyone we're grateful." Harold waved to the others, then met his wife and daughters on their way back from the garden. The four of them walked up the steps and into the now too-quiet kitchen. On the table was a bouquet of scarlet, pink, and mauve gladiolus, a fresh-baked cherry pie, and a still-warm loaf of bread, along with a note: *roast in refrigerator.*

"More food!" said Clara. "Does it say who from?"

Loretta lifted up the Pyrex pie pan. On the bottom was a piece of white medical tape with a name written in ink. "The Slaymakers," said Loretta. "And it looks delicious."

"Looks like we have supper tonight," Carol Ann said.

"We already had supper from all the leftovers. And I'm still not hungry after the meal at church. We won't have to cook for a week! We're blessed to have such neighbors."

"Yes, we are," said Harold. "God is good."

From their bedroom, Harold and Clara heard the screen door. A woman stepped into the kitchen and called, "Here are the tomatoes, and some peppers and cukes. See you later."

The neighbors were gone by the time the Unruhs were back in the kitchen. Clara spread the tomatoes out on old newspapers. They came in different sizes, and a few were split or splotchy, but most were perfectly ripe. The table and counters were soon completely covered. When Loretta and Carol Ann came down the stairs, their mother said, "Looks like we'll be canning. These tomatoes are ready, and we can't let them go to waste."

"I think Papa plans on me helping him in the beans tomorrow," said Loretta, "but that depends on whether it rains tonight or not."

Carol Ann sighed, "I guess I'll help." At sixteen, she would have preferred to be in Peabody visiting with friends and cousins or reading in the library or skipping rocks across the creek, but she knew she was needed and what was expected of her. Still, she regularly came up with excuses to get out of jobs like canning. She never really thought any of them would work, but she enjoyed the challenge of saying something clever that would amuse or shock her family. Tonight, however, she was too tired to entertain them, so she offered her services quickly, which drew surprised looks from both her parents and Loretta.

"We could do them tonight, but I don't want to be up late. I'm tired. How about we start first thing in the morning, before it gets too hot."

"If we have to," Carol Ann hmphed again for effect. "What shall we do this evening?"

"Let's clean up a bit, get the furniture back where it belongs, and make sure all the dishes and glasses are put away, then have some pie. Does anyone want anything else to eat?"

"Just that pie. It's calling my name." Harold loved all sweets, especially fruit pies.

The sun was low over the tree-lined creek west of the farmstead by the time the house was back in order. Carol Ann walked to the mailbox by the road while Loretta brought four slices of pie and tea out to the shady porch, which wrapped around three sides of the house. Harold and Clara sat beside each other on the swing. Loretta poured thick, heavy cream on Harold's piece, and smiled. "Just the way you like it." She took a seat in one of the rocking chairs facing the big barn and the road beyond it.

"Thank you, daughter." Then to Carol Ann, he called, "Any mail?"

"Looks like some more sympathy cards." Walking up the steps, she thumbed through the envelopes, then exclaimed, "Oh! Here's a letter from Joe!"

The others perked up. "Go in and open it with a knife," Clara commanded as she reached into a pocket for her glasses. She dusted the lenses with a handkerchief until Carol Ann handed her the envelope and took a seat beside Loretta. Clara coaxed two pages out, unfolded them, and scanned both sides of each sheet. The mere sight of Joe's chicken-scratch handwriting overwhelmed her with relief.

Harold tried waiting patiently. "What does it say? Is he all right?"

"I'll read it," Clara replied.

*Dear Mama, Papa, Grandma, and Sisters,*

*I'm writing to let you know I'm still in one piece.*

A lump in Clara's throat made it impossible to speak, except in a whisper. "Thank you, Jesus," she said. Harold put his arm around her shoulder. She composed herself and continued:

*My unit saw a lot of action recently. Some friends were*

*hurt and a good buddy since basic training was killed. It's hot and dusty here, but my sweaty feet don't ever get completely dried out. I've had some trouble sleeping because of all the noise at night, but lately it's been better. The food is still terrible too. Mama, I'd give anything for some of your rhubarb pie about now.*

Looking at her plate, Carol Ann said, "He'd love this pie, even if it's not yours, Mama."

Clara read on:

*Papa, I hope you're not working too hard. We've made progress, but it's slow going. Now we're getting ready to move. I can't give any details, except I'll say again that it's HOT here!*

"Sounds like he was still in Africa," Loretta said, "But now he's somewhere else."

Her mother nodded and returned to the letter:

*The main thing is I love you and miss you. I hope you're thinking of me too. Please tell John I say hi when you write to him. I've tried writing him a couple times, but don't know if I have the right address. Mama, I pray every night, like I promised. Every day too. Loretta and Carol Ann, I look at your pictures every chance I get. My friend Charlie says you're quite a dish, Loretta. I told him to lay off, that you're my sister!*

Loretta blushed, Carol Ann giggled, and Clara scowled:

*Your pictures always make me smile, even on the roughest days. Grandma, I hope you're feeling better. The last letter I got from home, you weren't doing too well. I gotta go now. Back to work, will try to write again soon.*
> *Your loving son, grandson, and brother,*
> *Joe*

Clara said, "It's dated July 8th, so a month's gone by."

"Operation Husky, the Allied invasion of Sicily from North Africa, started around that time. I'll bet that's where he is now, in Sicily," said

Loretta.

"And he doesn't know about his grandmother's death," Harold said, with pain in his voice.

"I wrote to him the Monday after Grandma died," said Loretta. "I wrote to John, too, since we couldn't get a call through to him, so the news is on the way to them both, but they won't get it for a while. That makes me sad."

Harold bowed his head and prayed aloud, "Thank you, Jesus, for Joseph's continued safety. We ask you to continue to bless and keep him in your loving care, wherever he might be." They went back to nibbling at their pie, but even Harold was no longer much interested in eating.

Clara reverently put the letter back in its envelope and tucked it into her apron pocket. Later, she'd place it in the top drawer of her nightstand with all the others. The family sat in silent melancholy. The whistle of a Santa Fe train rumbling north on the other side of the creek sounded especially mournful. Joe's letters were a relief, but every mention of death and injury brought the battlefield into their home and reignited their smoldering fears for his safety. And this one, coming on this particular day, was especially painful. Loretta wondered what her brother was doing at that moment. Hopefully sleeping. She couldn't stop thinking about the dangers he faced on a daily basis. It tied her stomach in knots.

Just a year apart in age, Loretta and Joe were always close. They were the most inquisitive of the four Unruh children. Each loved school, music, walks in the Flint Hills, and playing practical jokes on one another and the rest of the family. When they had crushes and started dating in high school, each was the other's confidante. Loretta could tell her brother anything; she trusted his advice like no other's.

The train had passed by the time Carol Ann returned from taking the dishes in. The porch was now dark, save for fast-fading glints of sunlight in the west and golden light coming through the kitchen door and windows. The swing creaked as the parents moved forward and back, and Loretta's rocking chair squeaked along at its own pace. Frogs croaked, crickets chirped, a heifer mooed low and deep, and a pair of coyotes started their nightly serenade. The evening breeze finally overtook the oxygen-sapping heat that had nearly smothered everyone earlier in the day.

At last, Loretta was ready to interrupt their solitude. "Papa," she began, "it was a nice funeral. Grandma would have been pleased."

"You're right. Such a big crowd, both last night and today, so many kind words, her favorite songs and scriptures, most of her family here, such a beautiful sermon."

"It still doesn't seem possible that she's gone. It will be so different now," said Carol Ann.

"God granted her a peaceful death in her own home, her own bed, after a long, blessed life," said Clara. "Who could ask for more?" Death was on Clara's mind, and not just Elizabeth's.

"It's just so strange. As long as I've been alive, she lived here with us." The magnitude of their loss seemed to be sinking in for Carol Ann for the first time.

"Me too," smiled Harold. "I was born in this house in 1892 and my parents had already been living in it for five years. They built it in 1887, just seven years after they came here. In all, she lived in this same house for over fifty years."

"It's funny how she lived so long in one place after moving around so much earlier in her life," said Loretta.

Clara retorted, "What's funny? She and Grandpa found what they were looking for right here—a place to make a home and live a Christian life. Doyle Creek was their Promised Land."

More silence, then Loretta said, "I liked Aunt Dora's stories last night."

Carol Ann concurred. "I was surprised how much I enjoyed them."

Loretta silently debated before saying something else, then went ahead. "It's ironic."

"What's that?" asked Harold.

She chose her words carefully. "That our ancestors were persecuted because they refused to serve in the military. And now Joe is in an army doing what Grandma tried so hard to escape." No one responded. "It just seems so, so, I don't know what. Is 'ironic' the right word? That on the day Grandma is buried, we got a letter from one of her grandsons from a battlefront." As soon as she heard her own words, she sensed she would regret saying them.

Harold said, "Do you think one of them was wrong and the other was right?"

"No, Papa, I wasn't judging anyone. And Grandma didn't judge Joe when he enlisted, either, at least not to me, but I know the path he chose was hard for her to understand."

"It's hard for all of us to understand," her mother said tersely.

Now Loretta definitely regretted wading into a subject that the family generally avoided, but she felt obligated to go on. "For some reason, he thought he had to join the fight, and taking CO status like John wasn't enough for him. He's put himself in harm's way for what he feels is a just cause. But deep down, I think he believes that war is wrong, like Grandma."

"Then he should have held fast to those beliefs," Clara snapped. The swing quit creaking.

"I'm sorry, Mama." Loretta's eyes filled with tears. "I guess I'm just missing him tonight."

"We all are." Her mother was still agitated. "We all are."

"And even if he had gone with CO, he still wouldn't have been here today. The war would have kept him away, just like it did John. I'm just sorry about it all." No one responded.

Harold finally spoke, "I'm sorry about something else. I'm sorry you had to come home from college, Loretta. I know how much you want to be a teacher, and now that's on hold."

"It's all right," said Loretta, with even more trepidation that her father was steering them into another subject that might be provocative to her mother. "I know I'm needed here."

"You're not just needed, you're indispensable. We wouldn't have made it these last two years without you. You, too, Carol Ann. With the boys gone, and all the other young men, too, there's no one left to do the work. The farm would have failed without you here."

"I don't know about that." Loretta smiled. "You still do the work of two younger men in half the time. Sometimes I think I'm more in the way than I help, but I try, and I'm glad if it makes things easier for you."

"We're grateful," said Harold. "And after Carol Ann goes back to school in a few weeks, the burden will be even greater on you again, Loretta."

"I'll be okay, really. We'll see this through together until the boys get home."

Clara, who'd been holding her tongue, finally spoke, "Well, you know my feelings on the subject. I was not in favor of you going to Bethel in the first place."

"Yes, Mama, I do know that." She looked up at the sky and fidgeted.

"Your place is here, not in Newton or someplace else. Women don't need to be going to college, that's just how I feel." No one spoke until Clara added, softer now, "That said, I appreciate your coming back too. You're a great blessing to us, Loretta. And maybe while you're here, you'll see that this life isn't so bad."

"Oh Mama, I never thought it was bad. I love it here. This will always be home. I just think my calling is to be a teacher. That's where I can do the most good." She felt her father looking at her in the dark. He'd encouraged her to follow her dream, though he was reluctant to say much in front of his wife in view of her strongly held beliefs to the contrary.

Gently, Clara said, "I'll keep praying that the Lord reveals His plan to you. In the meantime, thank you for being here, especially now, as we get into the harvest."

Harold saw an opportunity to steer the conversation in a different direction and took it. "Speaking of the harvest, I have what might be some good news."

"What's that?" Loretta was ready to talk about something else too.

"Remember, a couple weeks ago I went to a meeting in Peabody about maybe hiring some POWs to work for us? Well, Frank Becker told me at dinner today that there's going to be another meeting with the county agent tomorrow night to place actual orders for how many workers each farmer would want. If enough orders are placed, he'll petition the War Manpower Commission for us."

"What does that mean?" asked Loretta.

"It means the Army could send some German prisoners to Peabody and let us hire them."

"Where are they now?"

"The Army built a camp in Concordia to hold thousands of them. From there, they're going to move some around the State to places that want them."

"I remember reading about that in the paper. Are they dangerous?"

"I don't know. And I don't know what kind of condition they're in, if they're injured, or even willing to work. Last time, the county agent talked about how much we'd pay them and about guards coming along. I don't know more, but I want to find out."

"We'd have to pay them?" Clara was tense again. "Pay the very

Germans who were just shooting at our son? And they're dangerous enough to have to be guarded?"

"I know it sounds kind of queer, with them being the enemy, but we wouldn't have them be our slaves, would we? If they work, they should be paid. The plan is, we'd pay the Army, and it would keep part of the money to cover expenses and give the rest to the prisoners. The rate hasn't been set, but it would be less than what we'd pay Americans, if we could even find some who are willing to work. What do you girls think?"

"Well," Loretta paused, "it's strange to think that we might have German soldiers here. But as long as the Army is sure they wouldn't cause trouble, it would be good to have the help."

Carol Ann was unequivocal. "I'm all for it if I don't have to bale hay anymore!"

"There will still be plenty for you to do," said Clara. "I want to know more about this plan before we bring a bunch of Nazis out here."

"I'll find out the details tomorrow night," said Harold. "Even if it does work out, it doesn't mean things would get easier right away, but it might take some of the pressure off and help us get caught up. Maybe you girls wouldn't have to work so hard in the fields this fall."

Following prayers, Loretta stayed behind in the kitchen to write to Joe:

*Dear Joe,*

*It's very late here and I am very tired, but I wanted to write at least a few lines to you tonight, then will finish the rest of this letter tomorrow.*

*Today was Grandma's funeral. The wake last night and the funeral today were both well attended and very nice. I will tell you all about them tomorrow, but my eyes are drooping, and I don't know how long I will be able to keep my head off the table!*

*The things I wanted to tell you tonight? First, I wanted to say, again, that I respect you for making the decision you made to go to war, even though I still don't like it. It was courageous of you to do what your conscience told you was right.*

*Last night, Aunt Dora told us about what she and Grandma went through when they were children and afterwards. They were very courageous too. I guess it runs in our family!*

*I don't know if I could do what they did or take the path you took. I've never had to be courageous. Guess maybe I'm lucky in that sense.*

*Okay, I think I just drooled on this piece of paper. Ha! A sure sign that I should put down my pen and go to bed. More tomorrow.*

# Chapter 15
# DOYLE CREEK

The wall clock chimed five tinny dings as Loretta and Carol Ann made their way down the stairs, lured by the enticing smell of bacon sizzling in the cast iron skillet, one of a pleasing mélange of aromas emanating from the bright kitchen—floury baking powder biscuits just out of the oven, fresh-perked coffee, and the tangy-sweet earthiness of all the spread-out tomatoes.

Clara smiled in her daughters' direction, then turned back to the dozen eggs she was beating with milk in her favorite, most-used bowl, a fawn-colored crock with spider web cracks and a chipped lip. She and Harold had already been up for an hour, preparing for the day.

"Good morning, girls," Harold said welcomingly from his place at the table, which had been partially cleared of tomatoes to make room for them to eat. "And how did you sleep?"

"Well, thank you," said Loretta. She kissed her parents' cheeks and filled a cup with steaming coffee. "I'm surprised we have coffee left, and it looks full strength."

"It is. We're about out, but I heard on the radio that coffee rationing ended last month," said Clara. "Since we should soon be able to buy as much as we like, I splurged this morning."

"That's good news." As she poured cream in and stirred, she asked, "And how about you, how did you sleep?"

"Fine, just fine." Harold was comically swatting at a pesky swarm of gnats circling his head, the inevitable uninvited guests who'd followed the tomatoes into the house.

"Me too," said Carol Ann, still wiping sleep from her eyes. "It was cool in my room last night. Perfect sleeping weather."

"Yes, it was. I wish it would stay that way all day, but it's gonna get hot. And it doesn't look like rain, so we'll be in the beans again today, Loretta.'

"I figured. Maybe we'll get them done today."

As soon as the last bites were eaten and the last sips of coffee were swallowed, the family stood in unison as if a starting bell had rung and headed off in the direction of waiting tasks. Carol Ann cleared the table and washed dishes, while her mother sorted the tomatoes and got the jars and equipment out. Then she stepped outside to the well and pumped the seven-quart canner full of water, added wood to the stove, and went back out for more. Along with multiple canning batches that day, Clara and Carol Ann would tend to the chickens, gather eggs, hoe and pull weeds in the garden, water the garden from the well, and pick cucumbers and okra for pickling in a day or two. They would gather up the ripe apples that had already fallen in the orchard for applesauce. They'd also have the other family meals ready at the appointed times. Breakfast was at five every morning, dinner was at noon, those working in the fields got a snack around three, and supper was served around sunset, when everyone was finally back in for the night.

Loretta and Harold headed outside. The faint promise of light foretold the arrival of dawn, but they wouldn't wait for sunrise. Their first job would be milking the Holsteins already lined up at the gate into the pen next to the milk barn. By the time the sun had crested the eastern hills, the milking would be done, and the cattle and calves would be fed. Then, father and daughter would tend to the hogs and feed the horses before heading into the soybean fields to hoe out the weeds that were so close to the plants they hadn't been uprooted by the cultivator Harold had earlier pulled down the rows behind the family's Allis Chalmers tractor. After an hour-long dinner break, they'd be back out in the field in the heat of the day until it was time for the cows' second milking, after which they'd roost the chickens for the night.

Chores varied by day and season and were determined in part by factors beyond anyone's control—like weather, funerals, insects, equipment breakdowns, and now, war-mandated fuel rationing. The regular, everyday tasks set the farm's general rhythm, while the sporadic jobs, like fence-mending, planting, haying, shocking, canning, and sewing, were added in as necessary. Summer brought the longest workdays, but every day of the year dawned with something that had to be done. "There's no rest for the weary," Clara liked to say, quoting Holy Scripture. Even on the Lord's Day, which the family kept holy by attending church, there were still meals to fix, cows to milk, eggs to gather, and livestock to feed.

Aside from the deprivations brought on by war, the rationing, shortages of parts, the absence of their beloved sons, life on the Unruh farm in 1943 was comfortable and secure. There was food on the table, a roof over their heads, and enough money to buy what they couldn't grow or make. But the price of this stability had to be paid by every family member. Each's contribution was essential. Even Elizabeth was shelling peas, making noodles, and darning socks until a few days before she fell asleep and died. Watching her fade, Harold and Clara urged the old woman to slow down, but she kept on, giving what she could right up to the end.

The day flew by. Harold and Loretta left the field early, and Carol Ann helped her sister with the milking and outside chores so Harold could clean up for the POW meeting. Clara took twenty-four sealed quarts of tomatoes to the root cellar beside the house, then she washed up and changed too. At noon, she'd announced that she was also going to the meeting.

The girls were dozing in the front room when their parents returned around nine o'clock. Clara woke them when she turned the radio off.

"How'd it go?" Loretta asked sleepily as she followed her mother into the kitchen.

"Good," her father said.

"Are you going to hire some Germans?" Loretta yawned.

"We put in an order for four workers."

"Four? That's a lot. Do you think we'll get them?"

"I don't know. The county agent received over a hundred orders, which might be enough for the Army to open a sub-camp here."

"That's good, isn't it? What do you think, Mama?"

"I still have a few doubts, but everyone there seemed to think it will help us all, so I'm willing to give it a try."

"A few doubts?" Harold smiled. "At the meeting you sounded a lot more emphatic than that. You gave it to the county agent when he said he was sure there would be no trouble."

"That's because he can't be so sure. These are captured Germans who just got out of a war. That alone should be enough for us to want to be absolutely sure we'll be safe. Beyond that, we have no idea what any of them is like, except that they're all *außenseiter*. I thought the county agent was not taking those worries seriously."

Loretta, now awake, asked her mother, "How do you feel now, after the meeting, Mama? Do you think it's still a good idea?"

"I'm willing to give it a try because it's harvest time and we need the help so badly. But we must be careful around them."

Harold said, "We will be, won't we, girls?" His daughters nodded.

"When will we know something?" asked Loretta.

"Soon, maybe in a week or so," said Harold.

By 9:30, the house was still and dark. Drifting off to the hoots of a pair of barn owls, Loretta wondered what it would be like having men on the farm again. She was too tired to worry about whether they might be dangerous. Besides, her father would always keep them safe.

# Chapter 16

# HEINIES

In late August, Carol Ann started her junior year at Peabody High School. By then, the garden was about done, and the canning was mostly finished, but the field harvest was in full swing, and her absence was felt. Not least because she was a light-hearted, upbeat soul whose company was genuinely appreciated. Harold said there was never a dull moment around his rambunctious youngest child.

One still-warm September afternoon, the school bell signaled day's end at Peabody High, an imposing two-story brick structure with classic Greek columns built into its facade. Students and faculty alike poured out into the hallways, where Carol Ann and her friends shared a few last tidbits of teenage gossip before heading home. At her locker, she was selecting books for her evening homework when several boys approached. In the lead was Tommy Ferguson. She paid them no attention until they stopped next to her. Tommy looked nervous. "Is your family gonna hire German POWs?" he asked confrontationally in his country-twang voice.

Carol Ann was surprised and annoyed. "Maybe. I don't know. How'd you hear about that?"

"My folks was talking about it this mornin. Other guys said they heard it too."

"I'm not sure. Papa went to some meetings. Tell me, why does this concern you?"

"We heard they was settin up a camp for 'em here, and we don't like it." Tommy nodded to the others. "Heinies is the enemy, or did you forget? Why in hell would you bring 'em here?"

"I'm still not sure why that matters to you," Carol Ann said dismissively, "but in answer to your question, I'm not bringing anyone anywhere. All I know is we need help, and the Army told us the Germans might be able to work on farms."

"You're German, and the POWs is German. Ain't that just pretty damn cozy?"

Carol Ann laughed out loud. "What? Why in heaven's name would that matter? The Germans wouldn't just be going to German farms. The Slaymakers and others talked about hiring them too. Besides, my family's been here for fifty years. We're as American as you are, Tommy Ferguson. It's not like they'd be sending us friends or relatives."

"But you're all krauts. Maybe you're all Nazi sympathizers."

Now she bristled. "And maybe you're crazy. No one I know is pro-Nazi. My brother is even in the war."

"So is mine. So why would you want German scum working on your farm?"

Glaring directly at him, she replied slowly, "First of all, they're not 'scum' or 'krauts' or 'heinies.' Now try to follow along here: We can't find enough help to get the harvest in. Boys like you could do it, but you don't want to work on farms."

Tommy interrupted her, "We all have jobs."

"Well hurrah for you, and that's my point. There aren't enough men or boys around to work like there used to be. There's no one left to ask. So maybe it will be good having the prisoners here if they're willing to work."

"It's plain wrong. My parents think so too."

"I'm sorry, but that's their problem. And yours. Now I have to go. My ride is waiting."

Tommy stepped closer. "You tell your father we don't want any heinies around here."

Carol Ann refused to be cowed. "You bet. I'll do that the minute I get home from school."

⚊⚊⚊

When the sisters were alone doing the milking that evening, Loretta was just about to ask Carol Ann why she was so quiet, when she spoke. "Have you heard anyone complain because we might be hiring German prisoners?"

"No, why?"

"Tommy Ferguson came up to me after school today. He made it sound like we'd be anti-American if we bring them here. He called us all 'krauts' and implied we can't be trusted."

"I'm sorry, but he's a fool. His brother was in my class and just as foolish."

"More than anything, I found him rude. But it did make me wonder if there's going to be trouble if the prisoners come."

"I don't think so, but some people may talk. That's nothing new. People around here have complained about Germans for years, long before this business with prisoners. Americans with German heritage have been accused of all sorts of crazy things, and not just us Mennonites, but the Catholics and Lutherans too."

"Really? I guess I missed all that."

"Mama said that it was especially bad during World War I. Back then, people like Tommy Ferguson tried to say that every German in America was still loyal to the Kaiser."

"But our family didn't even live in Germany! We came from Russia."

"That didn't stop people from treating us like the enemy. There were demonstrations in town. Papa was even threatened by a gang in front of the feed store. Cletus Slaymaker came to his aid and put a stop to it before anything happened, but it was pretty shocking at the time."

"I never heard about any of this before."

"Papa even had to register for the draft in 1917."

"Wait, did he go into the Army?"

"No, he was exempted because farm workers were classified as essential to the war effort back then. But even that had some questioning his loyalty. They said he should have gone to war with the other young men and that he was a coward."

"Papa's never said anything about that to me."

"Me, neither. It was Mama who told me, and just a couple years ago, when John and Joe were deciding what to do." Loretta stepped out of the barn to move a reluctant cow along, then returned and continued. "That's when people quit speaking German on the streets and teaching in German in schools, because everyone was so suspicious of them."

"Good grief!"

"Mama said many of the Germans who weren't Mennonite felt like they had to volunteer to go to war just to prove they were real Americans. And some Germans' homes in Hillsboro even had their windows broken out by a mob."

"War does such horrible things to people."

"It does. I think that's why Grandma didn't talk about the 'good old days.' It really must have hurt when people accused her family of being anti-American and hazed her son like that."

After cleaning the equipment, making sure the milk and cream were properly stored, and sending the cows out to the pasture for the night, they paused on their way to the house to admire the sunset. While they took in the gorgeous array of color in the western sky, Loretta put her arm around her sister's shoulder. "Forget Tommy Ferguson. It's not worth worrying another minute about people like him."

"You're right," said Carol Ann.

"If Papa does hire German prisoners, it'll be because we need them. And the Army needs something to do with all the prisoners they're capturing. It could be a win-win situation, even for loud-mouths like Tommy, who get to eat what we 'krauts' grow. I think it will all turn out okay."

"I think I'd rather have German POWs here any day than nit-wits like him."

Loretta laughed. "No question about that."

# PART

## III

# Chapter 17
# CAMP PEABODY

September weather in Kansas is always a your-guess-is-as-good-as-mine kind of thing. Blast-furnace heat is the norm in summer, and accepted, and finger-numbing cold in winter surprises no one. But inbetween, September can be perfectly beautiful or it can skid off the tracks in either direction, or both, sometimes in the same afternoon. Fall officially starts in September every year, but Kansas weather rarely takes a cue from the calendar.

September in 1943 was a noticeable improvement over stifling-hot, bone-dry July and August, but there were still days in that year's ninth month when temperatures spiked into the upper nineties just to irritate people. Saturday, the 11th, the day for the first POW transport from Concordia to Peabody, was one such day, cruelly hot. Rolf Mueller had hoped to get a good look at the countryside on the ride, but the glowing sun, unrelenting wind in his face, the truck's rocking movement, and the exhaust fumes that enveloped them in the back of the truck lulled him into drowsiness almost from the moment they left Concordia. It was hard to keep his eyes open even when they passed through Minneapolis, Salina, McPherson, and Newton. The convoy seemed to speed up through the towns anyway, maybe so the prisoners wouldn't be tempted to jump off, or maybe because the Army didn't want them to be conspicuous to the locals. Twice along the way, the trucks pulled over in open country so the men could relieve themselves and stretch, but those were their only respites. Few bothered to eat their C-rations.

Around four in the afternoon, the convoy reached Peabody from the west on Highway 50 and turned south onto broad, tree-lined Walnut Street. They passed imposing, well-maintained homes with Victorian gingerbread and cupolas and broad porches surrounded by tidy lawns, then came to the downtown, several blocks of sturdy brick and stone buildings occupied by small shops, groceries, hardware and dry-goods stores, a pool hall, and a bar or two.

Rumors had been circulating for weeks, so the locals were ready as soon as the first vehicle left the highway and the rumble of the twenty-odd vehicles was heard. Children's shouts—The Nazis are here! The Nazis are here!—called young and old alike to the street. Some gawked from porch steps. Any parade was news in sleepy Peabody, population thirteen hundred, give or take a few and not counting those living on nearby farms, but this one was especially noteworthy. Folks tagged along with the slow-moving military vehicles on foot and bicycles and in vehicles. A few waved cheerfully, and guards smiled and waved back.

The Germans were confused. A guard said this was Peabody, but the convoy kept rolling, all the way through town until it reached a large field outside the city limits, bordered by roads on two sides and a brush-lined creek on the others. A two-storied building, apparently vacant, stood off to one side. The entire area looked forlorn. "Here we are," said a guard gruffly when the last vehicle had come to a stop. "Get down."

"Where is here?" asked one German. For a split second, Rolf thought he might have been wrong not to worry about being taken to an isolated location and shot. This would be a perfect spot. He was just wondering if they'd be executed in the building and whether their bodies would be thrown into a river or buried in a trench when his morose speculations were interrupted by the guard telling them to grab their gear and line up.

As soon as all sixty Germans and the thirty-odd guards were on the ground, a young lieutenant, George Stevenson, tall and slender and wearing wire-rimmed glasses and a smile, stepped forward with a corporal who quickly called off the POWs' names. Sixty names got sixty *jas* or *ja wohls*. The guards seemed relieved that they hadn't lost anyone along the way, and their relaxed demeanor helped calm the Germans. When the roll was complete, Lieutenant Stevenson, speaking in easily-understood German, introduced himself as the camp's commanding officer and said, "Welcome to Camp Peabody."

One brash POW called out, "There's nothing here. Did we bomb it off the map already?"

Stevenson laughed. "Not quite." Gesturing, he said, "It's just new, but we brought everything we need. Before sundown, we're going to have tents pitched and latrines dug. There's no time to waste, so let's get to it, unless you'd like to sleep on the bare ground tonight." The Germans smiled, they were ready to have something to do to shake off the trip's lethargy. Rolf took off his outer shirt and immediately felt better as a breeze reached his sweat-drenched T-shirt and skin. And he noticed how sunburned his forearms had gotten on the ride.

Water coolers were set up, and the Germans were divided into teams. The trucks were emptied of tools, canvas, hardware, cots, bedding, heavy cook stoves, large metal water tanks, buckets, and wash tubs. Much of the equipment looked brand new. The inmates did the unloading and setting up while the guards kept a wary eye on everyone, gave instructions, and helped as necessary. By sunset, a rudimentary camp had taken shape, with tidy rows of sleeping tents, larger mess and administrative tents, and several latrines. It was more than adequate. The Germans had all bivouacked in far worse locations. Tent assignments were made, and more C-rations were distributed to the now-hungry men. A low barbed-wire fence was hastily uncoiled along the perimeters and guards were stationed along it—two with machine guns—but there would be no strobe lights or towers. To a larger degree than they might want to admit, the Americans would have to rely on German acquiescence as much as firepower to keep the POWs confined.

Along the road to the north, a group of locals had gathered to watch, including Tommy Ferguson. He and his friends were guzzling beer and growing more animated with each bottle, until Tommy was emboldened to shout, "Not so high and mighty now are you, fucking krauts!" His taunts amused his friends, but chagrined the rest of the crowd. "You slimy sons-a-bitches, why don't you jump in those holes you're digging, and I'll come piss on you." People glared or shook their heads in dismay.

The Germans were too far away and too busy to hear, but Tommy caught the attention of two guards, who quickly approached. "Folks, this is a U.S. Army installation," said one of them. "Your interactions with the prisoners are not permitted, so please disburse and go back to town."

"So you're coddling them heinies, are ya?" said Tommy. "We don't want 'em here."

The guard, not much older than Tommy, but several inches taller and very well-built, stepped close to the boy and looked at him condescendingly. "Sir, it's not for you to decide whether they should be here or not." He paused, then added in a slow, emphatic cadence, "I'm going to tell you one more time to back off. Leave, and do not disrupt us."

Sober enough to realize that this guard was not to be trifled with, Tommy and his friends grumbled, but slowly backed down and drove off. Other townspeople nodded their approval; some even thanked the guards before leaving.

One woman said to another, "That Tommy Ferguson is a bad apple, just like his father. I'm glad the guard gave him the what for."

"What a pest, but at least this time he's not harassing our girls."

Tommy was not much appreciated in the community.

As they walked back from the road, the guard who'd spoken, PFC Jerry Flannigan, said, "You gotta wonder if it's a good idea putting POWs near civilians like this, don't you?"

The second guard, an older man named Greg Jordan, responded, "I know what you mean, but what else are we gonna do with them? They have to be close to the jobs they'll be doing."

"I know, but I wonder whether we'll be spending more time guarding the prisoners or protecting them. The Germans seem to be pretty decent for the most part."

Rolf and the others were exhausted but pleased when they unfolded their cots. Setting up camp was a solid, constructive accomplishment. It engendered a satisfying sense of teamwork and cooperation between the Americans and Germans that put everyone at ease.

A southwest breeze during the night refreshed everyone, but the more citified German POWs and American guards felt eerily exposed in such open country. To be sure, those who'd survived combat had camped out in open spaces before, but in those days, they were always surrounded by thousands of other soldiers and encapsulated in the incessant din of war. For some, it was unsettling to be in the middle of such dark, pervasive stillness, a quiet punctuated only by occasional fast-moving trains and yelps and hoots and shrieks from unfamiliar, unseen creatures. Those first residents of Camp Peabody didn't sleep well that night.

That was not a problem for Rolf.

# Chapter 18
# BROTHERS IN ARMS

After his best night's sleep in years, he woke, slowly and lazily, to surprising serenity. Pearls of dew sparkled in the sunlight beneath a deep blue sky. Three deer, larger than their European cousins, ventured timidly out from the trees in search of clumps of wet, green grass still to be found in the tawny carpet that spread from the creek to the camp. Unseen birds cooed from fall-tinted branches, and a solitary hawk searched for breakfast from high above in broad, graceful sweeps. As Rolf inhaled the earth-infused air, he was carried back to a hay meadow where he and his brother, Kurt, and Schatzy, their beloved longhaired pointer, often slept in warm weather. From this meadow straddling the rounded crest of a hill east of the family house, they could see over the farm's demarcating stone fence, down into the forested valley to the south and beyond, out into the world. It was a magical place where young boys could be whatever they wanted. Often, these two were heroic knights just returned from the Holy Land after the German Crusade, a romanticized twelfth century saga widely known to German schoolboys in those days. From the castle keep in their grassy fief, the Mueller boys regaled each other with their warrior exploits. They would tick off how many infidels they'd slaughtered and describe how enemy blood dripped from their heavy swords. They gloated over the splendid treasures they'd carried home. "Someday, I'm going to have adventures of my own," Kurt would tell his little brother. "Someday, I'm going to be a real crusader."

Recalling Kurt's crusader dreams snapped Rolf out of his reverie. What would Kurt have to say about his youthful ambitions today, after years of fighting real battles? And the contrast in their situations stung: Here was Rolf, cozy on a clean cot in relative safety, but what about Kurt? Was he still wallowing in the muck of war on the Eastern Front? Or worse, was he dead, or captured by the barbaric Slavs? Rolf involuntarily tucked his legs into a ball and shut his eyes to the rising sun, but he couldn't escape a cascade of wildly conflicting emotions—fear, relief, anger, selfishness, confusion, shame. And worst of all, there was guilt, the most powerful weapon a person can use against himself.

But what should he be guilty of? Having fought? Being duped into believing in Hitler's jingoistic mumbo-jumbo? Having lost? Having lived? Having killed? Suddenly, familiar faces from France and Libya burst into his consciousness. Old faces, young ones, innocents, enemies. *No! I was only following orders. I will not feel guilty! I did what I had to do.*

Unable to concede that he might be guilty for something and incapable of imagining what that might mean, his troubled mind settled on anger instead. But why was he angry? For thinking that war could be glorious? For getting captured and now being unable to help protect his family? For no longer being certain of anything?

He was still awash in emotional turmoil when Greg Jordan stood outside the tents and shouted for the Germans to get up and dressed, then line up for roll call and breakfast. In short order, they'd eaten and were assembled in front of the administrative tent to be told their work assignments.

Rolf felt marginally better when learned he was being sent to a farm. Most of the others were also going to farms, but some were assigned to local businesses, including a creamery, a hatchery, and a poultry operation. Any job would have been fine, but his first choice had always been farm labor, something he knew. Something familiar, something black-and-white.

Lieutenant Stevenson announced that the POWs going out would work Monday through Saturday. They would be picked up at seven and returned by six-thirty and accompanied by guards. The Peabody POWs would receive an extra eighty cents per day in wages, and their noon meal would be provided by the employers. They were warned against fraternizing with Americans and admonished to be respectful and courteous at all times. They were not to operate heavy equipment or drive vehicles, and they were told not to enter their employers' homes for any reason. A POW must never be alone with any American female, and if a man's work or attitude was deemed unsatisfactory in any way, Stevenson said, he would be re-assigned, Too many re-assignments and a prisoner would be sent back to Concordia and barred from further work "outside the fence."

The rules were not unreasonable. Rolf's only disappointment was that Otto Hecht was assigned to the same farm as he, along with two others. He barely knew the others, Erich Zimmerman and Anton Gralke, but Hecht was another story. He'd been exceedingly pompous and arrogant on the train and in Concordia. Rolf and Willy generally avoided him, but he would be hard to avoid working on the same farm. Willy said Zimmerman and Gralke were Nazis. Rolf wasn't sure if that was true but wondered if the three of them would try something stupid.

As the assembly broke up, Hecht walked brusquely past Rolf, taunting him, "What a great opportunity this will be."

"What do you mean?" Too late, Rolf regretted responding at all.

Hecht turned around. "It will be the perfect opportunity to see how loyal you really are to the Fatherland."

"Good God, Hecht, don't you have anything better to do than worry about me?"

"Worrying about you is one of my duties," came his quick response. "It is more important now than ever that we all live up to our obligations to the *Fuehrer*."

"Obligations to the *Fuehrer*?" Rolf laughed darkly, couldn't help himself. "Here, in the middle of the United States, under armed guard, in a prison camp? You're completely insane!"

"Am I? And I suppose Major Streicher is insane too?"

Rolf said nothing.

"Just remember, you can't hide your loyalties. I'll be watching."

"You're a fool."

"It's you who's the fool, Mueller, and you'll find out soon enough," he crowed as he turned to walk off.

Suddenly, Rolf's lingering emotional mish-mash flared into rage. He lunged at Hecht from behind, spun him around by the arm, and gripped it tightly. "Listen carefully—I am not afraid of you. And I'm not going to play games out here. A farmer will be paying our wages and I will do whatever he tells me to do. You understand, don't you, that the food we'll be harvesting is going to feed us too? You arrogant bastard."

"Is that right? Even though you yourself heard Major Streicher's orders that we must do all we can to thwart the American war effort?"

"I don't give a damn about Streicher or his orders!" Rolf was shouting now. "I did not sign up to sabotage a civilian's farm. That has nothing to do with duty to the Reich! Things have changed, don't you get it?"

"You're a feckless coward and a traitor! The major will hear about your attitude."

"Let me tell you something." As Rolf stepped in closer, now Hecht sensed danger. He tried to get away, but Rolf's hold was tight, and painful. "You are a sniveling bully who thinks he's tough, but you're not, you're just Streicher's bitch. And you're the one who'd better be careful. If you pull any shit out there, it's you who'll be reported. How would you like to be stuck in here washing my dirty underwear or shoveling shit out of latrines? That would probably suit you better anyway." He lowered his voice but glowered. "Don't ever threaten me again. I know perfectly well what I must and must not do. I've always done my duty. Now, I just want to be left alone. Got it?" Hecht nodded meekly without looking at Rolf, who released his grip with a final shake of the other man's arm.

Hecht knew he'd be no match in a physical altercation with Rolf and, besides, he had nothing to gain from a fight here, out from under the watchful eye of the officers he catered to. So, he stepped away and silently vowed to bide his time until he could settle the score.

Rolf immediately regretted losing his temper. Hadn't he warned Willy repeatedly to avoid talking too much and letting others know how he felt? And now he'd done just that, to Hecht of all people, and in front of witnesses.

One of the POW witnesses was Anton Gralke. As Hecht walked off, he approached Rolf and introduced himself. "I agree with you, I'm not going to do anything to hurt civilians here, especially if they're paying us and feeding us."

"I'm glad to hear that. What about Zimmerman? Do you know him?"

"Yes, pretty well. He's not going to cause trouble. But he knows Hecht well and doesn't trust him."

"Is that so?"

"They served in the same unit in North Africa. Erich says Hecht is only out for himself. He said Hecht would stab his mother in the heart to curry favor with his superior officers. I think we must watch him carefully."

# Chapter 19
# GOD PROVIDES

Well before dawn on Monday morning, cars and trucks were gathering in the shadows along the road near the entrance to the Peabody POW camp. A dozen local farmers, including Harold Unruh and Cletus Slaymaker, friends and neighbors for decades, stood along the fence, milling around and talking. Middle-aged men with weathered faces, missing digits, bowed legs, and backs bent from years of hard labor, they were all nearly giddy with excitement. Finally, they were getting help after two years of barely scraping by, and that help was coming from a most unexpected place. Some had qualms about having German prisoners of war in the community, but not these men. The difficulties they'd endured since the war took their sons and farm hands away trumped all their reservations about hiring the enemy. Manpower was manpower, and that was what they desperately needed if their farms were going to survive.

Yet the irony was not lost on Mennonites in the group: Peace pilgrims were hiring battle-hardened soldiers to work on their farms. Harold turned to a man from his church and said, "When we asked God to provide, this isn't exactly what we had in mind, is it?"

"The Lord works in mysterious ways," sighed his friend. "Who are we to comprehend His ways? Or look a gift horse in the mouth?"

"As long as that horse knows how to pull the plow!" They both grinned.

Promptly at seven, groups of POWs and guards strode to the entrance led by Lieutenant Stevenson. He looked as excited as the farmers, who were now joined by several businessmen. The camp commander spoke exuberantly, "Good morning. How are you all this morning?"

"Very well, sir, thank you," said one of the employers-to-be.

"We're pretty darned happy to see you," said another.

"Welcome to Peabody," said Cletus and Harold in unison.

"Thank you! Now we've got some men here ready to work for you, would you like that?"

"Yes, sir!" Everyone in the group nodded. A few even clapped.

"Excellent!" said Stevenson. "All right, we have your labor requests and our assignments. Private Flannigan has the lists right over there," he said, turning and pointing to Flannigan, who'd set up a table and covered it with papers. "We're going to ask you to come up one at a time, review and sign the forms, then we'll make the introductions and send you on your way."

The fifty or so Germans waited farther back with some guards. Even from a distance, their nervousness was obvious, and one of the guards made it worse when he turned to another guard and said, with a snicker, "This must be what it was like when the Negroes was getting sold during slavery. All we need now is an auctioneer."

Rolf glared at the guard, then turned to his fellow POWs and said boldly, in German, "We are not slaves! We're going to do some work, get some exercise, get out of camp for a few hours, and get paid for our efforts. Is there anything wrong with any of that?"

Erich Zimmerman looked up nervously. "No, but I've never worked on a farm. I come from Dresden. We're porcelain makers. How the hell am I supposed to know what to do?"

"You didn't know how to fight before the war, but you learned. You can learn farming too. It won't be as hard as fighting, and no one will be shooting at us. At least I hope not."

Many of the men smiled and relaxed.

"Zimmerman, you and I are going to the same farm," continued Rolf. "I'll help you get the hang of it if you want. The most important thing? Watch where you're walking and stay out of the cow shit." He was determined to lessen his countrymen's anxieties, and their laughter said it was working.

While the Germans waited, the Americans completed the paperwork. Stevenson reviewed the terms and rules with the employers individually. As soon as he was finished answering their questions and the Americans signed the documents, a guard stepped forward and escorted groups of four to eight prisoners out the gate to the waiting vehicles. When it was Harold's turn, Greg Jordan called Rolf, Hecht, Zimmerman, and Gralke forward, introduced himself as the guard assigned to the Unruh farm, and identified the Germans by name.

Harold beamed at them, then said, "Good morning, gentlemen, and welcome!" in German. The POWs were taken aback. "Surprised? Well, my family is German, and we still speak it, so that should help us get along, shouldn't it?" He then shook hands warmly with each man, including Jordan, and thanked them for coming. His dialect was archaic and hard to understand at first, and it felt a little odd to be thanked for coming, as if they had a choice, but the fact that he was making such an effort to be friendly was appreciated.

"Okay then, shall we go?" Harold continued in German and motioned the men toward his pickup, a shiny black 1942 Ford. The Unruh pickup was one of the newest vehicles in the county. Harold had ordered it just before Pearl Harbor and was very happy it arrived before American auto makers stopped making civilian cars and trucks and converted their assembly lines to the production of war-related vehicles and equipment.

Wood railings ran along the top of the pickup's sides, so the Germans and Jordan crawled onto the truck bed, with Jordan leaning against the tailgate. Harold said, "Private Jordan, don't you want to ride up front with me? It would be more comfortable."

Jordan replied, "Thank you, sir, but I have to sit back here with the prisoners."

"All right." Glancing at the guard's rifle and pistol, Harold sighed. "I wish you didn't have to bring those along."

"I'm sorry, but I do."

"This is the first time a weapon meant to kill human beings has been in my truck. I have guns for hunting, but not for violence against another soul. I don't like it."

"I'm sorry, sir, but I have orders to carry a weapon at all times when I'm on duty at your place. I'll do my best to keep it out of sight, though."

"Thank you." A smile returned to Harold's face. "Okay, men, my place is about four miles northeast of here. If you're all in and ready, we'll head out. It's a beautiful morning, isn't it? We have plenty to do today, but my family will want to meet you first."

The men in the back said nothing on the fifteen-minute drive, which took them north through Peabody, then east onto Highway 50 until it veered north, while they continued east on a gravel road. As they drove along, Harold called out the window from time to time to point things out—the park, the Carnegie library, a school, stores, churches. He was clearly proud of his community and happy to be showing it off. The Germans and Jordan all smiled at the royal treatment they were receiving. Even Hecht couldn't help himself and grinned once or twice.

Rolf took it all in—the town's quaintness, the stately homes with Victorian cupolas and large verandas, the business district coming to life, all the cars parked along its streets, people greeting one another. Outside of town, he noticed the good roads, fields of ripe corn and ripening grains, pastures specked with blue and orange wildflowers where large herds of cattle grazed, with rock-strewn hills in the distance. It was very different country from around Olpe, with fewer trees, and very interesting. He was especially impressed with how well-organized and neatly-maintained everything seemed to be. *Everything seems so new and fresh here*, he thought, *and prosperous. So much space, and no scars from war. Do Goebbels and Hitler have any idea of what America really is?* He laughed to himself thinking that after two months in America, he probably knew more about the country and its resources than the Nazi leadership.

# Chapter 20
# TEAMWORK

The pickup crossed Doyle Creek and slowed to turn north onto a long gravel driveway. On the left of the well-worn lane was the creek, and on the right were tidy rows of sweet-scented fruit trees and yellow-splotched grapevines ambling over fences. Beyond the orchard was a cluster of sturdy red barns and outbuildings. The largest one was massive, more than three stories tall. It was wooden like most of the others but sat atop a high stone foundation.

The path disappeared into a wide, partly-graveled area in front of the big barn. A large white house with green trim sat on the opposite side, nestled in a shady yard enclosed by a fence of wire mesh and tall stone posts set twelve feet apart. A whitewashed gate opened to a shaded grassy lawn and a stone walkway leading to the house.

Jordan stood up as soon as the truck came to a stop near the gate, but the Germans hesitated until Harold came around, lowered the tailgate with a bang, and gestured for them to step down. "Welcome, gentlemen. Have any of you worked on a farm before?"

Rolf raised his hand. "Yes, sir, I was raised on one."

"Very good, my boy," Harold responded heartily. "You'll be at home here in no time."

"Thank you, sir, I hope so."

As they spoke, Harold spied two figures coming out of the milk barn, a low cinderblock structure next to the big barn. "There you are, ladies! Come over so I can introduce you to our new workers!" Clara smoothed her cotton dress, and Loretta tucked stray strands of auburn hair into her kapp as they approached, both looking tentatively at the newcomers.

"Gentlemen, this is my wife, Clara, and my daughter, Loretta. And let's see, this is Herr Hecht, Herr Zimmerman, Herr Mueller, and Herr Gralke. Did I get that right?"

"Yes, perfect," said Zimmerman, as the Germans acknowledged the women with timid nods and furtive glances.

"And this is Private Greg Jordan, who must guard our new friends."

"It's a pleasure meeting you, ladies." Jordan shook their hands warmly, then turned to Harold. "So you have one child?"

"No, we have four—two sons and two daughters. Our oldest son, John, is in Maryland, our next, Joseph, is in the Army. Then there's Loretta here and our baby, Carol Ann, who's at school. We're richly blessed."

While the Americans exchanged pleasantries, the Germans stole more glances at Loretta. Even with no makeup and dressed in an unadorned blue dress, heavy work shoes, and the kapp covering most of her soft hair, her beauty was inescapable. Her simple attire actually seemed to accentuate her lovely face, its silky-smooth skin, high-cheeks, slender nose, and cerulean eyes, and amplified her tall, slender figure. Even the way she stood, demurely looking at her parents, was somehow endearing and sensual.

Rolf was embarrassed for staring, but he couldn't help it—he was thunderstruck. He was certain that he'd never seen a woman more lovely than the one standing in front of him. Finally, he managed several deep breaths to slow his racing heart and turned away in search of something— anything—else to focus on. He shook his head at the absurdity: He was having palpations over a total stranger, and an American at that!

The others' gawking was less discreet, prompting Clara to interrupt Harold's chit-chat with Jordan in a no-nonsense tone. "It's good you are here. I hope you will earn the money you're paid and deserve the trust we're placing in you." She looked directly at the ones she'd caught leering at Loretta. "Now, we all have work to do. We'll see you at dinner." With that, she led her daughter by the arm toward the house and said, "Don't encourage such looks."

"I wasn't, Mama."

As the women were about to disappear behind the gate, Rolf dared one more glance and was jolted to see Loretta peeking back at him too. Their eyes met for just an instant, long enough to make him wobble like he was on a ship again.

Harold was now talking to the Germans. "Let's get started. Today we're going to be hauling hay." Walking to the big barn, he explained that, a few days earlier, he'd cut two fields of alfalfa, a legume used as livestock feed, with a blade attached to the tractor. After drying on the ground, the alfalfa had been raked into windrows and baled into eighty-pound bales that were still in the fields. Their job today would be to bring them in and stack them in the loft.

"Simple, yes?" Harold said to their confused looks. "It's not hard, really, just hard work. This is the fourth cutting this year, and the last. My daughters and I did the first three ourselves, so I think we'll be able to do it. Rolf, have you ever baled hay?"

"I cut hay with a scythe and raked it into stacks at home, but only by hand, and it was meadow grass, not alfalfa."

"This will be easier than what you're used to then. We have some good equipment to help us. When we get to the field, I'll show you." He stepped around the barn and returned shortly on a tractor pulling a flat-bed wagon with no sides. As soon as his crew was aboard, legs dangling over the sides, Harold slowly released the clutch and off they went. The tractor chugged and occasionally belched out huffs of black smoke as it pulled them down the driveway to the road, then east a quarter-mile, where they turned into a serpentine field tucked in between rocky hills and the creek. Bales dotted the ground in winding, parallel lines that disappeared in the distance around the field's last curve.

Beside the first row, Harold set the brake and handed out sharp-pointed metal hay hooks, each about fifteen inches long and attached to a wooden handle, and thick gloves. Of the latter, he said, "You're gonna want these at least 'til your hands callous up." While the men pulled on the gloves and considered the hooks, Harold explained that two of them would walk alongside to hook bales and throw them up onto the moving wagon. He demonstrated, nimbly stabbing, then heaving and landing a bale on the wagon bed in one fluid motion. He motioned for Gralke and Hecht to give it a try. After a few awkward attempts, they started using their arms and knees to control the direction of the bales and were able to put them where they wanted.

Rolf and Zimmerman would stand on the moving wagon and stack the bales in snug, alternating layers. Harold warned them not to overload any one side or the wagon would tip over. Seeing their apprehension, he added, "Don't worry, I'll go plenty slow to start. If you have any problems, just yell, and I'll stop."

There would be no room for Jordan on the wagon, so he walked to the edge of the field to find a place to sit. He was a city boy, from

Pittsburgh, Pennsylvania, and had never been on a farm. Until just a few weeks earlier, he'd never been west of the Mississippi River. Drafted at age thirty-eight, he was assigned to the 480th MPEG, sent to Michigan for rudimentary training, then shipped out to Kansas. This was all as unfamiliar to him as it was to the Germans. And he felt useless. The Germans were now armed with weapons they could use to overpower the Americans if they wanted. And unless he walked alongside the wagon, which would soon be out of sight, they could easily escape. Hell, they could easily escape even if he was walking right beside them. But since his induction, he knew the Army expected all orders to be followed, no matter how inane. So, he sat down to "guard" his prisoners in the field, as ordered.

Harold yelled over the engine, "All right, here we go!" With an ornery grin, he added, "Watch out for the rattlesnakes, boys!" and with that, they were off. Rolf and Zimmerman initially struggled to find their balance on the rocking, creaking wagon floor. It was especially hard when the wagon tilted, even slightly, but after some wobbling and missed tosses, they and their cohorts on the ground and Harold on the tractor were all working as a team.

Before the end of the first row, the Germans were covered with an itchy paste of alfalfa sprigs, dust, and sweat. The work got harder for the men on the ground as the wagon filled up and they had to toss bales higher and higher. For Rolf and Zimmerman, getting the bales to fit together tightly on a moving platform was ever more challenging as the stack grew.

At six layers, the wagon could hold no more bales, so Hecht and Gralke climbed on top with the others. Near the road, they picked up Jordan, who stood on the hitch behind the tractor for the ride home. To Rolf's great relief, the load swayed and creaked a bit, but it held.

Back at the barn, they set up a long, mechanized conveyor to send bales high up to the loft skewered onto the spikes of a thick chain that rolled up and back in a continuous loop. As soon as one end had been placed through the open loft door, Harold attached a belt to the other end and fired the tractor engine back up. After some sputtering, the conveyor loudly rattled to life.

Harold sent Rolf and Zimmerman up to stack the hay in the loft since they'd done a good job on the wagon, then he showed Hecht and Gralke how to toss bales down onto the conveyor. In much less time than it took to load it, the wagon was empty, and the hay was stored for winter. As Rolf and Zimmerman climbed down from the sweltering loft to join the others in the shade of the barn, Harold exclaimed, "Excellent work, men! You're learning fast. Soon you'll be doing as good a job as my sons, and that's saying something!" He patted each one on the back and thanked each man individually as they guzzled cool water from the well and wiped their gritty faces. "Careful, don't drink too fast or you'll get a bellyache."

Bringing the second load in from the field that morning went more quickly and smoothly than the first. As the last bale from that load rode the conveyor into the barn, Clara called from the house that dinner was ready. "I wonder what we'll be eating," said Gralke. "Hopefully not C-rations."

"I don't even care, as long as there's plenty. I could eat a bear," said Zimmerman.

"I'm going to be sore tonight. That's the hardest I've worked in a while," said Hecht, who seemed strangely satisfied with himself. Rolf glanced at him, but Hecht pretended not to notice.

Zimmerman chided his comrade. "In 'a while?' I'll bet that's the hardest you've ever worked!" Hecht just smiled. "And we're only halfway through the day. How in the name of God did an old man and some girls manage to do this three times by themselves?"

Rolf thought, *As long as we're baling hay, I won't have to do push-ups and sit-ups.*

# Chapter 21
# BREAKING BREAD

As they finished washing up at the well, Clara called from the kitchen for everyone to come in. The Germans didn't move, knew they weren't supposed to go inside, and looked to Jordan for guidance, but he also looked confused. Harold was already on the porch, saying, "Come in, come in! It's time to eat."

Jordan replied, "I'm sorry, Mr. Unruh, but it's against regulations for POWs to go into houses. I assumed Lieutenant Stevenson told you that. They have to eat outside."

"But everything is ready inside. There's plenty of room, so come on in."

It felt rude, silly even, to press the issue, so Jordan thought for a moment, then shrugged. "Well, okay, if you insist and if your wife and daughter are comfortable with it."

"To be honest, my wife was not in favor of having them eat inside, but I told her it would be too much trouble for her to set up a separate table for them outside every day. She'd be running herself silly, and there's room in the house. Plus, I told her if she wants to know if they're going to work out, the best way to do that is by getting acquainted over the table. So, I hope you'll come in."

"Okay."

"But no weapons in the house. Please leave them out of sight outside. I will not countenance weapons in our house." Harold waited at the screen door.

Jordan turned around. "All right, we're going inside. I guess it won't hurt, but be polite, and let's keep this to ourselves." Rolf translated Jordan's instructions and the five of them slowly walked up the steps and in, careful not to get dirt on the floor or bump into anything.

The focal point of the well-equipped kitchen was a large rectangular wooden table, at least six feet long, surrounded by eight pressed-oak chairs, covered with a blue cloth and set for the meal. And the room was filled with the most intoxicating food aromas, the likes of which the Germans had not enjoyed in forever. They gave each other wide-eyed grins and tried to stifle childlike giggles.

Harold eased into his regular spot at the end of the table by the door while Clara and Loretta filled dishes at the cast-iron stove and the humming GE refrigerator on the other side of the table. As the clock on the wall chimed twelve, he said, "Please sit. Any chair, except the one on the end. That's for my wife, and she doesn't like sharing it," which made Clara smirk. Jordan sat next to Harold and the others followed. Harold said, "If it's all right, Private Jordan, I'll pray in German this afternoon."

Silence commenced with heads bowed and eyes closed, then Harold intoned, "Holy God, all we have and all we are comes from you. With humble hearts, we thank you for the food we are about to enjoy, for the beauty of this day, for life, and for the friendship of those who break bread with us. Your ways, O Lord, are inscrutable. Teach us to follow you more fully. Nourish us to do your will today. Keep our feet on the path of peace. We ask your blessings on John and Joseph and Carol Ann, and on these men and their families, and on all your children. Keep us all safe and in your loving care. We ask this through Jesus Christ, your Son, our Lord. Amen."

As the last Amens were said, Clara and Loretta swung into action, carrying mountains of food to the table—roast beef, mashed potatoes, gravy, green beans with bacon, corn, pickled okra, a salad of tomatoes, onions and cucumbers, cheese, and golden-brown wheat bread, still warm, with home-churned butter and honey. Loretta filled glasses with iced tea, then, at last, she and her mother wiped their hands once more and took the last chairs. Loretta sat to her mother's left; Rolf was directly across from her. His nervousness at being in such close proximity to her was mitigated by all the food, which was proving to be a powerful distraction.

The Unruhs started passing dishes, but the Germans hesitated until Harold interjected, "Don't be bashful. You worked hard, and you're hungry, so eat as much as you'd like. We can't have you starving now, can we?"

"Well, I haven't worked very hard, Mr. Unruh," said Jordan, "But I'm grateful to be here. What a feast! Thank you, ladies." They smiled as he filled his plate.

Taking their cue from Jordan, the Germans took modest helpings and started to eat, heads down and quietly at first, like skittish mice. Soon, though, their faces brightened, and they relaxed. The meal tasted even better than it smelled.

Hecht looked at Clara and said, "This is incredible, the best I've ever eaten."

"Thank you. I'm glad you like it," she replied with a modest smile.

Jordan turned to Harold. "I haven't seen this much food at one meal since rationing started. How are you able to get so much?"

"We grow it ourselves, and we butcher our own meat. We even have a smokehouse. Food rationing hasn't affected us much, except for store-bought things like sugar. Most everything you're eating comes from this farm, right down to the honey. Food has never been the problem around here. Tires and gasoline and tractor parts, now that's another story."

"I didn't know what I was missing in the city! Ladies, do you always fix so much?" asked Jordan.

"Our big meal is always at noon," Clara said, "We made a little extra today because it's a special day, having a field crew again."

Harold smiled at his wife. "But even on a regular day, no one goes hungry around here."

As plates were emptied the first time, Harold and Clara passed various dishes to the men for seconds, and Loretta re-filled empty serving bowls. Only the corn bowl was still mostly full. None of the Germans had tried it, prompting Harold to ask, "You don't like corn?"

They looked at one another, unsure what to say. Then Zimmerman replied apologetically, "We've never seen people eat corn. In Germany, we feed it only to pigs."

Harold put several spoonfuls of sweet, yellow kernels on his plate. "Well, you have lucky pigs because it's delicious!" He took some bites with mock seriousness, chewed exaggeratedly, and grunted playfully. Clara told him to stop, but then she had to laugh too.

One by one, the Germans politely sampled the tender corn, lightly buttered and salted, and were surprised at how good it tasted. "Not bad at all," said Gralke.

Just when the men thought they couldn't eat one more bite, Loretta went to the oven for a brown betty made with apples picked that morning in the orchard. To the incredulous looks of the Germans and Jordan, who groaned, she dished portions into bowls and sat them on the table with an ironstone pitcher filled with heavy cream.

"There, there, you can eat a little more, can't you?" Harold prodded as he poured cream onto his portion. "Dessert is a requirement in this house!" So, they followed his lead.

The Germans were mostly quiet that first day around the Unruh table. They answered direct questions, but weren't comfortable initiating conversation with the Americans, not even in German. Even Rolf was hesitant to speak too soon, ask too much. And apart from all the other reasons to refrain from speaking, they would have been tongue-tied in front of Loretta. They were like schoolboys in the presence of a pretty girl for the first time.

With Clara and Loretta mostly quiet, too, carrying the conversation fell to Harold and Jordan, which was not a problem, for Harold was a natural at drawing people out with questions and at listening to their answers. To him, dinnertime guests from other parts of the country and the world presented a great opportunity to learn new things. And with Jordan so engaging, Harold felt free to ask him about life in Pennsylvania, about his family, work, church, all sorts of things. While personal questioning can feel intrusive, like an interrogation, Harold was so obviously interested and sincere that Jordan gladly opened up. He talked about the barbershop he owned with his father. He beamed when he spoke about his wife and three sons and his love for Pirates baseball.

Jordan answered Harold's questions and asked his own. He wanted to know more about farming and this unfamiliar part of the country, so Harold gave him a little history of Kansas and the Unruh family and told him about the farm and their crops and the joys of farm living, and also the pitfalls—the droughts, winds, hail, flooding, and dust storms.

"Farming sounds like it's pretty risky with so many things that could go wrong."

Harold laughed, "And have gone wrong at one time or another. But the Lord has blessed our labors with a comfortable life and almost everything we need."

"Do you mind if I ask how large your farm is?"

"We own 240 acres outright, most of which is cropland like that alfalfa field we're working in. And we rent another 160 acres of pasture for our cattle. That tract is up the hill to the east of where we're sitting."

Rolf, who was still translating for the other Germans, said, "Please excuse me, sir. You said your farm consists of 240 acres and 160 acres, 400 in total?"

"That's right."

Rolf's eyes widened. "That's around 125 hectares, then, isn't it? That's very large for a farm in Germany, at least in my part of Germany."

Harold smiled. "Actually, 400 acres is around 161 hectares. Here in the United States, we don't measure land in hectares, but my father knew how to calculate hectares because that's what he knew back in Russia."

"Thank you, sir." Rolf turned to translate to the others, who were similarly impressed when they learned how large the Unruh farm was.

In German, Zimmerman said to Rolf, "They must be very rich to have such a large farm and big house and barns."

Harold overheard and replied, "God has richly blessed us, Erich."

Zimmerman blushed, embarrassed that his comment was understood, then asked, "Is this a normal farm for America?"

"Around here, there are farms larger than ours, and there are farms that are smaller. We're grateful for what we have."

As the meal finally came to an end, Harold told the Germans and Jordan to use the outhouse and rest for a few minutes in the grass under the cottonwood trees. It was his routine to take a fifteen-minute nap in his easy chair every afternoon after dinner, "to let the food settle." Rolf offered to help clear the table, but Clara said that wasn't necessary. The men thanked the cooks profusely. Loretta thought to herself that she'd be happy to cook all day every day as long as they were helping out in the fields. She marveled at how surreal it was to have German soldiers in their kitchen. And how strangely normal it felt, feeding strangers. She was rinsing and stacking dishes at the sink and turned to look toward the door just as Rolf stole a last glance on his way out. She smiled and felt her heart skip a beat. Silently, she thanked God that her mother wasn't looking.

By mid-afternoon, the first field was finished, so the crew moved on to a larger one a little further east. It was now cruelly hot, which was hard on them all, even Jordan. With nothing to do and being stuffed, he struggled to stay awake in the heat. Once, when the tractor and loaded wagon came by, he was so sound asleep that Hecht had to jump off and rouse him from his food coma. Jordan was embarrassed, and the Germans and Harold had a good laugh.

Around four, the pickup pulled into the field, honked, and stopped by a hedgerow. Loretta and a younger girl got out, opened the tailgate, and began unpacking a picnic basket and another box. Jordan walked over as the tractor and half-full wagon pulled alongside the truck.

"Hello, girls!" said Harold. "Did you learn anything at school today, Carol Ann?"

"Maybe. I had a history test and think I did pretty well."

"Good for you," he said as he motioned the Germans and Jordan over to be introduced. More outgoing than her sister or her mother, Carol Ann shook hands with each of them.

"More food?" Rolf said. "But your mother and your sister already fed us so much."

"Maybe so, but here's a little more in case anyone's hungry. And we have a Coleman thermos of iced tea for each of you."

Loretta spread roast beef sandwiches, cheese, and apples out on cloth napkins. The workers stepped forward, helped themselves, then sat down in a shady area littered with softball-sized, rough-skinned, chartreuse balls.

"What are these?" asked Rolf.

"They're hedge apples. They grow on these hedge trees," said Loretta.

"Can I eat one?" he asked, secretly thrilled. It was the first time she spoke directly to him.

"No, don't. They're not really apples. They're very hard and may be poisonous."

Jordan thanked the young women but said he couldn't eat another bite. "At least have some tea," Harold chided, "it will help you stay awake."

As he chose a sandwich, Rolf turned to Carol Ann. "Thank you very much. What was your history examination about today?"

"The Battle of Gettysburg. Do you know about it?"

"Only a little, that it was in Pennsylvania and the Union won the battle and then President Lincoln visited and gave his famous address there." Taking a thermos, he saw an opening to say more. "And now, here's a little bit of a different kind of history for you. If you'd like, that is." Carol Ann nodded. "Do you know where the thermos was invented and why it's called that?"

"No, I don't."

"It was invented in Scotland by a man named Dewar, but the company that produced thermoses for sale first, maybe around 1900, was in München, Germany. That company was called 'Thermos,' which comes from the Greek word, 'therme,' which means 'hot.' But a thermos has a vacuum inside, so it can keep hot things hot and also cold things cold."

Carol Ann smiled. "How do you know that? And how do you know English so well?"

Rolf feared he might be coming off as a know-it-all and blushed. "I love history, so my head is filled with all sorts of irrelevant data like that. And I studied English in school."

"Well, irrelevant or not, thank you for telling me."

"Of course." Out of the corner of his eye, he was relieved to see Loretta smiling. By the look on her face, she didn't think he was showing off. Then he shuddered, realizing that the most beautiful girl in the world had smiled at him not once, but three times in one day. At him!

As soon as the day's last bales were stacked in the loft, the men loaded themselves into the pickup for the ride into town. At the camp, Harold got out to thank each one of them again. "I think maybe you weren't honest with me. I think maybe you were all raised on farms. You seemed to know just what to do."

The men smiled and thanked Harold sincerely.

"So I'll see you in the morning?"

"Yes," the Germans said in unison.

"What's for dinner?" laughed Zimmerman.

Harold smiled. "That's not my department, but I'm sure it will be good. If the weather holds, we'll finish the haying, then go on to some other jobs."

"We'll be ready at seven," said Jordan, shaking Harold's hand.

"Very good. Have a good night."

"Thank you, sir," said Jordan as they walked through the gate with other POWs and guards coming in. Flannigan was there again, checking off names.

On the walk toward the tents, one of the Germans who'd been on another farm said, "That was not at all what I expected."

"It was much better, wasn't it?" said Gralke. Most of the others nodded their agreement.

"The war seems far away tonight," added Zimmerman. "I think I want to be a farmer. This is what life should be like—honest work, good food, and...."

"And beautiful women," added Hecht, finishing Zimmerman's sentence. "And I think the most beautiful one wants me. I'm sure of it."

Rolf turned toward him. "You're a pig, Hecht. Last night you were going to blow up a farm and now you're commenting disrespectfully about an American woman. You really are disgraceful." Hecht glared but knew better than to say anything more.

Rolf walked to his tent alone and was quiet. He had been so content when they left the farm, but then homesickness quickly descended upon him, and it was pricklier than usual. It began when he thought about his family. He was sure they hadn't eaten nearly as well as he had nor enjoyed their day as much. He wished they could have been with him today, imagined that they'd like the Unruhs, then felt guilty for enjoying himself. And to top it off, he thought, *I was flirting with an American girl. What kind of inconsiderate bastard must I be to be thinking about a girl and my own selfish desires at a time like this?*

He took a cold shower in the newly-installed outdoor stalls and put on clean clothes but skipped the camp's evening meal. He sat down on his cot to write in his journal, but only got a few lines scribbled before the sadness bit too deeply. And a line from Harold's noontime prayer kept replaying in his head: "Keep our feet on the path of peace." *This damn war! Damn it all! And Goddammit that I was forced into it! I did things I never wanted to do.* At first, he wanted to scream, blame someone, hit someone, but instead of lashing out this time, he let go, let himself be submerged in sadness. He didn't understand why he should feel so bad after such a good day, but he wouldn't resist the darkness. Resistance was always futile anyway.

# Chapter 22
# WAYFARING STRANGERS

C lara was wringing out a dishrag when Harold came in from the descending darkness. He'd been outside making sure everything was put away for the evening. Carol Ann was at the table working on homework, and Loretta was writing a letter to John.

"Finished?" Clara smiled at her husband.

"Yes, it's nice out there now, really cooling down. Feels like September again. Would you like to sit on the porch with me?"

"I've got mending to do, so I need to stay in here in the light."

"Then I'll take a look at the *Gazette-Herald* and get caught up on the news."

Clara went to the bedroom for several items of clothing and her sewing basket, then joined the others at the table. The kitchen was quiet until Carol Ann slammed her book shut with a *Whump!* and emphatically pronounced her homework "Done!"

Clara jumped, "Don't do that!" Then, "It's just eight. Not much homework tonight?"

"No, just English."

"You say you had a history test today?" Harold looked up from the paper.

"Yes. And I have tests in English and science coming up, but I'm ready."

"You've had a lot of tests already. Are you keeping up now that you're a junior?" her mother asked.

"So far, so good." Carol Ann changed the subject, "How'd it go with the POWs today?"

"To my mind, very well," said Harold. "What do you think, Clara?"

"They seemed friendly and polite enough, Private Jordan too. How did they do out in the field?"

"Good. I took extra care to explain what I wanted and showed them how to do everything. And I drove slower than usual so I wouldn't lose any of them." Harold smiled.

Loretta finished addressing an envelope and looked up. "Well I'm glad they were here."

"Only one of them, Rolf, said he'd ever worked on a farm before. The rest are from cities, so I was surprised at how fast they took to handling bales. They did good."

"Rolf is the cute one," Carol Ann chimed in.

"Carol Ann! Why do you say such things?" Clara's sixteen-year-old daughter had recently developed an annoying penchant for saying whatever popped into her head and regularly gave her mother heartburn. Sometimes Clara thought that was her goal.

"Because he is, Mama! He has the bluest eyes I've ever seen and a dreamy smile. He's shy, but smart too. He was telling me about where thermoses come from."

Clara and Harold looked at each other. "You better not be going boy-crazy over that young man," said her mother, alarmed. "Or any other boy."

"Please, Mama! I'm not boy-crazy for anyone. Besides, he only has eyes for Loretta."

Loretta's jaw dropped. "What on earth are you talking about?"

Carol Ann laughed. "Rolf may have been talking to me, but it was you he was looking at. I saw how he smiled at you."

"Nonsense! He was just being polite. They were all just being polite."

"The other ones looked at you, too, but Rolf was for sure the most interested. And you smiled back at him."

"Carol Ann!" Her sister's insinuations were getting annoying.

"It's true!" And don't say that you don't think he's handsome." Carol Ann loved teasing her sister about her romances, real or imagined. Loretta's reaction confirmed that she'd hit the bullseye this time.

Loretta blushed again. "He's here to work, Carol Ann. If I'm smiling, it's because we have help again and I'm in the kitchen and not in the hay meadow. He's *außenseiter*."

"Outsider or not, he's handsome and smart and you think so too. He's a real dish!" Carol Ann's comments were now met with sharp looks from both her sister and her mother.

"Enough, Carol Ann! We'll have no more of your suggestive comments." Clara's tone was unusually harsh, especially when she was addressing her family, but she wasn't going to hide her anger. "Are you listening to me?" Her youngest daughter nodded meekly. "Those men are here to work. Do we have to keep you away from them so they aren't distracted? Or send them away because of your lewd suggestions?"

"No, Mama, I'm sorry," said a chastened Carol Ann. Turning toward her sister, she added, "I'm sorry, Loretta." She stood and got a glass of milk, then stretched and looked out the front door and let the breeze cool her embarrassed cheeks. Loretta looked up at her, still annoyed but less with her sister than with herself for having been so free with her smiles that afternoon.

Harold's eyes stayed glued to the newspaper until his wife and daughters were quiet and again relaxed, then he led them back to finish the conversation he'd started earlier. Laying the paper on the table, he began, "So, it sounds like we're in agreement that we should have those boys come back to work again tomorrow? Is that what I heard?"

"Yes," the other three said in unison.

"Good, because it was a great relief today having a real field crew out there with me today. Not that you girls didn't do great, but having four strong men here just makes things so much easier for all of us." His family nodded in unison as Harold continued, "It's a strange set-up, I know, having foreigners among us, and not just any foreigners, but German POWs. On our farm. I never thought I'd live to see a day like today."

"It's a blessing to have able-bodied men here to work for us again," said Clara. "And I must say, there were moments during dinner today when I almost forgot they're prisoners."

"It's kind of hard to forget with those big 'Ps' and 'Ws' on their pants," said Carol Ann.

"I know, but around the table they could have been boys from Peabody. Maybe not fellow Mennonites, but it was nice to hear them speaking German. Things felt almost normal for a little while today, with Loretta in the kitchen with me and Carol Ann in school and men in the fields. That in and of itself is a great blessing, thanks be to God."

"They do seem to want to work hard, like our boys." Harold paused for a moment. "Now let me ask this, did any of you feel like any of them might be dangerous?"

Clara answered, "I don't think so. We don't know them, but I am comfortable enough with them here." Harold and the girls nodded in agreement. "I admit, I was worried to begin with, but now that I've met them and observed them, I feel better. That said, we need to be watchful in case they start to show too much interest in the girls. They must not be left alone with either of you." Clara looked up from her mending to look directly at Carol Ann. "And as long as our daughters act respectfully at all times, I think we'll have no problems."

Carol Ann walked from the door to where her mother was sitting at the kitchen table and kissed her sweetly on the cheek, then gave her a hug. "I'll behave, Mama, I promise." She walked over and gave Loretta a hug too.

"So, then I guess it's settled, at least for now. But if anything should happen in the future with these men that makes any of you uncomfortable for any reason, you have to speak up. I don't want anyone here we couldn't trust."

Loretta hmphed, "I don't think we'll ever have to worry about Carol Ann speaking up on any subject!"

"Well, while I'm speaking up, I'll say this: I would trust any one of them already more than I would Tommy Ferguson," Carol Ann said.

"Why do you say that?" asked her mother.

"Because Tommy's rude and arrogant and lazy too. I wouldn't want him out here. He's more *außenseiter* than those prisoners are." Clara looked at her, eyebrows raised. "I'm just saying that it's not just because someone is American or German or a soldier or a prisoner. I think some Americans are worse than these prisoners."

Clara replied, "I don't even like calling them 'prisoners.' I know that's what they are, they know that's what they are, but 'prisoners' or 'POWs' makes it sound like they're in a labor camp and being forced to work against their will. Like slaves or a chain gang."

To his daughters, Harold said, "You know we're paying them for their work, right? They're not being forced to come out here, and they're not in bondage, at least not in the usual way. They're not hardened criminals. And even if they were, they still deserve to be treated with respect, like all God's children."

Carol Ann nodded. "Even though they're marked with scarlet letters. Well, not scarlet, but white ones. I think those 'Ps' and 'Ws' are humiliating."

Harold stepped into the front room and returned with the family's

German Bible. Turning to Exodus 22:21, he read: "You shall neither mistreat a stranger nor oppress him, for you were strangers in the land of Egypt."

"Strangers," Carol Ann repeated, "like how Aunt Dora said we were strangers in Russia, then here in the United States. Our people should know how to treat strangers."

"Yes, we should," said Harold.

The room fell silent again until Clara started humming as she stitched. Then in a clear voice, she sang, *"I'm just a poor wayfaring stranger a-traveling through this world of woe. Yet there's no sickness, toil, or danger in that bright land to which I go."*

Her daughters joined in. *"I'm going there to see my father, I'm going there no more to roam. I'm just a-going over Jordan. I'm just a-going over home."* They sang all three verses of this favorite, melancholy song. And tonight, the words were especially poignant. Harold closed his eyes. He loved listening to his family sing.

"Amen," he said with a smile when they finished.

Loretta said, "I think we should agree to not call them prisoners. We should just call them workers or helpers. It's a little thing, so they know we respect them. What do you think?"

Clara smiled. "That's a good idea." She stood and patted both daughters' hands and added, "Our workers, our farm hands, our helpers, the Germans. Just not boyfriends. No more of that."

Loretta went on. "I do wonder about what they saw growing up in Nazi Germany. Were they taught to believe that Germans are the master race? And what did they go through when they were fighting? What did they see? What did they do?"

Harold took a few moments before replying, "We can assume our new helpers learned evil things and committed evil acts in Hitler's army. We know this because all war is an abomination, and they were in the middle of it."

"And now we are too," said his wife, sadly.

Harold continued. "Knowing this, how are we to proceed? There's an answer for that in here too." He scanned the gospels until he came to Matthew 18:21-22, and he read: "Then Peter came to Him and said, 'Lord, how often shall my brother sin against me, and I forgive him? Up to seven times?' Jesus said to him, 'I do not say to you, up to seven times, but up to seventy times seven." Harold looked up. "Whatever the sins of their past, we must now forgive these men and show them the way to righteousness."

Clara smiled, "Amen. Since our sons can't be here, let's be grateful that the Lord sent them to us to help with the harvest."

"And let's hope they think it's good to be here too," Loretta said.

"When I dropped them off, they were already asking what's for dinner tomorrow."

"It's nice to know our cooking is appreciated," said Clara, looking at Loretta.

Harold feigned hurt. "Don't I tell you all the time how much I love your meals?"

"Yes, you do, but it's nice to know that others enjoy it too."

Harold laughed. "Especially those poor wayfaring strangers." Then, as Clara turned to go into the bedroom with the mending basket, he leaned into Carol Ann next to him and added, "And maybe especially the ones with the 'dreamy smiles.'"

# Chapter 23
# AUßENSEITER

After the long months of soul-numbing idleness in Bizerte and Concordia, and on the journeys in between, the cadence of farm life, long busy days, and quiet restful nights, was agreeable to all the Germans. And their hard work was greatly appreciated by the Unruhs. For weeks, they baled hay and loaded it into barns. They picked and shocked corn, cut milo, and loaded the grain into borrowed trucks for Harold to drive into Peabody or Hillsboro to sell, and they filled several silos on the farm with silage to feed to the Unruh's dairy cattle.

In a matter of weeks, the fall harvest was mostly done, and Harold began to prepare for planting wheat, the red winter variety his grandparents had brought from Russia, which was perfectly suited to the Kansas soil and climate. Wheat planting is not labor intensive, Harold could handle it by himself, but numerous maintenance projects on Doyle Creek had been deferred for two years because the Unruh sons were not there to help. So, when the first contract to hire the four Germans for the harvest was nearing completion, Harold signed a second one with the Army to continue to employ them to help him with the maintenance. They repaired barbed wire fences, cleaned the milk barn, cleared out stalls, sties, and coops, trimmed overgrown brush, pruned trees in the orchard, chopped wood, patched roofs, and painted the big barn and several outbuildings. Gralke was an experienced mechanic, so Harold asked him to tune up the tractor and service the other large implements. The work was hard and sometimes they returned to camp filthy, especially whoever got stuck inside the silo tamping down the silage as it was being blown in over the top, but no one complained. The farmstead was soon restored to its normal well-maintained condition. The Germans were proud, and the Unruhs were happy and relieved.

In spite of how well everyone seemed to be working together, Rolf couldn't forget Hecht's comments about sabotaging American farms. He didn't think Hecht had tried anything yet, but still he wondered. He considered casually complimenting Hecht for taking to farm work so easily but decided against it. Since their earlier confrontations, Hecht had been careful to avoid Rolf as much as possible, and vice versa.

The subject of allegiance did come up one afternoon while the four of them were painting. Gralke was coming down a ladder when he turned to Hecht and, out of the blue, said. "You're a good painter. So, I guess you don't feel like you're betraying the Fatherland by working for Americans now? At least I haven't seen you poison the cows or choke the chickens."

Hecht shrugged. "The work keeps me from going crazy. Besides, what we do around here isn't hurting the Reich. Whether a barn gets painted or not makes no difference to the war effort. And as long as they pay me to eat their cows and chickens, I won't be hurting them."

The others smiled, then Zimmerman said, "Does your new outlook perhaps also have something to do with wanting to impress a certain beautiful woman?"

Rolf looked at Hecht, almost daring him to say something rude, but Hecht deflected, "What? I hadn't noticed any beautiful women here, except maybe for you and Gralke."

Neither Gralke nor Zimmerman teased Rolf about Loretta, though they both sensed how smitten he was. Rolf refrained from sharing anything about his feelings with anyone. And Loretta was equally discreet, though from a distance they shared smiles with each other when no one else was around. Rolf thought he'd seen her looking at him on other occasions, and the way she blushed when he caught her confirmed it for him. In such unusual public circumstances, with hardly any words exchanged other than in the presence of others, and with no opportunity to ever be alone or touch, a connection that started with flirtation was deepening into something more.

After a few weeks, all the Unruhs were all more relaxed around the men. Loretta enjoyed practicing her German with them, then decided to turn dinner conversations into English classes. There was shyness and laughter over misuse of a word or phrase and good-natured teasing over mispronunciations, but she and her parents all urged them to at least try to speak a little English, and they complied. Harold and Jordan enjoyed the banter. Clara did, too, to a point. She monitored everything that was said very carefully.

"You should be a teacher," Hecht said to Loretta one rainy afternoon as they finished their dessert.

Harold smiled, "That's what she wants to do." His daughter gave a thin smile; Clara pursed her lips.

Hecht went on, "Excellent! You should come to Germany and teach English after the war. There will be many new dealings between our countries then, and many Germans will need good English skills. The *Fuehrer* wants America and Germany to resume strong ties. You would be most welcome back in your ancestral homeland." His obvious efforts to engage with Loretta backfired spectacularly because neither Loretta nor anyone else knew what to say. His boorish assertions that Germany would win the war and that Hitler would remain in power were arrogant and insulting.

An awkward silence ensued until Rolf intervened for Loretta's sake. "I think you'll be a wonderful teacher, but I'm guessing you want to teach children here in Kansas."

Loretta smiled at him with relief and said confidently, "You're right. And yes, I could be a good teacher." She carefully avoided looking in her mother's direction as she spoke.

Following Army rules, Harold did not allow the men to operate the car or truck or other motorized equipment, but one afternoon without thinking, he asked Rolf to back the Allis-Chalmers up so he could hitch the plow to it. Surprised but eager to please, Rolf stepped aboard and shifted the tractor into gear, but he missed reverse and didn't know where the brake was. As he fumbled around, he got the throttle stuck open, whereupon the tractor shot off away from Harold and toward a fence going far too fast. Rolf was lucky to be able to get it to turn just in time to avoid the fence, but he still couldn't get it to stop. All he could do was steer the tractor around in wide circles in the grassy area between the fence, the big barn, and the house. Harold couldn't hobble fast enough to catch up. Arms flailing, he shouted and waved instructions, but wide-eyed Rolf couldn't hear him over the tractor engine and didn't understand Harold's hand gestures. The other Germans and Jordan got clear of the tractor and tried to help him understand what to do, but nothing helped.

After several wild loops with no end in sight, Loretta came around the barn and saw the unfolding spectacle. Without hesitating, she raced to the tractor, jumped up with catlike agility, squeezed her body tightly into the narrow space between the steering wheel and Rolf's lap, unstuck the throttle, pumped the clutch and brake, and brought it to a grinding halt. And just as fluidly, she jumped off the tractor, then bent over to catch her breath.

Red with embarrassment from not controlling the tractor and blushing at getting sat upon by the most beautiful woman he had ever seen, Rolf squeaked out a little, "Thank you." Then out of nervousness and without thinking, he tried to lighten the moment. "We make a good team, you and I, don't you think? But I think you will have to be the one to drive when we're married."

Loretta was dumbfounded. She glared at him and lashed out in German, "Are you insane? We are not a team! You shouldn't have been on that tractor. It costs a lot of money. You could have wrecked it or crashed into the barn or killed someone! Do you understand how dangerous that was? I could have been killed saving you." Now Rolf blushed to an even deeper shade of magenta. He wanted to try to apologize again, but Loretta was turned around and striding back toward the house. "*Außenseiter*," she called out over her shoulder.

As she walked past her mother near the gate, Clara, who had witnessed the chaotic scene, said, "Thank God you were there to stop the tractor, but I must say I do not approve of how you pressed yourself onto that man. That was very immodest of you."

"Mama! For Pete's sake! Do you really think I was trying to be immodest? That I wanted to jump up there? That I have nothing better to do? Did you want to wait until the tractor ran out of our rationed gasoline? Who else could stop it? Papa? You? Him?" Pointing to Rolf, "He was stupid to be trying to drive in the first place. I did what had to be done, that's all."

Clara pursed her lips and silently followed Loretta into the house, astonished and chastened. She couldn't remember her daughter ever raising her voice to her like that. She thought about it and decided to say no more about what happened. *Maybe it's just the excitement of having to do something so dangerous*, she decided.

When Harold got to Rolf, he said, "I'm sorry about that, my boy. I shouldn't have asked you to get up there. I'll explain it to Loretta and Clara later. My mistake." Then with a good-natured smile, he added, "I'll have to commend Anton. That engine was definitely firing on all cylinders there, humming right along." Rolf had to smile at that and was happy to know that he wasn't in trouble, at least not with Harold.

Jordan met him as Harold was driving the tractor off. Shaking his head, he said, "Dear God, I'm glad she got that stopped. There would have been hell to pay if you'd crashed. Now here's one more thing for us to not report to Lieutenant Stevenson."

Glancing over at Hecht smirking and Zimmerman and Gralke still laughing, Rolf said, "I think some are happy that I was made the fool."

"Maybe, but no damage was done and you gotta admit, it was pretty funny. If you'd seen that in a Laurel and Hardy picture show, you would have laughed your ass off," Jordan twirled his hand in wide circles in front of his face, eyes crossed. Rolf had to smile again. "I couldn't believe how fast and fearless Loretta was to run up to a moving tractor like that, then jump up and get it stopped."

"True, but she was not at all happy. Did you hear her shouting?"

Jordan nodded with a grin "I think they heard her in town. She was worked up." He paused for just a few seconds. "Maybe a little too worked up."

"What do you mean?" asked Rolf, but the American just shrugged and smiled and told him he'd better get back to work.

After enduring some final good-natured ribbing from Gralke, Zimmerman, and Jordan when they returned to camp, Rolf took out his journal and began to write:

Date: Wednesday, 6 October 1943, Location: Camp Peabody:
I made a fool of myself today. First, I got a tractor stuck in gear and I couldn't get it to stop. No one was hurt, thank God, except my pride.

But that's not the worst of it: The worst is that Loretta had to jump on the tractor while it was moving and sit down on top of me to get it stopped. She could have been killed and all I could do was make stupid, presumptuous jokes, which made her very angry. I should have told her how sorry I was and left it at that. I am very ashamed.

For the last month, I've been thinking (and writing) about

how amazing that such a wonderful woman seems to like me. I've been fantasizing that we might find a way to be together someday, while still worrying that may never be possible since I'm a POW and she's American.

After today, I don't need to be worrying about that. Loretta made it clear she's not interested in someone as stupid and insensitive as me. How could she be? Someone as caring and intelligent and beautiful as she? I'm a complete *dummkopf.*

The following Sunday, Harold and Clara had dinner for the extended Unruh family in or near Peabody. Once a month, Harold's sister and brother and their families all came out to the farm for an afternoon of catching up. Margaret Koehn, the oldest of Harold's siblings, lived in Peabody with her husband, Kurt, and their three daughters. Margaret was a teller at the First National Bank, and Kurt raised cattle on a ranch just east of the home place. The younger Unruh brother, Tobias, was eight years younger than Harold and farmed south of Doyle Creek with his wife, Gladys, and their six young children. Margaret, Harold, Tobias, and another sister who died when she was young, were all born and raised on Doyle Creek homestead, so these get-togethers were a coming-home. The Unruhs had always been a close-knit family.

On this Sunday, the "tractor-go-round" incident was the first topic of conversation. The night it happened, Loretta had shared the story with her cousin and best friend, Doris Koehn, and no one else. Yet by that Sunday the entire Unruh clan knew about it.

As soon as they came into the house, Loretta's uncles and aunts and cousins walked over one at a time to where Loretta was peeling potatoes. Each one ceremoniously placed a dollar bill on the table next to her.

"There she is! Our tractor heroine!" exclaimed Aunt Margaret.

"What?" Loretta turned toward Carol Ann, assuming she was the blabbermouth, but Carol Ann shook her head; she hadn't gossiped about her sister, not this time anyway. Loretta then remembered telling the story to Doris and glared at her across the table. "Doris…?"

Doris smiled and began a little prepared speech. "We were talking…"

Loretta stopped her. "Apparently you've been doing a lot of talking if the whole family knows about the tractor, since you were the only one I told."

Doris ignored her and began again. "We were talking, and we would each like a turn around the yard on the tractor. Then, when each one's turn is up, you can jump up and bring it to a stop. Papa brought a stopwatch, and we'll time you and try to help you improve your technique and speed." Doris paused for effect to growing chuckles. "And even though we'll actually be helping you, we'll pay a dollar a ride, cash money." Clara and Harold looked nervously at Loretta, hoping the family hadn't gone too far with their kidding on such a sensitive subject. And initially she was clearly peeved, but then her face relaxed and she laughed along. She was no longer upset, and so far, no one had mentioned the part about her ending up on a man's lap. Maybe Doris had shown a little discretion after all.

Uncle Tobias said, "From what I hear, kiddo, you're aces at tractor wrangling, better than most of those rodeo cowboys. Harold, maybe we should ask the County Fair Board to add tractor jumping to the fair next year, what do you think?"

"I'd like to see you in action today," said Aunt Margaret, barely containing her laughter. "A little preview, if you will."

When the laughter and jokes died down, Loretta wiped her hands on a tea towel and moved to the table. "Thank you so much for your encouragement." Her voice was sweet as molasses. "I am really sorry to disappoint, but there will be no tractor jumping this afternoon." As she spoke, she swooped in and snatched up all the dollar bills and slipped them into her apron pocket.

"Why not?" asked one of her young cousins. "I want my dollar back then!"

"Because I'm going to be busy putting arsenic in Doris's food!" She feigned complete seriousness, leaving the gullible younger cousins to stare at her wide-eyed while the adults laughed. "But thank you for the money, and no, there are no refunds. I've been needing a few things from town and now I have the money to pay for them. Thank you very much!" The donors protested, but to no avail.

"She's as nimble as a cat, that one, and twice as sneaky," laughed Uncle Tobias. "I've never seen anybody get to the money so quick. No wonder she got up on that tractor so fast."

"Well done," said Carol Ann as Loretta ran upstairs to stash her winnings. "I get to go with you!"

The afternoon passed pleasantly. After the meal, the older women stayed in the kitchen to wash and dry dishes, clean up, and share the latest church and town news. The men stepped into the front room to talk about crops and herds and commodities prices and their harvests and fall plantings and plans for the spring. Having worked together their entire lives, they were each other's most trusted advisors on farm matters. Most everything else too. Carol Ann led the younger cousins in games in the yard while Loretta and Doris put on sweaters for a walk. They strolled out into the orchard, where the trees and bushes had lost their leaves and fruit, but the lingering scents of apples, peaches, pears, blackberries, currants, elderberries, and mulberries mingled in the crisp fresh air to create an intoxicatingly wonderful fragrance. Their grandmother liked to say the orchard is what heaven smelled like.

After the orchard, the young women walked along Doyle Creek to watch schools of glistening minnows swim in the clear water in the rocky creek bed. They were back at the farm by milking time and joined Harold in the milk barn. Carol Ann enlisted some cousins to help feed the other animals and roost the chickens while Clara and her sisters-in-law began supper. The leftovers, with fresh bread and two cherry cobblers, would be ready by the time Kurt and Tobias and two of the cousins returned from evening chores on their own farms.

As the women worked alone in the kitchen, Margaret brought up the tractor incident again. "When Doris was telling me and Kurt the other day, she told us everything, including the part about who was on the tractor at the time. I made her promise not to bring that part up with anybody else, especially today.'

Clara was standing beside Margaret and touched her arm. "Thank you. Loretta didn't need for everybody to be hearing the lurid details."

Gladys looked over from the sink, curiosity piqued. "What lurid details?"

Margaret waited for Clara to give the okay to speak. "The tractor wasn't going around on its own. One of the POWs who works here didn't know how to drive it and got it stuck in high. He had the good sense to keep steering it around in a big circle, but couldn't get it stopped. That's why Loretta had to hop on and when she did, she landed square on that man's lap! Did I tell it right, Clara?"

"First of all, so you know, we don't call them POWs, they're our field crew and helpers. But yes, that's what happened, in front of God and everybody!"

"Oh my," Gladys said, wide-eyed.

Clara interjected, "Please keep that to yourself, Gladys."

"Oh heavens, yes, of course."

"The poor girl," said Margaret.

"Well," said Gladys, "it does sound a bit racy." She realized her pun and said, "Oops," laughing. Margaret laughed, too, but not Clara. "She did what she had to do. Otherwise, the boy might have been hurt, and the tractor might have gotten wrecked. She really did save the day."

"I agree," said Margaret. "And the Lord understands and forgives in situations like this."

Clara knew they were right, but still she was bothered. "Yes, of course! But I've seen how men look at Loretta. She's a woman now. And I've seen her smiling back at Rolf, the one she jumped on. And I don't like it. He's *außenseiter*! I don't want either one of them getting the idea that they can keep flirting and somehow start courting! It's ridiculous, it's impossible, it's wrong! And what happened on the tractor could give them such ideas, or worse."

Her sisters-in-law felt Clara's anxieties and frustrations. Margaret hugged her shoulder as they stood side-by-side at the stove. They returned to preparing supper for a few moments in silence, then Gladys said quietly. "You remember that I was an outsider, too, when Tobias and I got married? I was called *außenseiter* more than once by some in the family, and not in a good way. There is no good way to be called that."

Slack-jawed with embarrassment Clara turned to Gladys. "Oh my dear, of course I remember. But you were from here, not Germany, and you weren't a soldier in Hitler's army. We'd known you forever."

"But I wasn't Mennonite or German, I was an Irish Methodist. And worst of all, Tobias was marrying someone not approved by your parents. From the time people found out we were dating until we got married in '22, I was *außenseiter*. Some even tried to stop us. Tobias never paid much attention to them, just said getting married was the right thing for us and they'd have to come round."

Margaret smiled at that. "Your husband was the baby in our family and was always more independent than the rest of us. More than once, he made our parents want to pull their hair out."

Gladys continued. "Even after I had my believer's baptism and put on the kapp and started having children, some still treated me differently. It was hard. Maybe some in the church still think that way about me."

Clara and Margaret both walked over to where Gladys was now setting the table to hug her. Clara spoke first. "Gladys, I hope you don't think I feel that you're an outsider. I love you as my sister. And I sincerely apologize if I offended you just now. I spoke without thinking."

Margaret added, "You've been a blessing to us all since you and Tobias got married. I know some of the older ones were cold at first, but you are loved, and not just by Tobias and those beautiful children of yours, but by all of us. You're our sister in Christ, and a better Mennonite than most. By the way, our mother loved you to her dying breath and was grateful that you 'settled Tobias down,' as she used to like to say."

Gladys dabbed at her tears. "Thank you. I couldn't be happier with my husband and our life and family and church. I only brought it up because that was one time the Unruh family learned to bend a little. I'm not saying that Loretta should be courted by a German man who was in the war, just that there's a little bit of a family history of allowing an outsider to come inside."

"True," nodded Margaret.

"I don't know this Rolf, but from what little I've heard, he's polite and a hard worker."

"That's also true," said Clara.

Gladys went on. "I do know Loretta. She's a fine young woman, so is Doris. You both should be proud of your grown-up daughters. They're blessings to the family and the church, and I'm sure neither of them would ever do anything that brings shame upon themselves or the family or jeopardizes their eternal salvation."

"Thank you, Gladys," said Clara. "You've said some things to think about and pray on."

# Chapter 24
# HARM'S WAY

That evening, after the other families had gone home, Loretta and Clara stepped out into the dark to go to the fruit cellar next to the east side of the house to restock the kitchen pantry for the week. Clara unlatched the door and lifted it up and over, then Loretta carefully walked down the seven concrete steps holding a candle to light the way until she could turn on two naked overhead electric bulbs. The cool musty cellar consisted of two large rooms. One was lined floor-to-ceiling with deep shelves holding hundreds of jars of canned fruits, vegetables, and jams, homemade root beer, 25-gallon crocks of sauerkraut, racks of potatoes spread out and sprinkled with lime to reduce rotting, and the last of the season's fresh fruit from the orchard, also spread out. Bunches of garlic and onions hung from the rafters. The second room was used to store canning, soap-making, and smokehouse equipment, extra jars and crocks, crates, pails, and assorted tools and implements. There were also stacks of blankets, candles, a Bible, prayer books, and other provisions stored down there for those times when the cellar was used as a safe haven when thunderstorms and tornadoes threatened the farm. More than once, the family had spent the night in the cellar while storms raked across Marion County.

As they filled their wood crates, Loretta spoke. "Mama, I'm sorry for raising my voice in anger at you on Wednesday. I was agitated, but I should not have spoken to you so rudely. I ask for your forgiveness, please."

Clara was bent over, reaching for jars of tomatoes. She straightened up, arched her back to stretch, and replied, "Thank you, dear. Of course, you're forgiven. It was terrifying to watch. I was afraid you might fall and get run over. That had me agitated too. I apologize for reprimanding you like that when you were doing what had to be done. I wasn't thinking clearly."

"Thank you, but you were right to remind me of the need for modesty at all times."

"I know you couldn't have done it without getting into the seat to take control of the tractor. After you climbed aboard, you couldn't just politely ask Rolf to move over or jump off now, could you? He must have been terrified. And that night, your father told me he was the one who told Rolf to get up on the tractor in the first place. Rolf was just doing what he was told. Harold was in the wrong for asking."

Loretta smiled. "It was just crazy."

"I never thought I'd see the circus come to Doyle Creek!" They both laughed.

"At least I got a little extra money for my troubles from the jokesters who thought they could tease me about it this afternoon," and they laughed more.

"Well done." Clara turned around with her nearly-full crate. Pointing to the shelves beside Loretta, she said, "Would you get three quarts of the beans, please? I have room for them right here." As Loretta handed them to her, she said, "I would like to address one other thing since we're down here alone, if that's all right."

"Of course, Mama." Pulling up a bench, they sat down, side-by-side.

"The thing with the tractor brought to mind something I've been worrying about for a while now, actually since the Germans came to work here."

Loretta knew where her mother was heading, but still said, "And what's that?"

"I've noticed the way you and Rolf talk to each other and the way you look at each other. I would go so far as to call it flirting."

Loretta felt her heart beating faster and hoped the dim lighting would hide how much she was blushing. "Mama, I'm so sorry if I gave you that idea. I was just trying to be friendly, and Rolf is the easiest one to talk to. But I see how I may have given the wrong impression. And now I understand why you were so upset on Wednesday. I'm sorry for worrying you. I'll do better at being friendly without overdoing it."

Clara hesitated just a bit, then said, "Are you sure that's all it is, friendliness?"

Loretta was surprised at her mother's follow-up question and inquisitorial tone. "Yes, Mama." She hoped she didn't sound defensive. "Why? What else could it be?"

"What else, indeed." Loretta felt her mother's body tighten. "I'll be blunt. There's no future for you with him." Loretta nodded. "Rolf is polite and a hard worker. And he's interesting and good at conversation, just like your father, and he's attractive."

"But?" said Loretta.

Now Clara's words came quickly. "If he wasn't Catholic and from Germany and if he hadn't gone to war for Hitler and if he wasn't incarcerated and you'd met in normal circumstances, maybe you and he would have been able to court properly. But that's not the situation."

"That's a lot of 'ifs,' 'ands,' and 'buts,' isn't it?" Loretta said, trying to lighten the moment. "And you're right." She felt a little twinge of sadness and looked away.

"Your father and I are not going to choose your husband for you. We hope we've raised you to love the Lord and make the right decision on who to marry when the time comes."

"There's not much of a decision to make now."

"Even so, Rolf cannot be a husband for you, and you should resist any temptation to think otherwise. And you shouldn't lead him into thinking about you that way. I want to be clear on that. Since the day you were born, even before that, we've tried to guide and protect you from all danger, temporal and spiritual."

"And I'm grateful, Mama."

"One last thing: If all those other things I just said weren't enough, when this war is over, he won't be allowed to stay here. He and all the others will be sent back to Germany. It's mandatory."

"I didn't know that."

"Thank you for listening to me"

"Thank you, Mama, for your love and guidance." Loretta paused. Her mother sensed that she had more to stay. "And thanks for not calling Rolf *außenseiter* just now."

Clara gave her a curious look. "Please, tell me why you say that?"

"Because I think it's demeaning. Yes, he's all the things you said, but he's still a human being. I've used that word, too, but it's wrong. It makes it sound like they have no right to be treated with dignity and are unworthy of our hospitality. To me, it's worse than calling them prisoners. They're strangers brought here involuntarily. I don't think we should make them feel inferior or let ourselves think we're better than they are."

Clara nodded, started to speak, but then stopped, lost in thought.

"May I say something else?"

"Of course."

"Classifying people and saying they don't belong here is what the Nazis do. As Americans and as Mennonites, we should avoid the sin of judging and condemning whole groups of human beings because of what they look like or what they believe or how they worship or where they came from. Or who they fought for. '*Außenseiter*' even sounds a Nazi word. And remember that we Mennonites get accused of being un-American because we're pacifists and called 'heinie' because we're German. To some red-blooded Americans, we're the *außenseiter.* Carol Ann told you, but she was practically called a 'heinie' at school a few weeks ago."

"She did mention it to me, just a few days ago," said Clara sadly.

They sat in silence for a few moments, then Loretta added, "I'm not saying we're as bad as the Nazis. All we want is to worship with people we know and trust and who share our beliefs. But just because we love and serve the Lord as Mennonites, that doesn't mean everyone else is bad." She looked over at her mother and said with a tired grin, "Okay, I'll stop now or you'll think I want to become a preacher!"

When Loretta finished, Clara's eyes were glistening. "You have the heart of the Good Samaritan." She turned and held her daughter tightly. "Just this afternoon, I was thinking the same thing about that word, and it was right after I had used it too. And I was ashamed. Just the way it sounds is ugly, so guttural. And if it sounds degrading, that's because it's meant to be degrading. And I had never really thought about that until today. Words have power. Words can become weapons. You're right, we can do better. And we will from now on."

"I love you, Mama."

"I love you too. Now we'd better get back inside. It's time for evening prayer. Light the candle and be careful on the steps, they may be slick from the dew."

⌁⊸⊱⊶⊰⊸⊱⌁

When the house was dark and they were in bed, Clara seemed a bit restless. "Did you have a good day?" asked Harold.

"Yes. Elder Ratzlaff's sermon this morning was inspiring and our family time was good. I had some meaningful conversations today too. It's given me a lot to think about and pray over."

"Is that right?"

"Today I realized all over again how fast our daughters are growing up. The boys are gone, and it won't be long before Loretta will have a home of her own. I can't believe she's 21 already. She's a fine young woman; thanks be to God. I just hope we taught her all she needs to know to find her way. She's going to face so many challenges in this changing and troubled world. More than we did."

Harold rolled over to spoon his wife and said quietly, "These are trying times, no doubt about it. I think Loretta's going to be just fine. Carol Ann, too, although she's got a bigger ornery streak in her than Loretta."

"You're right about that." She snuggled against her husband. "I love you, Mr. Unruh."

"I love you, too, Mrs. Unruh. Good night now." He gave her a little squeeze and in a whisper began, "The Lord is my Shepherd, I shall not want. He maketh me to lie down in green pastures: He leadeth me beside the still waters." As he recited the words of her favorite psalm, Harold felt his wife let go of her burdens and relax into sleep.

⸎

Upstairs, Loretta lay thinking about how good it was to speak with her mother so forthrightly about important matters. Her mother had treated her like an adult, more as an equal than ever before. When she went to Bethel after high school, her father seemed to realize she was grown up, but Clara clung to the notion that Loretta was still a child in need of maternal protection. True, tonight Clara still gave her daughter unsolicited advice in a tone that brooked no dissent, but she also listened to Loretta's views about how people should be treated and actually said she agreed with her. Afterwards, Loretta began to think of herself as an adult, maybe for the first time. She liked that.

But then she thought of Rolf and remembered how childishly she'd acted when she yelled at him that day. He'd avoided all contact with her, not even said hello since it happened. Clearly, he was hurt. For all her sanctimony about not using that word, she was the one who had hurled it at Rolf, and her weapon had found its mark. Why did she do that? She must apologize to him at the first opportunity.

After asking the Lord's forgiveness once more, she got into bed and slipped under the covers. She was tired and ready to rest, but just as she was crossing the threshold between awake and asleep, her quieting mind wandered into her most private space, where all her vital secrets were hidden from everyone except herself. In that quiet little nook, sealed away from all the ifs, ands, and buts the world would impose, her heart's whisper could be heard: *I am drawn to Rolf Mueller, and I hope one day he will feel the same.* No explanation or justification necessary here in her safe place.

When she woke the following morning, Loretta was ready to apologize, but Rolf wouldn't make it easy. At dinner, he sat next to Harold at the opposite end of the table from where Loretta sat. He never looked in her direction and seemed unusually interested in the food and whatever those around him were saying. He spoke infrequently, only when necessary to ensure there were no lapses, no moments where Loretta might try to engage him in conversation. It was the same for the rest of the week. Loretta had to give him credit for being so adept at avoiding her. She decided to accept his challenge and find a way for them to speak.

At the very end of the work week, on Saturday evening, Rolf headed toward the outhouse, which was discreetly located between tall Rose of Sharon bushes east of the house. The Unruh outhouse was elaborate as outhouses go. Made of native stone, not wood, built on an elevated concrete platform, and twice as large as regular wood privies, it featured a red-trimmed gabled roof, a circular paned glass window above the wood door, screened ventilation ducts, a tiny wood stove that stayed lit on especially cold days. There were even candles, a lantern, and Scott toilet paper in lieu of the corn cobs or newsprint found in most outhouses of the day. The structure was an unusual extravagance but deemed a necessity because Harold's mother was deathly afraid of snakes and particularly terrified at the thought of encountering one in an outhouse when she would be vulnerable. So Harold built the "most elaborate Mennonite privy in the State of Kansas," he liked to say, for his mother's security and peace of mind. What he didn't mention was that he had inherited her phobia of all types of snakes, from garter snakes and blacksnakes to the poisonous rattlers and copperheads that thrived in Marion County. So a fancy, well-built, protected privy was an acceptable extravagance, even for simple-living Mennonites.

Loretta was in the milk barn when she happened to see Rolf go into the outhouse. She told Carol Ann she had to use the outhouse and hurried in that direction too. She and Rolf almost ran into each other as he came out, which startled him. They just stood there facing each other awkwardly until Rolf stepped off the stone walkway to allow her to pass. As he did, she began. "Rolf, I apologize for what I said that day. I had no right to yell at you and embarrass you in front of everyone. I'm especially sorry that I called you that awful word. I ask for your forgiveness. I wanted to apologize before now, but never seemed to get the chance."

When she was finished, Rolf stood looking at her without saying anything for so long that she began to worry that he might be weighing whether to forgive her or not. In truth, however, after recovering from his surprise, he was just relishing being so close to her and alone for the first time. When she realized she was growing nervous, he spoke, "Of course." He paused again, then said, "I would forgive you for anything, Loretta." Before she could respond, he went on, "I ask you to forgive me for being so reckless and then for making bad jokes."

"You have nothing to apologize for. I was the one in the wrong." The way he looked at her made her happy and nervous. She blushed. "I'd better get back to the milking."

"As you said, we are not a team, but I hope we can be friends."

"Yes, I would like that."

He smiled and gave a little bow. "Thank you again, *mein Freundin*, for saving my life."

She smiled and gave a little nod. "And thank you, *mein Freund*, for forgiving me."

The truck horn honked, and Harold started calling out for the Germans. "It's time to go," said Rolf. He began to jog to the truck, then turned to watch her as she returned to the milk barn. "*Auf Wiedersehen, mein Liebster,*" he said quietly. She couldn't hear him, but he thought he saw her glancing in his direction. The entire encounter didn't last more than a minute or two, but it gave him days of smiles.

In October, Army higher-ups figured out it wasn't necessary for guards to accompany the POWs to work. Henceforth, Jordan would stay in camp and assume other responsibilities. He knew he wasn't needed on the farm, but was sorry he'd no longer be spending time with the Unruhs and even sorrier that he'd be giving up his place at their table. In addition to all the familiar American dishes, Clara introduced Jordan to many German specialties she prepared for the workers—schnitzel, bierocks, strudel, pflaumenkuchen. "So they feel at home," Clara would say. Jordan loved it all. After he'd been reassigned, the Unruhs stayed in touch and regularly invited him out to Sunday dinner. "So he won't be too homesick," Clara would say.

Also during that last week in October, Rolf received the first mail from his family since before he was captured, more than a dozen letters delivered by the Red Cross. He stayed up late the night they arrived to read them all. The first ones, written in the spring, were worried pleas for information since his family didn't know what had become of him. Once they found out he was alive, the tone of the letters was calmer, but still each letter was soaked in anxiety. A particularly poignant one from his mother was written in July 1943. Her formerly graceful handwriting was barely legible:

*Dear Son,*

*Thank you for all your letters. We thank God you are recovering and hope your injuries will not cause permanent problems.*

*What a surprise that you are in Kansas. Do you recall that my cousin, Leo Steffes, and his family live there, in a town also called Olpe? It was named for ours because so many of its settlers came from here. What a coincidence that you are in Kansas.*

*Papa and Maria send their love. Maria had a bad cold but is better. We've not heard from Kurt in many months, so I can't tell you anything about him. The silence is terrible. I will let you know when we hear from him.*

*Papa is being drafted. He had to register last week. We hope he will be assigned to the* Volkssturm *and not the* Wehrmacht, *which might keep him closer to home.*

*Maybe you've heard what happened to Hamburg. Fires from air raids destroyed the entire city. Thousands were killed. There've been more raids on Köln too. There's not much left. Many of our relatives had to flee. A few of them are here in Olpe now. Tante Ursula is all right, but she lost everything. The Allies are so cruel!*

*We are struggling to keep the farm going. Our* Fuehrer *tells us that Germany will ultimately prevail. We trust him.*

*I will end with a bit of happier news. We had twin calves a few weeks ago. Maybe it's a good omen. They are both bull calves and seem healthy. Maria named them Kurt and Rolf! Ha!*

*Stay strong, do your best, and remember us. Your letters are always a great relief, so please write when you can. Maria promises to take good care of your namesake.*

*With love and affection,*
*Mama*

How could his mother and sister run the farm alone if his father was taken away? How could Germany possibly think about winning when its cities were being destroyed? Köln, heavily damaged in massive raids in May 1942, was still being bombed? And Hamburg was gone?

His mother's letters confirmed how the war was really going. In North Africa, Rolf had seen firsthand the superior might of the Allied forces once America got in the fight. Then, traveling across the United States and seeing all the rail yards and factories and fields, he had to acknowledge the vast resources the Allies could now bring to bear against Germany.

In Kansas, the POWs got war updates from the guards and had access to newspapers, magazines, and radios which told of the conquest of Sicily and the Allied landing on the Italian mainland. They learned that Mussolini had been overthrown in July, then Italy surrendered in

September. They learned about Russian advances in the East. Rolf might have been tempted to dismiss American news reports as propaganda had he not seen so much that confirmed what he read and heard. Now his mother's account of great cities destroyed and middle-aged men drafted provided further corroboration. To anyone paying attention, these weren't temporary setbacks. The war was going to end badly for Germany. While Rolf sat safe in the heart of America, his family was exposed in ways he could hardly bear to think about.

Out of consideration for one another, the Americans and the Germans on the Unruh farm did not generally discuss the war, though they sometimes unintentionally veered off into it. One rainy afternoon, Harold asked Rolf to tell them more about his family's farm. "How large is it?"

"It's small, sir. Mostly grazing meadows and small cultivated fields, about twelve hectares in all."

"And what do you raise?"

"We have a couple cows for milking, a few more for meat, and some hogs, sheep, chickens, geese, and ducks. We grow a little corn for feed, some sugar beets, and a few different grains—wheat, oats, barley, rye. Our fields are much smaller than yours."

"Do you have a tractor?"

"No, we still do everything with horses and by hand."

"So that explains why you had such a hard time driving ours!" Harold smiled. "And how's your family these days? Have you heard from them?"

"Yes, sir, I've gotten letters from my parents and my sister." Rolf took a breath. "They're having a hard time without my brother and me there. There's no one else to help them."

Clara frowned. "It must be especially hard since so much is still done by hand."

"Yes, ma'am. And now my father has just been drafted too."

"What?" Clara exclaimed. She and Harold exchanged startled looks.

"How old is your father?" Harold asked.

"He was born in 1892, so he's fifty-one."

"Good gracious, that's the same as me. He's not exempt because he farms?" Rolf shook his head. "The situation must be serious there if they're drafting old men like us."

The Germans shifted uneasily. Rolf thought for a moment before going on. "Yes, sir, it is. The war has created many problems—casualties on battlefields, of course, and civilian casualties and damage from the bombings and shortages. My family is doing the best they can." He was reluctant to say anything more in front of Hecht or the others that might be construed as unpatriotic.

The Unruhs grimaced, and Harold spoke for the family, "I'm so sorry. It must be terrible being away at a time like this. I hope I've not upset you by asking."

Rolf smiled feebly. "It's all right. I know it's hard on you having your sons away from home, too, and it's just as difficult for the others."

Hecht spoke up, "My home was destroyed in an air raid on Mannheim last month. My parents and sisters barely escaped with their lives. It was a beautiful home. My father is an important industrialist." Looking at Rolf, he added, "You should be thankful. At least you have your farm to go home to." Everyone squirmed at Hecht's crass implication that Rolf's troubles were insignificant compared to his own, while throwing in his higher social status for good measure.

No one knew what to say, until Gralke spoke quietly, "My mother and my uncle and aunt were killed in Essen, and my brother was lost at Stalingrad."

Seeing the look in the eyes of the men at their table, the Unruhs were silent, even until Clara said, "Anton, I am so sorry for your loss. We will pray that God will comfort you."

The following day it was cold and cloudy when the men arrived for work, but as they stepped inside the house for dinner, the sky broke loose. Cold rain poured down in torrents mixed with mid-sized hail stones, lightning flashed, and thunder rumbled.

"We made it in just in time," said Harold with a smile as he took off his hat and jacket.

"It's not fit for man nor beast out there," said Clara.

The storm continued through the meal and into the afternoon. There wasn't much Harold and the men could do outside, but instead of driving them back to camp, where their canvas tents wouldn't provide shelter or warmth, Harold asked his wife, "What do you think about our helpers staying inside with us this afternoon until around milking time and then

I'll drive them in? We can't very well make them sit in the back of the truck in this weather anyway, can we? Maybe it'll be done raining by then."

"That would be the Christian thing to do. Loretta and I aren't going to be doing anything outdoors, either, so we'll join you. I'll do some mending."

"Since you boys came out here to work a full day and aren't able to through no fault of your own, I'm thinking we should still pay your wages to the Army like always."

All four Germans smiled and thanked Harold.

"Just don't go telling anybody we were playing hooky. They might frown on that."

"That is not a problem. We can keep a secret," said Hecht as Clara stepped in to remove the dessert plates and carry them to the sink.

Loretta joined them at the table with a fresh pot of coffee and plates of mincemeat and oatmeal cookies. "I love days like this. What shall we do? We could play dominoes or checkers."

No one responded immediately, then Rolf said, "Mr. Unruh, yesterday you asked about our families in Germany. Thank you. We appreciate your concern." Hecht, Zimmerman, and Gralke nodded. "Now, if you wouldn't mind, there's something I would like to ask you about."

"What would you like to know?"

"I know you're Mennonites and you've told us how your family came to Kansas. Today, would you mind also telling us about your church? I don't know anything about it except that you're devout Christians. What makes the Mennonite church different?" Looking around at the other Germans, he said, "We four are Catholic or Evangelical Church members. You're the only Mennonites we know."

"I would like to know too," said Zimmerman, "if it's not improper for us to ask." He looked over at Hecht and Gralke, who nodded in agreement.

"Heavens, no! We're happy to share our faith with whoever wants to listen." Harold stood up and walked to the bookshelf in the front room.

Rolf was back at his usual seat, across from Loretta. He looked at her and said, "I hope you don't mind my asking this. We can still play games later, yes?"

Loretta smiled. "Our beliefs are important to us. I'm glad you asked.

Papa and Mama love to share the Good News."

Hecht heard her and smiled, "I will start. Are all Mennonite women required to cover their hair?" Hecht asked, pointing to Loretta's kapp.

Loretta was surprised by the banality of his question but was polite. "No. There are many different Mennonite communities, and each has its own rules. Some require specific clothing for women and for men. The church we attend does not require women to wear anything in particular, only tells us that our clothing should be simple and modest, and without extravagant adornment."

"Then why do you all wear it?"

Clara answered for her daughter. "To remind us that we are servants of the Lord and sisters in Christ. Mr. Unruh's mother, who died this past August, wore one her entire life and believed it was godly, so we do too."

As she was speaking, Harold returned to the kitchen with the family Bible and several Mennonite books, pamphlets, and hymnals. Looking at the men, he laughed. "I'll bet you're thinking, now we've opened a can of worms for sure! Don't worry, I'm not going to read all of these to you. I just got these in here in case you ask something that I can't answer off the top of my head." He sat down and put the books on the table. "Where shall we start?"

Zimmerman replied, "How did the Mennonite church come into existence, and why?"

Harold explained that the Mennonite church had its origins in the Anabaptist movement that began in Switzerland and the Netherlands during the Reformation period, four hundred years earlier. "Anabaptists were more radical in their views about the corruption of the Catholic Church and the need to return to a truer, purer form of Christianity than Martin Luther himself. That got them into trouble with Catholics and leading Protestants alike."

"What sort of trouble?" asked Rolf.

"Our ancestors believed that only true believers should be baptized only when they could choose to become a Christian, so baptizing infants was not biblical. That went against Catholic and Protestant teaching. And when the Anabaptists started baptizing themselves again as adults, 'anabaptist' means to get baptized again, that really got Catholics riled up. That's when the burnings and persecutions began."

"And other things the Anabaptists believed were contrary to

established laws and rules," Clara said.

"Oh, yes," said Harold. "Anabaptists believed in nonviolence, that aggression of any sort against another human being is a violation of God's Commandments, even resistance to an aggressor if you're under attack. And that Christians should live simply and share God's gifts with others and that there should be a complete separation of church and state. And that got them into more trouble with the emperors and kings and princes who were running things, not just the churches."

Gralke asked, "Is that what you believe?"

"Yes," Clara answered. "It is."

Zimmerman began to speak, then frowned before continuing. "Was it hard for you to have us come out to work for you? Because we're soldiers and our ancestors might have been persecuting yours?"

Clara answered for the Unruhs. "The truth is, yes, at first it was hard. But we needed help, and when we got to know you and saw how polite and hardworking you all are, we felt better. We may disagree with you on many things, but we're all sinners in God's eyes. Only He can judge any of us."

Harold made a few final points about the church's history. When he was finished, Hecht said, "Your commitment to nonviolence is interesting, but if I may ask, is it realistic? Are you saying that if someone attacked you or threatened to kill you, that you would not resist, not even to defend yourself or your family?"

Harold turned to a dog-eared page in the New Testament and said, "Before I answer that, let me read you this from the Gospel of Matthew. 'Ye have heard that it hath been said, An eye for an eye, and a tooth for a tooth. But I say unto you, That ye resist not evil: but whosoever shall smite thee on thy right cheek, turn to him the other also.'" He looked up. "There are other verses in the Bible that say the same thing. It was radical when Jesus said those words. It was radical when Menno Simons preached them and people were being burned at the stake for believing him. And it's radical today, isn't it? But the words are clear. There's no getting around them. We believe that's what Jesus expects from his followers if we want to see him in heaven." Putting the Bible down, he added, "Back to your question, Otto, I hope we are never threatened or attacked like that. But if it happens, I pray that the Lord will give me the strength to be faithful to His Word and not resist, right up to the end if necessary."

Hecht shook to register his disbelief. "I can't imagine ever being that...." He stopped, thinking. "I can't imagine giving up my life without a fight. I love my life too much to just throw it away without a fight."

Clara grimaced "We love life, too, but we love the Lord more."

Rolf had been listening intently and thinking. "It's remarkable to hear you say that you are literally willing to live and die for your faith. I'm Catholic. Our priests and bishops read the same words you just read, but then they find a hundred reasons why they don't apply today. I remember listening to those words when I was young, but I don't think I heard them until today. And your whole church is made up of people who feel the same way. It's inspiring."

Gralke added, "And after four hundred years of Mennonites getting killed or forced into exile, your church lives on true to its beliefs.

Zimmerman said, "Thank you for helping us understand what you believe. I also can't imagine being able to live up to those standards like you do, but sometimes I wish I could."

"All things are possible in the Lord," said Clara.

Rolf said, "You've given us a lot to think about."

The conversation continued for a little while longer, then Harold put some pamphlets on the table near the Germans. "One of these is our church's Confession of Faith. Another one is about the life of Menno Simons. Please help yourselves if you'd like to take them back to camp with you." Each of the men took a pamphlet or two. "Now I'll say a little prayer, and when we're finished maybe someone will pass those cookies down here. And then, who's up for dominoes?"

<hr>

That same month, it was learned that a local priest had offered to drive over to Camp Peabody from Florence to say Mass for the Catholics there. Rolf attended church weekly with his family as a child, but after he joined the *Hitlerjugend* in 1934, his interest in his church faded. Since 1939, he hadn't gone to Mass at all, except once or twice for Christmas or Easter. When he learned an American priest was willing to come to Camp Peabody, he was impressed at the gesture, but ambivalent about attending. However, the Sunday after the conversation about religion with the Unruhs, he joined fifty or so POWs and guards at the outdoor altar the guards had erected. The afternoon was cool and sunny. As they sang traditional hymns and recited familiar prayers, Rolf's mind drifted back to a simpler, better time in his life. And he was struck by the vast difference between his faith and the Unruhs'.

# Chapter 25

# AN OPEN SECRET

The same day that Rolf attended Mass for the first time, Doris visited Doyle Creek to spend the afternoon with Loretta. Three months apart in age, the cousins attended school together in Peabody from first grade through high school. They worshiped at the same church, at age fifteen they professed their faith and were baptized on the same day, and they were together at nearly every family gathering since before they could remember. Although Loretta was taller and slenderer than Doris, family members remarked that they acted more like twins than cousins. Small wonder, then, that they had been best friends forever.

After the dishes were put away, the young women walked out to the gravel road and turned east to head up beyond the hay meadows to a big pasture. The Flint Hills aren't ostentatious in the fall like the forests of New England, but Loretta and Doris loved the subtle beauty of the low hills folding into each other and stretching on for miles, now covered with gently-waving grasses turned brown, umber, and gold and dotted with splotches of vivid red sumac and limestone outcrops. The clear blue sky and cotton ball clouds above contrasted perfectly with the earth tones below.

Walking arm in arm through a gate into the pasture, Doris looked up at her cousin and smiled, "I haven't been out here to see you since the last family dinner. I hope you're not still mad at me for spilling the beans."

"I hope you're not mad at me for keeping your dollar."

"Of course not. It was Papa's!" Doris laughed. "You didn't say it was a secret or I wouldn't have breathed a word. But you didn't and since it was so funny, I had to tell my parents. And it took off from there."

"It was funny," said Loretta with a smile. "I was mad at first, but when no one mentioned me ending up on Rolf's lap, I felt better." The two walked on. "Thank you for not telling them that part of the story."

"Well, actually," Doris stammered.

"Doris! Did you tell that too? Does everybody know Rolf was on the tractor?"

Her cousin squirmed. "That was the best part!" Watching Loretta scowl, Doris said, "I am sorry, Loretta. Truly I am. I really didn't think it was a big deal."

"It was a big deal to me!" Loretta voice carried in the breeze. "There I was, jumping up onto a man in front of God and everybody!"

Doris grinned impishly. "And there's not much space between a tractor's steering wheel and the seat if there's a handsome man sitting on it!"

"No, there isn't, and you're terrible! And what makes you think he's handsome?"

"Oh, probably because you and Carol Ann have only said so maybe twenty times." Doris laughed. "Each!"

"Of course you're exaggerating, as usual, but I do need to be more careful." Loretta sighed. "Okay, so honestly? He is handsome, very handsome. And polite and smart. And when he smiles at me, it makes me feel something. I don't know," she looked for the word. "Okay, it makes me feel good. Special. Like he really sees me." She caught her breath and turned to look straight at Doris. "And if you ever tell a single soul what I just said, I swear I will jerk your arm and beat you to death with it! Pacifist or not!"

Doris laughed. "Good heavens! Swearing and threatening violence! Who are you?" She put her hands up in surrender. "I promise, not a word. And once again, I apologize from the bottom of my heart for what I did say."

"Apology accepted. I guess you can still be my best friend," she said with a smile.

Doris smiled too. "Good, and here's a little good news for you, best friend. After I told Mama everything, she gave me strict orders to not tell anyone else about you getting up there on a man's lap. She said it would embarrass you. So, nobody knows, except my parents and me."

"Aunt Margaret has more sense than you!"

They walked along arm in arm to the edge of a rocky crag that tumbled down to a lower pasture beyond which were the trees lining Doyle Creek. The crag was high enough for them to see over the creek. The view was marvelous, one of Loretta's favorite spots on their farm. As they took in the beauty of the afternoon, Doris said, "Are you ever going to tell me the whole story about Rolf?"

Loretta looked off to the horizon. "What is there to tell? He's from Germany, he was captured, and he's here working for us, at the end of the war he'll go home. End of story."

"Really?"

"Yes."

"That's all there is to it?"

"What more is there to say?"

"Ten minutes ago, you were having a hard time coming up with the right word to say how you feel when he smiles at you. Was 'tingly' the word you were looking for?" Loretta rolled her eyes and tried to reply, but Doris continued, "It's an honest question. And here's another one: What are you going to do about it?"

Loretta frowned. "Doris, what exactly do you think can happen here?"

"I don't know. I'm just asking."

Loretta took a slow breath, looked out to the horizon again, and finally began to speak, as if to the wind, "There's nothing that can be done. Let's say, hypothetically, that he makes me feel 'tingly.' What then? There are so many reasons that it could never work. I don't really know him, just impressions I've gathered during our dinner conversations. He and I have barely spoken directly to each other. I don't know what he believes or what he wants. Did he go to war because he wanted to or because he had to? What does he think about Hitler and the Nazis? For that matter, what does he think about me? I know so little and don't see how we'll ever be alone long enough to really know each other. It seems pretty cut and dried. Mama says courtship is absolutely out of the question. She may be right," Loretta said with a sigh.

"Maybe."

"But the other day, he did say he hoped we could be friends."

"Really? Were you two alone when he said this?"

"Yes, a few days ago, we were by the outhouse for a few minutes."

"Ooh lala!" Doris teased her. "Was this the first time you were alone together? How romantic!"

"Yes, I guess."

"How did you answer?"

"I said, yes, I would like that."

"It's hard to see true love springing from a first date at the outhouse door, although it is a very nice outhouse," Doris said with another laugh. "But that's something, isn't it? And there's no harm in befriending a stranger. That's something even Aunt Clara couldn't object to. How would you go about it?"

"It wasn't a date, you silly goose! If we want to become friends, we'll have to get to know each other at dinnertime. That's about the only time we see each other. There's always good conversation when the Germans are here. Papa knows how to ask the right questions. Mama's talking more, and I'm helping them with English. I can try to be a little more like Papa. As long as it's not too personal or directed only to Rolf."

"Sounds like a good plan."

"Maybe so."

"What about the other Germans, what are they like?"

"They're nice, but they don't speak much English and seem less interesting. Rolf went to a university in Berlin before the war. He seems more worldly than the others, but I like them all. One of the others is overly friendly, always smiling at me and trying to get me to talk to him. He makes me a little uncomfortable sometimes, but I just ignore him."

"Do any of the other ones make you feel tingly too?"

Loretta snorted, "Don't be ridiculous, of course not! What do you take me for, some floozy?" Loretta laughed at her own words, as did Doris.

"I know you better than that. And I also know that you haven't been excited about another boy since you were in college a couple years ago. What was his name?"

"Leon Farthing. Yeah, we got along when we were at Bethel. Then I came home, and he went back to Halstead and we lost touch."

"You lost more than that, you lost interest too. But you never gave me details."

"Yes I did, we talked about it. How Leon is hardworking and from a farm and our families like each other. And things were a little exciting at first, but not really. When I came home, I was sorry to leave Bethel, but not sorry to say goodbye to Leon Farthing."

"It's all a little fuzzy for me, so how about you refresh my memory?" Doris loved teasing her cousin.

Loretta gave her an exasperated look. "You just want me to say it, don't you?" Doris gave a look as if she had no idea what Loretta was talking about. "All right, I will. Leon was dull as dirt. Happy?" Indeed, her cousin was—she was laughing out loud. "I don't know why he was in college at all. He had no interest in anything besides farming. I don't think he ever read a book for fun or went to a picture show, and he never asked my opinion on anything. Leon had all the credentials—Mennonite, good family, a farmer, decent looking. But if I ever felt tingly around him, your word again, that feeling died a tragic early death." She stopped, remembering more. "He even told me it was a waste of time for me to go to college, that godly women didn't get jobs outside the home. I wondered if Mama put him up to saying that!"

Doris stifled a laugh and said, "So I guess you never wanted to jump on his lap and drive him around the yard on a tractor?" She and Loretta both guffawed.

"You're right about that!"

Her cousin grew more serious. "I'm glad you've met someone who makes you feel special. Friendship would be a good thing for both of you. Maybe frustrating since you might want more, but half a loaf is better than no bread at all. And maybe someday things will change, and if it's meant to be, you'll have a head start because you'll already be friends."

"But what if this situation is impossible?" Loretta sighed.

"Do you think it is?'

"I don't know. But why waste time wanting something that can never be." She sighed again.

"It's not a waste of time figuring out whether it's possible. Get to know him. Maybe he would convert. Maybe he's not a Nazi. Maybe he's a good man. Or maybe he turns out to be a terrible human being. You've got the time to figure that out, and from a safe distance."

"I suppose you're right. Thank you." Loretta hugged her cousin tightly. "It's time we were heading back, back to reality." The northerly breeze was starting to pick up as they turned around and headed back to the road.

In bed that night, Loretta smiled because it felt good to share part of her secret with her cousin. But she felt guilty for not being completely candid, because she did not, could not, tell Doris that when she was sitting on Rolf's lap, those fleeting seconds pressed tightly against him were the most erotically charged moments of her life. "Tingly" didn't come close to describing what she experienced that day. And aside from it happening in broad daylight and in front of the whole world, which caused her harsh overreaction, Loretta was not ashamed of what she felt. Not any longer, anyway.

In the dim light from her nightstand lamp, she saw her copy of *Little Women* on the bookshelf. It was a favorite book of hers since she was introduced to Louisa May Alcott in high school. Seeing it called to mind a memorable quote from it: "I am not afraid of storms for I am learning to sail." Loretta said the words out loud, twice. For all the storms that would follow if she allowed herself to think of Rolf Mueller as more than a friend, Loretta was surprisingly calm. Maybe she really could learn to sail.

In November, a virulent strain of influenza struck Camp Peabody. For days, at least half the Germans and their guards were sick. Three of the four men who worked on the Unruh farm were bedridden. Only Rolf stayed healthy, so he continued to work.

On Tuesday, the second, Harold and Rolf took a load of grain to the Hillsboro Elevator. On the drive, Rolf didn't say much. "Are you all right my boy?" asked Harold. "You're not coming down with it, too, are you?"

"No, sir, I'm just thinking."

"I'll leave you to your thoughts then."

They were back at Doyle Creek just in time to wash their hands and pray before dinner. As they ate, Harold updated Clara and Loretta on the excellent rating their corn received and the good price it sold for. Rolf asked a few questions about the factors considered in determining the sale price but was still quieter than usual.

"Rolf, are you okay today? You're so quiet, do you have the flu too?" Loretta asked.

Rolf smiled at her and then turned to Harold. "Your father also asked me that. I'm really fine but thank you both for asking."

"Is something troubling you?" asked Clara.

"Today is *Allerseelen*. Do you know this day?"

"All Souls Day," replied Clara. "We're familiar with it."

"When I was young, we would go to church for a Requiem Mass and then to the cemetery to light candles and pray for our deceased relatives. It was a good way to remember them. There was a Gregorian chant sung during Mass called the *Dies Irae* that I especially liked. In German it means *tag des zorns*."

"Day of Wrath," said Harold.

"The melody was haunting. I haven't even thought about *Allerseelen* for years, but for some reason, today I woke up hearing that song."

Loretta looked across at him, "Are you missing your family today?"

Rolf nodded. "Yes, but I miss them every day."

"I'm sure you do," said Clara. "I can't imagine being so far from family for so long, and in such circumstances. I'm sorry for you, Rolf."

"Thank you, Mrs. Unruh. But you do know what it's like, since your sons aren't here with you. I'm sorry for your family too." Clara nodded.

"Is there something else, something out of the ordinary bothering you?" asked Loretta.

"I've been thinking about all the dead today. Not just the ones in my family, but everyone who's died over the past four years. No one could even know how many."

"It's unimaginable," said Loretta sadly. She sipped her water and continued, "May I ask you a question?"

"Of course."

Loretta laughed a little. "And as I'm thinking about it, I may have more than one question. Is that still all right?"

Rolf smiled. "Ask me as many questions as you would like answers."

Now she chose her words carefully. "When the war started, were you already in the *Wehrmacht*? Did you volunteer or were you drafted? Also, how long were you in actual fighting?"

Harold and Clara looked at Loretta apprehensively. Harold said to Rolf, "I know Loretta means well, but if answering is something you'd prefer not to do, we understand."

Loretta interjected, "Absolutely. Rolf, I'm sorry if I shouldn't have asked you these questions."

Rolf looked at the others. "I really don't mind. Especially because the questions you asked are easy to answer: no; no; yes; and a long time." He smiled nervously and waited to see their reactions, but none of the Unruhs knew what to say. "I didn't mean to sound like I was making a joke. I can share more details if you'd like."

The Unruhs relaxed and smiled. Loretta said, "As much as you want to share."

"As to your first question, when the war began in 1939, I was not in the *Wehrmacht*. I was in my second year of medical school at the University of Berlin."

Harold smiled, "Really? That's impressive, Rolf. Earlier when you said you went to the university, I never asked what you were studying. Did you like medicine?"

"Medicine was my passion, sir. Since I was young, I dreamt of becoming a doctor. But then I was drafted into the *Wehrmacht* in October 1939, and my dream ended." He paused. "Like the dreams of many others." He looked at Loretta. "And I guess that answers your second and third questions."

"Thank you."

Rolf went on. "If you'd like, I can elaborate and provide a little background regarding the questions about volunteering or getting drafted." The Unruhs all nodded. "My parents were members of the Catholic Centre Party in Germany until it was dissolved in 1933. I was twelve when Hitler took power. My parents weren't Nazi party members, but they didn't oppose them, either. My brother, Kurt, who is two years older than me, believed in the Nazi policies. He joined the *Wehrmacht* voluntarily in 1937. I was drafted right after the war started, but if I hadn't been, I still might have enlisted like my brother."

"Did you believe in the Nazi policies?" Loretta looked at Rolf, and Clara looked at Harold, wide-eyed. She wanted Loretta to stop asking such personal questions, but the look on her husband's face told her that Harold didn't object.

"No, and yes." He gathered his thoughts. "Hitler's rhetoric was hateful and divisive. Also illogical and nonsensical. I read enough to know the Nazis were destroying German democracy. But I grew up hearing how much better Germany was becoming under the Nazis. That made my parents happy, so we children were happy. I believed in Germany's right to recover our lost territories, in *lebensraum*, but I didn't hate the French and I didn't think Jews were responsible for Germany's defeat in 1918. And I didn't object to the Nazis who promoted these beliefs and other lies. I loved being in the *Hitlerjugend* with my friends. And when I went to university, I was too focused on me to worry about much else."

"I appreciate your honesty," said Harold.

"I don't want to give you the wrong impression that I was standing up to the Nazis when the war started, because I wasn't. I was naive and self-centered and ignorant."

"When was the last time you saw your brother, or your family?" asked Clara.

"We were all together for a few days in December 1942, when Kurt and I were home on leave at the same time. Then he returned to the Soviet Union, and I went back to Africa."

Loretta hesitated, then said, "So you were in the war for three and a half years, from October 1939 until you were captured?"

"For the first six months I was in training in Germany, and I was also home on leave twice. So, from 1940, I was fighting on one front for most of three years." Quietly, he said, "I was in the war, and now the war is in me." He cleared his throat. "This is the first time in many years that I've not been in combat on *Allerseelen*. Maybe that's why I'm thinking about it today, because I have the time to think. I'm beginning to understand how wasteful and immoral this war really is." He looked out the door. "And I think this is the first time I've said that out loud."

"Amen," said Harold. "This one is no different than every other war that's ever been fought."

Rolf smiled nervously. "I envy you. You've known this all along." Turning to Harold, he said, "Thank you again for the pamphlets. I read them."

"You're welcome. I may have another one or two to share with you if you'd like."

"I would, thank you, sir." Rolf grew tense. "But to be honest, knowing what you believe about nonviolence and comparing it to the life I've lived since 1940 is very painful."

"Where you've been is less important than where you're heading," said Harold quietly.

Loretta decided to try to lighten the now somber mood. She turned to Rolf and smiled, "I have one last question for today, if you don't mind, and I promise, it has nothing to do with war."

He smiled too. "Please, ask."

"Is becoming a doctor still your dream?"

"Absolutely. One day I hope to finish my training and do something good with my life."

"Medicine is a noble profession," said Harold with a wink. "Almost as noble as farming,"

"Thank you for telling us about yourself," said Clara. "I hope it didn't feel like an inquisition, three against one."

"Not at all, Mrs. Unruh. I appreciate having the chance to talk so freely with you. But I must ask a favor of you all."

"What is it, my boy?" said Harold.

"Please, don't say anything about what I've told you to the others. I would not have spoken so candidly if they had been here with us."

"Why is that?" asked Clara.

"What I said to you could be construed by other Germans as unpatriotic or even treasonous. In Germany, it's dangerous to say anything disparaging about Hitler or the war. And maybe it's the same here." He paused. "I don't discuss my views with anyone in camp."

"We will abide by your wishes," said Harold. "Now let's bow our heads to pray for peace. Then let's you and I go take a look at that fence we were talking about, see if it needs mending."

When they were alone, clearing the table and getting ready to wash the dishes, Loretta said, "Were you surprised to hear what Rolf said?"

"I suppose, maybe a little. It would seem he wants to turn away from his evil past. We must continue to set a good example for him." Clara stepped out to the well for another bucket of water to heat. When she returned, she asked, "What did you think?"

"I think he's suffered more than he will say. Maybe God sent him here to us to help him find Christ. I think maybe he has a Mennonite soul."

Clara turned to look at her daughter angrily. "You don't know that! He's only just left the battlefield where he waged war for years."

"And Joe is still on a battlefield."

"Loretta!" Clara was offended. "You're comparing Rolf to your brother?"

"Mama, I'm sorry if I offended you. All I'm saying is that Joe is in the Army against your wishes and the church's teachings because he did what he felt was necessary. And we know he's still a man of God, even if he is taking a path that none of us would have chosen for him."

"A different path? Joseph has put his eternal soul in jeopardy by joining the Army."

Loretta put her arm around her mother's shoulders and gave her a squeeze, hoping to comfort her. Tenderly, she said, "And yet, we know Joe has a Mennonite soul, Mama, we do. And we also know that God is all loving and all forgiving." Clara nodded. "All I'm saying is that after listening to Rolf today, I think the Lord is pointing him in the right direction and he's starting to recognize that."

"Perhaps," Clara turned to wash the dishes, still upset. "That doesn't change anything."

"What do you mean?"

"There's still no future for you and Rolf. You know all the reasons. I will not repeat them, only will I remind you that you must resist the temptation to think otherwise."

Loretta turned to get a fresh tea towel from a cupboard. As she did, she whispered to herself, "Too late."

The following week, all four of the Unruh's German helpers were back at work, but rain had also returned, so for a few days they were mostly confined to working indoors. One drippy morning, Loretta was in a storage shed near the barn to get a box of housewares for her mother when Harold sent Rolf to the same shed to scrape and paint a pair of benches. Loretta was reaching up to a high shelf with her back to the door when Rolf walked in, too quietly. When he said, "Here let me get that," he startled her. She jumped, and they both laughed. "I'm sorry. Please let me help you."

"That's all right, I can do it." She smiled. "I just need something to stand on."

"Please, allow me. I can reach it easier than you can. It's the least I can do for my friend." Before she could object, he stretched up and brought the box down to her, but he held onto it with her for a few seconds before letting go.

"Thank you."

"Of course. It's heavy, though. Do you want me to carry it for you?"

"No, thanks. I can manage, and now I should be getting back to the house."

As she turned to walk away, Rolf was desperate to say something to keep her there with him even a few moments longer. What he settled on sounded feeble, but it was all he could come up with. "Actually, I should be thanking you."

She turned around eagerly and stepped back toward him. "Why is that?"

*Mission accomplished*, he thought with a smile. "Well, to start with, I just called you my friend and you didn't object. I think maybe I even saw you smile just a little."

Loretta blushed. "We are friends, aren't we?" She looked into his eyes and held his gaze for another eternity before she had to look away with a shiver. "Is that okay with you?" What a silly question, but her mind was suddenly blank.

He laughed. "Yes, it's very much okay with me."

Now Loretta played coy. With a sideways glance, she spoke, "You said 'to start with.' What else should you be thanking me for?"

He smiled to know she was playing a little game. "I can't remember," he laughed and she smiled. "Oh, only this." He took a deep breath. "I must thank you for being the most wonderful woman I have ever met."

"Oh my. I don't know what to say. Should I say, 'you're welcome?'"

Rolf laughed. "If you like." He reached out and squeezed her arm just firmly enough for her to feel it through her coat, then let go. Their eyes met again. He said, "If only…" but didn't finish the sentence.

"I know," Loretta said. "I pray that God will show the way for us to be together."

"You do?"

"Yes. Because I think you are the most wonderful man I've ever met."

"You do?" Rolf staggered back, only half in jest. "Then I think I should pray too."

Loretta smiled. "That's a very good idea. But now I really have to go." As she turned and opened the door, she ran headlong into her mother. "Mama!"

"Why are you taking so long? I need that box." Then catching sight of Rolf still standing in the shadows in the shed, Clara said crisply, "What are you doing in there?"

"Mr. Unruh sent me to paint these," he said, pointing to two benches. He was telling the truth but was sure he sounded like he'd just robbed a bank.

"Then get to it."

"Yes, ma'am."

Clara was exasperated on their longer-than-before walk back to the house. "What were you doing in there with him?"

"Rolf came in while I was trying to get the box. It was up on a high shelf, and he helped get it for me."

"You were gone a very long time. So, I'll ask you again. What were you doing alone in the shed with Rolf?"

Loretta was now equally exasperated. "He helped me, Mama, and afterwards, we prayed." Seeing her mother's disbelief, she repeated herself, "That's right, we were praying."

Clara wanted to reprimand her daughter for lying or disrespecting her mother or both, but the look in Loretta's eyes told her not to. She shook her head, annoyed at being outmaneuvered. "It's time we started dinner."

*It's not really a lie*, thought Loretta. *At least not a big one*. Rolf and she did talk about praying. That should count. Now if she could just keep from smiling so broadly, maybe her mother would calm down.

A week later, Loretta walked down to the end of the lane and saw the little red metal flag on the mailbox was up, letting the family know the mailman had left something for them. Inside was an envelope from Joe, but it was addressed to Loretta and marked *"personal."* In all the time her brothers had been away, Loretta had never before received a letter addressed to only her from either of them. She tucked it into her coat pocket and would open it in her room after.

*Dear Sis,*

*If anyone sees this and wants to know why I'm writing to just you, tell them I'm asking about Christmas. That should throw them off the trail. (So, how's Christmas?) Ha!*

*A little bird sent me a letter saying she thinks you and one of the Germans POWs are sweet on each other. She said all she had to go on are hunches, but she's sure she's right.*

*In case she is, I'll tell you what I think, even though you didn't ask for my opinion and even though I shouldn't be giving advice to the lovelorn. Here it is: If he's a good guy and you're sure of that, there's no reason you shouldn't be interested in him. (Assuming that he's not a real Nazi.)*

*Maybe it's complicated, but you've never been one to give up just because something was hard. I still laugh about when you learned to ice skate on the pond. You were around seven or eight and kept falling. It was bitter cold and so funny! John and I couldn't stop laughing. Mama said you should come inside, but you wouldn't quit. You wobbled like a newborn colt on roller skates at first, but then you skated on blades better than any of us.*

*Back to this German ex-soldier. One day, I'll be an ex-soldier too. Should I be judged by that alone? I hope not.*

*And here's a little confession. I've met women since I left home that I could see myself falling for. One, a Catholic Italian girl, might have stolen my heart if we'd had more time. (Don't tell Mama!) The Italians were enemies too.*

*You've always been a good judge of character. Get to know the guy, be sure he deserves you, then do what <u>you</u> decide is best. Good luck! I'll say an extra prayer for you too!*

*And don't hold it against Little Bird for spilling the beans. She's a doodle, that one. I miss you both so much!*

*Not much new to report from here. I'm always tired, my feet are always wet, and the food is terrible, but I'm where I'm supposed to be. If you get a chance to say an extra prayer for me, that would be great too!*

*Your loving brother,*
*Joe*

After finishing the letter a second time, Loretta called down the stairs to ask Carol Ann to come up and help her move a dresser. As soon as they were in Loretta's room, she closed the door and stared at her sister, doing her best to intimidate her before saying, "What did you think you were doing, writing to Joe about Rolf and me?" Loretta shook the letter at her sister.

Carol Ann was unbowed. "You heard from Joe? What did he say? Let me see the letter!"

"Forget what he said. Why did you do this?"

"Because it's true." Carol Ann was unperturbed. "I'm not blind, I've watched you two talking. I see how he looks at you. You like each other, plain as the nose on your faces."

Loretta's voice cracked. "I smile at all of them! I want all of them to know how glad I am that they're doing the work that you and I used to have to do! Remember those days?"

"Baloney!" Carol Ann was calm, even arrogant. "You're friendly with the others, but there's something special going on between you and Rolf and has been since he got here."

"I don't know how you can say that."

"Because it's true."

"You've been reading too many romance novels!"

"I know what I see. So, what did Joe say?"

"Never mind!"

"You and Rolf would make a good couple." And she asked again, "What did Joe say?"

"He said it was my decision."

"Aha! So, you do have a decision to make, eh?"

"I didn't say that."

"You didn't have to."

"You shouldn't be butting into other people's business!"

"I think you're having a hard time admitting you like him because of what the folks might say. Since you don't listen to me, I thought maybe Joe could help you figure things out."

"There's nothing to figure out!"

"Oh yeah? You still haven't said it's not true. Tell me I'm wrong about you and Rolf."

Loretta ignored her. "You've got me in a pickle, you know that? Getting a letter from Joe that's only for me? If the folks find out, they'll want to read it. Thank heaven I got the mail myself today. But now I'm hiding something from them. I hate that."

"You're only hiding something from yourself."

Loretta glared indignantly. "You have an answer for everything, don't you"

"At least I do have an answer. You still haven't answered me."

"Enough already!"

Carol Ann walked over to Loretta and hugged her. "I know I'm a bee in your bonnet sometimes, but I want you to be happy. And I'm glad Joe wrote to you."

Since the day she was born, it was hard to stay mad at Carol Ann for long about anything. "I love you too. Now it's almost time to say evening prayers so let's get down there. And not a word of this to Mama and Papa, you understand?"

"Of course. And I promise not to write any more letters to Joe. My work is done here." Carol Ann laughed and bounced down the stairs to the kitchen.

⌖⌖⌖⌖⌖⌖⌖

On the Sunday following Thanksgiving in 1943, the Peabody POW subcamp moved. It was originally supposed to be open for only a few months, from September until the end of the harvest in early November. But when the harvest was finished, farmers and business owners asked to be allowed to continue employing POWs indefinitely. The Army agreed but couldn't house the Germans and their guards in canvas tents through a Kansas winter, so after a brief search, the Eyestone Building, a large, two-storied brick structure close to downtown on Second Street, was requisitioned to serve as the Peabody POW subcamp. It was quickly outfitted with furniture and equipment, guard towers were constructed, and a fence was built. Guard quarters were upstairs and POWs occupied the first floor, which also had a kitchen, dining hall, and offices. The space was crowded, but adequate.

Shortly after the move, Rolf was half asleep on his bunk on a chilly Sunday evening when Jordan, who was on night duty, nonchalantly told him to come to the front office.

"There's someone here to see you," he said with a conspiratorial look as soon as they were out of earshot of anyone else.

Rolf shook his head in confusion. "What? Who?"

"Loretta Unruh." Jordan waited for Rolf's jaw to drop, then continued, "She came to see if I could give you something from her. I knew she liked you, so I said she should give it to you herself. She can't come in, but it's quiet outside and no one's watching, so you can step outside to meet her. She's waiting. But you have to be careful, and you have to come right back."

"You knew?" Rolf was dazed.

"Of course I knew. And you like her too. I may be old, but I'm not dead!" Jordan smiled.

"You knew that too?" He was sure Jordan could hear his heart pounding.

"It was pretty obvious. Since the first day you met, I've seen sparks fly every time you two look at each other. It's a wonder Mrs. Unruh hasn't had you shipped off!"

Looking at Jordan with continued incredulity, Rolf shook his head and repeated to himself. "You knew."

Jordan snapped his fingers twice like he was trying to bring Rolf out of a hypnotic trance. "Yes, you said that. Now do you want to go on debating this, or do you want to go out to her?"

"Of course I want to go."

"Then let's get going before we get busted." He handed Rolf an Army-issue winter jacket and flap cap. "Here, put these on, then go straight out and cross the street."

"Okay."

"And Mueller?"

"Yes?"

"Treat her with respect or I swear I will…"

Rolf cut him off and said seriously, "Of course I will."

"I'm trusting you, Rolf. Don't make me regret this."

Rolf nodded and stepped into the night. He moved tentatively toward the shadows across the street until Loretta stepped out of the darkness long enough for him to see her. "Follow me," she said anxiously as they set out going east on Second Street. The town was Sunday-night quiet; they saw no one else outside. After a block or so, they turned south and came to a small hedge-lined field near where the tent camp used to be.

"Where are we?" he whispered.

"The Slaymaker pasture. It's the only place close that I could think of where no one would see us." They found bales of straw near the trees and sat down on one. Side by side, they looked out into the pasture, waiting for their eyes to focus in the moonlight and trying to grasp the magnitude of what was happening. Loretta picked nervously at prickly pieces of straw clinging to her wool coat, until Rolf timidly reached over and took her hand in his. The resulting shock jolted them like they'd each put a finger in a toaster. It was the first time they'd ever held hands. He was afraid she would pull away, but she didn't.

"I'm touching you," Rolf whispered. "We're touching."

Loretta smiled, still looking out over the pasture. "I only came to town to give you something that I couldn't give to you at home. It's nothing, really. I had no idea I'd be seeing you tonight. I still can't believe Greg thought this was a good idea."

"He knew."

"He knew what?"

"That we like each other. He's just trying to help us out."

Loretta shook her head. "I can't believe we were so indiscreet."

Rolf laughed. "I don't think we were, but I do admit that I knew you were someone special since the morning we met."

"This is insane. What if we get caught?"

Looking up at the moon, he replied, "It is completely insane, but you're here and I'm here. And I'm glad." He squeezed her hand and leaned into her ever so slightly. "And if we get caught, I will still be happy. Of course, I'll have to say I was kidnapped and don't know how I ended up here in a meadow in the night."

"You would say I kidnapped you?" She laughed.

"I would have to," he said with mock seriousness. "I live in a prison camp, remember? I couldn't just walk out the door and start kidnapping you, could I?"

She laughed again and relaxed. "You don't think I'm too forward, agreeing to walk out here alone with you? I'm not like this, really!"

He laughed. "I think I have a good idea of who you are." He snuck a glance at her.

"But you barely know me, and I barely know you." She paused. "Even so," her voice quivered slightly, "we don't have much time, but it's more than we've ever had, so I should say something while I have the chance."

"Say what?"

"I'm sure that I want to be more than friends with you. And I'm sure this feeling isn't going away. And I'm willing to wait as long as it takes to get this all sorted out."

"Really?"

"Yes, really." Now she turned to face him and spoke more quickly. "I listened to you talk about your dream of going to medical school. I heard you encouraging me to become a teacher. I've listened to you talking with Papa about all sorts of topics. I know how much you've helped our family these past few months, and I hear how polite you are to my mother and tonight I see how much Greg trusts you." She drew a deep breath and sighed, "I feel like there's already a connection between us. And to me that's bigger and stronger than all the things that stand in our way. True, I don't know everything about you, but I see your goodness."

Now Rolf picked at straw with his free hand and hoped she wouldn't see the tears in his eyes. All he could say was, "Wow," in a voice barely above a whisper.

She laughed nervously. "But maybe this is all too crazy for you right now. Maybe you think it's pathetic how this American girl is throwing herself at you like this." When he didn't respond immediately, she added, trembling, "Rolf, is that what you think? If so, just tell me, please."

He was trembling, too, as he pulled her close. Looking into her beautiful, worried eyes, he slowly moved in and kissed her lightly and withdrew. Then they closed their eyes and kissed deeply and passionately. Nothing separated them. For that perfect moment, each inhaled the other's joy, and their trembling ceased. Each would never forget the sweetness of the other's lips that night.

"I love you, Loretta," he said as he again drew her in closer. He felt her heartbeat.

"I love you," she said, and kissed him again.

"Thank you." Gently, he wiped a moonlit tear from her cheek, then lightly traced the contours of her cheeks and chin with his fingertips as if trying to commit her face to his memory.

They held each other for a few moments, then she reached into her pocket. "This is what I came to give you. You can read it when you need me. And now we have to go."

They stood, embraced, and kissed again, then retraced their steps back to the Eyestone Building. After a last hug in the shadows, Rolf crossed the street to the door where Jordan was waiting anxiously, and Loretta ducked around a corner to the car.

The farm was dark when she drove up the lane. She tiptoed up the stairs and changed into her flannel nightgown. She pulled back her bed covers, but then walked across the hall instead, to snuggle beside her sister. Carol Ann woke up enough to say, "Hi, are you cold tonight?"

"A little. I hope you don't mind."

"No problem." Now awake, Carol Ann rolled over to face her sister. "How was church?"

"Fine."

"And how was Doris? You said you were meeting her there, right?"

"Yes."

"Well, that's odd," said Carol Ann, barely able to contain herself, "because Doris called while you were gone, asking for you. Quite a while ago."

"Oh, no! Dear Sweet Jesus!" Loretta was overcome with panic.

"I don't know if Jesus is listening or if He's gone to bed. It is very late. But I helped you out."

"How?"

"I happened to be the one who answered the phone and after we hung up, I told Mama and Papa that it was your friend, Agnes Spielbush, calling just to say hello to you."

"Did they believe you?"

"Of course," Carol Ann said with a giggle. "I'm pretty good when it comes to stretching the truth when I have to."

Loretta rolled her eyes and laughed. "That's not really something to brag about, but thanks."

"I'm thinking that you're also getting pretty good at doing the same thing." Loretta didn't know what to say. "Don't worry, I'm not going to ask you what you were up to."

Loretta laughed, "You wouldn't believe me if I did." She hugged her sister tightly. "Good night, Carol Ann. I love you," she said. "And thank you again." Then she turned over to face the window where moonlight was streaming in from the same beautiful moon that had just been shining down so brightly on Rolf and her.

"Good night, Loretta. I love you, and I'm happy for you."

In the dark dormitory, Rolf slipped off his clothes and quietly climbed into his bunk, not entirely unnoticed. He closed his eyes, but sleep would not come. When at last the room was sufficiently suffused with dawn's first light, he lifted a single sheet from the envelope. On it was a poem, *Nearness of the Beloved One*, by Johann von Goethe, handwritten in German, but with no accompanying letter or identifying signature. Von Goethe was a favorite poet of his—how could she know? He slowly read the familiar words and lingered over two lines:

*In the quiet grove I often go to listen when all is silent.*

*I am with you, however far away you may be, you are next to me!*

As he was dressing for work shortly afterwards, he looked out on the most beautiful sunrise he'd ever seen.

# Chapter 26
# A WOUNDED HEART

When he picked up his workers that morning, Harold was less jovial than usual. And when they gathered in the kitchen for dinner, Rolf thought Clara wasn't herself, either. As the women served dessert, Harold cleared his throat, signaling that he had something to say, but then he looked out the window. The Germans eyed each other warily. Rolf felt especially conspicuous. He risked a long glance at Loretta, asking with his eyes if she knew what Harold wanted to say, but she looked more apprehensive than he. Had her parents found out where she'd been the night before? Was he going to be reported? Were they all going to be fired?

Fortified by a sip of coffee, Harold finally began, "We have some news. But first, I can't tell you how much we appreciate all you've done for us these past three months. I've said it before—you've all been a godsend, even more of a blessing than we expected." Smiles around the table made it easier for him to continue. "The farm is in better shape today than since John and Joseph left, because of you men. We are very thankful."

Ingratiatingly, Hecht said, "You're welcome, sir. It's a pleasure to be here with you and your family." He glanced at Loretta. "I didn't expect to enjoy working on an American farm, but I do. Thank you for hiring me, and thank you, ladies, for feeding me so well."

"I'm glad," said Harold, "and now we have to make changes." He cleared his throat again and spoke faster. "With winter here, it doesn't make sense to have all four of you coming out every day. You've gotten so much done that now there's not enough work to keep everybody busy until we're back in the fields. I spoke to Lieutenant Stevenson. He said we could cut back to two men over the winter, so that's what we're gonna do."

The men said nothing until Hecht asked, "Do you know who you'll be keeping?"

"It's hard because you've all done such a fine job, and we work so well as a team, don't we? But I'm asking for Anton and Rolf to stay. Anton is the best mechanic, so he can help me with the machinery indoors while it's cold outside. And Rolf is the most familiar with farm animals, so I'll have him help with the livestock." Harold's expression told just how much he hated having to make this decision and risk hurting anyone's feelings.

Rolf and Loretta were relieved—their secret was apparently safe, and they would still get to see each other—but they did not want to seem happy at the expense of others. Gralke smiled slightly and Zimmerman gave a little frown, but Hecht's negative reaction was overt. His face flashed disappointment tinged with anger before it settled into a contrived, chalky smile.

Zimmerman spoke first. "We understand, Mr. Unruh."

"Thank you, Erich. And you, too, Otto." Hecht wouldn't look at Harold. "And there is some good news in all of this."

"What's that?" Hecht's tone was dismissive.

"The Army's going to keep this camp going next year because the demand for labor is still so strong around here, so neither of you will have to leave Peabody. The lieutenant told me they have winter jobs in town for you, but I can hire you back whenever I need you because agriculture still gets the highest priority. So, in March or April, we should have the whole gang together again."

"Do you know what we'll be doing until then?" Zimmerman inquired.

"For one thing, men are needed to cut firewood because of the coal shortage. That shouldn't be any harder than baling hay on a hot day, right?"

"When do we have to leave here?" Hecht looked and sounded like a pouting child.

Harold winced. "Well, I asked to have all of you through this week, but the lieutenant said you could start new jobs tomorrow, so this will be the last day for us to all be together." He continued to try to placate Hecht, "This is only temporary, Otto, only a few months. I hope you understand."

Hecht's eyes narrowed. "I understand perfectly," he said with exaggerated sincerity.

The afternoon passed slowly and awkwardly. On the drive into town, Rolf felt Hecht's glare. Feeling obliged to say something, he turned to Zimmerman and he as they walked into the Eyestone Building, "It's been good working with you both."

"Shut your fucking mouth!" Hecht spat the words out like a rattlesnake shooting venom. "And don't lie—you're glad about this! Such a worthless shit, always trying to make yourself look so smart. You probably set this all up."

"I didn't know anything about this until you did," Rolf said as Hecht stomped off.

Gralke shrugged. "He's pissed because he has this crazy idea about him and Loretta getting together. Now he won't be around her."

Rolf had suspected as much but still felt bad. "I hope he calms down."

"He's just a sore loser."

The next morning, Harold was picking Rolf and Gralke up when Hecht came out to meet his new employer. Harold greeted him warmly, but Hecht childishly walked by without a word.

⊹⊱⊰⊹⊱⊰⊹

With the changes came an unexpected gift: Harold asked Rolf to help Loretta with the milking each afternoon, meaning the two of them would be alone until Carol Ann got home from school. Clara strongly objected but had to allow it. A woman in their church was deathly ill and the congregation was caring for her, her husband, and their four children. Clara was asked to stay with the family from two to six every afternoon. Without hesitation, she said yes, but it meant she wouldn't be home to milk, and Loretta couldn't do it by herself.

Rolf and Loretta were thrilled. Their afternoons became get-acquainted sessions while they worked. They learned things about each other that they might have picked up if their courtship had been more conventional. Their conversations flowed easily. They joked and laughed and shared details about each other's families, childhood memories, past romances, favorite musicians and movies, pastimes, and the future. They found an unexpected degree of common ground in their core values, surprising considering their vastly different backgrounds.

There was one subject about which Rolf was not ready to share details with Loretta: His time in the *Wehrmacht*. Loretta broached the subject once, and he spoke generally about dates, times, places, and non-combat memories. Then he apologized and said he wasn't ready to talk about the fighting. By the look in his eyes, Loretta understood. "Only when you're ready," she said as she put a hand on his shoulder.

Out of respect for each other and fear of scandalizing others, which could cause their limited moments together to be taken away altogether, Rolf and Loretta avoided physical intimacy. There was, however, one afternoon when Clara was at the sick woman's house, Harold and Gralke were in Peabody to buy supplies, and Carol Ann was not yet home from school. With the farm to themselves, a little flirtation turned into hugging and kissing, then some serious kissing and hugging and several heartfelt I love yous.

When he finally managed to pull himself away from her and return to the milking, Rolf was both elated and guilty. "As much as I love to kiss you, we shouldn't do that here, even when we think we're alone. It's too risky, especially for you, and it's disrespectful of your parents."

Loretta saw him blush and said, "I love how you worry about me and my parents." She stepped out of the barn and surveyed the farm to confirm that the others were still gone, came back inside, and said, "It's still just us here, except for the cows." She gave Rolf a peck on the cheek, then walked up to a Holstein in a milking stall. She patted the cow, named Fannie, on the rump, laughed and spoke into her ear, "Fannie, you didn't see anything here today, did you?" After pretending to wait for a reply, she added, "No? Okay, that's good for my boyfriend and me, and it's especially good for you. Because if you had seen something and you were planning on ratting us out," and now Loretta spoke ominously, "you and your sisters will all be ground beef by tomorrow morning!"

Rolf laughed and said, "Boyfriend, eh? I like that. But remind me never to cross you!"

"That's a good idea!" And they embraced and kissed once more.

Coming in from work a week later at dusk, Rolf and Gralke saw Streicher with Stevenson in the Eyestone Building's brightly lit office. Hecht was there, too, and a translator.

"I wonder what's that all about?" said Gralke. "Nothing good, I'm sure."

At his bunk, Rolf's found his bed torn apart and his things strewn around, but before he could make sense of what had happened, a guard told him to report to the office, where Stevenson called him in immediately. "Mueller, do you know Major Streicher?"

Before he could reply, Hecht snapped to attention and saluted Rolf as his *Wehrmacht* superior, nearly shouting "*Seig heil!*"

Rolf almost laughed, and Stevenson's eyes widened. Salutes were rare in Peabody, usually just exchanged between the Americans, and even then, not often. But under Streicher's icy stare, Rolf's body stiffened instinctively, and he saluted everyone.

Stevenson said, "Major Streicher is here on behalf of the German officers in Concordia to inspect our subcamp and meet with your POW representative, Private Hecht."

Rolf looked puzzled. "Sir, I didn't know that Private Hecht was our representative."

Major Streicher interjected, "Of course he is, Gefreiter. You should pay better attention."

Warning bells ringing in his head, Rolf found himself reverting to the syncopated cadence and huskier resonance of a *Wehrmacht* soldier. "Yes, sir," he snapped, eyes fixed straight ahead.

"*Soldat* Hecht is authorized to speak for everyone incarcerated here and to report to his superior officers." By his sideways look at Stevenson and his inflection, Streicher made it clear that only German officers were the POWs' true superiors.

Stevenson ignored the barb. "As I was saying, in the course of his visit and conversations with Private Hecht, the major has learned of several possible infractions that you may have committed. He's just informed me of these allegations." Seeing Rolf's confused look, he went on, "According to him, you drove a tractor on your employer's farm, ate in his house, and fraternized alone with an American woman, all in violation of regulations."

"Sir, I can explain," said Rolf. Hecht stared blankly at him.

"Silence!" Streicher cut him off.

Stevenson shot the older German officer who outranked him a warning glance. "And there's a more serious allegation, that you left the Eyestone Building in the middle of the night earlier this month for more than an hour to meet a woman." Rolf was dumbfounded. "A search of your footlocker and bunk this afternoon found no contraband, but there was a note in German, perhaps written in a woman's hand, that may corroborate the statements made to Major Streicher." Rolf was sickened to think that his and Loretta's relationship had been discovered and violated by peering eyes and prying fingers.

"In light of all this, your assignment at the Unruh farm must be terminated. And while this alleged escape, perhaps with the complicity of a guard, is investigated, you're being sent back to Camp Concordia. Major Streicher is returning this evening, and you'll go with him. You'll have the opportunity to respond to these allegations there. Is that understood?"

Rolf felt weak in the knees. "Yes, sir."

With dripping sanctimony and shameless hypocrisy, the pompous German officer said, "*Gefreiter* Mueller, you were ordered to strictly comply with all the terms of your incarceration. Your actions bring dishonor to the *Wehrmacht*. You jeopardize the positive relations we are striving so hard to develop and maintain with the Americans."

Lieutenant Stevenson glowered at Streicher once more, then spoke calmly and evenly to Rolf, "Go get all your things, and report back here in ten minutes. We'll get you some C-rations to eat on the way. Do you have any questions?"

"No, sir."

"Then you're dismissed, Corporal."

Rolf barely had the presence of mind to salute before he left the room. As he walked back to his bunk, a hundred pairs of eyes were locked on him. The news had traveled fast.

Gralke and Zimmerman came over to his bunk to say how sorry they were, and Zimmerman added, "You know we didn't say anything to get you in trouble, right?"

Rolf scowled, "I know who's behind this."

"You won't tell anyone about us fraternizing with the Americans, too, will you?"

"Certainly not." The apprehension in their eyes reminded him of other friends in past battles. As then, he tried to reassure his comrades. "Don't worry, this will all get sorted out. The allegations really are bullshit. But Anton, would you do me a favor?"

"Sure, anything."

"Please thank Mr. and Mrs. Unruh for me, for everything. Tell them I'm really sorry I can't say good-bye, but don't let on about what's happened. Just say that I unexpectedly had to go back to Concordia for a few days." He paused long enough to decide that Zimmerman and Gralke probably already knew that he and Loretta were romantically involved, then he added, "And if you can do it quietly, please tell Loretta that I'll be in touch somehow. Tell her I've been in battles worse than this and always made it through, even if I did get shot once in a while." Rolf gave a wane smile. "Wait, don't tell her that last part." Neither of his friends was surprised that he would have a special message for Loretta.

Streicher was already waiting in the truck when Rolf returned to the front of the building. At the office, Stevenson called him in. "Mueller, I'm sorry about all this."

"Thank you, sir."

The lieutenant added cryptically, "Have you heard anything about Concordia lately?"

"No, sir, should I have?"

"Look, just be very careful about who you talk to and what you say up there. I'll send a letter telling them what an exemplary prisoner you've been."

"Thank you, sir." Rolf wished he could have learned what Jordan knew or what his story was, but he was off duty. Another guard motioned him toward the truck.

Hecht was waiting for him near the front door. An initial urge to punch the bastard in the face rose but then faded as he recalled Loretta's words—*I see your goodness*. Instead of striking him, Rolf looked at his rival and said, "I really did enjoy working with you. You did a good job." Hecht's only response was a triumphant, dismissive smirk.

As he stepped out into the dark, Rolf saw in a flash of clarity all of Hecht's pettiness, jealousy, fear, and, especially, his chronic sense of victimhood. Hecht personified perfectly all that was wrong with his beloved Germany.

# Chapter 27

# HONOR

They sat across from each other in the back of the small, dank Army transport, alone except for a guard near the tailgate. The canvas top kept most of the wind out, but it was still cold. And eerie. The flickering light from a kerosene lamp cast strangely elongated, swaying shadows on and around them as the truck rattled toward Concordia.

Rolf tucked himself down into his coat and avoided eye contact with Streicher as he calculated how much trouble he was in. When they arrived in August (how long ago that now seemed), the Concordia commander had said that escapees couldn't be punished more severely than with isolation, and escape was the most serious charge against him. Surely the punishment for the other infractions wouldn't be more severe than that. He might not get to work outside camp again and he'd been sent away from Loretta, but that should be the worst of it, he decided.

Across from him, Streicher was sizing Rolf up like a wolf eying a spring lamb. After testing the guard to be sure he didn't understand German, he spoke, "You never learned, even though you were warned."

Rolf gave no response, surprised that he felt no obligation to maintain the pretense of military decorum now or to afford Streicher any undeserved respect.

The major was undeterred. "I knew you were disloyal the day I saw you on the ship talking so freely to that guard. You're a discredit to the Fatherland." Still getting no reaction, he went on, "You think your oath to the *Fuehrer* no longer matters, but you're wrong. Your friend, Stultzman, was mistaken too."

Rolf's eyes opened involuntarily at the mention of his friend. "What about Willy?"

"Stultzman was a traitor! He was a provocateur who spoke against the *Fuehrer* and the Fatherland. He didn't care who heard, so now he's paid the price."

"What price?"

"He's dead," the major said, as nonchalantly as if he was mentioning a piece of trash lying on the truck bed, but he quickly sharpened his next words into daggers, which he thrust into Rolf. "The traitor hanged himself last week. You didn't know? Well, now you do."

Sucker-punched, Rolf exhaled audibly. "Is this a joke? Willy would never, ever commit suicide. He was glad to be in America and out from under goddamned officers like you."

"Ah, but he did. And this is no joke, I assure you."

"There's no way he would have taken his own life."

Streicher looked toward the dozing guard, then smiled cruelly, "Of course he wouldn't. But when given the choice between ending his pathetic life and having his family punished for his crimes, he suddenly became heroic. Too late though, since the authorities in München are already being notified. His family will likely still be arrested for encouraging such a traitor."

Rolf wiped his eyes. "You forced him to kill himself? Why? Whatever he said or did, what possible difference could it make now?"

"Cowards like Stultzman and you are the reason the Reich is struggling! We lost North Africa not because the Allies were stronger, not because our leadership erred, but because scum like you wouldn't fight harder. All miscreants must be disciplined or eliminated. Loyalty and order are more crucial now than ever."

"Cowards? While you were sitting on your ass and watching the war from the rear, we were wallowing in blood and guts. I did what I was ordered to do. I did things I never wanted to do, all for the Reich and all for Hitler. I fought to the end. Willy did too. I was captured while lying unconscious in a fucking hospital bed! Willy..."

"Stultzman surrendered! Gave up! And then he had the audacity to brag about it."

"Bullshit! He and some others were trapped! One was severely wounded. They were out of ammunition. What did you want him to do—attack the Americans barehanded?"

"Yes! That's exactly what any German soldier with a drop of honorable blood would have done! That is what our *Fuehrer* expects, nothing less."

"You're crazy! And Hitler's fucking crazy too!" Rolf could not hold back.

Streicher leaned forward and smirked. "And there we have it, another traitor!"

Words poured out in an angry torrent. "I'm a traitor? After I fought through Belgium, France, Algeria, Tunisia? After I did my best for the Fatherland even though the *Fuehrer* and feckless officers like you put us in a hopeless situation? You got Germany into war on two fronts, stretched the *Wehrmacht* beyond sustainability, made America our enemy when that could and should have been avoided. After all that, I'm the traitor?"

"Your own words indict you. You think you know better than your superiors? You, a student from a shit-hole Westphalen farm?" Seeing Rolf's surprise, he went on, "Yes, I know all about you, Mueller. You swore to fight to your last breath. Well, you're still breathing, but I don't see you fighting. Instead, you're aiding our enemies and happy to do so as long as your belly is full and an American woman bats her eyes at you. You're a traitor, and you'll pay the price too."

The guard looked their way and told them to keep it down.

The major continued quietly, but still emphatically. "You dare to complain about the *Fuehrer* now, when things are difficult. But if you really thought he was so wrong, why didn't you object before? I'll tell you why, because when the *Fuehrer* and the Party were making our country strong again, you were happy to ride along on our coattails. Parasites like you and Stultzman cheered the loudest when the Sudetens and Austrians were brought back into the Reich as our country grew powerful, prosperous, and proud again, when once more there was food and work for everyone. You were all cheering then."

Streicher's words hit their mark. Rolf flinched remembering how ardently he'd supported the *Fuehrer* in the beginning. He loved his years in the *Hitlerjugend*. He was proud when Germany tore up the Treaty of Versailles. He bragged when his brother marched into Austria and Poland. He was thrilled when his parents took the family to Nürnberg in 1935 for the Nazi rally. The Muellers weren't Party members, but it was exhilarating to be part of the glorious future that Adolf Hitler was creating for them all. It all came back in a bitter rush.

And the major wasn't finished. "Now look at you. Things become challenging and you crumble. You dare to presume the Reich will fall, you wave the flag of surrender. You whine and complain, blame everyone except yourself. Look in a mirror if you want to blame someone. If you and Stultzman and men like you had fought to the end, the war would long be over, and Germany would be at peace and stable. Even now, you had a perfect opportunity to serve your country right here in the belly of the beast, but instead you helped the enemy feed that belly."

Rolf was rattled. "Tell me, what did your lackey do to sabotage America? Hecht and I worked side by side for three months. I never saw him do anything to further the cause of the Reich on that farm, but I recall him eating at the same table with me."

"You coerced *Soldat* Hecht through your superior physical strength. You threatened him. He told me what happened. And now you blame him. So disgraceful, using your strength against a fellow German, but not against the enemy!"

Rolf slipped into a jumbled maze of thoughts and emotions. His best friend was dead, and now the major's truth-laced diatribe burned like fire. The familiar loop began in his head again: *I did things I never wanted to do. I did only what I had to do. I'm only twenty-three. I only did what you made me do!* He felt his foot tapping involuntarily on the truck bed. He hoped Streicher wouldn't notice.

But the major did notice. With a sneer, he said, "I loathe you, Mueller."

After a few minutes, the voices in his head quieted and his foot relaxed. Languidly, he asked, "Why now?"

"Why now what?"

"Why are you telling me all this now? We'll never agree. I'm not going to sabotage American farms or hurt civilians, regardless of what you try to order me to do. Are you telling me this out of pure hatred because Willy was my friend? Are you that morally contemptible?"

"Because your time is almost here."

"What is that supposed to mean?" he asked trepidatiously.

"You're to be tried at once by a tribunal of those German officers you despise so much. If found guilty, as Stultzman was, you'll be sentenced and punished accordingly. Since I've heard your treasonous words myself, it will be a very short trial."

Willy's warning in Tunisia came back like a slap to the face: The real danger to them came not from the Americans, but from their fellow prisoners. The foxes were in charge of the henhouse. But how? They were all POWs. "You have no authority here. I'll tell the Americans everything and refuse to participate in your kangaroo court." Even as he said the words, he sensed danger, and that realization was bringing him out of his grief-and guilt-induced stupor.

Streicher laughed. "Please, tell the Americans everything I've just said. Do you really think they'll believe a German *gefreiter* who's broken their rules and slipped out of their prison, probably aided by one of their own guards? No American officer will want to have anything to do with you or your wild accusations. Their Army, like the *Wehrmacht*, is based on order and discipline. They'll never let you speak freely because you might embarrass them too much. How would it look if it became known that the Americans can't keep their enlisted men from helping German escapees or, worse, can't control the German officers? Go ahead, tell them everything."

Rolf's silence told Streicher that he was still in control.

"But if you become too outspoken or incite further insubordination, do you really think that you'll go home one day and fall into the loving arms of your family?"

Rolf's body tightened, and he began to respond, but couldn't.

"We managed to confiscate a couple letters out of your personal belongings today, so we know exactly how and where to find your family if necessary."

"You'll regret these threats," Rolf spat the words out through gritted teeth.

"Will I? Well, here's one more: Don't forget that *Soldat* Hecht is still in Peabody. With you gone, he hopes to return to the farm where you both worked, where he can now take steps to render it unproductive. And if you do anything particularly stupid, I will order him to eliminate your American girlfriend." He smiled at Rolf's wide-eyed, slack-jawed expression. "I mean, how hard would it be for her to accidentally fall into a well? He awaits my orders and is prepared to fulfill his duties without hesitation. He will serve the Fatherland to his last breath."

"If you had any honor, you'd keep innocent people out of this."

"This is war, Mueller! Honor comes only from serving the *Fuehrer*! Nothing else! It's really quite simple: If you cooperate, the girl will be spared. But if you commit further acts of sedition or treason, she and her family will suffer, and it will be because of you."

He knew he could not trust Streicher, but his only option at the moment was to switch tactics to sound compliant. "I'll do what you want, as long as my family and the Unruhs will not be harmed."

"It's all up to you." The major paused. "When we get to Concordia, you'll await instructions on the time and place for your trial. Until then, keep your mouth shut. There are still loyal *Wehrmacht* soldiers like Hecht there, so I'll know everything you do and say. Do I make myself clear?" Rolf nodded weakly, whereupon the major dismissed him, saying, "Now, I'm tired of talking to vermin like you." He leaned back, pulled his collar up, and turned away. Even with his eyes shut, the major looked consummately evil.

Rolf closed his eyes, too, to separate himself from that evil. For several minutes, maybe longer, he was paralyzed with fear, but then he began to calm himself down enough to evaluate the situation logically. First, he knew he would have to wait to grieve Willy properly until after the threats to himself and those he loved were neutralized. Secondly, taking Streicher's words at face value, he realized he'd have to act quickly if he was going to make it through this.

The major had underestimated Rolf. True, he was young and the son of simple farmers, but after so many life-or-death battles, he excelled at staying calm under fire. Streicher, Germany itself, had just declared war on him. It would be unlike the war he'd recently fought in, but the principles of engagement were the same. He would identify and prioritize the threats, then inventory his strengths—weapons, skills, possible allies—and his vulnerabilities. After that, he should know what to do.

Streicher slept, but not Rolf. By the time they arrived in Concordia, his threat assessment was complete and a rudimentary outline for action was taking shape. There were variables to consider and much more information was needed, but his emotions were back under control.

It was after 10 o'clock when the truck came to a stop on the road between the sprawling camp's compounds. Streicher strode off with a guard without acknowledging Rolf further. Another guard confirmed Rolf's identity and looked at his clipboard. "There's a bunk open in Barracks 3 of EM Compound 2. Let's assign you there for tonight. Do you know your way?"

"Yes, sir, I do. That's where I was assigned the last time I was here."

"Good," and the guard escorted him to the barracks door.

He found his way to the empty bunk and smiled. Willy had likely stayed on in the same barracks after Rolf left for Peabody. With a shiver, he wondered if this was the same bunk that Willy had slept on a few days earlier. The thought saddened him, but then he found a strange comfort in the coincidence. A coincidence that Willy would have liked. And being in this barracks meant that someone still here might know more about what happened. Reconnaissance would start in the morning. First, though, he needed sleep. Rolf was in combat mode, but not restless. Knowing a battle was imminent had never rattled him as long as he had a plan. And now he did. He was going to escape.

# Chapter 28

# ONE LUCKY DUCK

Daybreak, however, brought harsh rays of reality. Rolf had slept well, but was wide-eyed at first light with a stark awareness that the idea of trying to escape from this prison was patently ridiculous. But what else could he do to try to protect everyone? With one foot tapping against his bunk's footboard, he forced himself to reopen his internal deliberations and re-review the options. He could tell the Americans in Concordia what had happened to Willy, but Streicher was right—they might not listen to him. He could offer to let the Americans use him as bait to expose the Nazis' subversion of their authority in camp, but who knew if the Americans cared what Germans did to one another so long as they didn't threaten any Americans. He might try to enlist like-minded Germans against the officers, but that would take time and risked exposing himself to men who might betray him and make his situation even more precarious.

Another option was to go on a physical offensive, bash a few heads, and send the message to Streicher that he would not go quietly. Rolf was strong enough again but had no way of knowing how outnumbered he would be. And this approach would commit him to a long-term struggle, and it would probably do little to protect his family or the Unruhs. Moreover, he was no longer certain that he had what it would take to be so violent. With increasing frequency since Tunisia, he'd found himself looking back with detached amazement at how brutal his life as a soldier had been, how savagery seemed so normal then, so acceptable. Each memory now made him queasy. He questioned whether he could revert to such ruthlessness, no matter how reprehensible Streicher was nor how necessary he might tell himself violence was. Merely threatening Hecht a few months earlier had left him uncomfortable. What's more, after seeing firsthand how the Unruhs lived and how seriously they are committed to their faith, Rolf felt that using violence against anyone, even the most heinous of men like Streicher, would violate Loretta's trust in him.

And so, he returned to his previously inescapable conclusion: Escape was his only option. No more second-guessing. Now he must prepare to act, and soon. The officers would surely move quickly in order to make another example of him and maintain their control by intimidation in Concordia. He expected they would try to force him to commit suicide, like Willy. Failing that, they would probably kill him outright, and the sooner, the better. Even staying in Concordia a few more days would be dangerous.

Escape was the best option for his family too. If word got out that a POW had attempted an escape in the heart of America, how could he be a traitor to the Fatherland? To his knowledge, no German had done so. His family might even be commended for his bravery. At the very least, authorities in Germany might be unwilling to arrest them, regardless of what Streicher said. It wasn't foolproof, but it was better than nothing. And escaping could also ease the threat to the Unruhs, assuming he made it back to Doyle Creek. Even just a few minutes there would be long enough for him to warn them about Hecht and tell them not to hire any other Germans. He was sure they would believe him.

Before he was out of bed, Rolf was mentally outlining his next steps. Based on the fact that he was sent to a regular barracks last night and not to the disciplinary barracks, it was likely that he would have the ability to move about Camp Concordia as he did when he was there in the summer. So, he'd begin by discreetly searching for an escape route. Armed guards in towers scanning the camp's floodlit, barbed-wire perimeter would make jumping the fence difficult, if not impossible, so he'd focus on finding some other way to slip out. Secondly, he'd try to find out what really happened to Willy.

Dressing quickly in the cold, he muttered hellos to those near him, but there were no familiar faces until he was returning from the latrine, when a vaguely recognizable man came toward him. "Haven't seen you in awhile," said the man. "Were you at some subcamp?"

"Yes, I got back last night." Rolf was circumspect but wanted to seem friendly.

"Did you work on a farm? Like it?"

"It passed the time, but the harvest is done, so I'm back."

"Home sweet home, but everything's different here. The barracks are all full now."

Encouraged by the man's friendliness, Rolf decided to try out a little story he'd come up with. "Have you been here the whole time?"

"Yes, I work in the laundry."

"Do you know if a guy named Willy Stultzman is still here? He owes me money from a card game, and I want to collect it."

"You're too late. Stultzman is dead. He hanged himself last week."

Rolf feigned surprise. "Really?"

"He was spying for the Americans. Before he could be punished, he killed himself."

It was hard to hold his tongue, but he forced a smile and came up with a reply. "Then I guess the bastard won't be paying off his debts, will he?"

"No, looks like you're out of luck."

"Do you know if anyone else who came early is still here?" By way of explaining his interest, he added, "I wondered if any of my other card-playing buddies are still around."

"Almost everyone here is new. Most of us who came early got shipped out to sub-camps. Only the ones with jobs inside, like me, are still around." The man shivered and rubbed his hands briskly. "Gotta go," and he headed into the latrine.

When Rolf's name was called at the morning roll, a guard took a second look at his clipboard and ordered him to report to the admin building at nine. There, a duty officer told him he'd be notified when his hearing was scheduled. Until then, as he had hoped, he'd bunk in the barracks where he'd spent the night, and for the moment he had no job assignment. Then the officer rubbed his chin and said, "Stay here, I need to check something." While he stepped into another room, Rolf fretted that he'd come back to tell him that he was being put in isolation until the hearing after all, which would make escape even harder. He fidgeted until the American returned carrying a cardboard-covered package. "Did you know Private Wilhelm Stultzman?"

Rolf's eyes widened. "Yes," he replied questioningly.

"You may have heard that Private Stultzman died last week, on the eighth."

"I heard, just now."

"A day or two before that, he came in and asked if he could send this to you. It was an unusual request, but my CO opened it and said okay. We were waiting until we had other deliveries for Peabody. I guess it's lucky we held it because now you're here."

"I guess so."

"So, you and Stultzman were friends?"

"Yes, sir. We were in the same outfit and got sent here together."

"I didn't know him, but I heard he was a funny guy," which gave Rolf a smile. "Do you have any idea why he'd kill himself? It took us by surprise, but maybe not some of the other internees. No one's talking, though. And he was acting strange the day he brought this in. I know, because I happened to be here when he brought that in."

Warily, Rolf stuck to his plan and avoided involving the Americans in what had happened. "I have no idea, sir. I know he got very homesick sometimes."

"It seems odd. We're looking into it. If you hear anything, will you let us know?"

He nodded affirmatively, then stepped out, now melancholic, but determined to press on. He would open the package later, after a stop at the mess hall where he assumed Willy had worked until he died. Several men were cleaning up there, including Peter Frankel, the POW who'd spoken to them the day after they arrived. Later, Willy and Frankel worked together, and they'd all become friends. Rolf was very happy to see him. "Frankel! How've you been?"

The feeling was mutual. "Mueller! When did you get back?"

"Late last night."

"Did you like working outside the camp?"

"Yes, very much."

"I'll bet. Willy talked all the time about how he wished he would have been assigned to a farm so he could meet real Americans." Frankel's face darkened. "You heard what happened?"

"I know he's dead, but I'm not sure I know what happened."

"The bastards forced him to hang himself, that's what happened," Frankel blurted out loudly, before stepping back and looking down almost apologetically.

"What do you mean? How could anyone force him to do that?" Rolf proceeded cautiously, even with a man who'd spoken so bluntly.

Frankel went on, now in a low, nervous tone. "He was so damn tired of pompous German officers telling everyone here what to do, and he said so. He thought we were free of their bullshit, but they didn't see it that way. When he railed against Hitler, some Nazi ass-kisser reported him. The officers gave him a choice: Commit suicide or they'd kill him and round up his family. I'm the only one he told. It's unbelievable, what they did to one of our own."

Rolf sighed deeply. "Where did it happen?"

"Right here, in the storeroom. I saw him just before. It was at the end of our shift. I was checking the lights and opened the storeroom door. Willy was in there, standing on a crate with a rope tied around his neck. The other end was wrapped around a rafter."

Rolf blushed with anger. "He wasn't dead? Why the hell didn't you try to stop him?"

"Because as soon as Willy saw me, he shouted at me to get out. He wasn't alone."

"What?"

"Two men with clubs were in the corner, I guess to make sure he went through with it. I know Willy was trying to protect me, but I've been sick about it. I'll never forget the look on his face." Frankel shook his head. "Maybe I should have done something, but I panicked."

"Who were the other two?"

"I only recognized one, Gerhardt Braun, a real prick, Streicher's errand boy. He works in the officers' compound." Frankel paused. "I'm really sorry. I liked Willy, I know you did too. And he really liked you. I wish I could have done more." His grief was sincere.

Rolf suppressed his frustration enough to acknowledge that there probably wasn't much Frankel could have done, then he added, "I wish Willy would have been more careful."

"Me too. I've got to get back to work now." Frankel looked around one last time. "Watch out, Mueller. Bastards like Braun keep an eye on everybody. They love to report everything to the officers, even made-up shit. It gets them easy jobs and money. They're whores for the Nazis."

Under his breath, Rolf said, "Weren't we all?" On his way out of the mess hall, he scanned an announcement on the notices board, but it barely registered at the time:

## Christmas Concert

Friday night, December 17, 1943, Brown Grand Theater.
Music provided by the 47th Grenadier Band.
Limited seats available for internees. Those interested
should assemble on Main road at 1800 hours.
First-come, first-served.

Willy's gift was a ten-by-fourteen-inch painting of a North African scene—Moorish buildings in rich earth tones with minarets and domes and red-tiled roofs, all set against a pale blue sky. In one corner of the canvas was written "Tunis AFRK" and, below that, the initials "WS." Simple and folksy, it captured the essence of the place. Rolf recalled Willy saying he would paint what he saw without the war damage, and that's just what he'd done. He winced remembering how his friend had hoped to return to Africa one day.

The canvas was stretched over a thin sheet of plywood and held in place by upholstery tacks. As he turned it over, he noticed something sticking out from under a tack in one corner. It was barely visible, white and out of place. Carefully, Rolf pulled up the tack, lifted the canvas, and gently coaxed out a square of folded paper. On it was written in tiny script:

*If you find this and I'm dead, they murdered me. It's all Streicher's doing. Tell my parents I love them. Thanks for everything. You're the best friend I could ask for. Long live free Germany! Willy 7-12-43.*

Rolf read and reread his friend's message, written just ten days earlier, until tears filled his eyes. *My God!* With a lingering lump in his throat, he refolded the paper and carefully tucked it into his shoe. After tacking the canvas back in place, he returned to looking at the painting and let it carry him back to the beauty of the Tunisian spring when they were reunited after each thought the other was dead. So long ago.

Back in the mess hall for lunch, he met two men who'd come out on the train with him. Their small talk didn't reveal anything significant, but he felt others watching him during the meal. As he was about to get up, an almost comically erect man in a crisp *Wehrmacht* uniform strode over and sat down next to him, but said nothing at first, just sat there. Rolf looked at him impatiently, then finally gave the man a questioning shrug of the shoulders to demand that he say what he had obviously come to say.

The officious stranger's eyes narrowed. "Be at the entrance to the officers' compound at ten tomorrow morning. Someone will tell you where to go from there. Don't tell anyone, come alone, and don't even think about bringing a weapon." Immediately, he rose and left.

From across the room, Frankel's eyes darted from Rolf to the departing man and back, then he motioned slightly with his head and eyes as he silently mouthed "Braun." As soon as Rolf gave a slight nod of acknowledgment, Frankel slipped into the kitchen.

*So, you're one of the bastards who watched my friend die*, he thought, *and now you think you're going to get to watch another 'suicide.' Well, fuck you!* His resolve bolstered, Rolf took a purposeful stroll around the compound to confirm the perimeter's impermeability, then he walked over to the library, which was now filled with books and periodicals and notices of classes offered by the University of Kansas. Perusing the shelves, he wasn't sure what he was looking for until he saw it: An atlas of the United States. Immediately, he knew that he'd struck gold. Turning his back to the guard near the door and to the other internees, Rolf anxiously opened the atlas and, sure enough, found a detailed map of Kansas, complete with main highways and county roads. As quietly as possible, he tore it out, folded it, and stuffed it into his pocket. He hated desecrating a book, but this map was clearly meant to be his. With it, he would be able to find his way back to Peabody and Doyle Creek.

Even so, he was disappointed that he hadn't made more progress, and the clock was ticking. Momentarily out of next steps, he wrote a short letter to his parents, did his exercises, and then laid down on his bunk and fell asleep. In the middle of a strange dream about a boat on a wide river, an incongruent flash jolted him awake and popped his eyes open: Could that Christmas concert be the opportunity he was looking for? He had no idea whether they'd let him go since he was being investigated, and there was no way to surveil the theater beforehand, so he'd have to extemporize if he made it that far. But this was the best, perhaps only, option he had, so he began to cobble a plan together. Quickly, he showered, then discreetly bundled himself up in layers of clothing and tucked in a few extra items that he might need.

On his way to the mess hall for the evening meal, two POWs looked at him oddly, then one said condescendingly, "Why are you so dressed up? It's not that cold out."

Rolf was ready. "It's none of your business, but I'm sick and have the chills. Come closer and let me sneeze on you." The men quickly stepped aside to let him pass.

The crowd was so large by the time he got to the assembly area that he worried he wouldn't be selected. As soon as four guards appeared, one of them announced that fifty seats in the theater were reserved for enlisted men, and they immediately began to count off the first fifty in line. Rolf held his breath as the line inched forward in the dim evening light until he was motioned through—number forty-four. Relieved, he said with a smile, "Made it!"

"Well, aren't you just one lucky duck?" chided a guard with a roll of his eyes.

Rolf did feel lucky, and relieved, until a commotion arose from behind. Were they coming to pull him out? He turned and saw another guard pushing through the crowd with a POW. The new guard said to the others, "This man gets to go to the concert."

"Why's that?" asked the guard in charge.

"His brother is a band member, so Jones wants him there tonight."

"But we already have our fifty, and we're starting to load them up."

"There'll be an extra seat, so take this one too. Just be sure to bring him back."

"You got it." The guard in charge turned to the Germans, "Listen up. Colonel Jones is letting you go to this concert to show the good people of Concordia what a civilized bunch you are. He'd better not be disappointed." The POWs smiled. "You will act at all times with utmost respect and decorum. There's no smoking in the theater. You will not talk during the concert. Under no circumstances are you to speak to the townspeople, not even the ushers. We'll be seated in the second balcony. When the concert is over, remain in your seats until the public is gone, then we'll leave. Any questions?"

"Will there be beer? A Christmas concert should have beer," said a jovial young prisoner.

"If there is, it won't be for you. Now let's go." And with that, fifty-one Germans and six guards loaded into three cold trucks for the short drive into town.

The Brown Grand Theater, located on Sixth Street at the west end of downtown Concordia, was a stately, beautiful brick and stone structure with two balconies, private boxes, soaring ceilings, lovely ornate fixtures, and 650 seats. Built in 1907 as an opera house, it was converted into a movie theater in the twenties, but still used for concerts. When the concertgoers arrived, thirty-five members of the 47th Grenadier Band were tuning up on the instruments that had been captured along with them in North Africa.

Rolf deftly maneuvered himself into an aisle seat, feeling conspicuous, but he didn't stand out because the others were excited too. For the first time in years, they were celebrating Christmas properly. Wreathes were hung in the entrance hall and a huge, festively-decorated cedar tree stood near the stage. Its spicy, sweet scent wafted all the way up to the second balcony.

His spirits sank momentarily when he saw a group of German officers in dress uniform entering with Colonel Jones and some other Americans. Streicher was among them, strutting like an honored patron. Streicher didn't see Rolf, of course; it was beneath the major's exalted dignity to glance up at enlisted men. They were invisible to him until he wanted to exert his authority over them. He repulsed Rolf, reminded him of a preening, self-admiring peacock.

As soon as the officers were seated, the doors opened to the public and the theater buzzed with conversations and warm-up notes. A group of nuns, Sisters of St. Joseph from Nazareth Convent, took seats on the main floor. They and other local people looked around curiously, and some pointed up at the POWs, but they weren't unfriendly.

At seven, everyone was welcomed, including the POWs, and the talented musicians began to play. The evening quickly became sentimental. For a few minutes, adversaries put aside their differences to unite in familiar songs of love, peace, and goodwill. Some in the audience began to sing along, and soon everyone was joining in. *Stille Nacht* was especially poignant, thanks in part to strong male harmony coming from the second balcony.

Rolf could hardly believe his good fortune at being there. For a few moments, he relaxed into the music and was filled with warm memories of childhood joy at Christmas time. Even nervously anticipating all the risky, uncharted steps that lay ahead, he felt strangely calm. A voice inside kept telling him to pay close attention, trust his intuitions, let events unfold as they would, and all would be well.

Twenty minutes into the concert, in the middle of a brassy rendition of *Angels We Have Heard On High*, with everyone singing along, Rolf saw an opportunity. He gestured to an older guard that he was sick and needed to use the restroom. The guard, more a store clerk than a soldier, may have been lax by nature, or maybe he wasn't properly trained, or maybe he was caught up in the holiday spirit, or maybe he didn't know what else to do since the other POWs still had to be guarded. Rolf was never sure why, but the guard directed him to the bathroom down on the second floor without accompanying him. It was the moment he'd been waiting for. Heart pounding, he tried to appear as casual as possible as he walked to the steps. The other guards either didn't see him, or they didn't care either.

Alone in the second-floor hallway, Rolf hurried over to a railing and peeked down to the first floor. People were standing in entrances to the auditorium, but they were all facing away, toward the stage. This was it! Taking a deep breath, he backed up to get a running start, then launched himself down the carpeted stairs in three steps without tripping. He landed with a light thud, unheard over the music, found the unguarded front door, and shot out into the night.

If he'd been to a place once, Rolf could usually find it again. Now, that keen sense of direction was going to be put to the test. He knew he had to head east to get back to the highway, Highway 81 according to his trusty map. North would take him back to camp, and south would send him toward Peabody. A block east of the theater, he slipped into a dark alley that he hoped would parallel Sixth all the way to the highway. It did, and soon he was sprinting south. He stayed in the shadows and darted behind bushes or buildings when vehicles approached, but almost no one was out, and anyway, the streets weren't well-lit.

In minutes, he was at Concordia's city limits, an invisible demarcation between his past and all that lay ahead. He crossed the line knowingly and ran on for another mile or two before taking a knee to catch his breath. A look for headlights and a listen for sirens revealed nothing. The air was frosty-cold, not perfect for running, but at least it wasn't snowing. He commended himself for bringing extra clothing, even though it was bulky, including the pilfered towel that he now pulled from his waistband to wrap around his face to keep the cold air out of his lungs.

Looking up at the pristine sky, full of the same stars that had so recently shone down on Loretta and him, he laughed out loud. He really was on his way! Grateful, he stood, stretched, and then set a long-distance runner's pace that he hoped would carry him to Peabody, and beyond.

# Chapter 29
# ALONE

Maybe he was a lucky duck, or maybe a lucky star was shining down on him that night. Whatever the reason, Rolf's road trip was off to a good start. Not only had he managed to slip out of the Brown Grand Theater unnoticed, but he wasn't even missed at first. The guard who'd sent him to the bathroom promptly forgot about him. Then, because it was cold when the trucks got back to camp, the guards didn't check IDs, just counted off fifty men as quickly as possible and sent them to their barracks, overlooking the fact that they'd taken fifty-one to the concert.

The significance of the guards' mistakes weren't realized until Rolf didn't answer at the Saturday morning roll. By the time the Americans confirmed his absence, he'd already been gone more than twelve hours, and they had no idea how he got out. At first no one even knew for sure that he'd gone to the concert; the guards hadn't bothered to write down the attendees' names. It was after noon before they had it sorted out and started a search outside the camp, an effort hampered at the outset by a lack of physical evidence and an overabundance of territory to cover, with nothing concrete to point them in any particular direction.

Major Streicher was much more chagrined than the Americans. Had he known that this insolent *gefreiter* would live long enough to tell the tale, he would not have been so candid with him. Braun was sent to investigate, but he reported back that no one knew anything.

As the sun rose that Saturday morning, Rolf was already thirty miles south, near Minneapolis, tucked into a well-insulated but itchy little nest high in the full hayloft of a large barn on a prosperous farmstead west of Highway 81. In the dawning light before he headed up the ladder, he'd chipped off chunks of ice from a stock tank. Once he was settled in, he wished he'd brought more, but the sun was rising fast and he couldn't risk going back down, so he ate a slice of the bread that he'd squirreled away, sucked on some of the ice, put the rest in the tin cup he'd brought, and rested. Several times through the day, unseen people entered the barn below him, but they never stayed long nor came up into the loft nor realized that they were in close proximity to a runaway.

After eating more bread and sucking on the last of his ice in the evening darkness, Rolf climbed down, careful to leave no trace of himself behind. Glancing at the farm's brightly lit house, he tried not to think about how warm it must be inside. Instead, he silently thanked his hosts for their unknowing hospitality and stretched his stiff legs, now tinged with a dull throbbing near old shrapnel scars. *Shake it off*, he ordered himself as he trotted out to Highway 81 and turned south on his course for Peabody. Thanks to the map, he knew that Kansas was platted into square-mile sections with roads generally at one-mile intervals, which helped him calculate distances traveled and yet to go. Again, he would stick to the schedule he'd set for himself the night before: Every hour, he would run for fifty minutes, then rest for ten.

Once again, the pristine night sky brimmed with sparkles of starlight and arcing meteor showers. Yelping coyotes and passing vehicles entered his consciousness from time to time, but mostly there was only the crunch of boots on gravel and his deep steady breathing to mark the journey. Once back in his rhythm, the aches and pains subsided. For long stretches he didn't sense his body at all, but felt as if he were floating on a magic carpet that kept him from touching the ground, freeing his mind to wander.

How long had it been since he'd been completely by himself like this? It had to be the summer of 1938. Kurt was already gone when his parents and sister went to Köln to visit relatives, leaving him alone on the farm for two days. Five years ago! Since then, except for a few moments scattered here and there, he'd been in close proximity to relatives, classmates, friends, adversaries, teachers, fellow travelers, soldiers, officers, guards. Someone else, always.

What does it do to a person when all his waking hours are spent with others? Can he claim a single idea as his own, or is each thought just a regurgitation of someone else's? Or is every cogitation actually just a mental plea for another's acknowledgment and approval? To some, aloneness was dangerous. The *Wehrmacht* certainly didn't want a man spending time by himself, thinking for himself. Armies run on soldiers who take orders *without* thinking. And the *Fuehrer* was categorically opposed to independent thought or any resulting free expression: He told the German people exactly what they should believe. That's what the *Hitlerjugend* did, too—molded young minds to conform to the *Fuehrer's*. Even well-intentioned people and institutions—parents, churches, businesses—tolerate only so much intellectual independence. Conformity in this world is far more valued than individuals trying to figure things out for themselves.

Rolf pondered how his life would have been different if he'd spent more time alone. Maybe it wasn't too late. Of course, he wanted to be with Loretta and his family again, but he should also try to make time to be by himself. With a laugh, he punched out words in time with his footsteps, "But-I-don't-have-to-run-a-hun-dred-miles-eve-ry-time-I-want-to-be-a-lone." A few minutes in a field on a summer day or by a lake at sunset would do.

Around two in the morning, he came to a Skelly station and an all-night diner on the north side of Salina. The diner's neon *OPEN* sign buzzed on and off erratically, reflecting red on a lone car parked in front. He was about to step inside for something to eat when he caught himself. In the first place, he had no money. Secondly, his pants were emblazoned with a *P* and a *W*. Alarmed at how fatigue was clouding his thinking, Rolf recoiled and picked up the pace to get through the town as quickly as possible. He stopped only once, for some badly-needed water. At the first well he came to that was far enough away from a house that its slumbering occupants wouldn't hear him, he pumped up an icy stream and drank greedily, filled his cup, and juggled it until he was out of town. There he took his ten-minute break, gulped down the rest of the water, and ate the last of the bread. It wasn't much, but it revived him.

After Salina, his pensiveness dissolved into drudgery. Now every step hit the ground with a jolt, his energy waned, he again knew every ache and pain. But on he went until he was west of Assaria and the first rays of flickering light in the east announced that it was time to find his next hiding place. This time, it was a small farm right on the highway. Lights were already on in the house as he slipped into an outlying shed. Minutes later, a man and woman came out with the bang of a door and headed toward a barn, not the shed, probably to tend to livestock. Rolf sighed and folded himself into a dark corner. He wasn't sure how long he'd been asleep when he heard them again. It was full daylight now as they headed toward a garage and spoke, but not in English. Scandinavian maybe, because he could partly understand them. From their words and clothing, he concluded that they were going to church. Soon a motor sputtered to life, then a car pulled out and headed north on the highway.

Judging by the couple's age, any children they had should be grown and gone, so he decided to risk it and try to get into the house to warm up. As he hurried across the yard, an angry German shepherd came racing toward him, barking ferociously. *Shit!* Too late to run, Rolf froze and spoke calmly in German. The dog carried on loudly until he was a few feet away, but then he stopped and lowered his head submissively. "Some guard dog you are," Rolf chided the animal as he scratched his head, "all bark and no bite, thank God!"

The house was small—just a kitchen, front room, and two tiny bedrooms. On a 1943 Swedish wall calendar from Assaria Lutheran Church, he saw that Sunday services started at nine. Since it was only eight forty-five, Rolf figured he had at least an hour before the occupants returned. Now he felt guilty, but he was going to have to steal to keep going. First, he looked through the man's clothes and found a pair of pants, a flannel shirt, and a thick wool sweater. The man was stouter and shorter, but the fit was close enough. He changed, then took a knitted hat, a pair of gloves, and two pairs of thick socks for his blistered feet. In the kitchen, he came across a knapsack into which he packed his telltale old clothing.

On a kitchen counter was fresh bread, cured ham, and a soft white cheese covered with a flour-sack towel. He ate ravenously and washed it all down with thick fresh milk and still-warm coffee from the pot on the stove. What a relief! Now if only he could take a quick nap on the couple's Jenny Lind bed. It was calling to him, but he couldn't trust himself to even sit on it for fear that he'd doze off like Goldilocks and not wake up until these Swedish bears came home and caught him. Instead, he gulped down the last of the coffee.

Done eating, he stuffed extra food into the knapsack, then opened a cupboard and found a bottle of J.R. Watkins Pain Relieving Liniment. Vigorously rubbing its thick, oozy contents onto both legs produced a wonderfully soothing sensation and filled the room with intoxicating camphor vapors. He put the bottle in the knapsack, too, along with a box of kitchen matches and two candles. In the same cupboard was a chipped bone china sugar bowl holding twenty-seven dollars and change. He already had the money in his pocket when the pangs of guilt became too strong, so he kept just one dollar and put the rest back in the bowl.

Before leaving, he wrote a short note and placed it on the kitchen table: *I'm sorry for taking your things and a dollar. One day I'll pay it all back.* The owners would surely feel violated, but perhaps his contrition and his gesture of goodwill by not stealing all their money would keep them from contacting the authorities.

In light of his larceny, he could not hide out all day in the shed, and running would call too much attention to himself, so his best bet was to walk along the highway and hope for a ride, assuming that news of his escape had not reached the area yet. Before he'd finalized the story he would tell anyone he met, the opportunity arose for him to try it out. Just minutes south of his last refuge, an older model Ford pickup driven by a middle-aged bald man came up on him from the north. Rolf listened nervously as the truck approached, then watched it pass him and pull over. Assuming that meant he was being offered a ride, he jogged up to the passenger door and said, "Good morning," in his best accent-free English.

"Need a ride?" Without waiting for a reply, the portly driver with a friendly round face and rosy cheeks commanded, "Well, get in. It's cold out there."

"Yes, sir, it is." The cab was musty and stale, but toasty warm.

"Where you headed?" The man wasn't shy about sizing him.

"McPherson."

"Where?" His pronunciation must have been off, but before Rolf could try again, the man went on, "Oh, McPherson. That's on my way. I'm heading to Wichita, so I can drop you off."

"Thank you." Rolf breathed a sigh of relief.

"I'm Nels Thogerson. And who might you be?" He stuck out a hand.

Storytime. As Rolf shook his hand, he said, "I'm Joseph Unruh. It is nice to meet you."

"Same here. You live in McPherson?"

"No, my family is picking me up there."

"So where's home?"

"Peabody." He was being forced to spin his yarn on the fly, which made him nervous.

"I see. Are you on leave?"

"Yes, from the Army." It would be too odd for a man Rolf's age not to be in the military.

"Why aren't you in uniform? You'da got picked up a lot quicker."

"It's rather embarrassing." Rolf sighed, "I ripped it when I was out with friends in Kansas City. I left it to be mended and will have to pick it up on my way back."

"Well now." Thogerson's brow was so furrowed that Rolf thought he wasn't buying it, but then the other man's face relaxed. "Musta had yourself quite a time if your clothes got tore up!" His knowing smile said he was very worldly, that he knew all about big city life.

"It was, but I can't let my parents find out just how much fun it was."

"Your secret's safe with me. Did you go to the Muehlebach while you were there?"

"The Muehlebach?" Rolf had no idea what that was.

"You know, the Muehlebach Hotel. Right downtown? I was there once. It's real fancy."

"Oh, yes. No, we didn't go there. We went to a place by my friend's house with some girls he knows. He lives near the Kansas City *bahnhof.*" *Shit!* Too late, Rolf realized that he'd inadvertently used the German word for railway station.

Thogerson pretended not to notice. "Oh, I see. And that's where you had yourselves that fun, eh?" He winked.

"Yes, sir." Rolf was on pins and needles.

Thogerson was quiet for a moment, then said, "I see. Unruh, you say?"

"Yes."

"That's German, ain't it?"

"Yes, sir."

"Did you speak German growing up?"

"Yes, sir. And English."

"Well, that explains why your accent is kinda funny."

Rolf relaxed. "Sometimes I think I still speak German better than English."

"My family is Norwegian, but we didn't speak it growing up. So, how'd you end up out here on the highway?"

"I got to Salina on the train last night. Another friend was supposed to meet me, but he didn't show up, so someone else gave me a ride until the last town back." When spoken out loud, his tale sounded far-fetched, and he feared that he was mispronouncing Salina.

Thogerson just said, "That's a heckuva story. I hope the rest of your leave goes better."

"Me too." Rolf smiled and rolled his eyes for effect. "It will be good, unless my parents figure out what happened in Kansas City. Then I'm in trouble, for sure."

Looking into his rearview mirror, Thogerson snickered, "If ole' Saint Nick finds out how naughty you've been, you'll be getting coal in your stocking for sure!"

Rolf had no idea what the man meant, so he nodded as if he did and said nothing.

"I'm on my way to Wichita to pick up a load of supplies for work."

Only too happy for the change in subject, Rolf asked, "Where do you work?"

"A printing company in Salina. I'm driving down today so I can spend the day with my brother and his family, then I'll get my supplies and go back tomorrow."

"Do you have a family?"

"In Salina? No, it's just me. My mother still lives in Wichita too. That's where I'm from."

"I see. Thanks again for picking me up."

"You look like you could use a little shut-eye. Go ahead, and I'll let you know when we get to McPherson. It shouldn't be too long."

Rolf was snoring before they reached Lindsborg. He was still out a half-hour later when Thogerson shook him. "Son, we're coming to McPherson. Where you meeting your folks?" Rolf's eyes opened, but he was so befuddled that Thogerson had to repeat the question twice.

"Um," Rolf wiped drool off his cheek, "the railroad station would be fine."

"You sure? But the train don't go from Peabody to McPherson."

Now Rolf was wide awake. "They're coming for me after church and told me to wait at the station." He had no idea if McPherson had one, but minutes later he was getting dropped off in front of a long narrow brick building with a red tile roof beside some railroad tracks. Stepping out of the truck, he nodded gratefully and thanked Thogerson for the ride.

As soon as the truck was out of sight, Rolf quickly walked east along the tracks, hat down and collar up, until he reached Main Street. It wasn't noon yet, and McPherson's downtown was quiet. He'd wait somewhere until nightfall, then either start running again or catch a freight train to Hillsboro, thirty miles to the east. He'd been to Hillsboro with Harold to sell grain and knew it was only twenty miles north of Peabody. By his map, a train eastbound from McPherson should go through Hillsboro. If he could ride there, maybe he'd make it the rest of the way to Peabody on foot that same night. But the challenge now was to get out of sight, and soon—no more nerve-wracking conversations like the one with Thogerson.

He found a spot at Poehler Mercantile, a large warehouse on the east side of Main next to the tracks. In the parking lot were three panel trucks emblazoned with the company name and logo—polar bears—a play on *Poehler,* a German name. No one was watching as he tried the first truck, found it unlocked, and climbed in. It was dark and empty, except for a few wood pallets. As long as Poehler didn't make deliveries on Sundays he should be okay. And if he was found, he'd pretend to be an American vagrant.

Train, vehicle, and pedestrian sounds punctuated his sleep throughout the day, but he still got some badly-needed rest. Between naps, he ate, but left enough food for one more day, which should be all he needed until the Unruhs re-supplied him for the next leg of his journey. He still had to come up with a final destination. A large city might be good for hiding, maybe Kansas City or even St. Louis. Or maybe he should head to Olpe, Kansas, in hopes that a long-lost relative there would help, at least until he could figure out something else.

While he was hunkered in the truck, pregnant clouds rolled over McPherson on a brittle north wind. By nightfall, it was snowing so hard that running to Hillsboro was out of the question; hopping a train was now his only option. After an hour of anxious waiting, a train finally wailed in the yards to the west and sounded like it was moving in his direction. Sure enough, a freight locomotive was soon crossing Main Street. He had just enough time to throw his pack and himself aboard through an open boxcar door.

The dimly lit car, cavernous and creepy, turned pitch-black as soon as the train was outside of McPherson. Rolf had an unnerving sensation that he wasn't alone in there, but he couldn't tell for sure. He thought about jumping off, but then he calmed himself, stayed close to the door, and tried not to think about what might be hidden in the encroaching shadows. It was miserably cold now, too, another reason to shiver.

The train chugged across the dark, lonely Flint Hills until a single light twinkled in the distance, followed by a few more. A town lay ahead, but Rolf wasn't sure it was Hillsboro. In case it was, he readied himself to jump off as soon as the train stopped, but it wasn't stopping. Almost as soon as he saw a sign on a grain elevator confirming that this was his destination, the train was accelerating, so he took a quick deep breath and leapt.

It turned out to be a bad landing spot. Hidden beneath the snow was a large uneven rock; one foot struck it hard. The pain was instantaneous and stunning. With moans and curses, he grabbed his knapsack and hobbled away from the tracks while a shadowy figure in the back doorway of the passing caboose shouted, "Stay the hell off our trains, ya damn bum! I hope ya broke your foot."

Every step on his fast-swelling ankle was so exquisitely, excruciatingly painful that it was hard to concentrate. Only with supreme effort could he force himself to get his bearings. On the east side of town was the road to Peabody, but there was no way he could run that distance— any distance—now. He'd have to find shelter for the night. But where? An abandoned house at the edge of town came to mind from his first visit to Hillsboro. He remembered it because he'd asked Harold at the time why such a study-looking structure was abandoned. Harold didn't know.

*Think!* Slowly, he visualized it—the house, a wooded area in back, a corn field to the east, open prairie across the unpaved road. If he headed east, he should find it, and it shouldn't be too far. He whimpered with each miserable step, but finally got himself moving again, slowly, and the terrain began to look familiar.

The large native-stone house still stood straight and proud, except for its sagging porches that creaked in the wind. No longer able to put any weight on the ankle, Rolf had to crawl up its steps on his belly. On the porch, he slowly rose up on his good foot and hopped in, bracing himself against the doorway and walls. The first room was vacant, except for some empty boxes and broken furniture. Something useful might be found in another room, but he could go no further. He chose an inside corner, far from the broken windows and door, and sat down hard. While unseen animals scampered and scratched on the second floor above him, he arranged some cardboard boxes to try and block the wind, covered himself with his extra clothing, and curled into a tight ball to conserve body heat. Utterly miserable, he wondered if his tracks in the snow would betray him. Maybe that wouldn't be such a bad thing, as long as someone found him before he froze to death and took him someplace—anyplace—warm.

Loretta looked out at snowflakes dancing around like whirligigs falling from maple trees on a warm spring day. She couldn't tell how much was still coming down and how much had already fallen and was now just floating on the breeze. The big barn's outline was eerily visible against the murky sky in an ethereal light that seemed to rise from the snow-covered ground and bathed everything in a haunting luminescence amplified by silence. The entire world was padded in giant cotton balls that had swallowed whole the humdrum of life. She shivered and touched a few snowflakes that had made it into her frigid room on the wind coming in under the closed windows. Anticipating warmth, she crawled under the thick goose-down featherbed made for her many years earlier by her grandmother, then thought of all her elders and how they'd survived winter nights like this in boxcars. How did they do it? And more importantly tonight, what about Rolf? *Where are you,* she thought.

Earlier that day, the phone rang and Clara answered, then quickly handed it to Harold. He mostly listened, injecting a few "oh mys" and "yes sirs" and "will dos" before hanging up and turning to his family. "Well, well," he began.

"Who was it?" Loretta was sure she knew who they'd been talking about, but not why.

"Lieutenant Stevenson. He got a call from Concordia that Rolf escaped. Two days ago."

"Escaped?" The word startled Clara. "Why would he do that?" The family knew that he had been sent away suddenly, but not why. His escape now only deepened the mystery.

"The lieutenant doesn't know. He only said that if he shows up here, we have to let them know or we could be charged with aiding a fugitive."

"What will we do if comes here?" asked Carol Ann.

Harold replied dismissively. "We'll cross that bridge when we get to it."

With her family that afternoon, Loretta tried to appear surprised, but she wasn't. She already suspected that Rolf had been sent away as punishment because someone found out about them. And now, in the dark of night, she was certain he was coming back. For her.

# Chapter 30

# IF WISHES WERE FISHES

By morning, the storm's disruption had moved on, leaving in its stead a whitened landscape that refracted the sun's rays into fields of dazzling diamond-sparkles under a magnificent blue sky. Rolf was sleeping when a beam of light crossed his face and the inside of his eyelids glowed pink. He opened them, squinting.

Somehow he'd stayed warm enough and felt surprisingly good—until he moved and woke the ankle. The joint was invisible under a grotesque mass of blue-black flesh molded into the shape of his boot, but it didn't appear to be broken and at least the pain was less insistent than the night before. Grimacing, he rubbed it with liniment and gingerly tucked it back into his boot for protection and warmth. By nightfall, he hoped to be able to hit the road again.

In the meantime, he had some one-footed foraging to do, first for water. His tongue hadn't felt so thick and rubbery since North Africa. In the kitchen was an old zinc pail that he filled with snow conveniently drifted by the back door, which was well-hidden from view beyond the property by a thick cedar windrow. The gnarled old trees' spicy pungence, especially noticeable in the purified air, reminded him of the Christmas tree in the Brown Grand Theater.

The kitchen still had a cook stove and there were enough pieces of furniture for a fire, but smoke from the chimney could attract attention, so he lit a candle instead and held it under the pail. The process was slow, but the result—a quarter-bucket of rust-flecked water—was more valuable to him than gold. It took three more trips to the back porch for him to feel re-hydrated.

Before sitting back down, Rolf searched the rest of the house for anything else useful. Negotiating the stairs was challenging, but a smelly old quilt with stitches missing and batting coming out that he found upstairs would help insulate him from the biting cold. Up there, he also saw his housemates' frozen scat, but not the critters. They must have been out foraging too.

Back in the front room, he moved his pallet closer to a window for the sun's warmth and a better vantage point. The house sat a safe thirty yards from the road. He was glad to see that his tracks had disappeared in the snow. Having survived what would surely be the worst night of his journey, he was back to not wanting to be caught.

Stuck there waiting, alone, felt very different from being alone on the run. Instead of exhilaration, now he felt vulnerable. And for the first time in weeks, he was bored, so he returned to his thousand-questions game. Who were the people who'd lived here? Where did they come from, where had they gone? What was Hillsboro like? He conjured up answers and imagined the house with the moist yeasty aroma of bread baking in the oven and laughing children running up and down the stairs. It must have been nice to sit on its shady porch after a long hot day in the field.

He wasn't able to bring writing paper or a pencil and regretted not being able to write out his questions, especially since he had so little else to do. Then he realized that all his journal entries were probably lost, confiscated by the Americans or stolen by Streicher. *My story—just one more thing the war has stolen from me,* he thought.

Without the need to focus on immediate tasks, Rolf's mind meandered into a thicket of less pleasant what-ifs. What if Hecht hadn't been so jealous? What if Willy had kept his mouth shut? What if he'd told the Americans what happened instead of running away? He sighed thinking about a favorite saying of his father's. He couldn't remember it exactly, something about if our wishes were fishes, we'd never be hungry. It was pointless to try and wish away things that had already happened. Then he slipped into even more dismal reflections.

From their first meeting, Rolf knew Streicher was evil, but when he learned of the major's complicity in Willy's death, Streicher became the personification of malevolence. But were they really so different from one another? Hadn't Rolf committed his own detestable deeds? He'd killed enemy combatants as soldiers must, but what about the others? Zombie-like, *the others* trudged back into his consciousness, the unarmed enemy soldiers and civilians he'd killed along the way. At the time, he hadn't given his actions much thought. He didn't have to—he was always just following orders. But wasn't that exactly what Streicher would say he was doing? Was he really morally superior to Streicher, or was the major detestable only because he'd killed Rolf's friend? But wasn't every single victim of Rolf's someone's friend?

These thoughts weren't new, but they were becoming less avoidable. Why? Because he'd had an epiphany after almost dying? Because he'd been captured? Because he was on the losing side in a battle? If might makes right, does losing make wrong? By definition, are losers guilty? What right did he have to complain about America, or about Streicher? Hadn't he been defeated by both? Wouldn't they have become his spoils if he had won? He lost, they won. End of story.

For the Fatherland! For the *Fuehrer*! How those mantras inoculated Rolf from personal culpability. And his personal mental mantras, unwelcome though they were, had served to insulate him from his own evil acts even more. *I only did what I had to do, what they made me do. I never wanted to do what I did. How could I be guilty of anything?* He may not have agreed with all of National Socialism's tenets or methods, but with sworn duty came the luxury of getting to remain quiet and not questioning what he was doing.

Until now. Now, cold, alone, hungry, and hurting in a house that had been forsaken, all the questions he never asked himself were fermenting inside him like cabbage rotting into kraut. Soon they would be demanding honest answers, not self-serving justifications.

How could he have been so malleable? How could a Westphalen farm boy have become so willing to kill other human beings, and so adept at it? If recompense was due, to whom would it be paid? How could he atone? Was it even possible? If Streicher's behavior was unforgivable, why should anyone forgive him?

Who could he talk to about this? The person who would best understand—Willy—was gone. What about Loretta? If they managed to be together one day, would his complicity in this war be something they discussed or would they have to set it aside just to get on with life? Would he have to concoct excuses so he could live with himself? Would she buy them?

Loretta. She said she saw his goodness, but how could she when she didn't really know him? How could someone like her, the embodiment of goodness, see good in someone like him? Would his evil taint her? Or would her love rescue him from his past? Was it too late? Why had he not taken a different path? *If wishes were fishes....* His head throbbed worse than his ankle until he dozed off.

At sunset, he wrapped his ankle tightly with strips of towel and covered it with three socks. Teeth gritted, he shoved the thick-shrouded foot into the boot and started off. The road to Peabody had been plowed, but was still splotched with crunchy, hard-to-see snow and ice. With a bad foot and treacherous pavement, the pace was slow, but he could reach the farm by morning if he pushed himself. And he was in the mood to push himself.

By five on Tuesday, he was just north of Peabody, heading east along Highway 50. Traffic was already rolling on this familiar, busy stretch of roadway, so he moved a fair distance off the shoulder and ran parallel to it, slogging through some rough, snowy fields until he got to the county road leading to the farm. Exhausted and nervous as he closed in on his destination, he reviewed for the umpteenth time what he would say. After warning them about Hecht, Rolf hoped there would be time for Loretta and him to tell her parents about their feelings for each other. Worthy of her love or not, worthy of redemption or not, it was time to be honest.

It was still dark when he crossed the bridge west of the Unruh driveway. Holding onto tree trunks and limbs, he slid down the embankment, slick with snow covering a thick mucky layer of leaves, and hobbled along Doyle Creek until he was near the house. The truck was gone. Harold must have gone to town to pick up Gralke or someone else. Hopefully not Hecht. Loretta and her mother were probably out milking. He wanted to sneak into the brightly lit house, so familiar and inviting, but that wouldn't be right, so he squatted down to wait.

When a screen door sprang shut with a familiar thwack, Rolf was up nervously dusting himself off. He could just make out the silhouettes of two women walking to the house as he stepped out of the trees. They were almost to the gate into the yard when both women saw him and stopped, then the taller one moved toward him. He still couldn't see her face, but was sure Loretta was smiling as broadly as he. As he got closer to her, however, there was only alarm in her expression. "Oh no, I'm sorry if I startled you."

Loretta was not smiling. She called out urgently, "Rolf! They're here!" and was reaching for his hand when three loud pops emanated from the big barn. He hadn't noticed its doors ajar or the men standing just inside. Struck, he stopped and sank to his knees, wide-eyed and bewildered, then crumpled face down into the snow at Loretta's feet.

"No!" she screamed as she bent down and turned him onto his back. "Dear God, Rolf!" Her first tears mingled with steaming blood already seeping out from him onto the snow. Gently, she wiped the snow off his face.

He winced and gave her a confused, dreamlike smile. "I made it, Loretta. I came back to warn you." Switching to German, he continued, "It's so good to see you." After a long viscous cough, he tried to clear his throat and looked up toward the sky.

"Rolf, look at me. You're going to be all right." She cradled his head on her lap, wanted to believe her words, was frozen in time and place.

"I am all right." Weakly, he turned his eyes back to her, "I'm with you."

When Clara reached them, she took charge. She'd never treated a gunshot wound, but like all Kansas farm women, she was no stranger to injury and didn't flinch at giving aid. Surveying the situation, she saw two holes in Rolf's coat and a third one below his left knee. That one was bleeding the worst, demanding attention. Clara ripped two long strips of cloth from the bottom of her dress, then spoke to her daughter with calm resolve, "Loretta, you've got to help. Can you?"

"Yes, Mama."

"First, we're going to tie these around his leg." As Loretta lifted the leg, her mother pulled the pants leg up to his knee and tied the tourniquet above a jagged hole in his shin. Shards of bone protruded in the wound. "Good," said Clara as she watched the flow of blood slow. "Now let's check the others."

"Thank you, Mrs. Unruh. I didn't mean to be such a bother." Rolf smiled bashfully.

"You're welcome." Clara smiled as she unbuttoned his coat and lifted up his sweater and shirt. A floppy hole in his chest wasn't bleeding as badly but gurgled with each breath he took. "Take your sweater off, dear," she directed her daughter, "and hold it down right here. Firmly." The final wound, a graze to his right shoulder, looked less serious but it was also bleeding, so Clara took off her own sweater, placed it on the right spot, and told her daughter to apply pressure there too. As she assessed what more they could do, she prayed. Clara was certain that only divine intervention would save Rolf's life.

From the barn, Greg Jordan, Jerry Flannigan, and an older man, a new recruit named Scott Davidson, came running. Jordan scowled when he saw Rolf. "Jesus, Davidson!" he shouted. "I said hold your fire unless we had to shoot. What the hell were you thinking? Three shots? For Chrissake! You could have hit a civilian, you idiot!"

"I panicked when I saw him getting close to her." Davidson looked more strickened than Rolf. "I've never shot anyone before," he mumbled, then stepped away and vomited.

"What can we do to help, ma'am?" Jordan asked as he and Flannigan moved in closer.

"We have to get him to a hospital. The nearest ones are in Hillsboro and Newton. We doctor in Hillsboro, so that's where we should go."

As she spoke, Harold was driving up the lane. He'd dropped Carol Ann off at school and was coming back alone because the Eyestone Building was in lockdown due to Rolf's escape. Based on the report of a strange robbery near Assaria, and on information given by a man who'd picked up a hitchhiker two days earlier on Highway 81, the Americans surmised that he was heading to Unruh farm. That's why guards were waiting in their barn that morning.

While Jordan and Clara filled him in, Harold knelt down. "How're you doing, son?"

Rolf struggled to focus. "Good morning, Mr. Unruh, I don't think I can help with the milking today." He offered a faint, delirium-tainted smile.

"That's okay. We can handle the chores until you're better. Now we're gonna go get you patched up. Looks like you sprang some leaks!" Harold hurried to the garage, backed the Chevy out, and pulled up near the group, and Clara ran into the house for blankets and towels. As soon as she returned, Harold said, "Okay, let's get him into the car."

Flannigan said, "Sir, I'm sorry, but we either have to take him back to Peabody or up to Concordia. We have orders."

Stepping away so Rolf and Loretta wouldn't hear, Harold spoke to the guards, "If we do that, he isn't going to live." Pointing at the growing crimson circle in the snow and the soaked sweaters, he added bluntly, "You shot a man on my farm, look and see how much blood he's lost already. We're going to Hillsboro, and that's that. If one of you wants to come along, fine."

In short order, the men fashioned a litter out of the blankets and lifted Rolf onto it, then carefully loaded him into the backseat. Loretta climbed in too. Crouching on the floorboard, she kept pressure on the wounds with fresh towels. With Harold and Jordan in front, the four of them sped off for Hillsboro while Flannigan and Davidson returned to Peabody.

Suddenly alone, Clara picked up Rolf's knapsack and looked at her bloody hands. Before she was on the back porch, she was shaking and sobbing. Calm and focused during a crisis, the emotional toll of what she'd just been through now caught up with her. She knew how badly Rolf was hurt, but there was something else. Now she saw what she'd suspected, how much that young man mattered to her daughter, which made what happened all the more anguishing.

As the car sped north, Rolf drifted in and out until he forced himself awake with such a shudder that it frightened Loretta. Between raspy breaths, he finally whispered, "Otto. Hecht. Stay away. From him. Tell your father." It took several tries, but Loretta finally understood his words, if not their meaning or significance, and repeated them to the men in the front seat.

Message delivered, Rolf relaxed. He would have liked to hold Loretta's hand, but she was using both of them to keep him alive. Instead, he focused on her beautiful blue eyes, so close to his, until just before Hillsboro, when he fell asleep.

# Chapter 31
# FESTERING WOUNDS

Major Streicher strode into the anteroom and demanded, in syncopated German, to speak to the officer on duty. "How can I help you, major?" an American lieutenant politely asked.

"The prisoner who escaped, *Gefreiter* Mueller, has been captured and was shot, yes?"

"Yes, sir. He's recovering in a civilian hospital. The IRC, the Swiss, and your highest-ranking officer here have all been notified."

"I'm here on behalf of Colonel Lutzke. Please tell me Mueller's current condition."

"The last I heard, he was stable. I don't have any other details."

"Colonel Lutzke has asked that I be allowed to visit him, which is our right."

"I'll notify Colonel Jones and let you know when arrangements can be made."

"As soon as possible." Streicher looked at the lieutenant haughtily. "The shooting of an unarmed German prisoner by an American guard is a most serious matter."

"Yes, sir. And as soon as the report's available, I'm sure Colonel Jones will provide it to Colonel Lutzke, or to you as his delegate. If you'd like to return tomorrow morning, we may have more information then. Now, is there anything else I can help you with?"

"I will expect the report tomorrow. It's already been nearly a week." The officers saluted and Major Streicher turned and walked out.

The lieutenant shook his head and said to the clerk sitting nearest him, "Can you believe that guy? You'd think he was the camp CO."

Streicher couldn't have cared less about Rolf's health, would have preferred him dead, but since he wasn't, the major wanted to know how he'd managed to escape. More importantly, he wanted to know who the troublesome *gefreiter* might have told about their last conversation.

Rolf woke from a nap to find Jordan thumbing through a magazine. "What time is it?"

"Around one," said Jordan, stretching and looking at his watch. "How are you feeling?"

"It is Monday, correct?"

"That's right, Monday the twenty-seventh. Things still a little fuzzy?"

"Yes, but better."

"You missed Christmas. We had a nice dinner for everybody in Peabody."

Rolf tried to sit up, but had trouble, so Jordan helped him. Finally situated, he said "Believe me, I would rather have been there than here."

"I'll bet that's right." A guard had been posted at Hillsboro's Salem Home and Hospital since he was admitted. For the last two days, it was Jordan. "But I'll be as glad as you to get back to Peabody. It's damn boring sitting in a hospital room watching a German sleep all day."

"Trade you places." Rolf smiled. "May I ask you a serious question?"

"What's that?"

"You were at the farm that day, weren't you?"

"The day you got shot? Yes, and I rode along when Harold brought you here."

"Did you shoot me?" Rolf was embarrassed to ask.

"No. It was Scott Davidson. Older guy, red hair."

"I don't remember him at all."

"He's new. And he still feels bad about getting over-excited when you came out of the woods. He asked me to let you know that."

"Thanks. And please tell him that I'm glad he stopped at three bullets."

With a laugh, Jordan said, "I will. As it is, he'll be filling out paperwork for a month. And some of your buddies have been giving him a hard time. When he walks by, they'll put their arms in the air and say, 'Don't shoot!' Even some of the guards are giving him the raspberries."

"Really?"

He chuckled. "He made the mistake of telling people that those were the first three bullets he ever fired at a human being. Now the guards are calling him 'Three Shot Scott!'"

"Three-for-three? He should be transferred to a sniper unit, one far away from me."

Leaning in closer to the bed, Jordan said, "I was wondering something too. Did you ever tell anyone about what happened the night Loretta came to town?"

"No, of course not. Did you?"

"Hell no! Are you kidding? If they find out about it, I'd be in more trouble than you. But there's talk going around that someone knows and reported you, but nobody can prove anything."

"It was Hecht. He found out and told the German officers, who told Stevenson."

"Hecht? Why would he do something like that? You and he are on the same team."

Rolf gritted his teeth. "No, we are not."

Jordan wasn't sure what to make of that. "Well, I'm pretty sure none of the Americans saw anything, so maybe you're right, but it still doesn't make any sense. I've already been questioned and denied any knowledge, but I wanted to be sure that's what you're saying too."

"Of course, I'll also deny it if I'm asked. I hope they won't bring Loretta into it."

"I don't think they will. Her name hasn't been mentioned. The story going around is that you were let out to meet a 'woman of the night' for some 'fun.' Do you know what I mean?"

"A prostitute?"

"Yes, but it's so crazy that our officers don't want to believe it."

"What would I pay a prostitute with—camp scrip?"

Jordan laughed. "Let me ask you something else. We were told you got sent back to Concordia for fraternizing with civilians and for this thing with a woman. But those charges aren't very serious. So why did you have to escape and run all the way back to Peabody? That's a helluva trip, especially on foot and in the winter, if you weren't facing much punishment."

"My trouble is with the German officers, not the Americans. Hecht fed them allegations against me, which they used as a pretense to get me back to Concordia so they could punish me."

"I don't get it." Jordan was genuinely puzzled.

"It's a long story."

"I've got time."

Rolf thought for a moment, then decided to trust Jordan and laid it out for him. He talked about Hecht's jealousy and how Streicher and other strident Nazis exerted authority in Concordia, how German enlisted men were told to disregard the orders of their captors, how they were supposed to sabotage farms and were obligated to further Germany's interests in America.

Jordan was flabbergasted. "But your officers are prisoners! How in the hell can they expect you to follow their orders in our camp?"

"They can, and they do. They say that refusing is treason. And because they have regular communications with *Wehrmacht* and government leaders in Germany, they have ways of threatening our families at home if we don't follow their orders here."

"Aren't the officers segregated from the enlisteds?"

"They live in their own compound but have access to the whole camp. Ass-kissers like Hecht love to help the officers. They spy on the rest of us."

"That's astounding." Jordan shifted and struggled to absorb what he was hearing.

"The German officers even hold secret tribunals to try and sentence other POWs. Right under the Americans' noses."

"You're kidding!"

"I wish I were. My friend, Willy Stultzman, was forced to commit suicide because he spoke against the Nazis and Hitler. I was told to appear before a so-called tribunal and knew what they had planned for me, too, so when the chance to escape came, I took it."

"We heard about that suicide, but didn't get details. How do you know what happened?"

"Because Streicher told me himself on the way back to Concordia! He bragged about it!" Rolf was relieved for someone else to know the truth about Willy.

"I'm sorry about your friend, Rolf. Do you have any proof besides what Streicher said?"

"I had a note, but I don't know what happened to it. Others in Concordia know, but it's our word against Streicher's."

"I have to tell Lieutenant Stevenson. He wouldn't stand for Nazis having free rein over other POWs in Concordia or anywhere else. I think he would believe you."

"Please don't say anything just yet. If Streicher finds out I've told you, it could be even worse for me if I go back there. That's why I didn't say anything to the officers when I arrived back in Concordia, and why escaping seemed like the only option."

"I'll try to do better at protecting you, but we have to get to the bottom of this. If we don't, we're all at risk."

"Please be careful or you could get me killed." Jordan nodded that he understood. "And there is one thing you can do now, though. If you wouldn't mind."

"What's that?"

"Please make sure Hecht never returns to the Unruh farm. I think he would hurt them if Streicher told him to," Rolf said. "Can you do that?"

"Yes. He already tried, after you left. He wrote the Unruhs this big, long letter apologizing for how rude he was when he got laid off. He said he was sorry for sounding skeptical about pacifism and that now he realized the Mennonites were right about war and everything. Gralke told me about the letter, he's the one who delivered it to the Unruhs, but Harold still asked for Zimmerman to come back instead. If what you say is true, Hecht shouldn't be assigned outside camp at all. He'd get sent back to Concordia for a disciplinary hearing."

Rolf listened, shaking his head in dismay. "What a bastard!"

There was a quiet knock on the door. When Loretta stepped in and saw their serious expressions, she said, "I'm sorry, am I interrupting?"

"Nothing important," said Jordan. "And I'm sure this one would rather see you than me anyway." He smiled and winked at Rolf. "I'll be right outside. Don't run away."

After kisses on the cheek, Loretta took off her coat and sat down. She'd been up to visit him every day. "How are you?"

"Better every day. And how are you?"

"Good, thanks."

"Is it cold? I'm too far away from the window to see much outside."

"Actually, it's warmed up. The snow is gone, it's sun-shiny, and windy from the south."

"Warmer? In the middle of winter?"

"This is Kansas." Loretta smiled. "We have a saying—if you don't like the weather, wait five minutes and it will be different. Are you still having much pain?"

"It's not bad." In truth, however, the injured leg was swollen, throbbed constantly, and the painkillers weren't helping.

"I don't believe you."

"Okay, my leg bothers me a little, but the rest of me is doing great. The doctor was in last night. He drew blood and said he'd be back this afternoon. Maybe he'll have some news." Ready to divert attention from himself, he said, "How are your parents?"

"They're fine. I'll tell them you asked. We had a long, interesting talk yesterday."

"Oh? About what?"

"You and me." Smugly, she let him fidget a minute before going on. "It's okay. They already knew. Mama said she knew even before you got shot."

"What do they think about that?"

"They're not angry. They both like you."

"That's good."

"But they say they're also realistic. And protective. Mama is not keen on me liking anyone who's not Mennonite, especially one from a world so different from ours."

"For sure, our romance is unexpected, like something Shakespeare would come up with."

"So now we're Romeo and Juliet?"

Rolf squeezed her hand. "Maybe, but let's stay away from daggers and poison, shall we?"

"Good idea. And yes, my feelings for you are something I never expected. And maybe I'm not ready to shout about us from the rooftops, but I'm also not going to lie about what I feel any longer, to my parents or to myself. I'm becoming more realistic, too, just not exactly in the way Mama thinks I should."

Rolf became serious. "I hope your parents won't interfere with your dream of becoming a teacher."

"Thanks again for your encouragement." She smiled and kissed his cheek again. "I'm just going to have to help Mama understand that it's my decision." Loretta's confidence as she spoke made Rolf proud.

"You'll be a great teacher. And I like the idea of being married to an educated woman." Loretta's eyes widened. When Rolf realized what he'd said, he blushed and stammered, "I, I just meant that I don't ever want to stand in the way of your dreams."

"Thank you, if that's what you meant," she said, laughing.

Rolf adjusted himself in the bed and said, "And please let your parents know that my intentions are honorable. And assure them there's no chance of me kidnapping you like you kidnapped me last month." He gave her a mildly suggestive grin. "At least not at the moment."

She pretended to be surprised. "And what is that supposed to mean?"

Rolf took her hand again, squeezed it, and tenderly massaged her palm with his thumb. "You know that my intentions are honorable, and my love is true. Every day I thank God that, somehow, we met. And I'm glad you're here with me today." Tears appeared in his eyes.

"Me too." Loretta rose up from her chair, touched his hair, and leaned in for a long, tender kiss. "I love you."

"I love you too." Looking into her eyes, Rolf believed the world could be theirs someday, somehow, against all odds.

They were sitting quietly, enjoying the moment when a doctor and a nurse stepped into the room. Paul Goering, tall, well-built, and still handsome in his sixties with thick silver hair, had been the Unruh family's doctor since before Loretta was born, but she didn't recognize the young nurse with him. "Hello," she said as she timidly backed her chair away from the bed.

"Hello, Loretta. I hope you had a happy Christmas."

"It was good, thanks. I spent part of it here with our friend."

"That was nice of you." The doctor was polite, but formal and vaguely nervous. Turning to Rolf, he said, "Hello again, Mr. Mueller. How are you feeling this afternoon?"

"I'm fine, Doctor." Loretta scowled at him for downplaying the pain.

"Let's have a look at that leg." The nurse was already pulling down the sheet and carefully removing the dressing.

"I'll step out," Loretta said.

"I wish you'd stay, if you don't mind."

"All right, if it's okay." Glancing at the un-bandaged leg as she spoke, Loretta unconsciously recoiled. Rolf saw her look away.

The doctor nodded. "Of course." He spent several minutes quietly pressing into flesh, taking measurements, carefully lifting it up and checking the drainage on the dressing. The movement hurt Rolf, but the expression shading the doctor's face was even more worrisome.

"How soon can I be walking again?" Rolf asked with excessive optimism.

Dr. Goering smiled noncommittally. He read the chart again and looked at the leg, then rubbed his face. "Mr. Mueller, it's not good."

"But it's just taking a little time to heal. The swelling will be down soon, won't it?" Rolf was resolved to keep the conversation light even as the mood in the room was darkening. "It's not going to look like this much longer, is it? I pride myself on my athletic legs, you see."

The doctor would not be sidetracked. "The situation is very serious."

"What do you mean?"

"The blood tests showed your white blood cell count is extremely high. That and what I see tells me that you have wet gangrene. It means..."

Rolf angrily cut him off. "I know what it means. I learned about it at university." He immediately regretted his rudeness. "I'm sorry," he muttered.

Dr. Goering remained calm. "Your leg's badly infected. As you know, we weren't able to remove the bullet. It's lodged in the bone. The necrosis is spreading and sending poison out through your blood." He pointed to a large area of oozing, black, foul-smelling tissue in the calf.

Rolf started to panic. "But antibiotics should be stopping the infection."

"You've been on penicillin for nearly a week and it's not helping. The situation is beyond the reach of medicine now. If something's not done, the infection could spread throughout your body and kill you. There's no easy way to say this."

"Say what?" Rolf was defiant. "What are you saying?"

"We have to amputate your leg immediately. This afternoon. Hopefully, we'll save the knee. There's no alternative."

The doctor's words were as savage as any bullet. Rolf gasped. "My God! This can't be happening! My lung is better. My shoulder is better. *I'm* better! I need my legs, Doctor! Both of them!" Loretta moved next to him, tears in her eyes, and took his hand.

"I'm very sorry, but I'm sure of my diagnosis." Now his tone was tinged with sadness.

"But can't we wait a little longer, see if it gets better on its own?" He was begging.

"We've waited as long as we can. I didn't want to alarm you earlier, but if we don't act now, we'll lose you. Unless you absolutely refuse, I'm going out to call the surgeon. If he's available, the operation should be done this afternoon. Shall I call him?"

Trapped like a bear with a bloody paw caught in a monstrous trap, Rolf couldn't speak as every drop of energy drained from every limb. Dr. Goering waited until finally, looking away, the young man managed a barely perceptible nod.

"All right, we'll be back soon."

Alone with Loretta, Rolf broke loose. He looked around wildly, hyperventilated, sobbed. "I'll be a cripple! A fucking cripple! Do you understand? Can't he give it a little more time before cutting my fucking leg off?" He raged, even tried to get out of bed, but the pain immobilized him. "How will I work? How will I become a doctor? This is so goddamn unbelievable! I'm only twenty-three." But even as he railed, he knew his objections were futile.

Spent, he shut his eyes, locked his jaw, and then convulsed. The world he'd envisioned in Loretta's eyes only minutes before was gone, stolen away forever. The cruelty was incomprehensible. Now all he wanted was to be at home in his own bed with his mother holding him, protecting him. Saving his leg. And all that was gone too.

Loretta cried with him, then cupped his face in her hands, wiped away his last tears, and spoke with clarity and authority, "Look at me, Rolf." At first, he wouldn't, but when he finally complied, she locked her gaze into his swollen eyes, and said, "If it's what must be done, then let's get it done so you can live. And you have to live. You will get through this."

His voice was now no more than a quivering whimper. "But how? How will I ever get over this?"

"With me. We'll get through this together."

The surgeon arrived, the same man who'd operated on him before. He examined the leg, reviewed the charts, and concurred in the verdict. Minutes later, Rolf was being rolled down a long-but-too-short hallway that stank of bitter antiseptic and palpable fear. Loretta walked with him to the open door of the lime green operating room and kissed him on the forehead. He looked back at her pleadingly, but neither of them could speak. As the door swung shut, he thought about how much he loved her, but part of him wished that he wouldn't awaken this time.

# Chapter 32
# NEW YEAR'S RETRIBUTIONS

Happy New Year!" Harold was finishing his first cup of coffee when Loretta and Carol Ann came down into the warm kitchen. Winter had returned with a vengeance the day before. It started with a harsh north wind and a dramatic temperature drop, then came tiny snow pellets that were still falling lightly as the Unruh family gathered at the breakfast table. "Did you girls make any resolutions for 1944?"

"Yes," said Carol Ann, shuffling her slippers heavily across the wood floor. "To stay in bed until six o'clock every morning."

"Oh dear, you've already broken it," her father said with affected solemnity. "Well, the sooner we get the cows milked and the animals fed and watered, the sooner we'll be back inside."

"Good morning, Papa. Good morning, Mama." Loretta was always more chipper than her sister in the morning. "How did you sleep?"

"Good. Sleeping next to your father is like having my own personal stove in bed."

"I'm happy to do what I can to keep those ice-cold feet of yours from freezing solid. By the way, Clara, your rolls smell especially good this morning."

"Do we have any plans today?" Loretta asked as she filled her and her father's cups with steaming black liquid from the pot on the stove.

"I don't think so. You have something in mind?"

"I thought we might all go see Rolf and cheer him up."

"Doesn't he really just want to see you?" Carol Ann hadn't been privy to all her parents' and sister's discussions, but she'd heard enough to confirm her suspicions about Loretta and Rolf, and she'd watched Loretta drive to Hillsboro every day since Rolf was shot to visit him.

Casting her sister a sideways glance, Loretta said, "He'd like to see everyone. Even you."

"What do you think, Harold? Should we venture out on a day like this?" Clara asked.

"It's not a bad idea if the snow stops. We haven't had so much that we couldn't drive, at least not yet. I can put the chains in the trunk, though, just in case."

"I'd like to go," Clara said, "I haven't seen him since that day."

Carol Ann said, "Papa, you can show him how you're doing after losing two fingers."

"Losing fingers isn't the same as losing a leg. He's got a hard row to hoe. With his family so far away, maybe we can fill in a little. What time are visiting hours?"

"Two to four."

"All right then. If the roads look good enough, we'll drive over in time to be there around two. How would that be?"

"Sounds good, Papa. Thank you," said Loretta.

"Should we take him a little care package?"

"Good idea," replied his wife. "Maybe some rolls, if you don't eat them all." After prayers for the new year, Clara added, "Let's not forget to take Rolf's pack to him too."

⌁⌁⌁⌁⌁⌁⌁

As they reached the hospital's second floor, the family saw several uniformed Americans loitering outside Rolf's room, including Jordan, who noticed their surprise and came over to put them at ease. "Happy New Year! How are you all?"

"A happy and peaceful 1944 to you," said Harold. "We're fine, thanks. And you?"

"I'm well, but I sure do miss your cooking, Mrs. Unruh." Jordan grinned.

"Is it all right that we came to see Rolf?"

"Of course, but he's meeting with a couple Germans from Concordia right now."

"So that's why there are so many guards here?"

"Yes, they came from Concordia too. I don't know them."

"Who are the Germans?"

"One is a Major Streicher. The other is a lieutenant. I didn't get his name."

"We'll go find a waiting room until they're gone."

Jordan looked at a clock. "They just went in, but it shouldn't take long." Then to Harold, he added, "Say, would you mind doing me a favor? A little eavesdropping?" He pointed to the half-open door to Rolf's room.

"What do you mean?" questioned Harold.

"None of us knows German that well. Could you let me know what they're saying?"

"Do you think I should? Isn't it a private conversation?"

"They're all POWs, so we have the right to know. Plus, I have a hunch that Mueller might want somebody to hear." Jordan lowered his voice. "He thinks this major was involved in some wrongdoing in Concordia. That's why he tried to escape."

"Well, if you think it's okay. I wouldn't want to get caught."

"If you stand right there," Jordan pointed, "you should be able to hear and not be seen. I told them not to shut the door completely."

"All right." Listening in felt devious, but with Jordan's reassurances, Harold agreed and found the spot.

Rolf was startled awake from a nap when he sensed two men lurking on either side of his bed. Streicher was waiting to be saluted, but when Rolf saw who it was, he refused even the pretense of military protocol. He looked from one to the other but said and did nothing. *What was it Willy used to say? Stick a fork in me, I'm done?* That's how he felt.

Rebuffed, Streicher began officiously while the lieutenant took notes. "*Gefreiter* Mueller, we are here pursuant to provisions of the Geneva Convention that allow us to inspect hospital conditions for injured prisoners. How are you feeling?"

Silence would probably prolong the interrogation, so Rolf replied tersely. "I'm fine."

"Your medical care has been satisfactory here in, what is the name of this institution? Salem Home and Hospital?"

"Yes."

"And the American guards are now treating you appropriately?"

"Yes."

"You will be returned to the hospital at Camp Concordia in a few days. Before then, is there anything your senior officers can do for you?"

Rolf laughed. "You've done enough." The lieutenant heard, but said nothing.

"The Americans' report indicates that you escaped by slipping out of the theater in Concordia during the Christmas concert. Is that correct?"

"Yes."

"Who were the Americans guarding you that night?"

"I don't know."

"Surely you know the name of at least one of them."

"I do not. I'd only been back in Concordia one day. Perhaps you do— you were there."

Streicher ignored him. "Did anyone assist you in planning or executing your escape?"

"No."

"Then how did you get so far from Concordia in such a short period of time?"

"I ran."

"At the time you were shot, were you acting in a threatening manner toward anyone?"

"No."

"Were you armed?"

"No."

"Do you know the guard who shot you?"

"No."

"Why were you at that particular farm?"

"I was familiar with it and hoped to secure food and provisions before continuing on."

"Is that all you were 'familiar with' at that farm?" Streicher said snidely.

"Of course, I knew the people I worked for there. Is that what you mean?"

"Did anyone living at that farm assist you beforehand in planning your escape?"

"No."

Streicher motioned for the lieutenant to move to a corner before continuing. "Do you recall our conversation the night we returned to Camp

Concordia from Peabody?"

"Yes."

"Have you shared what I said to you that night with anyone? Anyone at all?"

Rolf blinked. "No."

"Are you certain?"

"Your secrets are safe with me."

"As I expect them to be, *Gefreiter* Mueller." Streicher lowered his voice slightly, but continued emphatically, "Need I remind you that we still know where your family lives?" No reply. "Lastly, your hearing before our tribunal will be rescheduled when you return. The fact that you were wounded does not diminish your duty or absolve you of past wrong-doing or mitigate your punishment if you committed treason by aiding the enemy or by slandering the *Fuehrer* or the Fatherland." Then Streicher couldn't resist a final jab. "Stultzman learned the price of treason and slander. You will, too, regardless of how many legs you have to stand on."

Rolf eyed the major blankly, seeing while not seeing, would not give him the satisfaction of a response.

"This interview is concluded. We'll see you in Concordia shortly, *Gefreiter* Mueller."

The lieutenant stepped forward and brought himself to attention. "*Seig heil!*"

"*Heil* Hitler!" the major replied perfunctorily, while Rolf remained mute. In the hall, the Germans saw an old Kansas farmer hurrying away past the guards but thought nothing of it.

Rolf was still seething, but his spirits lifted as soon as the Unruhs and Jordan walked in. "How nice to see you all!" Amid handshakes and hugs, Clara was offering *pflaumenkuchen* and cinnamon rolls to him and Jordan even before her coat was off.

Rolf was even more surprised when Clara handed him his knapsack, or rather, the one he stole while he was on the run. Quickly opening it, he found Willy's painting, which he'd removed from its plywood back and rolled up. It was crumpled and frayed, but still intact, a sight for sore eyes. He explained its significance and gave it to Loretta for safekeeping. Then he found Willy's note hidden in a side pocket and quietly handed it to Jordan, who nodded.

Once his guests had found chairs, they chatted lightheartedly about the holidays and the weather. There was no talk of the amputation until Jordan announced that Rolf would soon be going back to Concordia for rehab and to be fitted for a prosthetic leg.

The young man's eyes widened. "The Americans will do that for me? I had no idea."

"The guards who were just here told me. The camp hospital has the latest equipment and supplies. It's got both American and German medical personnel."

"Incredible!" His hopefulness was unmistakable. The conversation then turned to the wonders of modern medicine and the functionality of the new prosthetics until Carol Ann, bored, returned to complaining about how she'd already had to break her New Year's resolution. Turning to Rolf, she said, "What about you? Do you make resolutions in Germany?"

"We do."

"What's yours for 1944?"

His expression grew very serious. "I resolve not to get shot for a whole year."

The group laughed, and Loretta said, "I hope you keep yours better than Carol Ann did."

"So far, so good." He smiled back at her. Both were grateful that they could be openly friendly even this much in front of her family.

The time to leave came too quickly. As he was putting an arm into his coat sleeve, Harold said, "It's good to see you, my friend. Now hurry and get back up to speed. Spring will be here before you know it. I'll need you then."

"Do you really mean that, Mr. Unruh?"

"Of course I do, Outside of our boys, you're the best farm hand I've ever had."

He looked forlornly at the sheet over the area where his lower left leg should have been, then up at Harold. He hesitated, afraid to ask, but the question came out anyway, "Even now?"

Harold gave him a heartfelt look of encouragement and patted his shoulder. "Son, you're a little banged up, and you've gotta get that new leg, but you'll be all right." Rolf smiled. "You've got a good head on your shoulders, you're strong, and you're a hard worker. As soon as you're fixed up, I want you back. And I'll be pestering the Army until they send you."

Rolf was so moved that he could barely speak, "Thank you, sir, very much."

Out in the hall, Harold told the family to go ahead, said he'd catch up, and turned to Jordan. "We must talk soon, Greg. I'll fill you in on everything I heard. It's quite the story. I'm gonna write it all down as soon as I get home, so I don't forget."

# Chapter 33

# AS YOU SOW, SO YOU REAP

Heavy boot-stomping announced the arrival of men at Camp Concordia's administration building, but they still brought big snow clumps inside with them, along with frigid air. In a corner, Peter Frankel and Rolf shivered and hoped they'd shut the door quickly.

"Hello, Mueller," Greg Jordan called, unrecognizable until he and George Stevenson had their hats and outerwear off. "Sorry we let all that cold in."

Rolf rose, leaning on his cane, and grinned. "Hello, Private Jordan and Lieutenant Stevenson. It's good to see you." Then his smile grew even broader when he saw the third man standing behind them. "Mr. Unruh? What are you doing here?"

"Hello, my boy, how are you? New leg, I see. How's it working for you?"

Rolf motioned downward. "Not as good as the old one, but much better than a crutch. I'm getting used to it, see." He demonstrated with a few steps, using the cane only sparingly, then introduced Frankel and turned back to Harold. "So really, what are you doing here?"

"Same as you—I'm gonna speak with Colonel Jones about Major Streicher." Rolf looked baffled. "Since Greg and Lieutenant Stevenson were driving up, they let me ride along."

Jordan interjected, "I didn't tell you before because I wasn't sure they'd want Harold to testify, but they do. He overheard your conversation with Streicher on New Year's Day and is here to tell them what he heard."

"That major of yours didn't think a dumb old farmer would overhear him threatening his own man. The ones in charge need to know what kinda troublemaker he is." He patted Rolf on the shoulder. "Now tell me, what are you doing with yourself all day? Are you working?"

"No, I'm still in the hospital in a rehab ward so nurses can keep an eye on the leg. I've had some swelling and a couple infections where the new leg connects to my old one, so they want to be sure it's under control. They're also helping me learn to walk all over again. It's different, but I'm getting better. It's been almost two months now."

"Glad to hear it."

"In fact, I expect that I'll be discharged from the hospital soon and returned to a general barracks, and then hopefully will be assigned something to do for work."

"So, you haven't run into Otto Hecht, have you?"

"Hecht is here? No, I didn't know he was back in Concordia. Is he up for a disciplinary hearing too?"

Lieutenant Stevenson replied, "Initially, yes." Rolf looked puzzled. "When I filed my report with the statements of Mr. Unruh and Private Jordan, Concordia ordered him brought back here to disciplinary proceedings along with Streicher and Braun. But now I hear that he's going to cooperate with us and give testimony against Streicher."

"Why would he do that?"

"He says he was only acting under duress, that Streicher forced him to find reasons to get you back up here because Streicher's out to get you."

Rolf replied, "But from the day we arrived in Concordia last August, Hecht was only too happy to spy for Streicher and do his dirty work. He even talked about committing acts of sabotage on farms right after we got to Peabody."

"He'll say that he had to say those things because Streicher was threatening his family if he didn't cooperate."

"That is something Streicher does, but Hecht will say or do anything to save his own neck. I don't trust him, not after what he did to me. And I don't think anyone else should."

"That's understandable." Stevenson replied. "We'll have to see what this hearing panel decides. They could still discipline him, but the ones they're after are Streicher and Braun."

Harold said, "And the truth is, we never had any problems with Otto at the farm. Far as I know, he worked hard and behaved himself. The only problem was when he got his nose out of joint when we were going down to two workers for the winter and didn't pick him to stay."

"You're right," replied Rolf, but he thought it highly suspect that Hecht's allegiance had shifted so suddenly.

At ten o'clock sharp, an American officer opened an inner door and invited Stevenson in. To the others he said, "Please stay here, and don't discuss the matter among yourselves."

As they sat down, Jordan leaned in to Rolf and said quietly, "I have Willy's note. I'll give it to the officers when it's my turn."

"Thank you so much." To Harold, he said, "How is everything on your farm?"

"Well, no one's gotten shot lately," he chuckled. "Last week, it was warm and dry enough to get some field work done. We're tired of winter now, ready for some spring. The wheat looks good so far. I've got Anton and Erich coming out every day to help. They're doing a good job. You taught them well."

"And your family?"

"Carol Ann is ornery as ever. Clara is good too. They both said to tell you hello if I saw you. And last we heard, John and Joseph were both okay. So, the family's good, the cattle are good, the farm's good. Let's see, is there anyone I'm forgetting?" Harold scratched his chin.

Rolf played along. "You have another daughter, don't you? Loretta, I think?"

"Oh yes, the older girl. I almost forgot." Harold winked. "Loretta's good, thank you for asking. She's keeping herself busy."

"If you don't mind, would you please tell her hello from me?"

"Happy to. And, let me see, oh yes—she told me to tell you hello too. I almost forgot."

Even this modest update was appreciated. Rolf had had no word from Loretta since he left Hillsboro, nor had he written to her. He wasn't sure he could write to Americans but decided it would be unwise to even try to do so through regular channels until everything was resolved.

After Stevenson, Jordan went in, then Frankel. When Frankel had finished and was making his way to the front door, he gave a reassuring look and nodded slightly. Then it was Rolf's turn. He followed the American into the conference room, where Colonel Jones and two other officers were talking quietly on the other side of a long table. At one end sat a dowdy older woman in a no-frills black dress who would transcribe Rolf's testimony and, next to her, a uniformed translator.

Jones looked up. "Good morning, Corporal Mueller." He pointed to the empty witness chair across from the panel. "Are you comfortable proceeding in English, or would you prefer that we speak through a translator?"

"English is fine, sir."

"Very well then, please raise your right hand. Do you solemnly swear that the testimony you give in this hearing is the whole truth, so help you God?" As soon as Rolf said yes, Colonel Jones stated that the hearing officers were considering whether continued placement of Major Streicher and Privates Braun and Hecht at Concordia or its satellites was appropriate and also whether Rolf's violation of camp rules and escape warranted discipline.

For an hour Rolf candidly answered rapid-fire questions about what he'd heard Streicher say about Willy's death, about the threats made to himself, about how Streicher had said that German officers had final authority over the enlisted POWs. By their questions, the Americans seemed to know what they were looking for.

Speaking so forthrightly would not have been possible a few months earlier, but Rolf knew he'd be in danger again as soon as he was out of the hospital if something wasn't done, so now he told the Americans everything. If he'd trusted them earlier, maybe he wouldn't have lost his leg, but there was no point in second-guessing himself. He was even ready to tell the truth about his romance with Loretta, including leaving the Eyestone Building in December. He would be honest about everything except the part Jordan played in facilitating their get-away because he didn't want to get his friend in trouble. He wasn't sure how he'd explain getting out that night, but he needn't have worried. The Americans never asked.

When the tribunal recessed at noon, Rolf was told to return at two. While the others went to get lunch, he hurried back to the hospital, found a tablet and pencil, and wrote:

*Tuesday, 22 February 1944*

*Dearest Loretta,*

> *You can't imagine how happy I am to see your father. He says you're well and that you said to tell me hello—music to my ears! Now I'm hoping he will deliver this to you.*

*I'm well too. It's still hard to get my balance, I fall sometimes when I go too fast. Some days I feel sorry for myself, and there are sores where the straps rub my knee and upper leg, but they will disappear as calluses develop. Sometimes I forget my leg is gone. I miss it, of course, but I have you to thank for encouraging me to do what had to be done so I could go on.*

*In Hillsboro you said you didn't care how many legs I had. Please don't think I am doubting you, but I must ask—is that still true? Is that still how you feel?*

*Right after it happened, I was afraid I'd always be a burden on you or someone. But now I'm starting to see that I still have much to offer. I hope you agree.*

*I read once in an English book that absence makes the heart grow fonder. That's true for me. I hope it is for you, as well.*

*With all my love,*
*Rolf*

Quickly, he sealed the letter in an envelope, pulled on his coat, and returned to the admin building. Before he was called back into the hearing, he inconspicuously slipped the envelope to Harold and asked if he would deliver it to Loretta for him. Harold nodded and said he would do so, and privately.

Just as the hearing was resuming, a loud commotion could be heard in the anteroom. A young officer seated in back was moving to the door just as Major Streicher strode in, uninvited and abrasive as ever. "What is the meaning of this? I was told to appear before this tribunal tomorrow. If testimony is being given about me by this man," Streicher looked down at Rolf, "I demand to be present, along with Colonel Lutzke." He thumped the table as the translator, lethargic after a morning of inactivity and a big lunch, lurched up and quickly began converting Striecher's words into English.

Jones and the other hearing officers were on their feet. The younger officer at the door had stepped out and returned with armed guards, who came up next to Streicher. Jones waited for the German's diatribe to be translated, then he leaned across the table. "You are out of order, sir. This is not a court martial proceeding. It is an administrative hearing regarding camp placement. Neither American nor German military protocols nor the Geneva Convention requires that you be present or that you be afforded legal counsel or the opportunity to question witnesses." While the translator caught up, Jones stared at Streicher calmly and authoritatively. "You're quite presumptuous to make these demands so disrespectfully. You will have the opportunity to be heard tomorrow. Now return to your compound. Do I make myself clear?"

Streicher was taken aback that the usually milquetoast camp commandant would speak so firmly, so he said only, "Yes, sir."

"One last thing, Major Streicher. Military protocols are followed in my camp. Never let me hear you address a senior officer, American or German, in the manner with which you've just addressed me. Are we understood on this point, as well?" Streicher nodded. "Good. You are dismissed." Jones straightened his uniform and sat back down with the other Americans.

His comeuppance complete, Streicher squared his jaw, saluted, and turned to leave with the guards. As he passed Rolf, he gave him the usual look of contempt, but this time there was something different, something new. Was it fear?

On the way out, Streicher saw Harold and knew he looked familiar, but couldn't place him. And Harold saw the major and stood to get his attention. "*Guten tag,* Major Streicher. *Sie müssen lernen, leiser zu sprechen. Ich könnte Ihnen hier hören ganz heraus.*" Stevenson laughed, but not Streicher, whose face flashed recognition. Suddenly he remembered seeing Harold in the hospital in Hillsboro.

"What did you say to him?" asked Jordan as soon as the major was out of the building.

"I said maybe he oughta think about speaking more quietly because we could hear him all the way out here. All the time he seems to be talking too loud. Anyone might hear anything."

Jordan cracked a smile. "That's excellent advice but looks to me like it's coming a little late to be of help to the major."

It only took a few minutes for Rolf to finish. He identified the note from Willy and corroborated Frankel's testimony about what happened in the storeroom. The only thing the panel asked about his escape from Concordia was why he did it.

As Rolf stood to leave, Colonel Jones looked up and said, "Before you leave, Corporal, a couple more questions." Rolf turned around. "Did you ever hear Private Hecht directly threaten harm to any member of the Unruh family or that he was going to commit sabotage on their farm?"

He thought for a moment. "No sir, I didn't. *Soldat* Hecht spoke about loyalty and remembering whose side I was on and who was the enemy and our obligation to further the German cause through sabotage, but I never heard him make a specific threat against the Unruhs."

"Thank you, and that's all, Corporal Mueller. You're dismissed."

Harold, the day's last witness, was stepping in as Rolf was coming out. They shook hands, then Harold smiled, tapped his coat pocket holding the letter for Loretta, and nodded.

The following afternoon, Rolf was in physical therapy when he was told to report to the admin building. As he entered, he met Streicher and Braun being escorted out by three no-nonsense guards. Neither spoke to him, but Streicher gave him a dead-eye stare with an odd smirk that sent a chill down Rolf's spine.

Then Hecht came out of the hearing room. Rolf had not seen him since December in Peabody. His jaw tightened with anger, but Rolf didn't act, didn't speak.

"Hello, Mueller. You're looking good," said Hecht, politely. Then he walked out unguarded and headed toward the enlisted men's compound.

Inside the stuffy hearing room, Rolf was thanked for his testimony. Jones said enlisted POWs like he and Hecht needed to be encouraged to report their officers' malfeasance. Then he announced that Streicher and Braun were being transferred immediately to a camp in Alva, Oklahoma, a maximum-security facility for incorrigible Nazis and other dangerous POWs. Rolf was told they would likely be court-martialed in the future for their part in Willy's death and that he might be ordered to testify at that trial.

Colonel Jones looked down at the papers in front of him, then continued, "As for Private Hecht, this panel has determined that his behavior, snitching on a fellow prisoner to gain favor with a German officer, was inappropriate, but he was likely coerced and at any rate the conduct is not sufficient cause for further discipline and he will be returned to Peabody." Rolf tried not to react, but the thought of Hecht getting off without punishment or even a reprimand was irritating. He was walking out on both his legs after costing Rolf one of his.

Regarding the allegations against him, the panel found that Rolf's escape was wrongful but justified. As for his conduct in Peabody, there was insufficient evidence to support a finding of wrongdoing, mainly because the Americans had assiduously avoided asking any questions that might have led to incriminating answers. Perhaps they felt he'd suffered enough. Perhaps they were being lenient because Rolf had helped ferret out the troublemakers. Or maybe Jones was just magnanimous because he'd not have to deal with the irksome major any longer.

⸺⸻⸺⸻⸺

Afterwards, Rolf shared the news with Frankel, then the two of them walked to the cemetery where Willy was buried. They stood next to his snow-covered grave in silence until Rolf offered an ancient prayer. "Eternal rest, O Lord, grant unto your servant, Willy. May his soul and the souls of all the faithful departed rest in peace."

Frankel, who was also Catholic, choked as he said "Amen," and he began to shake. "I'm so sorry that I didn't do more for him that day."

"Peter, there was nothing you could have done. He wouldn't have wanted you to die too."

"He was a good man." Wiping his nose and looking down at the grave, he said, "There's more. I'm ashamed to say that when Willy was buried none of us attended the service."

"Why?"

"Streicher made a big point of labeling Willy a traitor and said he deserved no honor in life or death. We were afraid to stand up to him and knew Braun would report us if we went."

Rolf sighed heavily. "Well, we're here now."

They stood quietly at the grave, then Frankel said, "Willy told me you saved his life."

"He saved mine, too, at least a couple times when I was exposed or out of ammo."

"Yes, but he was talking about a specific incident, and he told me the story a couple times so it must have been important to him. How you and he went into a tent in Libya that was filled with civilians. And hiding behind them were British soldiers hiding and waiting to kill you both. You saved his life, he said."

Rolf's tone turned angry. "Let's not talk about that day. I did what I had to do. That's all." His good foot began tapping the ground.

Frankel replied quietly. "I understand."

They stood there a bit longer, until it was time to move on. By then, Rolf was calmer. "Did he ever tell you about the time in Algeria when he fell into an open latrine? He came up completely covered in shit—only his eyes were visible. My God, the stench! I gave him hell about it for weeks. It was the funniest thing I've ever seen." Frankel smiled, and they shared more memories of their friend, funnier and happier ones, as they walked.

Before they parted at the hospital, Frankel turned serious once more. "Willy was right."

"About what?"

"About everything—the war, Hitler, the Nazis, how fucked up our country is."

"Yes, I think he was. It's a shame he didn't get to see what happened today. He would have been pleased. It's a small step, but it's in the right direction. Maybe things will be different around here from now on."

"Do you ever wonder how in the hell we got into this mess?"

"All the time. I shudder when I think about how we let ourselves be manipulated."

"I wonder what it will be like for us once this damn war is over."

"So do I. And I also feel guilty about how well-fed, warm, and safe we are while our families and friends are still in the war. How much more will they suffer before this is all over?"

"I know one thing, the Americans are not what I expected. The ones I've met are mostly decent people. Have you found that to be the case? You were treated well in Peabody, right?"

Rolf laughed. "More than you know, my friend. More than you know."

⊶⊷

Shortly after the hearing, Rolf was discharged from the Camp Concordia hospital and sent to an enlisted men's barracks. He was assigned to work in one of the camp libraries, where he organized, cataloged, and reshelved books and other reading materials. He missed farm work, but spending his days in a library was the best job he could hope for in Concordia. As libraries go, it was small, haphazard, and unremarkable, nothing like the great ones he visited as a child in Köln or as a student in Berlin. But still, it contained nearly a thousand fiction and non-fiction titles, plus newspapers and periodicals. He got to browse through it all and discuss books and authors with other internees as part of his job. His days in the library passed quickly and pleasantly.

One afternoon on his way from the library to the dining hall, he met Hecht. Rolf was surprised but managed to be civil. "Hello, Hecht."

"You're out of the hospital and back in a barracks?"

"Yes, as of a few weeks ago."

"I'm just going in for dinner too. Would you care to join me?"

Rolf eyed him suspiciously and replied, "No. Find someone else to snitch on."

Hecht smirked. "Come on, I only did that because Streicher made me. It's too bad we can't chat, since this might be our last chance." He knew Rolf wouldn't let that pass without commenting.

"Why? Are you dying? Or planning to escape?"

Hecht gave a hollow laugh and smiled in anticipation of what he was about to say. He even waited extra long for effect. "Oh no, tomorrow I'm returning to Peabody. And I get to ride in a truck. I don't have to run."

To Hecht's delight, Rolf couldn't hide his revulsion. "They're letting you go back?" Now Rolf felt his hands tingling and balling into fists.

"Yes, of course. Why not? I was exonerated, just like you." He winked. "Apparently, farmers are asking for all experienced and able bodied fieldhands to work this spring," he said, over-emphasizing *able bodied*. Rolf said nothing. "And I have you to thank."

"What?"

"Back in September, I knew nothing about farming, but you showed me how. You even said I was doing a good job. Mr. Unruh praised me too. And now I'm in demand, as are all *able-bodied* POWs." Hecht loved taunting Rolf. "I have you to thank, and who knows, maybe I'll be sent back to the Unruh farm. Wouldn't that be great?"

Rolf stepped closer until their faces were mere inches apart. His fists were clenched tight. It would be so easy to bloody Hecht's nose or beat him senseless. And he wanted to, so badly.

Hecht beamed at getting exactly the reaction he was trying to provoke. "Careful, Mueller, you don't want to get caught starting a fight with me. You might really get in trouble this time. Although with your peg leg, you're not as intimidating as you were before."

It took all of Rolf's internal fortitude to keep from pummeling the arrogant bastard right there at the door to the mess hall and taking whatever punishment the Americans gave him. But he stayed in control of his emotions and took a step back. As he did, he was ashamed to realize how close he was to resorting to physical violence once again.

Hecht savored his victory. "That's better. Maybe you're smarter than I thought. Or weaker." He paused. "I'm glad I got to see you before I go. If I get reassigned to the Unruh farm, I'll tell Loretta hello for you. I hope she's still irresistible." He grinned lecherously.

Rolf's anger surged again, but he held it back. "Let me give you the same advice you gave me once: Don't forget where your loyalties lie. You're no longer Streicher's trained poodle. You don't want to end up in Oklahoma."

Hecht replied quickly and sharply, "I know exactly where my loyalties lie." Now it was he who stepped in closer to Rolf with a swagger and his tone softened. "Poodle? Really? I'm a Rottweiler." With a haughty grin, he turned to walk into the hall.

⸺⸻⸺

Rolf headed for his barracks. He'd lost his appetite and wanted to seethe in private. But on the way, he detoured to go to Willy's grave. It was a perfect spring evening, clear and warm. The scent of new pasture grass floated on the mild breeze. By the time he reached the cemetery, Rolf was feeling less angry than sad.

With effort, he managed to get down on one knee at Willy's grave. The dirt mound over his friend was slowly settling. Dandelions and wild violets sprouted from seeds carried in on the wind were blooming, and clover and prairie grasses were slowly reclaiming the area.

"I hope you can hear me, my friend. I miss you." He paused and looked off toward the fields beyond the camp fence. "You were my best friend, Willy. You always had good advice when I got hot." He wiped tears from his eyes. "I want to ask you a question: How did you always manage to stay so positive, even when we were going through some rough shit? And there was a lot of rough shit. How did you keep from blowing up when people were assholes? You despised the officers and propagandists and apologists, and you got mad at them, but you never let that warp your convictions or dampen your enthusiasm for life. You never sold your soul." Fresh tears came now. "You looked for beauty in the face of evil, and you found it. I still have your painting of Bizerte and my lucky pig." He smiled sadly. "It cost you your life, but you lived free right up to the end." Rolf struggled to regain his composure. "Now I'm trying to be more like you, I want to learn to be free. So, if you wouldn't mind sharing some of your secrets for staying positive, I would be grateful." Rolf stood and dusted off his knee. "I gotta go now. Love you, my friend. And no wisecracks about how funny it is watching me kneel down and get back up! I can hear you laughing!"

A few steps from the grave, Rolf turned around, "The next time I come, I'll tell you about Loretta. You would have liked her."

# PART

IV

Chapter 34

# NO MAN'S LAND

On Tuesday, June 6, 1944, an announcement woke all the internees in Camp Concordia before dawn: The Allied invasion of France from England had begun. Rolf tried to gauge reactions in his barracks, but no one was saying much that morning. When he met Peter Frankel in the mess hall for breakfast that morning, he asked him what he thought.

"I haven't heard much, but it sounds like this is the real thing. And it's going to be brutal."

"And bad for us. The Allies are going to take back France, then it's just a matter of time before they're in Germany, and they're not going to stop at the border like in 1918. With the Russians moving in from the east, there's only one possible outcome."

"I just hope the Americans or Brits reach Dortmund and my family before the Russians."

"Same here. We should be okay since Olpe and Dortmund are both in the west."

Throughout the day, he listened to speeches by General Eisenhower, Prime Minister Churchill, President Roosevelt, and King George on the library radio, along with reports from London war correspondents. A staggering eleven thousand planes and four thousand naval vessels were reported to be taking part, making the invasion, dubbed D-Day, the largest in history. This was indeed *das Echte*, the big one, the attack everyone had been expecting since North Africa fell.

After lunch, Rolf pulled out his journal in the library and wrote:

Date: 6 June 1944, Location: Camp Concordia: The Allies have begun their invasion of France on their way to Germany. Are they unstoppable? I remember how hard I fought in 1940 when Germany conquered France. At the time, I thought we were unstoppable, and that France would be under German control for a thousand years. Now Hitler's fantasies have turned into nightmares for everyone involved. All that's left is death and destruction. What we didn't destroy the Allies now will. What will be left when the fighting is over? (If someone steals this journal and reads these lines, I could be branded a traitor. But I no longer care.)

That night, a fistfight broke out near his bunk over speculation about whether the Allies had secured beachheads in France and whether the Germans could drive them back out. After things calmed down, Rolf still had a hard time sleeping. Battle memories mixed with wonderings about Joe Unruh and his brother and acquaintances still in the *Wehrmacht* who all might now be warring in France. He suspected the battles in which he had fought would pale in comparison to the hell that was now unleashed so close to his home and family. Ghosts from France and Libya returned to haunt him, then he gasped when he saw the faces of his family intermingled with those of his victims. *I did what I had to do,* he thought while lying on his bunk with his foot tapping out its familiar cadence. Now, what will the Allies do because they had to?

Camp life returned to normal for a few weeks after D-Day. Rolf began each morning with a rigorous work-out. He couldn't run or play soccer, so instead he lifted weights and modified calisthenics routines to fit his new circumstances. Six days a week, he worked in the library. He also took classes offered by the University of Kansas on organic chemistry, anatomy, and physiology, and he attended history and geography seminars for fun. The medical courses were for officers only but a doctor he met during his convalescence recommended that he be allowed to take them. The same doctor also let him watch several surgeries. Sometimes he felt like he was back at university.

Most evenings, he and Peter got together. It wasn't the same as with Willy, but Rolf appreciated having a confidant again, even told Peter about Loretta. Often, they went to the movies, which were shown five times a week. Mostly American films, and also a few German ones from before the Nazi era. But beneath this superficial sense of normalcy, Rolf's and Peter's anxieties grew as the news from France grew more grim.

Early in July, Camp Concordia was rocked by a disturbing event. Germans were playing soccer on a field near the fence when a ball was kicked out into the no man's land. One of the players, Adolph Koehler, stepped out there to retrieve it and was shot and killed without warning by a guard in a nearby tower. He had assumed that Koehler was trying to escape, but other POWs had retrieved balls from the no man's land many times. Other guards told them it was okay. Koehler's death enraged the Germans, who were further enraged because the Americans seemed indifferent to the death, refusing to even consider whether a mistake had been made.

For three days, the Germans protested with demonstrations and marches. Camp Concordia went into lockdown. Outside work stopped, civilian workers weren't allowed in, classes were cancelled, and most Germans refused to work. Meals still got fixed, but little else. For those three days, Concordia looked and felt like a real prison.

Rolf didn't join in the demonstrations, but he also didn't report for work. Deeply depressed, he turned to his journal to try to sort out why:

Date: 10 July 1944. Location: Camp Concordia: I can't get over the death of the soccer player. Why? Willy is dead, my brother might be dead, I didn't know Koehler, so why does he matter to me like this? Maybe the question is, why shouldn't he matter? His death was so meaningless. An American had just casually ended the life of another human being for only one reason—the man was German. Like me. It's just one more life, but it's one more life wasted! Of course I should grieve for him and for his family. But then shouldn't I grieve for all the lives lost? For all the lives I took? How can I get through this?

When things finally started to settle down in the camp and in his head, Rolf forced himself out of the barracks for a walk. Near the hospital, he met an American surgeon, Fred Schulte, who had fitted Rolf for his prosthetic leg and helped him learn to walk again. In his sixties, kind and considerate, he initially took a liking to Rolf. Schulte's father was Swiss, and he spoke some German. And after Rolf spoke of his interest in medicine, they frequently discussed the profession. Rolf came to look up to him as a wise mentor.

"How are you?" Schulte was the kind of man who was genuinely interested in knowing the answer to that question whenever he asked it of anyone, even after a twelve-hour shift.

"I guess I'm okay."

"If you don't mind my saying, you don't look okay. What's troubling you?"

"I'm tired."

"Want to talk?"

"Can I ask you a question?"

"Ah, a question answered with another question." Schulte smiled, "Go on, please."

"How do you like practicing medicine in a POW camp?"

"That's an interesting one. How about we sit down over there for a few minutes." Rolf nodded, and they headed to a bench shaded by the hospital. "So, you're asking how I feel about treating the enemy, is that what you want to know?"

"Yes, I suppose it is. Your army's mission is to destroy my country's army. But if one of us gets captured and injured, you try to help him recover, like you did me. How does that make any sense?"

"I took an oath to heal the sick and treat the wounded. There was nothing about treating only the good guys. I became a doctor to provide medical care to everyone."

"Wouldn't you rather be treating Americans?"

Schulte smiled and looked up at the sky. "Some in my own family have been asking me that same question since I was assigned here. They want to know how I can help the very people who started the war in Europe and are killing Americans. My brother even called me a traitor. He told me what I should be doing is helping the Army execute you all."

"Good Lord!" Rolf was taken aback by the sharpness of the sentiment.

"My answer to him is the same as it is to you: On the operating table, I don't see a person's nationality or his religion or his color. I don't care about his past. I only see someone in need of medical help, which I do my best to provide. A human life is a human life."

"No exceptions?"

"No exceptions. It's not that I don't think Germans have done some terrible things. I do. I hope you don't mind my saying so, but I think Hitler and the Nazis have to be stopped.”

Rolf was surprised at how quickly he replied, “Me, too. At least now I do.”

“That said, all war is an abomination. But I’m lucky because I never had to be the one killing or maiming people.”

Sullenly, Rolf turned away. “Here you are saving Germans while on the other side of the same camp, guards are shooting them dead.”

“We’ve created so many moral and philosophical contradictions. Our leaders say this war must be fought for noble purposes—to rid the world of evil, to make us all safe, to rectify past wrongs, or, and this is my personal favorite, to promote peace. But to achieve these lofty goals, each one of us is forced to participate—some more, some less—in the wholesale slaughter of warriors and bystanders, ones like Corporal Koehler, who were just in the wrong place at the wrong time.”

“Lately I’ve felt death all around me again, like I’m being swallowed up by it.”

“That’s not surprising, is it? Look at all you’ve been through. You were expected to kill, and I assume you did. You were probably even told it was honorable and heroic to do so.”

Rolf recalled his pledge to obey Hitler and his concomitant obligation to kill whenever ordered without asking why. The contrast between his oath and Schulte’s made him shudder.

“You’ve been close to a lot of death, my friend.”

“How do I get beyond all that? How do you?”

“I’m lucky because I didn’t have to do what you did. I didn’t have to get my hands so dirty. But yes, I’ve still seen more than enough death in the past few years. To cope when I’m at work, I put everything aside except what I’m doing. If I have a patient with a chest wound, I focus on that chest. If a patient needs an artificial limb, I make sure it fits. I focus on a man’s needs. One man at a time, nothing else.” Schulte paused. “I grieve for every one who’s lost, but then I have to let go of the grief or else I couldn’t do my job.” The two men sat in silence. “And I hope people will turn away from war. I admire the courage of soldiers, but I’m thinking there’s no such thing as a just war, only unjust death and destruction and self-serving justifications. I wonder whether one country’s wrongdoing ever justifies another country’s wrongdoing in response. This tit-for-tat has gone on for centuries. Who will have the courage to end it and try something different?"

"You sound like a Mennonite family I know. To them, all war is a sin against God."

"I'm not religious, but there has to be a better way to solve our conflicts."

Rolf took a deep breath. "So, you don't judge me for having killed people? Can I tell you something?" He waited for a nod then spoke in a whisper. "I've killed people who were just as innocent as the soccer player."

"We've come to a deeper question, haven't we? No, Rolf, I don't judge you. That must be a terrible burden for someone who wants to cure people, not kill them."

"I was told it was my duty. And that's what the American said on Sunday, that the guard who killed Koehler was only doing his duty. Maybe he and I aren't so different."

"I know the guard who killed Koehler. He feels terrible."

"Me too," Rolf whispered.

"Well, that's a big step, isn't it? Remorse lets us know when we've made mistakes. Maybe your next big step will come when you're able to forgive yourself and let go of the guilt."

Sleep-deprived and out of self-control, his eyes filled with tears. "I'm sorry," he sniffed.

Schulte waited quietly. "Don't be. You're a good man, Rolf. Try to focus on that."

How strange, he thought later that night, that Dr. Schulte and Loretta could both see goodness in him when he couldn't see it himself.

# Chapter 35
# RECONNECTED

News of his transfer back to Peabody came with little warning. Late on Saturday evening, the twenty-second of July, Rolf was told he would ship out early the following morning. He barely had time before lights out to pack and find Peter. They promised to find each other back home. Peter was hoping to open a restaurant in Dortmund. Rolf said he would come visit. Dr. Schulte was off, so Rolf could only leave a quick note for him expressing his gratitude. After Koehler's death, they had more long chats. Rolf would miss his mentor too.

This drive, in the back of a hot transport with a dozen other POWs and four guards, was nothing like his first two trips to Peabody. This time there were landmarks to look for—the farms where he sought refuge, the diner he almost walked into, the Poehler building. He had a history in Kansas now. He smiled recalling the ridiculous story he told Nels Thogerson and made a mental note to try to identify the people from whom he'd stolen and to repay them somehow.

His arrival in Peabody was also different this time around. The townspeople were by now so used to the Germans that no one was gawking from porches or following the truck to see one more batch of enemy come to town. And no one was hiding in a barn to shoot at him.

While disembarking at the Eyestone Building, he heard singing, but it wasn't coming from the building. Twenty POWs soon came into view, marching down the street toward them and singing loudly. "Where've you been?" called a man from the truck.

"Playing soccer. There's not enough room in the yard, so they let us go to the city park to play on weekends." At the rear was Greg Jordan, bent over and panting.

Rolf smiled, but couldn't resist teasing his friend. "What's the matter, Private Jordan, too much exercise for you?"

"Those assholes were double-timing it to show off for some girls. Either that or they're trying to kill me in this heat. I'm an old man!" Jordan straightened up, wiped his face, grinned, and saluted. "Welcome back, Corporal Mueller. It's good to see you again."

"At ease, Private," Rolf laughed, then the two shook hands. "How are you?

"I'm glad you're back. With you on that peg leg, I'll have someone I can keep up with."

"Don't be so sure. And is Mrs. Unruh feeding you again? You've grown fatter."

"Shut up! And yes, I have been out there a few times on my days off. They wanted my help in getting you back, plus they know I love Clara's cooking. They're good people."

"You know I agree. Have I been assigned out there again?"

"Yes, sir. You start tomorrow morning."

"I understand that Hecht is back. Has there been any trouble with him?"

Jordan's expression grew serious. "Let's step into the office. Lieutenant Stevenson wants to talk to you. We can do that while your transfer paperwork is getting completed."

Rolf guessed what they were going to tell him, forced himself to stay calm and would let them do the telling. He followed Jordan into the office where Stevenson sat at his desk. Looking up, he said, "Mueller! Welcome back! How's the leg?"

Rolf straightened up and saluted the camp commandant. "Thank you, sir. It's good, and it's very good to be back."

"For all of us," said Stevenson, motioning for Jordan to shut the door and for the two of them to sit down. "It will mean a lot less paperwork for us. I'll bet Mr. Unruh wrote twenty-five letters to the Army demanding that you be sent back to work on his farm, and he hand-wrote a copy of every one for me. He played hard on their sympathies because you were shot by an American on his farm and lost your leg. I never knew the Army to have sympathy for anyone, but they made an exception for you. Or maybe they were just tired of reading his letters."

That drew smiles from Rolf and Jordan. "I don't know what to say, only that I'm grateful to him and to you."

"We're glad to have you back. You went through hell over the winter and helped stop some bad people. It seemed appropriate to honor Mr. Unruh's request."

"Thank you, sir."

"I wanted to welcome you back personally and also tell you that Otto Hecht is back too."

"Yes, sir, I saw him in Concordia, and he told me."

"Correct. And he's been re-assigned to work on Mr. Unruh's farm. He's been working there with Gralke and Zimmerman."

Rolf grimaced. "Sir, is this a good idea? He was exonerated at the hearing in Concordia, but he made direct threats against me and indirect ones against the Unruhs. I believe he is dangerous."

"That's understandable. I don't trust him, either, but here's the dilemma we're in: After Hecht helped put Streicher away, Colonel Jones didn't want him punished because that might discourage other enlisted men from speaking up. He sent him back here, where he isn't allowed to communicate with any officers. And since we know him, we're better able to watch him."

"That makes sense, sir, but why would he be returned to the Unruh farm after Major Streicher said he would order Hecht to hurt them if necessary? Did the hearing officers not believe me?"

"That's a fair question. Yes, they did believe you, but Streicher's in solitary confinement in Oklahoma and we think Hecht's a follower and lazy and wouldn't take the initiative to sabotage anything on his own. Jordan and Flannigan and Unruhs and I talked it over and agreed that the Unruh farm would be the best place for keeping an eye on him. Zimmerman and Gralke know the situation and agreed to help watch him. And I trust them."

"And the Unruhs thought this was a good idea too?"

Jordan looked at Rolf. "There's another reason the Unruhs were willing to hire Hecht back. Remember last winter I told you about the letter he wrote to them apologizing and asking for forgiveness and all that?" Rolf nodded. "When Mrs. Unruh heard he was returning to Peabody, she specifically asked if they could rehire him. She believes in her heart that God is calling the Unruhs to help Hecht find salvation."

Rolf shook his head in disbelief. "What about Mr. Unruh? Does he believe that?"

Jordan replied, "I don't think so, but he believes in forgiveness and second chances."

Stevenson stood. "So that's what we wanted to tell you. Can we count on you to watch Hecht and report any problems?"

Rolf thought for a moment before replying. "I still think it's a terrible idea to have Hecht working for the Unruhs or anyone else. But if that's what the Unruhs and you think is best, then absolutely, sir, I will do whatever I can to be sure he doesn't cause problems."

"Thank you," said Stevenson, "and welcome back."

Jordan stepped out of Stevenson's office with Rolf. "I still think Hecht is a piece of shit, but I think you're the best person to help us keep him under control. You pay attention to things, you notice what's going on, and the Unruhs trust you." Jordan laughed. "And if you get the tractor stuck in gear again and end up running over Hecht, my only advice? Don't do it in front of the family and be sure you don't just wound him." Jordan winked.

Rolf laughed, then grew serious. "Having to work with the man who is most responsible for all I went through is not going to be easy, but I can handle it if it helps keep everyone safe."

As he was stowing his gear, POWs and guards came over to welcome him back, including Zimmerman and Gralke, plus Flannigan and even Three Shot Scott. Then when he and his friends walked into the dining hall, they met Hecht. Rolf had had time to anticipate the moment, but Hecht didn't know Rolf was back and was caught unawares. An awkward silence ensued. Rolf stopped walking when he saw him and said nothing, just looked directly at Hecht and waited for him to pass in front of him.

As he did so, Hecht regained his composure and held out his hand. "Welcome back, Mueller," he said. "It's good to see you again."

Rolf didn't take Hecht's hand. Instead, he gave Gralke a sideways look and said, "Is it not customary for German soldiers to salute when meeting one another, with the one lower in rank offering his salute first, not a handshake?"

Hecht replied quickly. "Of course you're right, *Gefreiter* Mueller, I apologize." He straightened up and saluted crisply.

Rolf saluted back, but with a condescending flip of his hand, as if he were swatting flies.

"It really is good to see you, and you're looking well and recovered."

"Yes, you said that." When Hecht didn't move, Rolf and the others walked into the dining room without acknowledging him further.

Gralke said, "I'm betting he's not as happy to see you back as he keeps saying." Then he laughed, "And I'm so sorry, *Grefreiter* Mueller, that I failed to salute you when we met earlier."

Rolf laughed and said, "Don't let it happen again, *Soldat!*"

⸻⸻

When Harold pulled up the following morning and Rolf walked out with Zimmerman and Gralke to get in the truck with them, Hecht's initial surprise quickly gave way to a smile. "Isn't this great? The old team is back together. Did you miss working with us, Mueller?" Rolf ignored him and headed to where Harold was standing.

"Welcome back, my boy! It's good to see you again!" He shook Rolf's hand heartily.

"It's great seeing you, Mr. Unruh. Thank you for everything you did to get me back."

"They just got tired of hearing from me. I was writing letters every week asking for you."

Rolf laughed, "Lieutenant Stevenson told me. Thank you."

"The Lord may work in mysterious ways, but the Army's ways are even more mysterious. But you're back, that's what matters, and we need the help, although Erich and Anton and Otto are becoming quite the farmers." From the cab he called jovially, "All aboard!" but he let the clutch out too fast and the truck lurched forward. "Oops! Sorry! Hope we make it home! That hay isn't going to get itself into the barn, is it?"

"*Nein!*" the men called back in hearty unison.

"Alfalfa?" Rolf asked the others.

"Yes," said Zimmerman, "with all the rain, it's thick and the bales are really heavy. Lots of twigs. This will be the first time we've been able to get into the lower fields in weeks. And we have to be on the lookout for mold in the bales."

Gralke smiled. "Listen to you! Mr. Unruh's right, we are farmers now." Rolf closed his eyes and enjoyed the freshness of the morning breeze on his face. It was almost exactly a year since he first came to Doyle Creek. Almost a year since he met Loretta. How good it felt to be in the back of the Unruh truck again, in spite of his stomach jitters over seeing her again after six months.

She and her mother were under a broad old tree out by the garden next to a black kettle hanging on a tripod over an open fire. They were making soap, a smelly, grimy chore best done outdoors and in the cool of a morning. Even from that distance, and though blurred behind a thin veil of gray smoke rising from the fire, she was still intoxicatingly beautiful.

"Rolf?" said Harold. "Rolf!" He was trying to tell the men that he would bring the tractor around, but the young man was so distracted that Harold had to move closer. "For goodness sake, go tell her hello. And don't forget her mother too." He turned to the others. "We'll never get any work out of him until he does."

Rolf blushed and headed toward the women. When she saw him, Loretta put down the wooden paddle she was using and came his way. When they met, they smiled sheepishly and said hello.

Clara joined them. "Rolf, it's good to see you, and doing so well. But I told Harold not to make you walk too far or do anything too dangerous."

"Thank you, Mrs. Unruh, I'll be fine. The new leg is working well, and it's great to see you again."

"Thank you. Don't overdo it out there." As soon as they were out of earshot, Clara gave her daughter a cold look. "Remember who he is, Loretta. And who you are." She glided the paddle in broad loops through the simmering brew of tallow and lye. Loretta looked as if she would reply but just smiled to herself.

At the tractor, Harold asked, "Can you handle being on the wagon with Erich like before? I think that's a better spot for you than walking along on the rough ground."

"I think I can but put me wherever you need me. I'm here to work."

"Okay, but you let me know if it doesn't feel right."

It was hard, but Rolf managed, even overdid it to show Harold that he had not wasted his efforts to get him back.

⚬━╫━⚬━✴━⚬━╫━⚬━✴━⚬

Dinner at the Unruh table was as gratifying as ever, both food-and conversation-wise. Harold peppered Rolf with questions about Concordia, the new leg, his work there, the classes he took. Then he said, "Why don't you give us a look at that new equipment."

"Papa! Don't make him show it." Loretta looked at her father with embarrassment.

"It's all right." Rolf pushed his chair out and tugged his pants leg up above his knee. The middle portion of the contraption was made of solid maple and contoured more or less like a leg. On the bottom were shiny screws and hinges attaching it to a wooden foot hidden inside his shoe. At the top, a hollowed-out portion cupped what was left of his leg below the knee, and above that, leather straps and laces and a sleeve wrapped snugly around his thigh to hold it all in place.

"Looks like a good fit," said Harold admiringly "And you sure don't limp much."

"Does it hurt?" asked Clara.

"Sometimes. In the beginning there was edema, swelling around the stump, which made it hard to put it on, but we got it under control with pressure bandages. Then I got sores where the sleeve goes around. They're healed now and don't bother me as long as I don't get it too tight." He didn't mention how bad he was going to hurt that night after his first full day of strenuous manual labor in months. Apprehensively, he looked at Loretta, who instantly read his mind and smiled back reassuringly. She was not bothered by what she was seeing.

When Rolf finished speaking, Hecht looked at him and then at Harold. "Mr. Unruh, if I may, I would like to say something."

"Of course, Otto. What would you like to say?"

He took a long breath, then nervously and said contritely, "Rolf, I owe you an apology, and I must offer it before these people because they were all affected by my actions. Would that be all right?" Rolf said nothing and showed no emotion, then nodded almost imperceptibly for Hecht to get on with it. Hecht took another breath and began, "I've had a long time to think about what happened last December. Mrs. Unruh, your prayers helped me see how sinful my actions were in the sight of God. I was jealous of you, Rolf, for getting to stay here over the winter while I was sent away. My petty jealousy led me to tell lies about you to Major Streicher. I wanted to hurt you. Because of my sinfulness, you suffered greatly, getting shot and nearly dying and then losing your leg. My sins are great. I asked the Lord for His forgiveness, and now I'm humbly asking you for yours, Rolf." He looked down sadly. "I don't deserve it, but I want you to know how terribly sorry I am for causing you so much pain." At the end of his clearly rehearsed speech, Hecht managed a tear to underscore his sincerity. He gave Clara a sad little look, then bowed his head again, as if he was praying for Rolf to reply.

Rolf sat motionless and expressionless, until finally he said quietly, "I forgive you, Otto."

"Praise be the Lord!" Clara exclaimed, now with a tear in her eye. "Otto, your sins will be forgiven because you have repented." Hecht nodded and wiped an eye, then Clara turned and said with a smile, "Rolf, the Lord says, 'Forgive and ye shall be forgiven.' Thank you."

"Thank you, Mrs. Unruh." Looking across the table at Loretta, he saw her smiling too.

Gralke waited until they were out the gate and out of earshot of the others, then said to Rolf, "I'm from a city, but I've worked on a farm long enough now to know what horseshit is. And that was a big bunch of horseshit coming out of Hecht's mouth just now. It was all I could do to keep from laughing."

Rolf smiled and replied, "It was quite a show, wasn't it? I heard he's even asking about becoming a Mennonite."

Gralke laughed out loud. "I've heard him say it! Can you believe that shit?"

Rolf shook his head. "And the Unruhs are encouraging that?"

"Several times, always in front of Mrs. Unruh and Loretta, he's said how much he admires them for their beliefs and how God must have sent him to them to open his heart! He's even asked for more of the pamphlets Harold gave us that time and then he memorizes them so he can talk about his faith and show them how pious he's become. He's even asked to lead the prayer before dinner a couple times. It's all he talks about when we're at the farm. Such a hypocrite!"

Shaking his head, Rolf said, "Do they really think they're converting him?"

"Not Mr. Unruh or Loretta. I mean, they smile and nod along when Hecht starts getting all holy, but they don't say much. But Mrs. Unruh thinks that her prayers are working, and he panders to that. He asks her to pray for him, likes to tell her what an inspiration she is. I think she thinks he will return to Germany after the war and make Mennonites out of Nazis."

"*Gott in Himmel*! Why is he going to so much trouble?"

"I think he's still trying to get Loretta to like him. But mainly he loves being the center of attention. On the first day you're back, he decides to grab the spotlight for himself? Pathetic."

"Has he started going to church services in camp?"

"Of course not! At camp, away from the Unruhs, he's just as arrogant and selfish as ever. His excuse for not going to Sunday Mass is that a Mennonite service is the only one he wants to attend. He's been asking Mrs. Unruh to see if their preacher might come to the Eyestone sometime. Says he'd like the preacher to counsel him on getting baptized someday."

"He is such a kiss-ass. First with Streicher, now with Mrs. Unruh. Whatever he can do to get ahead. He lectures everyone about loyalty, but his only loyalty is to himself."

It was several days before Loretta and Rolf were alone. The opportunity arose during a raucous afternoon thunderstorm that drove the men out of the fields. Clara and Carol Ann were in town and Harold and three of the Germans were sheltering in the barn. Rolf was stranded on the porch, watching water pour down from the porch roof and cascade over the gutters in sheets when Loretta quietly sat down in the rocker next to him.

"Hi," she smiled shyly.

"Hi."

"Thank you for your letter in February."

"It made it? Good."

"Private Jordan said I couldn't write to you, so that's why I didn't."

"I know. I couldn't write directly, either, so I'm glad your father got that one to you."

"I missed you."

Rolf moved in ever so slightly. "I'm glad to know you still care."

"Of course I do. More than ever."

"The same for me. But, just so you know...." Rolf's look was serious, yet flirtatious.

"What?"

"I don't think we should plan any more midnight rendezvous."

Loretta frowned. "I've felt guilty ever since you were sent back to Concordia, I thought it was my fault because Otto found out and made trouble for you. Maybe if I hadn't come...."

"Don't think that, Loretta. Hecht was going to make trouble no matter what." Under his breath he added, "I would not have missed that night for anything. And I still love you."

"I still love you too." She was reaching over to confirm her words with a touch of his hand when, at that moment, an enormous, iridescent lightning bolt flashed from the ground to the clouds just beyond the creek, accompanied by an instantaneous KA-BOOM! Loretta and Rolf lept from their seats and heard rough German profanities coming all the way from the barn. They couldn't stop giggling.

"There's a sign!" Rolf said.

She was still laughing nervously. "From heaven or hell?"

"It has to be from heaven. Otherwise, we wouldn't be having this conversation."

⌁⌁⌁⌁⌁⌁⌁

A week later, as Loretta was clearing the dinner dishes, Clara stepped into the pantry and came out with an angel food cake with a single lit candle on it. She sat it down in front of Rolf, and the group sang "Happy Birthday."

"But my birthday was weeks ago." Rolf protested as he blew out the candle.

"We know, but you weren't here on the eighth, so we'll celebrate now." Loretta handed him a large flat package wrapped in newsprint with a red ribbon curled into a bow on top.

"What's this? A present? You really shouldn't have."

"Open it," Harold said. "None of us gets cake until you do." Inside was Willy's picture. It had been damaged on Rolf's cross-country adventure, but Harold cleaned and repaired it, then he put it in a simple homemade walnut frame. "Someday, you'll have to tell us more about this friend of yours who painted it."

Rolf was deeply moved. "You'd have liked him."

Zimmerman and Gralke took turns admiring the painting, each remarking how much it reminded them of North Africa. Hecht looked at it with a plastic smile but said nothing.

"He captured the best of it, didn't he?" said Rolf. "He was able to see how Bizerte looked before the war. He would look over the city and then paint what his mind's eye saw. He would have been a great artist." Rolf grew sad at remembering.

"Sounds like he was a special man," said Harold. "And now, in your honor and his, I think we should cut into that beautiful cake. Clara, do we still have any ice cream?"

Before Clara could answer, Hecht spoke up. "I apologize for interrupting, but before we have that delicious looking cake, I would like to say something about someone very special."

Harold did not like for anything to come between him and dessert. "Yes, Otto, please say what you'd like, but let's keep it short." Loretta, Gralke, and Zimmerman all smiled. Rolf sat expressionless, afraid Hecht was going to make some fawning comment about getting to celebrate Rolf's birthday with him.

"I promise I'll be short, sir." Then turning to Mrs. Unruh, he said, "I need to say how thankful I am to God for bringing you and your amazing wife and family into my life. Mrs. Unruh told me this morning that Elder Ratzlaff has agreed to come to the Eyestone Building to counsel me and prepare me for my true believer's baptism into the Mennonite Church. Hopefully before too long, I will be baptized, God willing." He made sure Clara noticed his rapturous expression. "I am so grateful to you, Mrs. Unruh."

Mrs. Unruh said, "We serve the Lord when we share the Good News, right, Harold?"

"Yes," said her husband. The others at the table said nothing. Rolf and Loretta gave each other furtive glances. Harold continued, "This is indeed a day for celebration. Now, let's eat some cake before Rolf turns another year older and Mrs. Unruh has to bake another one!"

⚬⚬⚬⚬⚬⚬

On a sweltering day toward the middle of August, Harold said he had an announcement.

"Is it going to snow?" asked Gralke, mopping his sweaty brow with a handkerchief.

Harold smiled, "Now that would be good news, wouldn't it? Sorry, no snow, but this is even better news. At least my wife and daughters think so."

"Very good news," said Clara as she sat down at the table.

Harold smiled broadly. "Our oldest son, John, is coming home. He'll be here next week."

"He works in a hospital, doesn't he?" asked Hecht.

"Yes, in Maryland." Clara beamed. "We haven't seen him in more than two years."

"God is good," said Hecht.

"What about your other son, the one in the Army?" asked Zimmerman.

Loretta answered, "Soldiers overseas usually don't come home because they're so far away. Joe's had leave in Africa and England, but hasn't come home, so we haven't seen him in two years, either. We think he's in France now."

"German soldiers get to go home on leave, usually every year," Zimmerman said.

"At least you'll get to see one of your sons again," Rolf said. "That's great."

"John will spend more time traveling than he'll be home, but we're still grateful."

"Will you do something special?"

"Yes, we're planning a picnic for Saturday the nineteenth. That's this Saturday.

"Then you won't be needing us that day?" asked Rolf.

"We won't be working in the fields, but we still want you to come out, as our guests. We'll invite Greg too. You can help us set up for the party and do the regular chores, but otherwise, it'll be a day of relaxation and celebration for all of us, you included."

Gralke smiled. "It's been a long time since any of us was invited to a family party."

Hecht turned to Clara with a smile. "You are so kind. I'll be happy to help in any way I possibly can." Clara gave him a nod of gratitude.

On Friday evening, Harold, Loretta, and Carol Ann were at the Newton Depot as the Santa Fe Chief, the premier passenger train from Chicago to Los Angeles, creaked and whooshed to a stop at ten, only an hour behind schedule. As soon as Carol Ann saw John walking forward from the back of the train, she raced ahead. When she finally let go of him, Loretta took her turn hugging her brother and didn't mind that he would see her tears of joy.

At last, it was Harold's turn. "John, my boy! It's so good to see you."

"It's good to see you, too, Papa." He bent down for kisses on both cheeks.

Carol Ann grabbed his hand as they walked to the car. "How long have you been traveling?"

"More than two days. First I took a train to Chicago, then I caught the Chief there."

"Was it crowded? Have you eaten? Were you able to sleep? Were you in a Pullman car?"

He answered his sister patiently. Yes, the train was crowded. No, he hadn't eaten much. Yes, he got some sleep, but not much because he couldn't get a sleeping berth. It was so crowded for part of the trip that he had to stand in the aisle.

"Take us home, son," Harold said, handing him the keys with a grin.

"No, thanks, Papa. I'm too tired. You drive."

Ever since he learned how, it was a family joke that John always wanted to drive. Harold only let him behind the wheel once in a while, but when it was just the siblings in the car, John never let anyone else have a turn. *He's really tired*, Loretta thought.

The moment she saw headlights, Clara was out the door. At the gate, she clutched her son tightly in the enveloping darkness. "Praised be the Lord, you're home!" As soon as they were in the light of the kitchen, she said, "Let's get a good look at you," then, "John! You're so thin!"

"That's because nobody cooks like you, Mama."

"I've got leftover roast and potatoes on the stove for you. And pie. It's all ready."

As he took off his coat, Loretta saw the weight loss too. Well over six feet and taller than Joe by a couple inches, John was always gangly, but now he was gaunt. "Mama's right, you do look thinner."

He gave a wane smile. "And everything here looks just like it did."

Carol Ann planted her elbows on the table beside him. "We have big plans tomorrow. We're having a party for you! Relatives are coming, and friends, including your old girlfriend, Emma Becker. And the Germans."

"The Germans?"

"Yes, the ones who work here. You'll get to meet Loretta's boyfriend."

"Carol Ann!" Loretta scolded her sister.

"Well, he is, isn't he? And he will be here, won't he?"

Loretta was glad their mother didn't hear. Quietly, she said, "You'll like him and the others," and waited for a positive comment or reaction, but John looked away.

When she reached the table with a plate mounded high with food, Clara said, "Here you are. There's bread, too, and let me get your coffee. Would you like anything else?"

"This is fine, Mama. Thank you. It looks great." John began eating without saying grace. *He really must be exhausted*, thought Loretta.

Carol Ann continued the interrogation. How was work? Had he made friends? Did he like getting their letters? Had he been to Washington? In the Capitol? John's answers were polite, but flat. After his mother had stuffed him with a second helping of everything, plus pie, it was time for prayers and bed. On his way upstairs, John offered to help with the morning chores, but his father told him to sleep in since it was already midnight and he must be tired. John didn't argue.

By nine on Saturday morning, the chores were done and party preparations were in full swing. Harold and John drove to town to pick up the Germans, then stop by the church for extra tables and chairs. Harold noticed his son's lassitude, but still tried to engage him. "So we've had the Germans working for us for a year now. Funny as it may sound, they've been a godsend."

"Is that right?"

"Yes, Carol Ann was tired of getting tossed around by the hay bales." Harold chuckled, but got no response. "The farm's in good shape thanks to them."

"That's good."

"You'll enjoy meeting them."

John kept his gaze on the passing countryside. "That's what I keep hearing. And you call them 'the Germans,' not POWs?"

"Yes, we decided that referring to them all the time as prisoners of war sounded inhospitable and judgmental."

"But that's what they are."

"Yes, indeed, and they're also children of God. We try to be kind."

"Everybody, this is John," Harold said proudly outside the Eyestone Building. "John, this is Greg Jordan, the guard." Gregarious as ever, Jordan told him how good it was to meet him. Then Harold introduced each of the Germans by name. John shook their hands, too, but without the eye contact or vigor he had shown with Jordan. Then Harold added, "They all speak English pretty well now, or you can converse in German if you'd like, which is probably easier for them."

"English is fine. This is America, after all," John replied, and got back in the truck cab.

Back at the farm, the men set up tables and chairs in the yard, then Harold and John went in to help the women with the food while the Germans stayed outside with Jordan and relaxed. The yard was soon filled with people. Several made a point of introducing themselves to the Germans and Jordan, including Doris Koehn, who then hurried off to give her assessment of Rolf to Loretta. And when Dora Jantz came over to say hello, she delighted them by sitting down and sharing family stories with them in her old-style, rich-toned German. She reminded each of them of a favorite *großmutter*.

After grace, Loretta led the Germans and Jordan through the line and to a grassy spot under a towering cottonwood tree in the side yard where they could eat on blankets she'd spread out for them. Once, Rolf saw John giving them an odd, vaguely hostile look from across the yard. *How strange,* he thought, or perhaps he was just misreading him.

When everyone had eaten, Harold thanked God again for bringing their son home and everyone else for coming, then announced the afternoon's activities: horseshoes on the pitch near the barn and a baseball game by the creek. The Germans were in for a treat, Harold said. They were going to play baseball! All four laughingly tried to get out of it, but the Americans' cajoling made it impossible for them to say no. Sides were chosen, with two Germans on each team. John, Loretta, Carol Ann, and Harold all played, while Clara looked after the other guests and cheered them on.

It was a perfect afternoon. The August sun shone brightly, and the ground was baked hard, but the breeze was cool and carried a sweet hint of apples from the orchard.

The seven-inning game was spirited, but lopsided. Rolf was put in right field with the idea that not many balls would come his way, but that assumption proved to be faulty when fly after fly headed his direction, He tried valiantly, but his slowness and errors contributed significantly to his team's double-digit loss and the good-natured ribbing that resulted.

By the time the winners had been congratulated, it was time for chores, so Harold, Zimmerman, Hecht, and Gralke went to tend to the livestock while Loretta and Rolf headed to the milk barn. They were starting on the first three Holsteins when the screen door opened. Looking over a cow, Loretta called, "Hey, John, what a nice party. I hope you're having fun."

Her brother said nothing, just stood there staring in a vaguely threatening way.

Rolf approached. "Again, it's good to meet you, John. Loretta has told me many good things."

When her brother didn't answer, Loretta joined them and said, "Is everything okay?"

Anger began to contort John's features. "What do you think you're doing?"

"What do you mean?" Loretta asked nervously.

"You know what I mean. What are you two doing together?"

"Well..."

"This man's a goddamn Nazi, for Christ's sake!" Loretta was shocked. She'd never heard him utter a single profanity or use the Lord's name in vain. Rarely had he even raised his voice in anger. Rolf stepped back, said nothing, wasn't sure what to do, kept working.

Loretta tried to placate her brother. "Maybe you're still tired, John, but that's unfair."

"Unfair? Where do you think he was before he came here?" Now his words erupted from him like molten lava. "First, I'll bet he was cheering on the madman, then he was happily doing his dirty work. He may even have been shooting at our own brother. Have you ever thought of that?" Even louder, he shouted, "Have you?"

Loretta couldn't believe what was happening. Apologetically, she said, "Rolf's a good man. And we have feelings for each other."

"You're being duped by a cold-blooded killer. It's bad enough German POWs are on our farm taking my place and Joe's place and everybody's so goddamn happy about it. And now, one of them wants to fuck my sister too?"

Loretta gasped. "What's come over you?"

"I've spent the last two years cleaning up the blood and shit and piss of good men who suffer because of bastards like him. Human misery you can't begin to imagine. And since D-Day, it's ten times worse. And now I come home and the sons-a-bitches are at my goddamn homecoming party? Have they won the war? Have they taken over America?"

Loretta started to cry. "I never thought you, of all people, would say such things."

"Why? Because I'm the cowardly brother? The CO? Because I'm not heroic or a daredevil like the other one? Maybe you thought since I'm such a pussy, I wouldn't care who you dated? Or that our farm is crawling with Nazis?"

"No!" Loretta shook her head. Now words tumbled out in heaves between gasps. "Because I've looked up to you my whole life. You're one of the kindest people I know. I thought you could look beyond Rolf's past and give him a chance before condemning him."

"Kindness? Ha! Any kindness in me is long gone. I'm sick to the depths of people like him. And my faith's gone too. How could a god allow such suffering? And not just because of what I've seen in one hospital. Don't you read the papers about what these barbarians are doing to the Jews and the mentally ill and Gypsies and homosexuals? How blind can you be?" John was shaking now, his eyes fullwith tears of rage.

"John," Loretta sobbed, "I don't know what to say."

He pointed a menacing finger at Rolf. "Don't ask me to forget what he and his kind have done. Don't ask me to say, 'How nice to meet you, Herr Mueller. Welcome to our farm, welcome to our family, have a nice life, and enjoy my sister, Herr Mueller. *Sieg heil!*'"

Rolf seethed and Loretta cried, "Oh, John," and she moved toward him.

"Stop!" he said, hands outstretched. "I won't have it." Turning, he nearly bowled their father over in the doorway, made it outside, kicked the gravel, and headed east toward the hills.

Harold had been walking to the milk barn and heard the last of John's harangue. "Are you all right?" he asked Loretta. She could not speak, only gave him a pathetic look. He looked out the door. "I think I need to go look after him. I'll be back as soon as I can."

Seeing her pain brought tears to Rolf's eyes, and shame because he hadn't protected her. But how? They clung to each other for a minute, then finished their work in silence. As the last of the cream was separating, her depleted father returned. "I don't know why he's so angry and took it out on you. Maybe we expected him to be the same, and he's not." Loretta hugged him. "And Rolf, I'm sorry you had to hear all that. John really is a good man." Rolf nodded, then Harold continued, "I think it's best if I take you men back now. It's close to time anyway."

"Yes, sir. I'll get the others and meet you at the pickup. Please thank Mrs. Unruh for us. It was a lovely picnic."

Harold inhaled deeply to try to relax, then went ahead. "I'll go find Greg."

Alone with her, Rolf said, "If I've contributed to his unhappiness and yours, I'm so sorry."

"I don't think this has anything to do with you." Her lower lip quivered.

He kissed her on the cheek, whispered, "I love you," and went out to find the others.

By the time Harold got back from town, his children were folding up tables and setting them against the porch. "It's not going to rain tonight, so let's take everything back tomorrow."

"Yes, Papa," said Carol Ann. "Mama's getting supper ready. The Jantzes are still here."

"Good." Harold smiled and walked to the steps. "Are we eating inside or out?"

"Mama said inside. It's too cool out here now for Aunt Dora and

Uncle Peter."

With some effort, Loretta and John were able to come inside looking calm and upbeat. As he made his way across the crowded kitchen to the sink, Dora touched his arm. "John, we haven't had a chance to visit, what with everyone else around, so maybe we can now, before we eat?" She motioned toward the front room, so he dried his hands and came over to help her up. Dora had always been his favorite aunt, and suddenly he realized he wanted to be near her.

When they were seated on the sofa, she turned to him. "Please tell me, how are you, really? And, by the way, you're too skinny! Aren't they feeding you in Maryland?"

Through the door, he saw Loretta and Harold looking in apprehensively. Slowly, John closed his eyes, opened them, and looked at the old woman's kind face. "It's been hard."

"You're still an orderly in the same military hospital?"

"Yes. I'm in a post-surgical ward. We get the worst cases. First, they came from Africa, now they're pouring in from Europe. Unbelievable injuries. Our doctors and nurses are great, but the mortality rate is still high. And those who survive are often left disfigured or paralyzed."

"That must be terrible to see. You've always been so sensitive, even as a little boy."

John looked down. "It can be too much."

"Do you get satisfaction from your work?"

"What do you mean?"

"Don't you feel like you're doing the Lord's work?"

"Sometimes...yes...I suppose," but then he checked himself, put his hands up, and shook his head. "No, not really. Not anymore. Mostly it feels hopeless, like God isn't there." He grimaced because of what he'd said.

"But He is, child." She patted his hand. "Even in our darkest hours. Do you remember Matthew's Gospel?" John nodded. "Chapter twenty-five, verse thirty-six, one of my favorites: The Lord said I was sick and you comforted me. Do you remember?" Another nod. "That was written about you, John. You're doing the Lord's work. I'm so proud of you."

John shrugged. "Can I tell you something else?"

"Of course."

"Sometimes I worry that I'll see Joe in our hospital. A time or two, I actually thought I did, but I couldn't recognize him at first because of the wounds and bandages."

"How awful."

"Some nights I dream he's there." His face twitched. "And it's all so real."

"But according to your mother, he's all right in France."

"Yes, last time he wrote. But who knows about today?"

"Who indeed, so let's keep praying for him. And if something does happen to him, God forbid, I will pray that someone like you is there to comfort him. Someone who cares as much as you do for your patients."

John tried to clear his throat. "You're so thoughtful, Aunt Dora. Thank you."

"You're carrying heavy burdens, child. Place your trust in the Lord and you'll find help when you need it most. That's His promise." She smiled and gently patted his face. "Now I see food on the table, so we'd better go in. And let's see if we can fatten you up a little."

"Food doesn't solve everything, Aunt Dora. But thank you for listening."

⊶⊷⊶⊷⊶⊷⊶

On Sunday, the family attended church and prayed afterwards at Elizabeth's grave, which was especially emotional for John. Otherwise, they spent the rest of his three days at home together. Carol Ann stayed home from school on Monday, and Harold gave the Germans a day off so the family could be alone. John helped with chores, relaxed, grew more talkative, smiled more, and began to act more like himself.

On Monday night, as his train approached Newton, John hugged Loretta last. "Goodbye, sis. I love you."

Loretta smiled. "It's so hard to see you go away again, and so soon. I love you."

Turning back to his parents, he smiled, "It was good to be home. Thank you for everything. Mama, your cooking was just what I needed."

Arm in arm, Harold and Clara watched the train pull away while their daughters waved to their son, who looked back at them until he was swallowed up by the dark. Clara dabbed her eyes. "No matter how old they are, it's never easy to see them go." Even Carol Ann was quiet on the ride home, and it was raining, which added to their gloom.

Sitting in the backseat of the car on the drive home and looking out into the night, Loretta wondered when she and John would talk about what happened. Until then it would hang over them like a cloud. She wasn't waiting for an apology, only trying to understand what had caused her brother to change so dramatically.

## Chapter 36

# LATITUDE

Loretta, telephone." Clara called out the kitchen window to her daughter, who was feeding and watering the chickens in the large yard east of the house.

"Who is it?"

"Doris, and she says it's important."

Loretta hurried up the steps into the house. "Hello! What's so important that you made me run all the way in with chicken poop on my shoes?"

Doris sounded conspiratorial. "Have you seen *The Wichita Beacon* from a couple days ago?"

"No, why?"

"Get a copy of it as soon as you can and you'll understand. It's the paper from this Wednesday. Now I have to go, I'm at work."

As Loretta hung up the phone, her mother said, "What was that all about?"

Loretta shook her head and smiled. "I'm not sure, maybe it's just Doris being Doris."

A short while later, Loretta volunteered to drive into town and pick Carol Ann up from school, then they stopped at a downtown drugstore and bought the last copy of the paper in question and immediately understood why Doris was so excited. The bold banner headline read: **Nazi War Prisoners at Peabody 'Coddled'**

"Oh Lord," Carol Ann said, then repeated herself several times as she read the article and looked at several photographs while Loretta drove home. "This is not going to be good."

After supper, the family took turns reading the article and looking at the photographs, including one of the POWs being escorted back to the Eyestone Building after seeing a movie in the Sunflower Theater. Loretta turned white as a sheet and stifled a gasp when she read the allegations about Peabody women being allowed to "check out" POWs from the camp. The rest of her family wasn't paying attention or they might have wondered about her reaction. She'd never told them about her and Rolf's December getaway, and she certainly didn't want them finding out this way.

"What do you think?" Harold asked when he came back in for the night. Loretta held her breath, hoping Carol Ann wouldn't start with a wisecrack about the salacious parts, but her mother took the lead by calling the article sensational.

"And ridiculous," interjected Carol Ann. "Just because we treat them like human beings doesn't mean we're coddling the enemy. And that part about them being able to sabotage the railroad tracks if they wanted to is absurd."

"That's some wild speculation, isn't it? What do you think, Loretta?" her father asked.

Glancing down at the paper still in front of her, she responded, "I agree with Mama and Carol Ann. Why shouldn't they get to see a movie sometimes? They work hard all week and should get to go to church and have recreation on the Sabbath, just like everybody else."

Clara said, "You catch more flies with sugar than vinegar."

Harold nodded. "The Army must be doing a pretty good job of weeding out the troublemakers. I haven't heard of anyone who's hired them here having a problem. Some don't work as hard as others, but that's just like the rest of us."

"I've never been afraid with them around, except when the guards started shooting at Rolf," Clara said. "Those we've had here are all hard workers."

"Yes," replied Harold, "even Otto."

"What do you mean, 'even Otto?' He's an exemplary worker, you said so yourself. And he's polite and most importantly, he's contrite." Clara sounded defensive.

"You're right, he's become a good farm worker."

"I wonder who the *Beacon* reporter talked to," Clara said. "They mention 'unnamed sources,' but it doesn't sound like they got their information from anyone we know."

Carol Ann said, "It looks like the whole thing got exaggerated to make it sound bad. Newspapers like to make mountains out of mole hills."

Clara agreed. "That's right. It's true the POWs here aren't guarded all the time. But they've proved they can be trusted and should be allowed some latitude. How else can you expect them to work? Put them in shackles? Draft more guards to follow them around everywhere? If we have enough American men available to stand guard over all the Germans at work, then we might as well just put the guards to work and not bother with POW labor at all."

Carol Ann said, "They're really not that much different from American farmhands, and people like us should know that after all this time."

After a pause, Harold said, "But I'm afraid this article will cause trouble."

"How so?"

"It will get people riled up. People who don't know better will start being afraid. The *Beacon* is stoking the fire with this talk about sabotage and undisciplined POWs here."

"What do you think will happen? Will the Army let them keep working for us?"

"I hope so. We need them, and what would they do without jobs? I'd be more worried about them having too much idle time than sending them to bed tired after a hard day's work, and I wouldn't want them in big, overcrowded camps where Nazi officers like that Streicher might still hold sway."

"We can't let people like Tommy bully us," said Carol Ann. "He was gloating about that article today."

Harold looked at her. "Does he worry you?"

"No, Papa, It's just annoying to hear someone say we're not good Americans because we're treating the Germans the way they should be treated."

Clara said, "I understand, but don't do anything to provoke him. That serves no purpose, either. It's important to be an instrument of peace in thought and word, as well as in action."

"I try."

"I know you do." Clara smiled. "Loretta, you've been pretty quiet."

She looked up. "It makes me sad that people are so hostile."

"I don't think they're the majority," said Harold, "but they are vocal sometimes. By and large, everybody in Peabody gets along pretty well most of the time."

"But, have you noticed something?" The others waited for Loretta to continue. "To me, it looks like some people are more hateful now than they were a year ago. Have you noticed that?"

"Now that you mention it, maybe. Why, do you suppose?"

"I'm not sure, but with it looking more and more certain that Germany is going to lose the war, shouldn't we be less afraid of the Germans than we were a year ago?"

They sat quietly until Harold responded. "Maybe Americans finally see how dangerous the Germans were all along, and that's scaring people after the fact."

"That's possible, but could it be something else?"

"Go on," said Clara.

"Maybe all this doesn't have anything to do with fear. What if now that the Allies have the upper hand, people just want revenge? What if they want to take it out on all Germans? Why else would we keep bombing their cities filled with women and children, except to punish them all? Maybe punishment is easier now because we're actually less afraid, not more."

"So, you're saying some Americans think it's time to begin exacting their pound of flesh?"

"I wonder. Starting with the ones right here." Loretta's tone was apprehensive.

Harold's prediction that the article would stir up trouble was proven right the following Monday at Peabody's Labor Day picnic. Several hundred people turned out for the annual event in the flag-festooned city park, its fences and tables decked out with red, white, and blue bunting. A potluck dinner started things off. Everyone brought salads and desserts to go with hot dogs provided by Peabody's American Legion Post #95. The Legion also provided watermelon and an unlimited supply of soda pop in bottles chilled in oval metal stock tanks filled with icy water.

As dinner was winding down, the mayor spoke first, noting American labor's many accomplishments, but his remarks were forgotten when the local American Legion commander began a rambling outline of the

Servicemen's Readjustment Act. The landmark legislation, just signed into law by President Roosevelt, provided educational, housing, employment, and other benefits to the millions of Americans who had served or were serving in the military. It affected almost everyone in some way. The commander's speech about the GI Bill, as it came to be known, was met with loud applause by all, but then he immediately launched into a scathing tirade about the evils of having German POWs in town. He declared that having the enemy in their midst was not only dangerous, it was also insulting to all the men serving in the military. With fire-and-brimstone fervor, the pudgy old man quoted *The Wichita Beacon* article extensively, ending his diatribe almost shouting, "A true American patriot would not have those Nazi bastards working on our farms and fraternizing with our women and children!" His words sent part of the crowd into a cheering frenzy, including Tommy Ferguson and his parents.

Up to that point, the Unruhs had been enjoying the picnic with other Mennonite families and neighbors, but after the commander's speech, Clara leaned over to Harold and said, "This is the first time I've felt like a stranger in my own town." They and their friends collected their dishes and left. Even Carol Ann was too put off to stay for the dance. Several townspeople made a point of coming over to say that they did not agree with the commander, but others watched them leave with icy stares.

The backlash festered to the point that the Army found it necessary to address the situation. On September 20th, a meeting was held in the packed high school gym. Along with hundreds of locals, representatives of the Army were there, including the commander of the main camp at Fort Riley. Also in attendance were representatives of Kansas State University's Extension Service, the Kansas Farm Bureau, and other farm organizations, along with dozens of people who drove over from Marion, Hillsboro, and Newton.

At first, Harold and Clara intended to stay away, but Cletus Slaymaker convinced them that farmers should be represented, so all four Unruhs came and sat with a group of friends.

From the outset, Colonel Lawrence Reed, Fort Riley's camp's commanding officer, made it clear that the employment of Germans outside the camps was not going to stop. He said he'd investigated the situation in Peabody and noted a few security deficiencies that would be remedied. For instance, he cautioned farmers not to let women drive

POWs to and from their farms alone, which he had witnessed that very day, and which, more than anything, just looked improper. Anyone who continued to do so wouldn't be allowed to hire POWs. He said he expected the rules to be followed, but he also encouraged employers to find a middle ground, being neither too strict nor too lenient with their POW laborers.

The colonel then addressed the main allegations in the *Beacon* article by explaining the Geneva Convention's requirements for the treatment of prisoners. Largely, he said, the Germans in Peabody were being treated appropriately. Speakers from the farm organizations then gave detailed statistics on how vital German labor was to food production. One expert from Manhattan said bluntly, "If you want all Americans fed, including our men in uniform, then you must stop complaining. These POWs aren't superfluous to the war effort, they're essential."

Colonel Reed ended by taking questions from the audience. Most seemed mollified, but the American Legion commander and others still muttered and scoffed at the assurances given. The last question came from Tommy Ferguson's father, who stood and struck a defiant pose. "Colonel, but you don't have all the facts."

"And you're going to enlighten me, I presume?" the colonel asked dryly.

"I will. Some of the Germans here is treating them prisoners like long-lost relatives, and for all we know, they may be!" There were audible groans. "And I'm not afraid to name names."

"What exactly are you complaining about? Is there a question in there?"

"Take Harold and Mrs. Unruh for starters," Ferguson said, but he wouldn't look at them just a few rows away. "They let these Nazi bastards take meals in the kitchen with their daughters present! I bet you didn't know that, did you? You think that's fine and dandy?"

Carol Ann looked mortified, Loretta stared angrily at Ferguson, and Clara shook her head in disgust.

The colonel asked, "So the Unruhs employ Germans on their farm, is that right?"

"Yeah."

"And you're talking about the meals they're contractually obligated to provide the men?"

"I suppose so. They're even feeding the one who escaped a year ago, right in their house. What do you say about that?"

Reed didn't hesitate. "First, that is technically a violation of Army rules."

"That's what I thought. It's not right, and they should be told to stop it. These are Nazis, not good people." Ferguson looked smugly at his friends.

"You don't know that,"quickly countered the colonel.

"Say again?"

"Most of the POWs here in the United States were never Nazis. Most of them are Germans, but not all Germans are Nazis; in fact not even a majority are. Most of the Nazi POWs have now been segregated. They were not sent to Peabody. I don't know who's working on the Unruh farm, but I can say with some certainty that they're not Nazis."

"But they're the enemy!" exclaimed Ferguson, "And they should be treated like it."

The colonel said, "I don't know all the circumstances, so I can't comment on why it's happening. Yes, it's a technical violation, but maybe the Unruhs have a good reason. Maybe it's easier for them. They must not be too worried, or they wouldn't be doing it."

Growing irritated, Ferguson spoke louder and his voice went higher. "If it's a violation of the rules, they shouldn't be doing it! It's goddamn ridiculous is what I say."

Reed stared across the room at him. "Clearly, you're upset, sir."

"Yes, I am."

"Can I tell you something that upsets me?" Ferguson could only nod yes while Reed's jaw tightened. "I'm troubled that citizens like you spend time worrying about who's eating what and where they're eating it. Haven't you got anything better to worry about?"

"Now hold on there..."

"No, sir, you're going to listen to me now. The Army has determined that the POWs here pose no danger, and the facts bear this out. Your own farm officials have just told us they're vital to our food production. Farmers around the state are begging me to send more POWs their way. I assume the Unruhs are satisfied with their help. Are you here tonight, Mr. Unruh?"

Harold stood up. "Yes, sir. The ones we have are keeping us going. And we feed them well because we work them hard. And if I do say so myself, my wife's a fine cook, so those boys mind their manners because they like eating what she fixes." Harold patted his stomach. "So do I." Clara blushed, while Reed grinned and others laughed.

"That's good to hear, thank you." Turning back to Ferguson, the colonel continued, "The POWs here are honorable men who laid down their arms. If I were you, sir, I'd stop worrying about how they're being fed and mind my own business." When he finished, most of the audience applauded politely.

Ferguson muttered, "That's bullshit," but he didn't try to engage the colonel further.

"That's it, meeting adjourned."

Harold smiled. "Now maybe this will put an end to the nonsense."

It didn't. Less than a week later, on a Sunday morning, the 24th, the Unruhs arrived at church to find congregation members standing near the south wall, but they couldn't see what the others were looking at. As they walked toward the church, the presiding elder was coming up from the basement with a bucket of paint and several brushes.

"Good morning, Elder Ratzlaff," said Harold. "Doing some painting before church?"

"Good morning, Harold. Ladies." The preacher was tense. "We have a mess." Walking around the corner of the building, they saw it—a large, sloppy, red swastika painted on the white clapboard wall. Next to it was scrawled, *GERMANS GO HOME*.

"Oh my," exclaimed Clara. "Is it because we're German or because we hired POWs?"

"Maybe both," said Elder Ratzlaff. "When I drove past the Slaymaker place this morning, there was one on their barn too. They're not German or Mennonite, but they do have POWS working for them."

Harold and several men quickly painted over the graffiti, careful not to get paint on their Sunday clothes. "Let's not make too much of it," Harold said, "It's probably just some kids."

That same evening, a group of Germans going to play soccer at the park were confronted at the entrance by twenty men armed with bats, clubs, and a few firearms. They brandished their weapons, taunted the POWs and their guards with crude insults, and told them they couldn't use the park. A few were even struck with clubs, beer bottles, and rocks. The guards quickly got the Germans back to the Eyestone Building. The rabble rousers followed them and continued with their insults and jeers while driving around the building in pickups. The guards and most of the town were soon as irritated as the Germans. Jordan said, "It's like the Wild West," but after a tense half-hour and a few more thrown beer bottles, the crowd dispersed.

The news reached the Unruhs before sunset. Harold, Clara, and Loretta were on the porch enjoying a gorgeous sunset when Carol Ann came out to tell them what her friend, Shirley Evans, had called to tell her. "She said the Germans got inside before any real fighting broke out, but she was scared by all the commotion." With Carol Ann in tow, Loretta went in to call Doris to see if she knew anything more.

Alone as dusk turned to dark, Harold said to Clara, "What a shame."

"It is a shame, and shameful," she replied. "Violence has taken root in some hearts here. The longer this war goes on, the more elusive peace will be." She sighed heavily.

"Violence and hatred are nothing new, are they?"

"No, but it feels different when it's so close to home."

"Perhaps. We have to stay the course, keep peace in our hearts."

"I try, but it's hard when war is all around, and for so long. When one of our own sons is caught up in battle and the other is traumatized by what he's seen. When one of our daughters is taunted by classmates and the other is enamored of a man who came here because of war. It's hard to see how peace will prevail."

"Now don't lose hope, Clara."

"I won't, but you know how much I worry."

"About Joseph?"

"Yes, and the others, too, especially Loretta."

"Why especially Loretta? She knows to stay away from troublemakers."

"I worry for her because she's grown so fond of Rolf. I can't see how they'll ever have a chance to find happiness together. Much as I like him, he's not right for her."

"You mean because he's not a Mennonite. But he's a fine young man."

"But he's not one of us."

Harold reached out for Clara's hand. "Things sure have changed, haven't they?"

"In so many ways." Her words bore her sad resignation.

"I think of my parents. Their marriage was arranged by their parents. They'd known and liked each other since Karlswalde, but they got married because their elders told them to."

"I know. It was the same for mine."

"We had more latitude, but it never even occurred to me to marry outside the church."

Clara squeezed her husband's hand. "We knew the boundaries. Now I wonder if we gave our children too much leeway. Maybe we should be telling them more forcefully to marry other Mennonites, for the sake of their happiness and their eternal salvation."

"Would they listen? You and I grew up around only our own folk, but our children know people from all backgrounds and religions. And they've been exposed to so many other things, what with the radio and movies and magazines. Now John is living in Maryland, Joseph is overseas, and young men from another country are working right here with us. I'm not sure how successful we'd be if we did try to tell them how to live their lives as adults, even if we're right."

Clara thought quietly. "I suppose Joseph's a good example of that. We couldn't keep him from enlisting. We taught him to make moral choices for himself, but it's hard to sit back and watch, especially if it looks like they're going astray."

"I think we have to do the same with Loretta. She knows right from wrong. Now she has to choose her own path, even if it turns out to be strewn with rocks."

"Maybe, but maybe the old ways were better." Clara sighed.

"How far back do you want to go? To when we were choosing each other or to when parents were arranging marriages for their children? Or to the time when the church shunned people who sinned or sometimes just because they disagreed with them? I'm not sure I wanna go back too far. Your parents mighta picked somebody else for you, and I'd have missed out on a wonderful life."

Clara kissed her husband, but had no answer for him.

# Chapter 37

# HOME FRONTS

A week and a half after the church was vandalized, Loretta and Clara were in the milk barn when Harold got home from dropping Carol Ann off at school and picking up the Germans. Turning into the driveway from the country road, Harold noticed odd movement in the little pasture just east of the orchard and behind the barns. As soon as he parked the truck, he walked through the big barn to the pasture gate, then he began running toward what he had seen from the road, now yelling at the top of his voice. The family's beloved Belgian draught horses, a magnificent pair of chestnut giants named Axl and Hans, were both lying on their sides on the ground. Axl was not moving, his one visible eye opened wide with a terrified gaze. His mouth was filled with thick froth, and his hindquarters were covered in excrement. Hans was nearby, muscles spasming, frothing at the mouth, and convulsing as explosive bloody diarrhea shot out from him. He was panting, gasping for air, and trying in vain to stand. By the time Clara and Loretta heard the commotion and reached Harold, standing helplessly a few feet from the animals, Hans exhaled heavily and lay still, too, with the same shocked expression as his partner.

Clara and Loretta burst into tears, and Loretta moved toward the lifeless horses, but Harold stopped her. "No! Don't touch them, we don't know what happened." Harold wiped his eyes and hugged his wife and daughter. "There now, there now." He tried to comfort both women with the Lord's Prayer.

Axl and Hans were the Unruh family's last team of Belgians. They were fifteen years old, stood sixteen or seventeen hands tall, and weighed around two thousand pounds each. Before Harold bought the tractor in 1938, these powerful creatures were the brute force that made farming on Doyle Creek possible—plowing, pulling wagons and the thresher, hauling rocks, and every other kind of heavy lifting. Although they weren't intended for riding, the Unruh children each had treasured memories of being hoisted up on the backs of these gentle Belgians for rides around the farm. The mild-mannered horses were incredibly gentle. When machinery replaced them, Axl and Hans went into retirement, except for occasional wagon pulling at church or family gatherings or parades in town. Farmers in the area asked to buy them, but Harold would say that would be like selling one of his children. "They're family," he said, "and they belong here with family."

The Germans and the family tried to make sense of what had happened. Rolf spoke quietly. "I remember seeing them last night when we were leaving. They had finished the oats in the trough and were turning to go out to the pasture for the night. They looked fine then."

Harold said, "I saw them about the same time. Same thing. They were fine."

Clara asked, "Could they have eaten moldy oats or moldy hay?"

"I put the hay and oats out for them myself yesterday afternoon and I didn't see anything moldy," Harold said. "I suppose it's possible, but I've never seen a huge animal like these die so quickly from moldy hay. They would have had to eat bales of it to get this sick so quick." He turned to the others. "Any of you notice anything unusual about what they were eating yesterday? Or were they acting funny?" The Germans and Loretta all nodded no.

Hecht spoke up. "No, sir, I didn't see the horses doing anything unusual, but last night when we were leaving, I saw an old truck parked on the country road east of your driveway and next to the pasture where the horses were. Did anyone else see it?" The others shook their heads. "I don't see how it could be related, but I thought I should mention it. It was green and old and rusted, a Ford I think, with a bunch of dents. I've never seen it out here before, but I think I did see it outside the Eyestone Building one night."

"Thank you, Otto."

Clara dabbed her eyes, blew her nose, and said, "We all have work to do, let's get to it."

The day passed slowly. At dinner, Loretta and her mother quietly picked at their food. Conversations on the farm were subdued until Carol Ann got home from school and learned what had happened. Her sobs made her mother and sister cry again too. Harold walked out to the pasture with her to see the horses. She cried loudly again, then ran into the house. The heartbroken teenager said only, "We can't even hug them goodbye."

As the family sat around the table that evening after supper, Harold said, "We need to keep the other animals out of that little pasture for now. Tomorrow, the boys and I will scour the area to see if we can figure out what they might have gotten into. Maybe it was hemlock or elderberry or some wild blue flax. We've tried to keep the pastures clear of all that, but maybe there was something growing in the brush along the fence that they could reach."

"Be careful, Papa," said Loretta. "Please don't touch anything that looks suspicious."

"I agree," said Clara. "And check the stock tank for algae that might be poisonous."

"That's unlikely," said Harold, "Otto and Erich just repaired that tank and put fresh water in it a couple days ago."

No one spoke for a few minutes. Harold was staring at the newspaper, Clara was mending clothes, Loretta was writing to her brothers, and Carol Ann was trying to concentrate on her homework. Loretta broke the silence, "What about the truck that Otto saw?"

Harold answered, "I don't know. I didn't see it, but I guess it was there if Otto saw it."

Carol Ann looked up from her homework. "What truck?"

Clara answered, "Otto said he saw an old Ford pickup parked alongside the pasture just east of the orchard yesterday evening as they were being driven back into town."

Carol Ann squirmed. "What color?"

"Green."

Emphatically, Carol Ann said, "Tommy Ferguson's father has a green truck."

"Are you sure?" said Clara.

"Yes, I'm sure. I've seen his father dropping him off at school in it. It's green and dented up and rusted and always dirty. It's a Ford."

Loretta said, "That's how Otto described the truck he saw by the pasture." She and her sister and her mother all looked at Harold.

"Is this just a coincidence?" asked Clara in disbelief.

Harold let this new information sink in, then replied, "I'll call the Sheriff's Office in the morning. Maybe it's nothing, but we should try to find out." He thought a bit more, then added, "And I should also tell him this: This morning I thought I smelled garlic by the horses."

"Arsenic," said Clara quietly.

Loretta shook her head. "Do you think it's possible that someone could hate us so much that they would poison our animals?"

"We shouldn't jump to conclusions, but if someone is mad at us for hiring and being kind to our German workers, poisoning old Axl and Hans would be a surefire way to hurt us."

"Jesus Christ!" Carol Ann shouted and loudly slammed a book down on the table.

"Carol Ann! How dare you use the Lord's name in vain like that!"

"I'm sorry, Mama."

"And please stop slamming your books down. How many times do I have to tell you?"

"I'm sorry, Mama. But I just thought of something."

"What is it, child?" asked Harold.

"Do you remember about a week ago, we found four of the barn cats dead?"

The others gave her surprised looks. "I'd forgotten all about that," said Clara.

"We thought it was probably a case of them getting into rat poison. Probably from eating mice and rats that ate the poison, as sometimes happens."

Loretta said, "Yes, but it was unusual to have so many die at once. And I haven't seen a couple other ones since then, either."

Carol Ann continued, "Right, and what rat poison do we use?"

"Cowley's Rat and Mouse Poison," replied Loretta.

"Right again!" Carol Ann was now prosecuting her theory. "And what's the poison in Cowley's?"

"Arsenic," answered Harold.

"Bingo! So, what if the cats were poisoned on purpose? And so were Axl and Hans?"

"This is all speculation at this point," Clara said, "but my, that's a lot of coincidences, a lot of dying animals."

Loretta looked at her sister, then her parents. "Yes, it's a lot of speculation, but Carol Ann may be on to something. We saw how angry Mr. Ferguson was at the town meeting, and he was especially angry with us, calling us out by name. If he was prowling around here last night, it's reasonable to think he was up to no good."

Clara put down her mending and looked at her husband with troubled eyes. "What is the world coming to?"

Harold put down the newspaper and tried to sound reassuring. "Let's not get ahead of ourselves. But I think I'll call the Sheriff's Office tonight so he'll have the information first thing. But let's remember that our help comes from the Lord and bow our heads."

When the family was going to their rooms, Clara said, "Carol Ann, tomorrow at school don't say a word about any of this to anyone, especially the Ferguson boy. Let us get to the bottom of this first."

I won't say anything to anyone, Mama. I promise. After what happened to Axl and Hans and the cats, I'm afraid to."

"I admit, I'm a little frightened too," added Loretta.

Clara walked over to where they were standing near the stairs and hugged them tightly. "Don't be afraid, daughters. The Lord will protect us, as He always has. He is our rock and our salvation, in Him do we trust."

"I hope so," Carol Ann replied. "I love you all."

"And we love you too," said Loretta with a smile.

When the girls were upstairs and Clara had gone into the bedroom, Harold quietly opened the drawer under the counter, the catch-all drawer nearest the door. It took him a few minutes to find what he was looking for. When he did, he turned out the lights, walked to the window, and peered out into the night. Then he locked the outside doors in the kitchen and front room with the key he had retrieved from the drawer. He couldn't remember the last time he or anyone had felt the need to lock the house for the night.

⊸⚡⊸⚡⊸⚡⊸⚡⊸

Shortly before ten the next morning, Marion County Sheriff Leonard Dreyer drove into the Unruh farm, along with a veterinarian, Duane Jones, and a deputy. Clara offered them coffee and then Harold took them out to where Axl and Hans still lay. They examined the horses, the feed bunk, and the water tank. Next, they walked the fence lines for the entire pasture. Harold stayed with them for a while, answered a few questions, then returned to work in the little barn and let them finish their investigation.

At noon, Sheriff Dreyer and the others came through the big barn from the pasture. Harold told the Germans to go in and tell Clara to start dinner without him. The day was warm, so Harold invited the visitors to join him on the porch. Loretta brought iced tea for everyone, plus warm rolls with butter and honey. She invited them to have dinner, but they declined.

"Thanks again for coming," Harold began. "Did you learn anything?"

Sheriff Dreyer replied, "Nothing conclusive, but we've eliminated some possible reasons your Belgians died, and we have the start of a theory. Duane will give you his assessment."

Dr. Jones said, "Thank you. There's no indication of any hemlock, elderberry, cyanide, blue flax, Johnson grass, or any other toxic plants growing in or near your pasture. And there's no sign of mold in your oats or hay, we even checked the oats and hay in the barn, and we saw no sign of algae in the water. So, I think we can say with certainty that the horses didn't die from those causes."

Harold said, "Thank you for that. Now, do you know what they did die of?"

Dr. Jones said, "My preliminary finding is they died of acute arsenic poisoning. The symptoms they were showing, the garlic odor, how quickly they died, and the fact that both horses died of the same thing, all that suggests arsenic. I got urine and blood samples, and I'll have them tested as soon as I get back to Marion."

"How could they have gotten enough arsenic to die like that? They don't eat dead rats."

"Most likely it would have been put into their water for them to swallow enough to die so quickly. I've taken a sample of the water in your stock tank and we'll test it too."

"So you're saying they had to have been poisoned intentionally?"

Dr. Jones frowned, "If we confirm it's arsenic poisoning, then yes, I would say someone put the poison in their water and they drank it. Maybe their oats, but more likely the water."

Sheriff Dreyer asked, "Mr. Unruh, do you keep rat poison with arsenic around?"

"Yes, Cowley's Rat and Mouse Poison. But it's high in a cabinet in the tack room, far away from animals and people too. The horses couldn't have gotten to it."

Dr. Jones said, "I use it, too. It comes in small bottles, but even one bottle in the stock tank might have been enough to harm your Belgians, even as big as they were. And it has no taste, so they wouldn't have known not to drink it."

The sheriff asked, "Do you mind if we take a look at your supply?"

"Of course," Harold was heading to the barn while he answered. "I just bought a case of those little bottles and put them up on that shelf. There were already two other bottles there, so there should be fourteen in there now."

When they got to the barn and Harold opened the cupboard, all four of the men were rattled to see just two bottles of rat poison on the shelf. "Dear Lord, someone got in and stole the bottles and killed Axl and Hans on purpose." He shook his head in dismay.

The sheriff asked, "Does everyone on your farm have access to this cupboard?"

"It's never locked, but I'm the only one who ever takes a bottle out when we need it, or I ask someone else to take one out. That way I keep track of it." He thought for a moment, then added, "And this barn door that opens to the pasture is almost always open. If someone was set on hurting the animals, he probably wouldn't mind stealing the rat poison to do it with."

"But how would he know that you had rat poison here in the barn?" asked Sheriff Dreyer.

Dr. Jones answered, "Anyone who lives in Marion County would know that every farm in the county has some sort of rat and mouse poison on hand to control rodents."

"True," said Harold. "And it wouldn't have taken that Ferguson fella long to sneak in here while I was driving the Germans back to town. Clara and Loretta were milking and Carol Ann was in the house and they wouldn't have been able to see him."

"We're looking into him, Mr. Unruh. In fact, I had a conversation with him this morning on the way to your place."

"What did he say?"

"Ferguson says he is angry with you and other farmers coddling

POWs. But he said he was in Newton two days ago, spent the day there taking care of his mother, so it couldn't have been him out at your place poisoning your horses. Which he emphatically denied doing."

"Do you believe him?"

"I'm not sure. I haven't verified his alibi independently. His mother is in her nineties and unwell. Ferguson and his sisters take turns caring for her. I'm going to go see the sisters and see if I can find out for sure if he was there. So, I don't know for sure about his alibi, but I'm kind of inclined to believe him on this."

"You are? Why's that?"

"Well, he didn't deny that he doesn't like what you're doing for the POWs, so he gave me his motive. And then he admitted to some things he did do."

"Oh?"

"He told me he was part of that gang that was yelling at the POWs after a soccer game. He said he threatened them, threw rocks at them, then he and friends drove their trucks around the building to intimidate guards and prisoners alike. He openly admitted to committing numerous crimes—disorderly conduct, assault, intimidation of the guards, harassment, possibly drunk driving—and to me, the sheriff, of all people. He's proud of being pro-America and not shy about saying so. If he thinks he's righteous, it puzzles me why he would admit to some crimes but not others. Unless he's being crafty, and honestly, I don't think he's that bright." Harold nodded. "Plus, he didn't have time to come up with a story for me. I just showed up at his front door unannounced early this morning, got him out of bed."

"Well, if not him, then who? Who could have done something like this?

"We don't know, but we're going to continue to investigate, and if we have the evidence, I'll ask the county attorney to file criminal charges against whoever is responsible. It'll take a little while, but we'll let you know when the test results are back or when we have a suspect. After this and the vandalism and attacking the POWs, we need to get control of this situation. Now, it's time for us to head back to Marion."

"Thank you, Sheriff."

As they walked to the car, Dr. Jones said, "Mr. Unruh, did you say you had some barn cats die a week or so ago, all at the same time?"

"Yes, we did. At least four of them. We assumed they ate poisoned rats or mice."

"What did you do with them?"

"Burned them, the ones we found."

"Good. You should also burn the horses too."

"That'll be a heckuva job, but we'll get started this afternoon."

The sheriff spoke out the car window, "I'm sorry for your loss, Mr. Unruh. It's clear your Belgians were some beautiful horses."

"They were. The best."

All eyes in the kitchen were on Harold when he came through the door after 1:30 p.m. Everyone had finished eating and the table was cleared, except for coffee cups and dessert plates. Harold feigned lightheartedness. "Did you boys eat it all? What am I gonna eat?" The Germans weren't sure if he was being serious and was upset.

"Harold!" Clara said. "There's a plate in the oven for you and we have fresh coffee." Loretta was already getting her father's meal while he washed his hands in the sink.

"I'm sure you prayed already, but do you mind if we do so again?"

"Of course not," replied Hecht as the others nodded their assent.

Harold's prayer was short: "Heavenly Father, thank you for this food. We humbly ask for your protection and your peace." When he finished and looked up, Harold's expression was sad.

"How did it go with the sheriff?" asked Clara tentatively.

"Nothing is certain, the vet is running some tests, but it looks like poor old Axl and Hans died of acute arsenic poisoning." Harold choked up before he could get the rest of his words out with a trembling voice. "It looks like it was intentional." Finally, he got his throat cleared. "Sorry about that, it just got to me there. Axl and Hans have been a part of our family for fifteen years, they didn't deserve to die like that. I can't even imagine how someone could do that to them. We're gonna miss them."

"That this should happen to two of God's most innocent, most gentle creatures," Clara was unable to finish her sentence.

Harold looked down the table at his wife. "The Lord's ways are inscrutable. But He is our comfort and our joy."

"Amen," she said.

Pushing his half-eaten plate of food away, Harold looked up at the clock and said, "And now, we have some hard work ahead of us this afternoon, and not much time to do it. It's nigh on two o'clock already." The men looked at him, waiting for his instructions. "Dr. Jones said it was probably a high dose of arsenic that killed them, so we have to cremate them where they died. We'll have to use all the firewood already cut for winter and probably more. We'll need brush for kindling, and as much gasoline and kerosene as we can spare. If you boys are ready, we'll get started. I want to be done before Carol Ann gets home from school. I think that would be best, don't you think, Clara?"

"Yes."

"Clara and Loretta, it's best if you stay out of that pasture. This won't be easy to watch."

"I'm going to help," said Loretta. It wasn't a request. "I can drive the tractor and gather up what you need to get this done quickly."

"Okay, daughter. We'll start with the firewood that's stacked near the house and the barn. Loretta, bring the wagon over to save us so many trips to the pasture. Anton and Erich, you go to the brush pile along the creek and start gathering up dry brush and extra logs, even big ones, then load the wagon when Loretta gets there. Rolf and Otto, you'll help me tend the fires. It's gonna take a lot of fuel to get the fires hot enough to do the job. And everybody, you must wear gloves and cover your faces with bandanas. Clara will get them for you. Don't stand downwind of the fires and don't get any closer than you have to be. Be extra careful, or you could inhale arsenic ash or get it on your skin."

⌇⌇⌇⌇⌇⌇⌇

As the first wagonload was on its way to the little pasture, Rolf and Hecht followed on foot. Coming through the big barn and the gate into the little pasture, they passed the stock tank that the Belgians used.

Rolf was beside the tank when Hecht roughly bumped him with his shoulder. "Careful, Mueller," he laughed. You don't want your wooden leg to give out and fall into the water."

Rolf looked confused. "I'm not going to fall into the tank or into anything else."

"That's good. Because if you fell in there, you might end up getting baptized all over again. And what would your Catholic parents think?" Something about Hecht's grin and the way he emphasized "baptized" sounded and felt peculiar to Rolf.

"And you think you're going to be the one to baptize me?"

"I would love to be the one. But all in good time. First, I have to get baptized myself, and I will, thanks to Mrs. Unruh. That woman is a true saint."

"On that we agree."

"Are you happy that I'm going to become a Mennonite?"

"Why do you care what I think? I just hope you're being sincere."

"You don't think I'm being sincere?"

"I have no idea. But it seems odd when you're talking this way."

"But Mueller, I'm very sincere. And I have you to thank for opening my eyes."

"What?"

"When I saw how much pain I put you through last winter, I realized I had to do things differently. Try something new. You set me on the path of righteousness, you and this beautiful Unruh family."

"Congratulations," Rolf said indifferently. "Now let's get to work helping this beautiful family, shall we?"

"Of course, I'm here to serve."

"One last thing." Rolf stepped in front of Hecht to look him in the eyes. "If you're not sincere about becoming a Mennonite, you're even more despicable than I thought."

Hecht smiled as he looked past Rolf and said to Harold, "We're ready Mr. Unruh, please tell us what we can do to help."

An hour later, Clara walked onto the porch and saw thick dark clouds of smoke billowing from behind the big barn. She sighed and whispered, "Dear Lord, I know they were just animals, but please bless Hans and Axl. Thank you for sharing them with us."

Dr. Jones' tests confirmed deadly levels of arsenic in the horses and the water tank. Sheriff Dreyer returned to Peabody a few more times to investigate and to update the Unruhs. He couldn't corroborate Ferguson's alibi, so he couldn't rule him out as a suspect, but with the only evidence being the statement of a German POW who claimed he saw Ferguson's truck at the Unruh farm, charges would not be filed against him. Dreyer's men compiled a list of the other troublemakers in Peabody and questioned a few, including Ferguson's son, Tommy, but there was nothing to link any of them directly to what happened to the Belgians. Sheriff Dreyer told Harold they would keep working to find the culprit. In the meantime, he said, it was a good idea for the family to keep locking the doors in their house at night, and their barn doors too.

A week after the Belgians were cremated, the Unruhs were out on the porch to take in the moonlight and fresh air. As Harold and Clara were rocking slowly in the porch swing, Clara said, "I have some more good news. And a request."

Harold smiled, "Tell us. We can always use more good news."

"I was talking to Elder Ratzlaff at our Wednesday prayer meeting, He said that Otto has finished his counseling and classes and is ready to be baptized. Elder Ratzlaff says he believes Otto has had a sincere conversion and is willing to turn his life over to God."

Carol Ann said, "Really? Otto Hecht is going to join the church?"

"Why are you so surprised?"

"I don't really know him, but something about him makes me feel, I don't know."

"What?"

Carol Ann paused to collect her thoughts. "Whenever I see him, he seems more interested in impressing us than anything else, especially you, Mama."

Clara bristled. "Judge not, lest ye be judged, Carol Ann. You don't know what's in his heart, only God does."

Carol Ann didn't back down. "I'm not trying to judge anyone, Mama. I'm only saying that Otto Hecht seems to be a little bit too sincere."

"Your mother's right," said Harold. "It's not for us to say what is or is not in Otto's heart. If Elder Ratzlaff thinks he's ready to profess the faith, then who are we to disagree? It's inspiring to see how your mother was instrumental in bringing a former soldier for Hitler to Christ."

Once her father sided with her mother, Carol Ann knew there was no point in debating the matter further. She mumbled, "I guess," then said no more.

Harold looked at Clara. "You said there was a request too?"

"Because of the unusual circumstances, with Otto being confined and unable to come to the church, he asked Elder Ratzlaff if the baptism could take place here at our place. I said yes, but I had to ask you first." Her voice told her family how excited Clara was about Hecht's conversion.

Harold smiled and squeezed his wife. "Good heavens, woman. Who are we to stand in the way of bringing a lost lamb into the fold. Of course he can be baptized here. When?"

"We're going to be hosting the whole family again on Sunday the 22nd, so I was thinking that would be a good time to do the baptism. It's ten days away, which gives us time to get things ready." She paused, then added, "The family will be here, and I think we should invite Erich, Anton, Rolf, and Greg to come. Maybe they will be inspired too."

"What do you girls think?" Loretta and Carol Ann both nodded. It was dark enough on the porch that Carol Ann could roll her eyes without her parents noticing. But Loretta saw and had to look away to keep from laughing. "It's settled then. And Priscilla is right here in our midst, tending to the prisoners and bringing them to Christ. I'm proud of you, Clara."

Carol Ann said, "Priscilla from the Bible? Paul's friend? Mama, if you're Priscilla, you're looking good for being two thousand years old!"

Clara ignored her daughter. "Thank you, Harold, but I'm no Priscilla."

"You're a wonderful example for the world. After what we've all been through the past few weeks, it's nice to have something to look forward to, something to celebrate. God is good."

# Chapter 38

# IN THE NAME OF
# THE FATHER

The next day, Harold got permission for Hecht to be baptized on Doyle Creek and invited Stevenson, Jordan, Zimmerman, Gralke, and Rolf to festivities on the 22nd. Lieutenant Stevenson accepted on behalf of them all and said he'd be happy to drive to save Harold the extra trips. Hecht didn't know Stevenson and Jordan were coming to the baptism until the morning of. Initially, he seemed a little perturbed about the additions, but when Stevenson asked if it was all right, Hecht smiled and said, "Absolutely. It sounds perfect. The more, the merrier!"

The four German POWs and their two American guards pulled into the Unruh driveway at one o'clock on the 22nd. As they came up the stairs, they were greeted warmly with a chorus of hellos. Harold made introductions. More than two dozen people were there—the Peabody Unruhs, the preacher and his wife, the Slaymakers (Harold called them "honorary Mennonites"), and now the Germans and their American guards.

Rolf saw Loretta in the corner between the stove and the sink. When she turned around, gave him a nod and a warm smile. Next to Loretta was Doris. When her cousin turned to look at Rolf, she giggled and waved, then quickly turned back to whisper something to Loretta.

Clara walked around the table to greet them all, then hugged Otto. "Good afternoon, Otto. Are you ready?"

"Yes, ma'am," he replied, smiling. "I've been waiting a long time for this day."

Harold called for everyone to quiet down, then said, "Welcome to you all on this beautiful day that the Lord has made. It's so good to see family and friends gathered to witness our young friend's baptism." The group nodded and smiled. "We'll start things off with prayer led by Elder

Ratzlaff, and then we'll eat, because we're hungry!" Everyone laughed. "Elder, your sermon was a little long this morning, so we got out of church hungrier than usual."

"Sorry about that," the preacher said. Then he turned to Clara and added, "Not really," with a grin. Everyone laughed.

Harold said, "Then after dinner, we'll go outside for your baptism, Otto, since it's such a beautiful day. We'll draw pure water from the well, just like in the Bible."

"It sounds perfect, sir," said Otto. "Thank you so much."

Clara asked Hecht to sit next to her in the kitchen. Rolf and the other Germans and Jordan sat outside at a picnic table, alone until Loretta and Doris joined them. Loretta was not able to sit next to Rolf, but there wasn't much opportunity to talk anyway because Doris dominated the conversation from the moment she sat down. She peppered Rolf, Zimmerman, and Gralke with all sorts of questions, all the while sizing Rolf up, and not very subtly. Once or twice, Loretta tried to encourage her cousin to be less inquisitorial, but Doris ignored her. The Germans and Jordan didn't mind, they all enjoyed her verve.

When the meal was over, Elder Ratzlaff said another prayer and the children were told to bring all the dirty dishes and silverware in from the picnic tables and the porch. Hecht, even more annoyingly cloying than usual, volunteered to help the children. When he reached the picnic table where the other Germans and Jordan sat, he said, "Is everyone having a good time?"

"Yes," said Jordan. "And I'm now officially stuffed."

"Relax a few minutes, then, and please, let me take your dishes in for you."

Jordan smiled, "Thank you, Hecht." As Hecht made his way back to the house, Jordan said in amazement, "Maybe leopards really can change their spots."

But Rolf and Gralke weren't listening to Jordan, whose back was to the house. They were watching Hecht, who had stopped for a moment just before walking up the porch steps.

Gralke turned to Rolf looking astounded. "Did you see that?"

Rolf was also alarmed. "Yes! Hecht put a knife in his pocket."

"What the hell?" said Gralke "What does a man about to be baptized need with a knife?"

"He stole a knife?" said Jordan. "What the hell!"

Rolf was already up and heading toward Hecht. He caught up with him just as Hecht was about to go into the kitchen. "Hey, Otto." Hecht turned around. Rolf directed him away from the kitchen door so they could speak privately. "Did you put a knife in your pocket?"

Hecht rolled his eyes and sneered. "What? Are you crazy? Why would I steal a knife?"

"Just show me what's in your left front pocket."

"Why should I?"

"Because Gralke and I saw you put something in there. And it looked like a knife."

"You have no right to accuse me like this. And on my special day. Are you that jealous of me because I'm about to be baptized?" Hecht shook his head. "You are! You're jealous because Mrs. Unruh has taken me under her wing and helped me find salvation, but not you."

"Just show me what you put in your pocket."

Hecht sighed dramatically, then said, "If I do, will you stop harassing me?"

"Yes, and if you don't, I'll go find Stevenson. And there will be a spectacle on your 'special' day right here in front of everyone. If I'm wrong, I won't say another word."

With a gotcha smile, Hecht set the plates he was carrying down on a nearby bench and turned out all four pants pockets. Three were empty. In his left front pocket were two teaspoons. "Satisfied?"

"Why did you put spoons in your pocket?"

"Because the dishes were teetering, and I was afraid I would drop the silverware."

"From where we were sitting it looked suspicious."

"From where you're sitting, everything looks suspicious." He stepped in closer to Rolf and spoke in a low voice, "You really are pathetic, trying to make yourself out to be some hero to the Americans. Maybe you should think about your sad, one-legged life. And know this: You're never going to end up with Loretta. Not if her mother has anything to say about it. And she has a lot to say about it. I know what she really thinks of you."

Behind Hecht, the screen door opened with a squeak and Harold stepped out. "Everything all right here?"

Hecht's sneer dissolved into a sugary smile as he turned around.

"Yes, thank you. Rolf was just telling me how happy he is for me today. God is good."

"Amen," said Harold. "Mrs. Unruh sent me out to find you, Otto. She wants you to go down in the cellar and get the ten-gallon cask of apple cider. You'll see it in the corner. Bring it up and fill that crock dispenser over there by the punch glasses. We'll have a little toast after the ceremony."

Hecht paused for a second, then smiled. "That sounds perfect. Let me take these plates into the kitchen. Then I'll use the outhouse and pick up the cask on my way back." Then to needle Rolf, he added, "Rolf, maybe you'd like to go with me?"

"I don't think so."

Harold nodded, "Thank you, Otto." After he was in the kitchen, Harold said to Rolf, "I'm sure it's hard for you to believe that Otto has accepted Jesus as his Savior."

"Yes, sir, it is."

"I don't blame you for doubting him. But people can change. Men can turn from evil to good. And we have to give them the chance to do that."

"Do you think he will be a good Mennonite, sir?"

"I've watched him pretty close since he got back. I'm not a hundred percent sure, but the missus is. And I've never known her to be wrong in such matters. Her intuitions are good."

"I have great respect for both you and your wife, and I trust your judgment."

Harold stepped back inside, and Rolf returned to the table where Gralke, Zimmerman, and Jordan were all waiting to find out what happened.

Rolf shrugged. "False alarm. He had spoons in his pocket, he said he would have dropped them otherwise."

"That sounds like bullshit to me," said Jordan to the nods of the others after Rolf translated for them. "I think we should still keep a close watch on him."

Rolf nodded. "I agree, but discreetly. Mr. and Mrs. Unruh would be upset if we make a scene accusing their newest Mennonite of being a liar and a manipulator in front of everyone."

When the dishes were washed and put away, the women came out and called the children to the well. The ritual was short and simple. Elder Ratzlaff asked Hecht if he had repented from his sinful past, if he was ready to serve the Lord in all things, and if it was his free choice to be baptized into the Mennonite community. Hecht solemnly replied affirmatively to each question. Then Harold and Clara, standing on either side, leaned Hecht back while Elder Ratzlaff poured cool water over Hecht's head and spoke the ancient words: In the name of the Father, and of the Son, and of the Holy Ghost. When he stood back up, Clara dabbed his forehead and hugged him. Harold shook his hand, and the preacher said a brief benediction and welcomed Hecht into the church. The group cheered and clapped.

As the ceremony was ending, Rolf headed to the outhouse and was nearing it when he noticed something unusual. The ground was covered with a thick blanket of October leaves, but one spot near the rose of Sharon bushes was bare, as if the leaves had been pushed aside. Curious, Rolf walked over to investigate. Using his foot, he brushed the leaves around the bare spot and discovered a hole in the ground. It was partially hidden by a bush and looked freshly refilled, but haphazardly. And a piece of paper was partially sticking out of the dirt. It was a label, frayed around the edges and damp, but the words printed on it were easily decipherable: **COWLEY'S RAT AND MOUSE POISON**. Below the name was a skull and crossbones with a warning: **CAUTION** / This Bottle Contains A Deadly Poison / **ARSENIC**.

Rolf picked it up and read the words out loud a second time and thought, *Who would bury a rat poison bottle out here, away from the trash cans?* In a flash, he recalled the dead Belgians and that rat poison was missing from the barn. "Holy Shit!" he said out loud, then his racing mind recalled something even more alarming: Just before the ceremony, Hecht came out to the outhouse and went to the cellar, all out of sight of the family and friends gathered on the other side of the house. Then it all came together in his mind. "The cider! Hecht!" Rolf exclaimed. *"Gott in Himmel!* That son of a bitch!"

He raced to the cellar and flew down the stairs so fast that he was afraid he might land wrong and break his prosthesis, but it held. When he turned on the light, he saw what he feared he would find: Rat poison bottles lying in a corner, all of them open and empty, along with a pair of work gloves. And the cider keg was gone.

Now full of adrenaline, Rolf reflexively put on the gloves, grabbed one of the bottles, bounded up the steps, and hurried around the house. Everyone was still gathered in the west yard, chatting and laughing. And now every one of them was holding a punch glass filled with apple cider, even Tobias' and Gladys' youngest children.

Gladys was bent over talking to her five-year-old. "Yes, I know you're thirsty, but you have to wait. And no sips!" Margaret was shushing the other children, who were all growing impatient too.

When Carol Ann saw Rolf, she called out, "Finally! Get your apple cider, Rolf. Otto said we couldn't drink our toast until you're here. We're thirsty!"

Loretta saw by the look on Rolf's face that something was wrong and he was out of breath. "What's the matter?" she asked as she walked over to him carrying two glasses of cider.

Rolf retained his composure while conveying the urgency of the moment. "Please put down those glasses now, and do not get any of the cider on you." With his free hand he made a slow downward motion to illustrate what he was asking her to do. He was also hoping to God that he was right in his assessment of the situation or there would be hell to pay. But he was sure.

"Why?"

"It's poisoned." He showed her the little brown bottle in his gloved hand, then put the bottle behind his back. "Don't say anything yet." Loretta did as he said. Once she was safe, Rolf turned to the group and called out, "Everyone! Don't drink the apple cider! Please put your glasses down."

Some of the people complied and some didn't hear Rolf. Hecht was among the latter, couldn't hear because his back was turned and Cletus Slaymaker and he were engaged in a loud, jovial conversation.

Harold hurried over to Loretta and Rolf, alarmed, "What's going on?"

Rolf put his head down to talk discreetly. "I found the rat poison bottles, sir. They were buried by the outhouse and now they're on the cellar floor, empty." He lowered his voice. "Hecht put arsenic in the apple cider, I'm sure of it."

Harold was dumbstruck. For a moment he weighed whether to

believe Rolf. But as soon as he remembered sending Hecht out for the cider, he nodded that he understood. Like Rolf, he quickly switched into survival mode.

"What should we do?" asked Loretta,

Her father was already turning back to the group with a calm smile. In a friendly but authoritative tone, he said, "Everyone, please listen." He repeated himself until all heads were turned toward him. "I want you to take your cider glasses over to that picnic table and set them down. Don't drink any of it. Doris and Gladys, please help the little ones."

Clara looked annoyed as she hurried over to her husband, daughter, and Rolf. "What in heaven's name is going on?"

"Trust me," Harold replied, then he spoke to the group once more. "Loretta found hairs in her cider, along with what looks like a piece of a rodent tooth. A mouse or rat musta gotten into the cider keg before we sealed it up." Carol Ann and a few others gasped and made ewww sounds, but most were calm as they walked to the picnic table. Some carried their glasses gingerly, arms extended, as if they were holding hand grenades.

Standing near the porch, Hecht and Cletus heard Harold's warning. Without asking, Cletus took Hecht's glass from him. "Let me get that for you. We can't have the guest of honor getting sick on his baptism day now, can we?" Cletus said with a smile, then he walked both glasses over to the picnic table.

Hecht started to look panicky. He began to edge away from the group, heading toward the gate. But while Harold was still talking, Rolf had gotten Jordan's attention. Jordan was standing across the yard next to Lieutenant Stevenson. When Rolf nodded his head toward Hecht and rolled his eyes in that direction, that's all it took for Jordan to understand. He whispered to Stevenson, then the two of them glided over to stand beside Hecht before he could try to run. Rolf joined them and motioned for Gralke and Zimmerman to come too. In seconds, Hecht was cordoned off from the rest of the party, squeezed against the porch between Gralke and Zimmerman and behind Jordan and Stevenson.

Rolf showed the Americans the Cowley's bottle. "He put it in the cider," he whispered.

Stevenson and Jordan turned around to face Hecht. "You were going to poison the Unruhs?" Stevenson asked.

Hecht feigned surprise. "What? No, of course not! What are you talking about?"

The magnitude of Hecht's plans was now becoming clear. Jordan was livid, "You were going to poison all of us, with rat poison. Just like you poisoned their horses." Rolf quickly translated what Jordan said so the other Germans would clearly understand.

"*Du dreckiger Bastard!*" Gralke snarled. Jordan had to restrain him to keep him from beating Hecht on the spot.

All the glasses had been collected on the table and everyone was safe, but the Unruhs and their other guests couldn't hear what was being said by the Germans and their guards and kept their distance. Clara began to head toward the Germans and the guards to get to the bottom of what was going on, but Harold and Loretta stopped her and whispered what they'd learned. For a moment, it looked like Clara might faint. Her husband and daughter had to steady her.

Across the yard, Hecht tried to maintain his innocence. "I didn't kill those horses. Some crazy American did it because he hates Germans. I didn't kill them."

Stevenson took charge. "Turn around, spread your legs, and hold your arms out." As he complied, Hecht saw Clara and gave her a look proclaiming his innocence. She looked away.

Jordan patted him down and pulled out a table knife hidden in his underwear. Hecht shrugged as if he had no idea how it got there.

"I knew it!" exclaimed Zimmerman. He and Gralke gripped Hecht's arms tightly.

"And I found the bottles in the cellar where you emptied the rat poison into the cider." Rolf spoke calmly, but his voice belied the rage growing in him.

"I didn't put arsenic in anything. I don't know anything about those bottles." He looked at Jordan and Stevenson. "Mueller is making this up. He's jealous and trying to ruin my day."

Stevenson said, "So you didn't put rat poison in the cider?"

"Absolutely not!"

The lieutenant took a glove from Rolf, walked to the picnic table, and picked up a full glass of cider. "Drink it," he said when he returned. He reached out to hand it to Hecht, but the German refused to take it.

Game over, Hecht's expression switched from victimhood to fear to defiance. "Fuck you!" he said, swatting the glass out of Stevenson's hand to create a diversion so he could escape. "*Heil* Hitler!" he roared as he broke loose and ran, shoving Carol Ann and others down as he tried to get free. But before he got through the gate, Jordan and Gralke tackled him and pressed him down in the dirt face-first. Rolf pressed the shoe on his prosthetic leg into the small of Hecht's back to immobilize him while Stevenson procured rope from Harold and bound him. All the while, Hecht kept shouting expletives, "Fuck you, stupid Americans. Fuck your weak Mennonite God! And fuck you, Mueller, and you other traitors to the Fatherland! I act in the name of the *Fuehrer*! Glory to the *Fuehrer*! *Heil Hitler!*" It wasn't long before Zimmerman had had enough. He took off his shoes and socks, stuffed a sock into Hecht's mouth, and tied the other one around his head to hold the gag tightly in place.

Once he was securely bound, Jordan and the Germans got Hecht up to walk him to the car and put him in the back seat between Rolf and Gralke, Clara insisted on walking over to the car. Loretta held her mother's waist, afraid she might stumble, but Clara had regained her strength and her footing. She looked in at Hecht and returned his hateful glare with a kind, compassionate smile. "May God forgive you. I will pray for you. And I will ask the Lord to give me the strength to forgive you." Then she and Loretta stepped back and were joined by Dora Janz, Doris Koehn, and her mother, and Carol Ann. They bowed their heads in silent prayer, then began singing *Amazing Grace* until the car drove off.

Lieutenant Stevenson spoke to Harold. "I don't know what to say, Mr. Unruh, except I am sorry. We shouldn't have allowed this to happen. We failed to protect you and your family this afternoon."

Harold replied with a smile. "We invited the serpent into the garden, that's not your fault. And you did protect us, lieutenant, with God's help and without excessive force or violence. We are all grateful."

As they drove off, Rolf looked through the window to see Loretta looking at him with a sad, desolate expression.

# Chapter 39

# CONSEQUENCES

When Hecht was back in the Eyestone Building and handcuffed to a bunk in an impromptu isolation room, Lieutenant Stevenson thanked Gralke and Zimmerman for their help and asked Rolf to join him and Jordan in the office. The three of them sat there quietly for a moment, calming down and trying to process the day's events.

Stevenson pulled out a small bottle of bourbon from his desk drawer and motioned for Jordan to hand him three of the coffee cups sitting on a nearby file cabinet. "After that, I think we all deserve a little drink." As he poured three healthy shots, he smiled slyly. "I just remembered, I forgot to ungag Hecht after we got him locked up. Oops! Jordan, please remind me to get that taken care of later on tonight. Or tomorrow."

After they chinked cups, Jordan said, "I can't believe how close we all came to dying this afternoon." Jordan shook his head. "When I think of my family alone because that son of a bitch poisoned me, I want to go strangle him with my bare hands." He was shaking.

"I'm glad everyone is safe," said Rolf. "But I want to say something to you." He looked at both Stevenson and Jordan.

"Okay, but first there's something I want to say to you, Mueller," said Stevenson. "You were right about Hecht. We should have listened to you. I can't thank you enough for acting so quickly and so wisely. All of us, even those children, could have died from the poison or the knife if Hecht had figured out what was happening and used it. Had he gotten away with it, the results would have been catastrophic."

Jordan added, "He's right. You saved us, you literally saved us."

Rolf smiled. "I was just in the right place at the right time."

"Possibly, but there's more to the story than that. After you figured out what Hecht had done, you stayed calm and didn't make a scene or alert him. You made sure we had him surrounded and that no one panicked, then you made sure everyone was safe. Very few people I know could have handled this so well."

"Thank you for saying that."

Stevenson nodded. "What is it you wanted to say?"

Rolf thought for a moment. "I hope you don't become suspicious of all of us after what Hecht did. You've allowed us a great deal of flexibility and you've treated us with respect. Hecht abused the trust you placed in him, but I hope you will still feel like you can trust the rest of us."

Stevenson replied. "Hecht was an exception, not the rule, as far as the Germans here are concerned. Since this subcamp opened, I've been amazed at how decent almost all of you are. Almost everyone works hard and tries to get along. The farmers tell us the harvests this year and last would have been lost if you POWs had not been here to help them bring it in. Yes, some people complain about having German POWs in town, but they're just showing old prejudices. They don't realize how beneficial your presence has been. We have to guard you, of course, but I think everyone gets along with everyone else for the most part. That's not going to change now, except that I may rely on you more going forward to let us know if there's a problem we should know about. You know the difference between good and evil, Rolf. As I said, we should have listened to you about Hecht in the first place."

Jordan said, "I second everything the lieutenant said."

"And now," Stevenson said as he stood up, "if there's nothing else, I have at least a hundred forms and reports to fill out because of today, including a transfer order to get Hecht out of here as soon as possible, before I find some rat poison of my own!" All three men laughed.

Rolf stood and said, "Thank you for your kind words." Before he turned around to leave, he gave the lieutenant a crisp salute.

Around the table after chores that evening, the four Unruhs were still shaken and grateful to be alone after a day like no other. Loretta started to write to Joe and John to tell them what had happened, but it was all still too overwhelming and raw. "I don't know how to begin."

Sensing her family's exhaustion and sadness, Carol Ann knew it would be up to her to lighten the mood. "How about this: 'Dear Boys, you missed a swell party today. We invited the family and some others out to have dinner and witness Otto Hecht's baptism, but then he tried to poison every last one of us with arsenic like he did Axl and Hans and the cats. Then Rolf saved us. That was nice of him, but after that we weren't much in the mood for a party, so we're sitting here in the kitchen moping! Wish you were here! Love Loretta.'" By the time she'd finished, even Clara couldn't keep from smiling, at least a little.

"That's a pretty good summation of our day!" laughed Loretta.

"Wait! I left something out," said Carol Ann as she stood and walked over to her mother. She hugged Clara tightly and kissed her cheeks. "It's the most important part, about our mother."

Harold smiled. "Please, elaborate."

Carol Ann obliged. "Our mother, your wife, Papa, always looks for the good in others. She witnesses for Christ like nobody's business, even to those who don't deserve it." Carol Ann kissed the top of her mother's head. "Loretta, be sure to tell the boys that."

Clara's face was pale and sad again. She said, "If you're going to write that, you also have to be clear what a damn fool your mother is too."

"Mama!" Carol Ann shouted. "Cursing?"

"Just this once." Clara nodded to her daughters, then looked at her husband.

Harold smiled. "Well, if you're a fool, it's only because you're a fool for Christ. And no one can fault you for that."

"I love you, husband, but I let someone in who tried to kill us today." Her voice was quiet and weak, and her hand was shaking as she reached for her coffee cup. "I feel so betrayed."

"You were betrayed, wife, and I love you too. And we're all still kicking, aren't we? God protected us once again, like He protected our ancestors so many times. And with every cloud, there's a silver lining, even this one."

"I'm not seeing a silver lining here."

Carol Ann looked at her father and interjected, "Is the silver lining here that you'll have an incredible story to tell your grandchildren someday?"

"Ha! No, that wasn't what I was thinking. I was thinking that now we know it wasn't our neighbors who killed Axl and Hans. I'll sleep a little easier knowing that the perpetrator is locked up and won't be coming around here anymore."

The following afternoon, Lieutenant Stevenson and Jordan came out to Doyle Creek to speak with Harold, Clara, and Loretta about what had happened. Rolf, Gralke, and Zimmerman were all working in the barn, and Clara had a fresh pot of coffee and a pound cake ready when they arrived.

Stevenson began by asking how everyone was doing, then he apologized again on behalf of the Army for failing to take adequate measures to protect the family. Harold thanked him and reaffirmed that they did not blame the Army for what had happened. The fault, he said, was solely Otto Hecht's, who took advantage of the family's hospitality and betrayed their trust. He compared Hecht to the wolves in sheep's clothing that Jesus spoke of in the Sermon on the Mount. The family was saddened by his betrayal, they said, but grateful that they and all their guests were safe.

Clara added that the family was especially grateful to Rolf for acting quickly enough to save them. "And we thank you too," she said, "for protecting us without resorting to violence or bloodshed."

Then Harold said. "Back to what happened, have you decided for sure that it was Otto who killed Axl and Hans? And why on earth would he do that?"

Stevenson replied, "Yes, we're sure. Hidden in his mattress, we found calculations for how much arsenic it would take to kill someone. We think he found the rat poison in your barn, then decided to practice, first on the cats and then the horses. But the animals weren't the targets. You and your family and Mueller were. We're sure of this because we found a letter from Streicher in the mattress, probably written before he was transferred to Oklahoma and given to Hecht when he was still in Concordia. Streicher ordered Hecht to kill all of you in retaliation for testifying against him." The Unruhs shook their heads sadly. "Streicher's letter ended with these words, I translated and wrote them down. Stevenson unfolded a piece of paper:

*Soldat Hecht, time and again you have proven yourself a loyal son of the Reich. Now once more, do your duty, for the Fatherland, for your Fuehrer! Heil Hitler!*

Stevenson frowned. "I made the mistake of letting Hecht come back to your farm because I thought Streicher wouldn't be able to order him to take action against you, but clearly I was wrong."

Harold said, "Do you think maybe Otto was forced to follow that order? Maybe they threatened him or his family? Was he just following orders?"

Stevenson replied, "I don't think so. Hecht knew Streicher was locked up and couldn't communicate with anyone by last March, but he kept planning to kill you. It wasn't just a spontaneous action, it was an elaborate scheme. First, he had to convince the hearing board that he was being coerced by Streicher. Then he had to get close to you while Mueller was in Concordia. Then he had to pretend to have a religious conversion so you would trust him, and he was an opportunist. Once he found out about the arsenic, he tested it and waited for the right moment to execute his plan."

"That is truly diabolical, isn't it?" said Harold.

"Yes, much worse than just following orders. I believe this 'loyal son of the Reich' saw himself as brilliant for coming up with a way to wage war for Hitler right here. And it wasn't a momentary whim. Look how long it took for him to find the right moment to execute."

Jordan added, "And when the opportunity presented itself, he decided on his own to go beyond Streicher's direct order and kill not just you and Mueller, but everyone that was here yesterday, even the children. A couple dozen people! That's not following orders or doing your duty. That's heinous."

"I think he thought," said Stevenson, "that if he succeeded in killing people in Kansas, it would strike terror in the hearts of all Americans, maybe even worse than Pearl Harbor because it would bring the war to the American mainland. There would be chaos, possibly riots in the streets. Crops would go unharvested, there would be food shortages, and 400,000 POWs would be held in big camps with nothing to do. Imagine how people like Ferguson and that *Wichita Beacon* reporter would react if they were proven right, that German POWs really are a grave threat to America. There would be lynchings, Americans could be fighting Americans."

Loretta looked astonished. "I hadn't thought about all those consequences. It's stunning what could have happened here yesterday."

"Thank God, he didn't succeed," said Harold.

"Yes, sir," replied Stevenson. "But even the attempt is bad enough.

Which is why I want to ask one more thing: We're hoping to keep what happened out of the newspapers. My superiors and Marion County law enforcement have been notified, but we don't want a sensational story like this riling up the townsfolk again. Especially because overall the POW labor program has been such a huge success for everyone, and safe."

"We agree. Last night before the rest of our family and our friends left, we asked them to keep what happened to themselves. They will. We're all pretty tight lipped when we need to be."

Stevenson smiled. "That's good, because if this goes public, I think the Army would close Peabody down for good."

"And we still need the help," said Harold. "We won't say anything."

"Then we're in agreement. I'm glad. And now I suppose we should be getting back to town so you can get back to work."

As Stevenson and Jordan stood to leave, Clara said, "You think you know someone, you think you can help them, then something like this happens. It's so dismaying."

Jordan walked over to her and gave her a hug. "You're a good person, Mrs. Unruh, so kind and hospitable. Otto Hecht is a Nazi at heart, and a deceitful one at that. It's not your fault that he took advantage of you."

"Thank you, Greg. I hope you're right."

⋯⚬⋯⚬⋯⚬⋯

Harold decided to keep all three of the Germans on for the winter. They would do the regular chores and maintenance, restock the farm's depleted firewood supplies, and do some painting and other outdoor jobs when the weather permitted. And when it was too cold or wet, Harold would find work for them indoors. He didn't need three workers over the winter of 1944-45, but he and Clara felt they owed Zimmerman, Gralke, and Rolf a debt for acting so quickly to protect them from Hecht. Clara made a point of regularly thanking each of them.

One afternoon, Harold handed Rolf an envelope. Inside was a Hallmark thank you card with violet flowers and black and white kittens on the front. Inside, the printed note said *Thanks a bunch!* Under it, Carol Ann had added *For Saving Our Lives!!!* And everywhere there were squished little notes and signatures. Some weren't legible, but the sentiments were sincere.

Rolf read the notes and smiled. "I've never received a printed card. I love it. Thank you."

Clara said, "Without your quick thinking...." She was still very emotional about what happened and couldn't finish what she wanted to say.

Harold helped her out. "If you hadn't had to use the outhouse, we might not all be here today!" Everyone smiled and laughed.

But things were different. That night, Rolf wrote in his journal:

Date: 15 November 1944, Location Camp Peabody: Today the Unruhs gave me a beautiful card signed by everyone who was at their farm the day Hecht tried to poison us. Even the little children printed their names. And in one corner on the back of the card, Carol Ann forged Hecht's signature and wrote a note from him: "Sorry I tried to kill you! Love, Otto <u>Himmler</u> Hecht!" So funny!

I appreciate everyone's kind words, but since that day, Mr. and Mrs. Unruh have been different around us. Hecht betrayed Mrs. Unruh in the worst possible way. Her faith is more important to her than anything else except her family. For him to use that against her to try to hurt her family is probably the worst thing someone could do to her. Now it's like she's looking at us with suspicion. And not just me, but Zimmerman and Gralke too.

And Mr. Unruh doesn't seem to want to leave the three of us alone for long, and he's quieter. He put a lock on the cupboard where the rat poison is stored, and now he's tuning up the equipment himself instead of Gralke, who he used to call the best mechanic he's ever seen.

After such a betrayal, it would be natural for them to wonder about us. Maybe they're thinking if they could be so wrong about Hecht, are they wrong about the rest of us?

And Loretta? Honestly, I can't tell for sure, but I think things are not the same between us now. Is she hesitant? Sad? I would like to talk to her, but I don't think I should. If I'm right, it would make her uncomfortable if I confront her. I should let her tell me in her own time. And if I'm wrong, then I'm doubting her and her family and that would hurt her feelings. So I'm going to stay quiet for now.

Rolf's perceptions were correct. He and Loretta were still assigned to do the afternoon milking until Carol Ann got home. They still enjoyed being alone together and there was friendly banter and engaging conversation and some flirting, but it was different than before. And they both noticed it.

One Sunday afternoon in November, when Loretta and Doris were out for a walk in the hills, Doris asked, "How's Rolf?"

"Fine." After Rolf was shot, Loretta had shared the whole story of their friendship and romance with Doris, all her feelings for him and all the details of their limited interactions. But on this afternoon, Loretta's answers were uncharacteristically short.

"Are you and he still getting to spend a little time alone together?"

"Yes."

"Are you still friends?"

"Of course."

"Are you still in love?"

Loretta looked at Doris and scowled, "Yes."

Doris decided to press Loretta a bit more. "Okay, so what's going on here? And you have to answer with more than one or two words."

"Yes, we're still close, and yes I still love him, but…" Loretta thought for a moment. "I don't know."

"What don't you know?"

Loretta sighed. "After John was here in August and said the things he said, and then after what happened last month, I've been doing a lot of thinking."

"About Rolf?"

"Yes. I can't imagine being as wrong about him as Mama was about Otto Hecht, but—but what if I am? Am I just being naive, believing what I want to believe about a man I don't know very well? Could he be using me like Hecht used Mama?"

"After all that's gone on, it's normal to wonder. What does your heart tell you?"

"That Rolf is a good man, honest and kind, and that he loves me."

Doris feigned outrage. "That's positively awful! Now I must

intervene for your own good. You must never talk to him again! The cad!"

Loretta laughed too. "Okay, I get it. And you're right. I've never felt manipulated by him. I don't think he's ever lied to me. And we've known each other now for over a year. We haven't been together round the clock, but I think I have a measure of the man. But now I have these nagging little doubts about him, and I hate that. And I can't even talk to him about it."

"So, are you and he planning on eloping anytime soon?"

Loretta laughed. "No."

"Are you planning on busting him out of prison again?"

"No!"

"Has he given you the slightest reason to doubt his sincerity?"

"No."

"Has he ever given you reason to be uncomfortable around him for something he did, not something that crazy Hecht did?"

"Honestly, no. Not once."

Doris took her cousin's hand. "Then I don't think you have anything to worry about. Continue to get to know him. Continue to be his friend, Continue to love him. Let him love you back, and in time you'll know whether you have anything to worry about."

As she hugged her cousin, Loretta said, "Thank you, Doris. You should write an advice column for the paper."

On Tuesday, the fifth of December, Rolf was starting the afternoon milking when Loretta walked in, loosely draping her heavy coat around something. "What's this?"

"A surprise," and she pulled her coat back to reveal a cupcake with one lit candle.

Rolf's face brightened. "It's the anniversary of our first kiss!"

"Yes. It was a year ago today, under the stars."

"I will never forget that night."

She smiled. "It was, and still might be, the craziest thing I've ever done."

After they blew the candle out, Rolf said, "I know what I'm wishing for." He drew her to himself and she let him. And when they kissed deeply, he felt the excitement and desire that had changed his world a year earlier. And for that moment, she did too. "I loved you then, Loretta Unruh, and I love you still."

"I love you too."

"Will it be enough?" He hated asking, but had to.

With sad eyes, she stepped back and said, "Honestly, I don't know."

Things were also changing in Europe that fall. Events there were casting dark shadows over Rolf even in far-away Kansas. On October 21st, the day before Hecht's treachery, the Americans captured Aachen, their first German city. The front was now just 150 kilometers away from Olpe. Overwhelming forces had reached German soil. Armies would soon be on his family's doorstep. He knew what they had to look forward to.

Letters from home now arrived only erratically, and the few that made it through were dreary. There was still nothing definitive about Kurt. His mother was mostly resigned to her firstborn's death, but the sliver of hope that sprang from the uncertainty kept her from being able to grieve him properly. Maria was ill, his father was away with the Volkstrum, and the farm was in disarray. Klara Mueller no longer offered any pretense of having faith in the *Fuehrer's* ability to save Germany. Her letters only brought her son more anxiety.

# Chapter 40
# GOODWILL TOWARD MEN

For some Christians, Advent is a time for soulful reflection before Christmas. Advent in 1944 was filled with even more anticipation than usual. In the Eyestone Building, the guards and internees all sensed that the war was moving inexorably toward a climactic, cataclysmic finale. The timing may not yet have been known, but the writing was on the wall for anyone willing to read. The Axis Powers were in retreat globally and the status quo—military conflict devouring lives by the million and swallowing up resources at an incomprehensible rate—could not be sustained much longer. For some, that brought hope—maybe next year they'd be home for the holidays. For others, there was dreadful certainty that there would be no homes, or families, to return to by the time it was all finally over.

Early in the season, Jordan surprised Rolf one morning after Sunday Mass. "Are you still interested in carving something for Loretta for Christmas?"

"Yes, certainly."

"The Peabody Lumber Company owner has a set of tools that he'll loan you." In the office, he handed Rolf a seven-piece set of wood-handled chisels, gouges, knives, and a mallet, still in the original Craftsman box. One blade was chinked, but still usable. "Will these do?"

"Oh yes! They are just like my father's."

"What are you thinking of making?"

"Maybe a nativity set. Do you think she'd like that?"

"Yes, she'll love it. So you're gonna need a buncha pieces of wood. Here," and Jordan tossed him a sack of irregular squares and rectangles trimmed off of larger boards. "Also courtesy of the lumbar yard man. There's walnut, pine, and basswood in there."

Touched by Jordan's thoughtfulness, Rolf immersed himself in the joy of creating. For a model, he sketched out a set his grandfather had made that decorated their home every Christmas. He would make something similar—an ambitious sixteen-figure crèche including the Holy Family, an angel, wise men, shepherds, some sheep, a cow, a donkey, and a manger.

There were some initial mistakes, some ruined blocks, and the results were primitive, but Rolf was generally pleased. At least each figurine was recognizable for its intended purpose. Jordan also found him some sandpaper and tung oil to rub each piece to a fine luster. By Christmas, all but the kings were ready, and those he would have done for her by Epiphany.

Christmas was also on Harold's mind one afternoon in December when he asked the Germans how they celebrated the holiday. They happily described their favorite customs—*sternsingers*, Christmas markets and trees, *weihnachtsmann,* Christmas Eve gift exchanges, Midnight Mass, feasts, and visits from relatives.

"And how do Mennonites celebrate?" Rolf asked when they'd finished.

"Not as elaborately as you," Clara said, "but we still remember Christ's birth. Some in our church don't put up a Christmas tree, but we do. And we exchange gifts."

"Practical ones. I can always count on new socks and underwear." Harold smiled.

"And it's a good thing, because you always need new ones by then."

"We go to church on Christmas morning and then come home to a nice dinner. And Clara makes mincemeat cookies and *stollen*."

"I love *stollen*!" said Gralke. "My grandmother makes it for us, with currents."

Clara smiled. "Like mine."

Loretta said, "Santa Claus came with presents when we were little. And he always left a big bowl of apples and nuts and hard candies on the table for the whole family. And oranges."

Harold looked up from stirring his coffee and said, "We were wondering if you'd like to join us for Christmas dinner this year. It's on a Monday. We'd pick you up on Christmas morning around eleven. Do you know if Greg is going to be in town?"

Rolf replied, "That sounds wonderful, thank you. And Greg just told me he won't get leave until maybe in January."

"Then we'll be sure to invite him too. And we'll have you help with the afternoon chores, so we can say we brought you for work, and not just fun." Harold winked.

Gralke smiled. "I promise to work especially hard for a slice of Mrs. Unruh's *stollen*."

"She loves to share her *stollen*, don't you, my dear?"

"I will happily give you some, Anton, if I can keep my husband from eating it all first!"

Zimmerman seemed nervous. "It sounds wonderful, but I have a question." He paused. "I wonder if you should invite us after what happened in October."

Clara replied flatly, "We're trying to put the past behind us and not blame all of you for the sins of one, Erich. We're happy to have you join us on Christmas."

"Then thank you, I look forward to celebrating Christmas with you."

Clara's tone and the words she used and the look in Loretta's eyes told Rolf that it was not an easy decision for the family to invite the Germans to celebrate Christmas with them.

***

A week before the holiday, an unexpected blizzard swept across the plains, dropping a foot of snow on Peabody in a matter of hours, then sculpting it into massive pompadour drifts. Temperatures plummeted below zero, making it impossible to keep the Eyestone Building, with all its plate-glass windows, warm. At Doyle Creek, Harold got the driveway cleared, but mountains of snow blocked the county road in several places. It took days for the Marion County maintainers to get all the roads open. Rolf used the time off to carve, but he wished he could be helping the Unruhs because he knew how miserable outdoor chores would be in such weather.

Finally, on the 22nd, the skies cleared, the winds died, and temperatures rose from brutal to merely cold, and people were happy it was going to be a white Christmas. As if to remind them, Bing Crosby crooned *White Christmas* on their radios at least once every hour.

On Christmas Eve morning, the POWs cleaned their quarters like they would have done at home, and cooked. Once again, their government had sent Christmas money for them through the Red Cross. The amount was less than in 1943, but still enough to purchase several fat geese and ducks, rabbits, sausage, oranges, nuts, red cabbage, and the ingredients for *stollen* and *weihnachtsplätzchen*. By noon, the building smelled like a proper German restaurant.

When guards carried in a large cedar tree, POWs were already stringing popcorn and making aluminum foil-and-cardboard ornaments, then other guards showed up with store-bought lights, glass ornaments, and a star for the treetop. They even had candles and a few poinsettias, but couldn't find a nativity set, so Rolf carefully unwrapped his gift to Loretta and let them display it that night in a nest of cedar branches. He thought she would understand.

By the time the priest arrived for "Midnight" Mass at eight o'clock, the dining hall had been transformed into a sentimental, candle-illumined chapel. No minister could come for a separate Protestant service, so everyone was invited to join the Catholics. With German and American Catholics and Protestants and even nonbelievers in attendance, the night felt holy, a feeling enhanced by heartfelt singing and a guard's moving rendition of *Oh, Holy Night* on his violin.

Afterwards, as the dining hall was being set up for dinner, the Americans surprised the POWs with *glühwein mit schuss*, a German holiday tradition. And the Germans had a surprise of their own for the guards—cases of cold Falstaff beer—courtesy, ironically, of the Nazis in Berlin.

It was a fine meal. When he'd finished eating with his friends, Rolf slipped away to find Jordan, who was carrying on with a group of other off-duty guards, all of them drunk. When he saw Rolf, Jordan bear-hugged him and slurred effusively, "Merry Christmas!" Rolf laughed and asked him out into the hall, where he handed him a small package. "What's this?" Jordan swayed and opened his eyes wide as if that would enable him to actually see what he was looking at.

"In Germany, we give gifts secretly by tossing them in through the door, but I wanted to give this to you in person." Inside was a small duck carved out of walnut, perfectly proportioned and sanded and oiled to a satiny luster. On its pedestal, Rolf had carved his initials and 25-12-44.

"Oh my God, it's wonderful!" Then Greg frowned. "But I didn't get you anything."

"You've done so much for me already. This is just a small token of my appreciation."

"Thank you, my friend." Jordan hugged Rolf and they both wobbled. "My friend. I never thought I'd say that, but I'm glad we're friends, even though—you know."

Rolf laughed. "Yes, I know. And you've called me your friend before."

"I have?" Jordan flopped an arm over Rolf's shoulder and moved in too close. "You should come to Pittsburgh with me in January to meet my family! I'll give you a fine haircut."

"I'd like that, but probably not in January," Rolf laughed. "Merry Christmas, Greg."

On the way back to the party, he silently wished his family *Frohe Weihnachten*. A few days earlier, he'd received a letter from his mother. Written in early December, it was more upbeat than other recent ones. Maria was recovering, his father was back in Olpe, and they were hoping for extra rations for Christmas. A cousin and his wife were now staying on the farm after being bombed out of their home in Frankfurt. They'd managed to salvage a few valuables that could be bartered for food. It wasn't much, but by pooling their resources, they might all survive. There was still no word on Kurt and the future still looked impossibly grim, but her more positive tone let Rolf be less afraid, and feel less guilty, at least for a few minutes.

His mother also thanked him for the parcel he'd sent via the Red Cross. It contained canned meats, sugar, coffee, and chocolate purchased with funds in his POW account. He was pleased that it arrived in time for Christmas. More than anything, he was surprised that it actually made it through without being stolen.

It was after two when the last revelers finally staggered off to bed, so Christmas Day started slow in the Eyestone Building. Stevenson let the duty guards take a head count instead of calling everyone into morning formation after such a late night. Only a few men were out of their bunks when Rolf, unable to sleep past eight, headed into the dining hall in search of coffee.

After a cup of steaming black coffee and some *schnecken*, he began a long letter to his family. It would please his father to know that he'd taken up woodcarving. In addition to farming, Muellers had been woodcrafters for generations. Their home was furnished with a fine table, chairs, beds, dressers, and wardrobes made by his father, grandfather, and more distant ancestors. Rolf hoped to one day make his own furniture in the cluttered workshop attached to the barn. Its distinct smell—lacquer fumes and wood shavings mixed with stale pipe smoke—filled his consciousness. He could see the sunbeams streaming down from the south-facing windows through sawdust that never quite settled onto the workbench or the floor. He could visualize how his father organized his tools just so and how nails, tacks, and brads were kept in coffee cans and glass jars by size, so as to be able to find just the right one when needed.

⚯⚯⚯⚯⚯

At 10:45, the Unruhs' dinner guests were ready and waiting. At eleven, Jordan, badly hung-over, braved the painful sunlight to look outside for their car. "Maybe Harold went home after church to drop Clara and the girls off." At 11:30, he speculated, "I'll bet the preacher just talked extra long." Finally, by noon, he conceded, "This isn't like Harold. He's always early, never late."

"You think something happened? Car trouble? Maybe they slipped off the road. Should you call them?" Rolf fidgeted with the present in his hands. "Maybe we had the wrong time?"

Gralke shook his head. "No, I'm sure they said they'd be here at eleven."

"I don't think I should call," Jordan added. "If they had car trouble, they wouldn't be home, and if we just have the wrong time, we'd embarrass them by calling."

The reason Harold didn't show had nothing to do with the weather or getting the time wrong. Shortly after two that afternoon, Rolf was on his bunk when Jordan came up to him. "Cletus Slaymaker wants to talk to us." Rolf jumped up, and they hurried to the office.

Cletus and Lieutenant Stevenson were conversing solemnly when the others walked in. "I just came from the Unruh place," Cletus began. "They've had some real bad news, and Harold asked if I would come in and tell you myself."

"Is Loretta all right?" Rolf blurted out.

353

"Loretta's fine. It's their son, Joe. He's presumed dead in Belgium." The men looked from one to another while Cletus waited for the news to sink in. "That's all they know at this time. It's not confirmed, but..." He looked away and cleared his throat. "He was in what they're calling the Battle of the Bulge. Lotsa casualties."

"When did they find out?" Jordan asked for himself and the others.

Cletus coughed again. "Yesterday afternoon, from an Army officer outta Fort Riley."

"My God, on Christmas Eve. How are Harold and Clara doing? And the girls?"

"They're shaken up. The wife and I got the news last night. We went over this morning and went back this afternoon and that's when Harold said he forgot all about picking you up, so he asked if I'd come in to let you know."

⚊⚊⚊⚊⚊⚊

Loretta and Carol Ann sat side by side on the sofa. Across from them was the tree Harold had cut the day before, still bare. They'd just started decorating when the Army man came. Boxes of ornaments, tinsel, and strands of lights were still lying where they were when the news came.

Clara was in her bedroom behind the closed door. Harold sat at the table staring at nothing. Dorothy Slaymaker and Margaret Koehn were near the sink organizing the condolence food that was already starting to overrun shelves and counters. The kitchen clock tortured them all with its relentless tic-toc tic-tocs.

On the table lay the telegram that the Army officer—he couldn't remember his name—had handed him. Harold took a resigned breath. Maybe if he re-read it once more, slowly enough this time, he would see that it had all been a big mistake, a bad dream.

MAJ115 42 GOVT=WUX WASHINGTON DC 11 218 P
MR AND MRS HAROLD J UNRUH=1944 DEC 24 PM 12 13

THE SECRETARY OF WAR DESIRES ME TO EXPRESS
HIS DEEP REGRET THAT YOUR SON JOSEPH H UNRUH
HAS BEEN REPORTED MISSING IN ACTION SINCE

SEVENTEEN DECEMBER IN BELGIUM AND IS
PRESUMED KILLED IN ACTION PERIOD IF FURTHER
DETAILS OR OTHER INFORMATION ARE RECEIVED
YOU WILL BE PROMPTLY NOTIFIED PERIOD
        DUNLOP ACTING THE ADJUTANT GENERAL

"Harold, would you like coffee?" his sister asked. "It's fresh."

"Not just now." Harold heaved a heavy sigh.

Dorothy Slaymaker said, "When Cletus gets back, we'll go home for a while, then come back to finish your chores tonight."

"No, Dot, that's all right. We'll do 'em this evening. You've got your own to do."

"We're happy to come back."

"I know, but we'll need something to do. I'm gonna go in and see how Clara's doing." His eyes welled with tears. "Thanks again, ladies. Margaret, you should go home now too."

In those first hours, grief pulsed over them, waves rising and falling. For Loretta, it was as numbing as anesthesia until an exquisite pain broke through. Had it been flame, it would have consumed her. Then that anguish ebbed for a moment, and her soul was filled with sadness like a sponge soaked in vinegar. Numbness; anguish; sadness. Over and over and over.

Rolf peered into blackness as day turned to night. Once more, he found himself detachedly wondering why this latest death should be so painful. Shouldn't he be used to death by now? And this was a man he'd never even met. Was it because the news followed so quickly such a pleasant Christmas Eve? Did the starkness of the contrast sharpen grief's steely blade?

No, somewhere in the night, he understood. The ferocity of his pain arose out of something more powerful than death: It was inextricably interwoven with love. Rolf ached down to his marrow because he was keenly aware, even without being on the farm with her, that this brother's death would be grievously wounding the woman he loved. He would never be hurting so deeply, but for the fact that he loved Loretta more than he'd ever loved anyone else.

## Chapter 41

# ANOTHER SHOE

Grief takes many forms, depending on the person and sometimes depending on the hour. In the days following receipt of the telegram, Clara withdrew almost completely from everyone, from life itself. The death of a child, regardless of his age, sends his parents down a raging river of tears. Often the woman who bore the child experiences his death most savagely. The pain was unimaginable. There were no words for Clara to adequately convey what she was experiencing, so there was no point in her speaking of it.

Harold's grief was also fierce, but he told himself he couldn't withdraw from life. His wife and other children needed him. He'd failed to protect Joseph, failed to talk him out of enlisting. That would haunt him forever, but he had to go on. He had to carry the burdens of the rest of his family until they were able to do so themselves. He would not fail them too.

Joe's death forever destroyed Carol Ann's and John's dreams of life after the war, when their brother would be returned to them and their lives would be synchronized once more in peace with family, church, and farming on Doyle Creek.

As for Loretta, in the days following Christmas her grief grew from numbness, anguish, and sadness into something even more potent. She began to experience flashes of deep unrelenting anger. Anger at Joe for having willingly gone to battle in the first place and at herself for not having told him unequivocally that he could not. Anger at those who had killed him and those who had put him in harm's way. Anger at Rolf, her parents, the church, the Army, Hitler, the Nazis, God! Anger at the people who tried to comfort her, said they knew what she was going through, said at least she had another brother and sister, and they were safe! Everyone felt her rage firsthand, except for Clara, for whom Loretta felt only the deepest sorrow.

Shortly after the new year began, with its implications that it was time for everyone to move on and forget the problems of the year now ended, Greg Jordan was waiting one afternoon to talk to Cletus Slaymaker when he pulled up to drop his crew off. Through the open passenger door, he called, "Good evening, Mr. Slaymaker, do you have a minute?"

"Sure, get on in here, it's cold. And Happy New Year."

"Same to you. Say, we haven't seen or heard from the Unruhs since Christmas. How're they doing?"

"About like you'd expect, I'd say."

"Have they heard anything more?"

"No. They haven't found his body yet. It's a helluva thing."

"It is. At least, I'm sure, they're getting a lot of support."

"Yep. This is the third Peabody boy to die. The first one, Donny Johnson, was killed at Pearl Harbor, then the Shelby boy died in Sicily. I didn't know those two well, but Joe's different—well-known and liked by everybody. He was class salutatorian, captain of the basketball team, played baseball. Plus, he was just a nice, outgoing kid. He had his father's sense of humor and gift of gab. Joe never knew a stranger."

"Is that right?"

"This one has hit the town hard. And I'll tell you something else. It's really bad for the Mennonites. As you know, they don't believe in war in the first place, you know, so losing one of their own in a war is, well, they don't quite know what to make of it."

"Are they second-guessing Joe's decision to enlist?"

"I'm sure they are since he could easily have taken CO status and avoided the fighting."

"It was brave of him to do what he did."

"Yes, but poor Harold and Clara. When a child dies before his folks, it's all wrong. It's out of order. I've never had to face that myself, thank God. I don't know if I could take it."

Jordan grimaced. "If anything happened to my boys...." His voice trailed off. "How are the girls?"

"It's probly the worst for Loretta. Since they were itty-bitty, she and Joe were two peas in a pod. And Carol Ann's back in school, but this has taken the wind outta her sails too. But the family is close and strong.

They'll make it."

"Thank you for the update, sir. I'll let Zimmerman and Gralke and Mueller know. They're all worried about the family."

Most mornings, Rolf had a hard time pulling himself off his bunk. Unemployed, confined to camp, and unable to see Loretta, he was bored and isolated. And when he and the others were told they would be reassigned to another employer if Harold didn't hire them back soon, that was one more thing to worry about. He finished the three king figurines for the nativity set, but couldn't make himself start another carving project. Jordan did get him a condolence card for the Unruhs and then secretly mailed it for him, which was a small satisfaction.

One sunny afternoon, he was loitering alone in the camp yard when he saw the Unruh car. His pulse sped up as the Chevrolet slowed to a stop, then raced when Loretta and Carol Ann got out. As they approached, though, he couldn't read her expression. Was she happy or angry or sad or tired? All of a sudden, he was as tongue-tied as the day he first saw her.

Carol Ann took the lead. "Hi Rolf, how've you been? We were driving by and saw you. That was good timing."

"I'm okay, thanks. How are you?"

Carol Ann replied. "It's been terrible. But maybe it's getting a little better."

"How are you, Loretta?" Such a ridiculously inane question, but it had to be asked in moments like this.

"Oh, you know," Loretta's voice quivered, her eyes puckered, "Not so good." A fast-swelling lump cut off her windpipe, like it did every time she tried to speak about Joe.

Her sister rescued her. "Thanks for your card. Mama and Papa were touched." Then she said, "I'm going back to the car where it's warm. I hope we get to see you again soon."

"Me too," said Rolf. Looking back to Loretta, he was struck again by how beautiful she was, even veiled in such sadness. "I don't know what to say, except that I'm so sorry."

Her blue eyes met his, tears glistening on her cheeks. "I never imagined when Joe left home that he wouldn't be coming back." Shyly, she put her fingers through the fence in search of consolation.

He caressed them with his. "I love you," he said softly, but the words must have sounded more like a question than a declaration, a request in want of an RSVP.

The hoped-for reply did not come. "I know you do," was all she said. "I'd better go. Papa is waiting." He squeezed her fingers and watched her go. The spring was gone from her step. At the car, though, she turned and gave him a faint smile. That would have to be enough for now.

A few days later, Harold asked if he could rehire the three Germans starting on Monday, January 22nd. He was friendly when he picked them up, but subdued. And Clara's appearance shocked them. When they came in for dinner, she looked as if she hadn't eaten in a month. Silently, she moved around the kitchen like a ghost. Harold chatted in generalities, but his words were forced. Even his prayer rang hollow. *Has their faith been destroyed?* Rolf wondered.

Over dessert, Clara tried to speak, but all she could get out was, "I'm sorry I'm not myself today," before bursting into tears. Loretta hugged her tightly, and Rolf and the other Germans felt like intruders. It was a struggle, but Clara finally gathered herself enough to say, "Joseph was a good boy. We miss him terribly. I'm trying to find God's will in this, but it's hard."

After that first day, things got easier—at least their mealtime conversations regained some lightness. As soon he could, Rolf gave Loretta her Christmas present, but in the milk barn rather than in front of her parents. She brightened while unwrapping it and thanked him with a hug, but as their bodies pressed in, he felt stiffness instead of willing reciprocity.

As she was putting the pieces back in the box, Rolf said, "*Ach verdamm!*" which drew a laugh from Loretta because she'd never heard him curse, even mildly. "Sorry," he blushed, "I forgot the Magi. They weren't done when I wrapped this." He promised to bring them the next day, but he never got the chance.

The next day, Saturday, February 10th, started normally. After tending the animals, the Germans headed to the big barn to clean out stalls. They were breaking out and carting off half-frozen animal droppings and muck when a mud-splattered black car pulled in and stopped next to the gate. Two men in uniform got out and hurriedly strode up to house. Something about their gait gave both Rolf and Gralke the shivers.

"More news about their son?" Gralke asked gravely.

"Perhaps," said Rolf. He tried to concentrate on his work with an eye on the kitchen door.

After fifteen long minutes, the visitors left. Harold stood at the door with Clara, who was saying something Rolf couldn't understand. Then she screamed it out clearly enough, "I want them gone! I can't look at any of them any more!" After the door slammed shut, the men in the barn could hear more anguished cries coming from inside the house. It was impossible to work.

Then came another slam, and this time Loretta was marching to the barn. Her swollen eyes had an ominous quality when she said, "I'm going to drive you back to town now."

Rolf stepped toward her. "What's happened?" Loretta burst into tears. "What is it?"

She flinched and stepped back, forcing herself under control. "Just get in the car."

"Are you sure you should be driving us? Isn't that a violation of the rules?"

"You're going back to town! Now!" The men put down their shovels and followed her. No sooner were they in than she sped off as if she couldn't wait to be rid of them. The car fishtailed through muddy tire tracks in the driveway and sent gravel flying on the county road. She even ran a stop sign in town.

At the Eyestone Building, Gralke and Zimmerman quickly jumped out, but Rolf waited to try to find out what had happened. But neither he nor Loretta could speak. She stared out the windshield, rigid as a statue except for one palm thumping on the steering wheel. Finally, he garnered the courage to ask, "Can you tell me what happened?"

"I can't." Her voice gurgled; she was on the verge of hyper-ventilating.

"His voice filled with emotion, he said, "Okay. When you're ready, I'll be waiting."

"I don't want to see you again." She still wouldn't look in his direction.

Eyes filling with tears, he pleaded, "But why? What's happened?"

Now she turned to face him and spat out the horrible word that she'd been struggling to bring herself to say: "Malmedy." Then again, louder: "Malmedy!"

"Malmedy? What's that? I don't understand."

"Malmedy is in Belgium. It's where *you* killed my brother." She choked. "Get out." As he did, she spat out another word, "*Außenseiter*," and drove off, but she made it just a block before she had to pull over, sobbing uncontrollably.

Rolf stumbled on the sidewalk, still grasping for something, anything, to say to her, but she was gone.

Jordan saw him come in. "Hey Mueller, what are you doing back so early? It's only ten o'clock. And what's Loretta doing driving you? She shouldn't be doing that."

Rolf's face was ashen. "I don't know what just happened."

"What?" Something was wrong. "Should I get Stevenson?"

"We were working in the barn and two Army officers drove up and went in the house and then Mrs. Unruh was screaming and Loretta came out and drove us back. That's all I know."

"She didn't say why or anything?"

"All she said was that I killed her brother. *Me!* At Malmedy, and that it's in Belgium."

Now Jordan's color matched Rolf's. "Oh shit, is that where Joe died? At Malmedy?"

"I don't know, that's all she said. What happened at Malmedy?"

"You didn't hear about it on the radio? Seventy or eighty Americans were captured there in December. Once the Germans disarmed them, they shot them all in cold blood in the middle of a field. It was a massacre. I saw an AP newsreel about it at the movies just last night." Rolf looked at him, dumbfounded. "A couple of them escaped by playing dead and crawling into the woods. That's how the Allies first found out. Then a few weeks ago, after the Germans got pushed back, we recovered the bodies. Most were shot in the head at close range. Some were tied up, others' hands were frozen above their heads, like they were surrendering when they were killed."

"*Mein Gott.*" A high-pitched tinny sound rang in his ears. "Do you suppose that's where Joseph Unruh died. As a POW?" He didn't want to believe it, couldn't process it.

"With what Loretta said, and since he was lost before Christmas but the bodies were just found and identified, it looks like it."

"So that's why Mrs. Unruh couldn't look at us anymore. She blames us."

"It's understandable she might feel that way, but it's not your fault."

Shaking his head, Rolf sneered sarcastically. "Of course not. But who's fault is it, Greg? If it's not mine and no one else's in my fucking country, then who's fault is it? Tell me, please."

Jordan had no reply.

Rolf threw himself on his bunk and closed his eyes, trying to will this terrible world away, but escape was blocked by the echoes and faces of his own guilt. *You were only doing what you had to do. You did things you never wanted to do.* Then the familiar voices added, *Yes! And isn't that exactly what Joe's murderers will say? Your countrymen? You're all alike, you're all Nazis!* Now his foot was tapping so violently against the footboard that the entire bunk shook, but Rolf was so immersed in despair that he didn't notice.

That evening, at Gralke's insistence, Rolf made himself get up to eat. In the dining room, he was surprised to hear everyone discussing Joe Unruh and Malmedy. After he'd gotten his tray and was walking to a table, he overheard a group of Germans bantering about it. One arrogant man was pontificating, "This dead American was a soldier, so what's the big deal? Who knows how many of ours he already killed. Or how many he would have killed if he made it into Germany. I'm glad he was taken out before he could do more damage to the Reich."

Rolf exploded. "You ignorant bastard, he was an unarmed prisoner, like you! How about you, should you be 'taken out' too?" The man's smirk and a dismissive wave of his hand enraged Rolf. He moved in and quickly landed several powerful punches to the man's face. Blood gushed out his nose and mouth.

Gralke rushed over and pulled Rolf away. "Let's go!" he said, pushing him out of the dining hall. When they were alone, he said, "What the hell? What do you think you were doing?" Shaking and already ashamed, Rolf gave no reply. The only words he could hear were inside his head: *Only doing what you had to do, eh?*

⚬──⚬⚬⚬──⚬⚬──⚬

Joe Unruh's funeral was held the following Wednesday. Intended to be simple and prayerful in the Mennonite tradition, it was also the largest funeral in Peabody history and, for some, a flag-waving spectacle. Because their church was so small, the Unruhs acquiesced to holding the service in the high school auditorium, but even then, not all their friends and neighbors and townspeople and onlookers and reporters got a seat. People had to stand in the halls and even outdoors on a chilly February afternoon to pay their respects and show their solidarity with the town martyr's family.

There was no focal point for the assembly's grief and indignation that day, for there was no coffin, nor pallbearers to carry Joe's body to its rest. By then, he'd already been buried a world away, in Henri-Chapelle American Cemetery in Hombourg, not far from Malmedy, along with thousands of others who fell in the Battle of the Bulge. The same day they gave the family the news about how he died, the Army officers handed Harold a form letter telling them that their beloved son's body could be repatriated home after the war if the family wished.

# Chapter 42
# UNTO DUST

By quirk of fate, Joe Unruh's funeral was held on Valentines Day. For the rest of their lives, February 14th would be the day Loretta and Carol Ann said goodbye to their brother. No heart-shaped box of Russell Stover chocolates or bouquet of roses or tender Hallmark verse would change that. Their pain would gradually dissolve into a larger sea of happier memories, but neither sister would ever entirely forget how she felt on that day in 1945.

The 14th of February that year was also Ash Wednesday, the first day of Lent. As the crowd was remembering Joe at Peabody High that afternoon, an old sedan crept by and turned toward downtown. Behind the wheel was Father Clement Dreier, OFM, pastor of St. Patrick Catholic Church in Florence, on his way to the Eyestone to help the Catholics there get Lent off to a solemn start with confession, Mass, and marking with ashes.

A Franciscan friar and priest for fifty years, Father Clem had worked for decades in his order's New Mexican missions and later in parishes in the Diocese of Wichita. The son of German immigrants who homesteaded at Garden Plains, he was a gentle, practical man with a dry sense of humor who sincerely loved his work and people in general. Because he spoke German, he volunteered to make time from his already too-busy schedule to be camp chaplain as soon as he heard the POWs were coming to Peabody.

Rolf had recently been attending Mass most weeks, but he was in no mood for religion that Ash Wednesday. Loretta's four-word indictment—*You killed my brother!*—had left him disconsolate. At the last minute, though, for reasons as murky as the winter sky, he forced himself off his bunk and into the dining hall. Men kneeling on the hard linoleum faced the portable altar covered with a richly brocaded purple cloth. Soft candlelight reflected off the golden ciborium and out into the room. In a corner, Father Clem's robe-covered knees protruded from where he sat behind a three-panel folding confessional screen. Greg Jordan was kneeling in front of it, but just as Rolf walked in, Jordan touched his fingertips to his head, chest, and shoulders in the Sign of the Cross, rose, and moved over to a spot near the altar, where he knelt down again and bowed his head.

Without thinking, he would never be sure why, Rolf knelt down on his good knee where Jordan had been and straightened out his prosthesis. Through the thin cloth, a silhouetted head could be seen looking down, waiting silently for the next anonymous penitent to begin. At the sight, Rolf panicked. What was he doing? He hadn't been to confession since he was a child. The thought of it suddenly terrified him. He rose to flee, but Father Clem's head had lifted slightly in response to his movement and now, still looking away, the priest spoke softly. "Do you want to make your confession today, my son?"

He froze like a child with his hands in a cookie jar. Trapped, he had to kneel back down. *Oh, what the hell*, he thought. "Yes, Father."

"I'm ready when you are."

"Give me a minute, please." Could the priest hear him panting? Rolf squinted, as if that might help squeeze the right words out, and out they came: "Bless me, Father, for I have sinned. My last confession was...." He drew an ashamed breath. "I'm sorry, but I don't know how long it's been. Five years, maybe ten? I can't remember."

The priest was steady, reassuring. "Have you examined your conscience?"

"Not really," Rolf stammered. "I mean, it's been so long, I don't think I can remember everything I've done since my last confession."

"Being exact is less important than having the desire to seek forgiveness. The Lord understands the frailties of one's memory. Is that what you want, God's forgiveness?"

"I suppose so."

"Then start by thinking about the Commandments and how you violated them."

Oh yes, the Ten Commandments, God's guideposts for self-evaluation. As they seeped into his consciousness, a tidal wave of memories broke free. Slowly, then faster and in greater detail, sins spewed out—countless times when he'd lied, failed to honor his parents, had impure thoughts, fornicated, cheated, stole or desecrated others' property. Times when he'd made fun of people, when he was drunk or jealous or proud or covetous or profane or cowardly or angry or violent, including recently battering another POW. Farther and farther back he went. He began in English, but unknowingly switched to German, the language in which the worst of his memories were stored. The priest may have asked a question or two, but mostly Rolf talked, without subterfuge or pretext, until he reached the hardest part, where he paused. "And I've killed people, Father. Many people. Some were soldiers, some were not. I don't know how many. I don't know their names." The harsh words, spoken, made him start trembling.

"*Ich verstehe*," was all the priest said, with no hint of condemnation. After a short silence, he asked, "Are you finished, my son?"

Rolf was crying. "No, Father. There's more."

"Say what you wish for God to hear, my son, in your own time."

Rolf continued to cry softly, trying to get himself under control enough to speak. Finally, "There were two times when my actions were most sinful." He sniffled and took a long deep breath. Then in a quiet, controlled voice, he began. "The first was in France. We were clearing a street of partisans. They had kept fighting even after the French army had withdrawn from the town. Our orders were not to take prisoners. Three of us went into a house, including the *unteroffizier*, my superior. Upstairs we found twelve people hiding in a corner. Six of them were women, two were old men, one was blind, and there were four little children. I confirmed they had no weapons and my comrade and I were turning around to leave when our *unteroffizier* came up the stairs. He pointed to the people in the corner and said, 'Why are they still breathing? Do your duty!' And I turned around and shot everyone of them until the moaning and all movement stopped. One of the children, a little girl of around five years with curly blond hair, was looking right at me as I shot her in the face. She was the last one to be quiet." Rolf started crying in sobs.

"And the second time?" asked Father Clem.

Rolf regained his composure, barely, then went on, "The second time was in Libya. Thirteen women and children were hiding in a tent, Bedouins with no weapons. Only this time," Rolf choked, had to stop. "Only this time, no one ordered me to do my duty. There were British soldiers hiding behind them, so I shot them all. I shot them all." As he was speaking, Rolf gasped audibly, then cried out: Willy was kneeling beside him, just for a moment before vanishing. The priest waited. Rolf wiped his eyes and breathed deeply several times, then recited more words from his childhood: "For these sins and all the sins of my past life, I am heartily sorry."

The priest gave him a moment before asking, "Have you made a good Act of Contrition?"

"No, Father, but I will." And out came the long-forgotten prayer: "Oh, my God, I am heartily sorry for having offended Thee. I detest all my sins because of Thy just punishment, which I so richly deserve; but most of all because they offend Thee, my God, who art so good and deserving of all my love. I firmly resolve, with the help of Thy grace, to sin no more and to avoid the dangerous occasions of sin."

"Is it your intention to turn away from sin?"

"Yes, Father."

"For your penance, say the Rosary every day in Lent." Then Father Clem pronounced God's absolution, *"Et ego te absolvo a peccatis tuis in nomine Patris, et Filii, et Spiritus Sancti, Amen,"* and concluded in English, "God be with you, my son. Now go in peace."

"Thank you." As if he were awakening again from a coma, Rolf wobbled to his feet and walked over to where Jordan was still praying.

Jordan caught a glimpse of what he thought were sweat beads on Rolf's cheeks, but they were tears, unnoticed by the man who had just shed them. "Do you have a rosary?"

"No." Rolf shot him a look of surprise. "Why do you ask that?"

"Father makes everybody say the Rosary as penance. Here, take mine, I've got another one." Jordan crossed himself again and added quietly, "I gotta go to the office for a minute. I'll be back in time for Mass."

Rolf looked down at the twenty-four inch chain-linked loop of fine metal dangling from his fingers. He felt the cool coffee bean-sized walnut beads, oily from human fingers, and ran a finger over the silver crucifix. He began to pray, completely exhausted, but he made himself recite the entire devotional, one bead, one word, at a time. As he whispered the prayers over and over and focused on the candles flickering on the altar, the horrible burdens he'd been carrying for so many years seemed to grow lighter, if only slightly. Maybe he was on the right track. *I did what I did,* he thought. *I can't change that, ever. But I am heartily sorry, my God. Please forgive me. Please help me forgive myself. And help me atone for what I've done.*

---

After supper, Jordan was alone on guard duty at the front door. Hearing footsteps approaching from behind, he turned. "Hello, Mueller," he said, motioning to an empty chair, then pointing up at him. "You still have ashes on your forehead."

"Oh, I forgot." Rolf touched the sooty smudge traced onto his forehead during Mass and repeated the ritual's words. "Remember, man, thou art dust, and unto dust thou shalt return."

"That about sums it up, doesn't it?" Rolf nodded slightly. "Hey, after Mass, I went out to the Unruhs since I couldn't go to the funeral."

Rolf's body stiffened. "How are they?"

"They all looked completely wiped out, especially Clara. She just sat at the table and stared off into space. It was like she didn't know anyone else was there."

Rolf was afraid to ask what he most wanted to know. "Did you talk to Loretta?"

"I only saw her for a minute, but I got to tell her how sorry I am." Jordan saw the sadness. "I know how tough this is on you, not being able to talk to her."

"She doesn't want to see me again."

"She may have said that, but I don't think she meant it. I bet she doesn't even remember what she said that day. She was out of her mind with grief and lashing out, and you were the closest target. She knows you didn't kill her brother."

Rolf grimaced and cleared his throat. "It's hard to forget."

"I know, but what happened to Joe Unruh isn't on you. She knows that. You do too. That belongs to someone else. Can I give you some advice?" Getting a shrug, but no objection, he went on, "Be patient with her, and don't give up just because of what she said."

"It's too late for that."

"Give her some time," Jordan said. "She knows where to find you. You and she can still be friends. And don't beat yourself up for something that wasn't your fault."

"But in some ways, she is right." He then handed Jordan an envelope. "The next time you see Loretta, would you please give her this?" Jordan gave him a skeptical look but nodded affirmatively. "Thank you, Greg."

Later that week, with no jobs and no place to go, Rolf, Zimmerman, and Gralke lingered at the breakfast table in the Eyestone Building. Zimmerman mopped up streaks of egg on his plate with a crust of toast. "I wonder if we'll get reassigned to another farm. Or maybe the Unruhs will decide to hire us back."

"I wouldn't count on it," said Rolf.

Gralke looked at him. "I'm sorry for you, Rolf. I know how much you and Loretta meant to each other before this thing with her brother."

"Please don't feel bad for me." Rolf took a sip of cold coffee and looked at his friends. "It was a naïve fantasy. A case of opposites attracting if ever there was one."

"Even so, it must be hard to let it go. Erich and I had our own little fantasies after working for the Unruhs. We were treated with respect, fed well, and belonged out there. It was like a dream come true for both of us and we thought it would go on."

Zimmerman added, "They made us feel like family or neighbors."

"Like friends," Gralke said. "We arrived in America as prisoners, little more than chattel. Then an amazing family took us in and for a little while, they made us feel worthwhile again. And now, here we are, back where we started."

"Prisoners forever," said Rolf with a sad, resigned expression. "No less than we deserve."

A week after Joe's funeral, Loretta was sitting on her bed looking out into the night when she heard a car door shut and saw red taillights slowly disappear into the dark as a car drove down the driveway past the barn and turned, heading back to Peabody. On her lap was the envelope Greg Jordan had discreetly given her when he stopped by to check on the Unruh family again. Turning back to the light of her bedside lamp, she read Rolf's letter a third time:

*Dear Loretta,*

*I'm writing this the evening after your brother's funeral and will ask Greg Jordan to deliver it when the time is right.*

*I know what happened in Malmedy.*

*I've done things as bad or worse. I'm ashamed of almost everything I did before I met you. I am no better than Otto Hecht or the ones who killed your brother.*

*There's no future for us. I am not worthy of you. If you knew everything, you would agree. Now I have to spend the rest of my life living with myself. That's too much to ask of you.*

*Rolf*

She stared at the sheet of paper and then returned it to the envelope. She shed no tears the first two times she read it and didn't this time, either. She was numb, except for a sudden powerful urge to rip the letter to shreds and burn the pieces. But just as she began to tear the paper, she stopped. She couldn't. Instead, she looked at the envelope once more, sighed deeply, and put it into the drawer of her nightstand.

There was a soft knock on her bedroom door. "Yes?" said Loretta.

Carol Ann opened the door gently and peeked in. "Papa asked me to ask you if you'd come down and help Mama bathe and get ready for bed. But I can do it if you're busy."

Loretta stood and gave her sister a faint smile. "I'm happy to, but thanks for offering."

"Let's do it together. I'll brush her hair. Mama likes that." The Unruh sisters hugged tightly at the top of the stairs, then walked down together into the warm light of the kitchen.

# Acknowledgements

With humility and gratitude, I recognize the contributions of so many people who inspired and guided me as I researched and wrote *The Spoils of Victory.* Thank you, Trish Markowitz, Jerilynn Jones Henrikson, Jan Darting, Phil Witt, Steve Farney, Colette Bizal, and others for reading the original manuscript that included this story. Thank you for your honest reactions and detailed thoughts about what you did and didn't like.

Thank you, Antonia Felix, for brainstorming with me in your kitchen all those years ago when we first discussed POWs in the Heartland. Thank you for the syllabus you created to help me learn to write. Your guidance was invaluable, and your recommendations, *On Writing* by Stephen King, *The Scene Book* by Sandra Scofield, and *Inside Story* by Dara Marks, were transformative.

Cheryl Unruh, your *Flyover People* essays were my inspiration to start writing in the first place. Thank you for all your quiet, steady, practical encouragement. Thank you for sharing your own family history to guide me and for allowing me to use your family name in the story.

Thank you, Thea Rademacher, for answering the phone that day when the Universe said it was time for me to submit the manuscript to Flint Hills Publishing and thank you for sharing your sage advice and beautiful energy so generously since then. Working with you and the FHP team, including Amy Albright and Greg German, has been a wonderful collaborative experience. You are all appreciated.

Thank you, Nathan Fredrickson, for guiding me through the revisioning process with your uncannily-insightful wisdom and pragmatic suggestions. I can't imagine working with a better editor. Thanks to you, I'm learning to be a storyteller, not just a historian.

Lastly, I offer my special thanks to Teresa Markowitz for repeatedly encouraging me to tell this story and for gently prodding me to get at it when I got sidetracked, as frequently happened. Thank you, sister dear, for never doubting that this book would be published.

# Suggestions for Further Reading


*Prisoners of War in Kansas 1943-1946,* Lowell A. May & Mark P. Schock, KS Publishing Company, Manhattan, KS, 2007

*Camp Concordia, German POWs in the Midwest,* Lowell A. May, Sunflower University Press, Manhattan, KS, 1995

*The Helpless Poles,* Abe J. Unruh, Courier Printing Company, Grabill, IN, 1973

*In The Name of Christ, A History of the Mennonite Central Committee and Its Service 1920-1951,* John D. Unruh, Herald Press, Scottdale, PA 1952

*Nazi Prisoners of War in America,* Arnold Krammer, Stern and Day, New York, NY, 1979

*Nebraska POW Camps, A History of World War II Prisoners in the Heartland,* Melissa Amateis Marsh, The History Press, Charleston, SC, 2014

*Men in German Uniform,* Antonio Thompson, The University of Tennessee, Knoxville, TN, 2010

*Bomber Offensive, The Devastation of Europe,* Noble Frankland, *Ballantine's Illustrated History of World War II, Campaign Book, No. 7,* Ballantine Books, New York, NY, 1970

*Panzer Division, The Mailed Fist,* Major K.J. Mucksey, M.C., *Ballantine's Illustrated History of World War II, Weapons Book, No. 2,* Ballentine Books, New York NY, 1968

# Book Club Questions

1.  Did events of World War II like those described in *The Spoils of Victory* directly or indirectly affect your family or community? In what ways? Are the effects of World War II still being felt in your family or in American society today?

2.  How should the enemy be treated once they've been captured and are no longer a threat? Should valuable resources be used to house, feed, and care for them? Should Rolf have received a prosthetic leg courtesy of the U.S. when his leg was amputated?

3.  Which character(s) in *The Spoils of Victory* do you relate to most? Why?

4.  Can romantic love ever really flourish between people who, like Rolf and Loretta, come from completely different traditions, cultures, beliefs, and experiences and who are at profoundly different stages in their lives?

5.  Have you ever had to balance your own aspirations and beliefs with your family's beliefs and values, as the Unruh children had to? In what ways did your issues arise, and how did you resolve them?

6.  Should Joseph Unruh have enlisted in the Army in 1942 when he could have taken CO (conscientious objector) status like his brother, John?

7.  Should Harold and Clara Unruh have done more to try to stop Joe from enlisting? What could they have done?

8.  After all Aunt Dora Jantz experienced in her life, including when her family was forced to leave their home in Russia to be able to practice their Mennonite faith, why was she so willing to support Joseph when he chose a path that was contradictory to the Mennonite way?

9.  Is the kind of radical pacificism and hospitality that the Unruhs believed in and practiced realistic? Is it desirable? Is it possible for the world to achieve a lasting peace for all? What would it take for that to happen?

10. Is war ever moral? Under what conditions? Who decides? In your opinion, and based on the events in *The Spoils of Victory*, was American participation in World War II moral?

11. Are some wrongs unforgivable? Which ones? When and in what circumstances? Who decides?

12. Should Rolf have been able to forgive himself for the atrocities he committed?

13. Should Loretta forgive Rolf for what he did, especially considering what happened to Joe?

14. Did your opinion of Rolf change when you learned what he had done in France and North Africa? In what ways?

15. How far would you go to comply with an order given by a superior in wartime if you believed your actions would violate your own moral code?

# About the Author

Daniel Markowitz is a descendant of German and Slovenian immigrants who came to America in the late 1800s and early 1900s. Raised in Olpe, Kansas, at the edge of the Flint Hills, he grew up listening to his grandparents' and other beloved elders' stories of their home countries, traditions, and the hardships and joys experienced on their way to stability and prosperity. His love for history and storytelling grew out of their often humorous and sometimes hyperbolic oral chronicles.

He earned degrees from Emporia State University (social sciences) and the University of Kansas (law) and spent decades in quixotic pursuit of success in a career for which he was ill-suited, before embarking on a trial-and-error journey for authenticity and purpose.

Markowitz is a passionate advocate for peace, equality, justice, and respect for all, especially the marginalized and the forgotten. He has five children, five grandchildren, and lives near the beaches of Baja California, where the big skies, low horizons, and undulating waves of the Pacific Ocean remind him of the rippling tallgrass prairies of home.

*The Spoils of Victory* is Markowitz's first novel and Book 1 in the *Prisoners of War* series. Publication of the second book in the series is anticipated in early 2026.

www.djmarkowitz.com